Dark Elf Chronicles

Book 3

Pathways

By

Dave Willmarth

The story so far…

Mace and Shari are two survivors of the zombiepocalypse that turned nearly all life on Earth into mutant killing machines. Most living matter has become contaminated, down to the birds that fly in the skies above, the fish in the sea, and the bugs that crawl through the grass. The grass itself could be deadly. Plastic, latex, and other synthetic materials are the only protection. The humans and animals that didn't die outright have become viciously aggressive. Killing and eating other creatures makes them bigger, stronger, and possibly smarter.

After months of surviving alone before finding each other, Mace and Shari are now living together in an underground facility owned by a corporation that ran the largest VRMMORPG on the planet. Shari was a med student, nearly ready to become a full-fledged doctor, and Mace was a coder, newly hired by the company on the very day the world ended.

There is no option for long term survival in the real world. Lack of food, and the risk of contamination or being eaten every time they go to the surface to scavenge, will eventually bring about their end. The two of them, and a few other survivors they've found in a similar facility in England, are hoping to combine their expertise, to be able to upload their consciousnesses into the game servers so that they may live on. Mace has been designated Alpha Admin by the facility's AI, Peabody, who has connected with the game's AI, Elysia. Together the two artificial intelligences are attempting to assist the humans in their endeavors both in the game and out in the real world.

Mace plays a drow assassin/sorcerer hybrid known as a Darkblade. Shari plays a light elf druid who specializes in healing. The two of them, along with their adorable pets, are working to build a kingdom of their own within Elysia, the game world. If they can raise their sync levels with the game's AI interface high enough, and figure out the science of uploading their full consciousness into the game, they'll potentially reign for decades before the geothermal power runs out or the servers shut down.

Griff and Lisa, the only other two living humans our heroes are in contact with, both play Dwarves starting out in a newbie village in the mountains. They are working to level up and be able to join Mace and Shari as they adventure through Elysia, build their kingdom, and use the game to search for other human survivors.

It's a race against time. Can they figure out the technical requirements of uploading, and raise their sync levels to transfer into the game world before they starve, or get themselves killed.

This is the third book in the Dark Elf Series. If you haven't read the first two, you may still enjoy this story. But there will be some references that won't make much sense. I recommend reading the first two before going any further.

Chapter 1

Thieves and Liars

Keeping a wary eye on both T'enaj and her mate N'osaj, Mace invited them to sit by the fire. As she approached, T'enaj made a series of casual but rapid signals with the hand that wasn't holding N'osaj's chain. Mace looked into the darkness behind her, his drow vision impaired by the light of the campfire between them. He couldn't see whoever it was she signaled.

"How many of your people are out there, T'enaj? And do I need to demonstrate my abilities as a Darkblade?" he growled, daggers instantly in his hands. The others in his group all put hands to weapons as well.

The drow held up her hands, saying, "There are ten more in the trees behind me. And a couple back with our horses. I brought them merely as insurance, in case you were less than welcoming. It would be foolish of me to walk into such a group without *some* form of insurance, don't you agree?" She smiled sweetly at him.

"It may have been foolish of you to walk into this group, period. We shall see soon enough." Mace placed his daggers back in their sheaths. "Prove to me that it was not you and your people who laid that trap for us today. You've arrived rather quickly after the battle."

T'enaj tilted her head and dropped her hands to her side, the chain tinkling lightly. "It is… difficult to prove a negative. But I shall try." She tapped a finger to her chin a couple times, then asked, "You are aware your attackers were Black Flame?"

Mace and several others nodded their heads.

"And that any of their members of significant rank are also oathbound?"

"All that we've found so far." Shari contributed.

"Then it stands to reason that if I were one of them, I too would be oathbound. And thus unable to answer questions of any import regarding the Black Flame or its leadership, correct?"

Mace considered that for a moment. "Unless you are, in fact, the leader of the organization and unbound by any oath."

T'enaj sighed. "That is true. She is not bound by oath to her followers."

Shari asked, "She?"

Ian answered before T'enaj could speak. "Garya. The drow who leads Black Flame. A creature of pure evil if ever there was one, yes." Shari had never heard a bunny growl before, but she thought the sound Ian made probably qualified.

T'enaj smiled and patted the oversized bunny's shoulder. "Ian's last encounter with Garya was unfortunate. He was not always this lovely shade of green."

Ian's shoulders drooped, and his face gathered in a scowl as he kicked at the dirt. "I would gladly slit that woman's throat if given the chance. Oh, yes."

T'enaj explained further. "Ian was… observing her organization. On my orders. She detected and captured him. After some intense questioning…" Ian growled again, louder this time. "She decided to let him return to me with a message rather than kill him. She turned him green as a reminder of his failure."

Shari moved to the bunny and gave him a one-armed hug of support, saying, "And it ain't easy being green." Which caused Mace to snort and work to suppress a laugh as she smiled innocently at him.

T'enaj continued. "In any event, feel free to ask me any questions you like regarding the Black Flame. I am only too happy to share what I know in hopes that it helps you defeat them." She sat cross-legged by the fire, settling effortlessly as N'osaj moved to sit on her left. The male drow was slightly larger in frame than Mace, and bristled with blades. An aura of menace permeated the space around him. T'enaj, by comparison, was completely at ease and smiled amicably up at Mace.

Not wanting to trust too easily, though she had in truth convinced him already, Mace formulated some questions. "How many Black Flame are in Graf now?"

"Well, minus the group you just eliminated - and thank you for that, by the way- there should be no more than a hundred active members remaining. There are also another fifty or so murderers and thugs who wish to become members that would fight with them."

"And how many members of your Thieves' Guild?"

T'enaj gave him a wry grin. "Ah. I agreed to answer questions about the Black Flame, not my own little enterprise. But in the interest of friendship, I shall disclose that we have a similar number of associates."

Mace chuckled despite himself. He was starting to like this drow. "And where are Garya's headquarters?"

"She has several facilities within the city. Most large gatherings are held underground, in a chamber below a poisoner's shop she owns. It has numerous entrances and exits, both visible and hidden. There are adjoining chambers used by her people for sleeping and eating, training and such. Her main residence is a small mansion compound in the merchant's quarter. Heavily fortified with both mundane and magical protections and always guarded. Though she rarely sleeps in the same place two nights in a row. She has safe houses and hideouts scattered throughout the city and surrounding lands."

"A poisoner?" Shari asked, eyes wide. "Not an apothecary?"

T'enaj turned to smile at her. "Graf is… different than your home city, lady elf. It is a hub for illicit trade goods that flow from cities across the continent, above and below the surface. That trade brings with it the roughest and least morally refined customers, traders, and guards." She spared a glance at Mace, then added, "And the influence of drow leading two of the three major powers in the city might have something to do with it. Poisonings are a daily occurrence in Graf."

Mace smirked at the drow, "So why not embrace poison making as a legitimate, taxable business?"

"Just so." T'enaj nodded. "Though this particular shop is a front for the Black Flame and pays only a token tax to achieve some small semblance of being legitimate. The poisoner who runs it is quite talented. I, myself, buy from him on occasion and have never been unhappy with the product."

Behind her, N'osaj grunted and shook his head slightly. T'enaj smiled. "My mate feels I should add that I only purchase poisons from the Black Flame's poisoner to use on Black Flame members. I see a certain poetry in that."

Mace looked at the male drow carefully. "He doesn't speak." It was a statement more than a question.

Ian looked uncomfortable again. "When Garya sent me back to my mistress with a message, it came in the form of master N'osaj's tongue in a box, yes. While she tortured me, her people captured him and removed his tongue to 'gift' to my mistress. It was I who gave up his location, yes. I could not withstand the pain, no." He bowed his head, bunny ears drooping forward.

N'osaj stepped forward and placed a hand on the bunny's shoulder. T'enaj spoke softly to Ian. "There is no shame in your actions, Ian. All but the best-trained drow elite, like Mace here, would crumble under the ministrations of that bitch. She has had centuries to hone her skills." N'osaj patted Ian's shoulder and smiled at him. "You see? N'osaj bears you no ill will. He has always been the strong, silent type. I sometimes believe he enjoys having an excuse not to speak." She tossed her mate a suspicious look, for which he returned a wide grin.

Mace tried to steer the conversation back to more productive topics. "Let us assume I believe you are who you claim to be. If you have traveled out here to meet us, can we assume you plan to assist in our mission to eliminate the Black Flame for good?"

T'enaj leaned back, placing her hands on the ground behind her. "Let us say that I am open to the possibility. Under certain circumstances."

Captain Jorin, who'd been quietly observing up till then, made a guess. "One of those circumstances being that you and your guild be left in charge of the city when the fighting is done."

"Heavens no!" T'enaj grinned at him. "I have no interest in the boring politics and paperwork of running an entire city. No, I would leave it up to you and the Merchants Guild, the third power in Graf, to decide who runs the city. I simply want all of Garya's properties and assets."

The look on her face reminded Mace of every drow matron he'd ever set eyes on. Pure, unfiltered and unabashed ambition.

Mace shook his head. "Only a fool would agree to that here and now, especially when we don't know the extent or value of those assets." He thought it over as T'enaj stuck out her lower lip and did her best to feign disappointment. As a drow, she never expected Mace to acquiesce to her initial demand.

"There is at least one item that I hope is here in Graf, which I have a quest to retrieve. If it is in Garya's possession, I'll want it. And I believe my people should maintain a presence here in Graf, for trade purposes, of course. Maybe a dock and warehouse of our own, and a residence, for when we come to visit our friends in the Thieves' Guild."

N'osaj snorted and flashed a thumbs-up at Mace. T'enaj rolled her eyes. "It seems my mate approves of you, Darkblade. And I was never fond of Garya's manor in the merchant's quarter. It would make an adequate rest stop for the occasional visit by... I'm sorry. I'm afraid I do not know the name of your organization." She shot Ian an annoyed look.

Mace was taken aback. He took a breath to buy himself a moment, then replied, "We are not as... formal as your guild. Just a loose association of like-minded friends and associates helping each other survive."

"Yet you make plans to establish a permanent presence." She looked at him with a knowing smile. "Then, as I was saying, Garya's manor would make a fitting home for you and your... associates. As for the dock and warehouse, that can be arranged easily enough. Garya currently controls several. I'm certain you could find one to your liking." She bowed slightly to Captain Jorin.

"One that would remain off limits to your own... associates?" Jorin returned her bow, eliciting a laugh.

"Of course, Captain. We do not liberate items from our own members or our trusted allies."

Mace continued the negotiations. "Then let us establish a fair split of the more... liquid assets that will be seized. My people will take the personal possessions found on any of the slavers we kill, and yours will do the same. Any caches of gold, silver, or other valuables found will be split between our groups. Let's say... sixty percent to you and yours? The rest to my people. To help us better establish our 'organization'. This will include any bank accounts we manage to get access to."

T'enaj looked for a moment as if she might press the issue. N'osaj gently nudged her from behind, then gave her a look. She sighed and agreed. "That is acceptable." She reached out a hand, and Mace shook it, followed shortly by Shari.

The group all settled back around the fire and passed the next few hours planning their moves over the coming days.

*****

Griff and Lisa enjoyed a quick breakfast of granola bars and canned pears the next morning. When they'd cleaned up the kitchen properly, making sure to leave no crumbs or pear juice around to attract bugs, they each went to their rooms to gear up.

Neither of them had spent much time outside since the zombiepocalypse began. But Mace and Shari had given them good advice and filled them in on the many dangers the outside world posed. With this in mind, they geared up as best they could and met at the elevator.

Peabody had it waiting for them when they arrived. Without a word, he took them up to the ground level. The two of them didn't speak as they exited the lobby level into the garage, where Griff's Jeep awaited. He made sure to point out the contaminated blood splatter that still decorated the one rear section of window and frame.

Once safely inside, Griff took a moment. "You ready for this?"

Lisa shook her head no but said, "Yeah. Let's get on with it."

Griff started the Jeep and moved up the ramp toward the garage exit. Peabody obligingly opened the roll-up door just as the vehicle approached, then lowered it again behind them.   Griff took a moment to get his bearings, then headed toward the Tesco he'd visited previously. Taking Mace's advice, he didn't move in a straight path. He jigged left down one block, then right down another, taking a roundabout route that should throw off any undead creatures attempting to follow.

Parking in the same spot on the loading dock, Griff led Lisa inside. They each grabbed a shopping cart and activated forehead-mounted flashlights. They were just reaching the first of the aisles between the five-meter high shelves when Griff's faith in the effectiveness of the roundabout route was shattered.

A roar shook the building, glass bottles in crates on the shelves rattling against each other. Griff froze, the memory of that sound nearly causing him to void his bowels. Lisa grabbed onto his arm with shaking hands, gripping with all her strength as she partially hid herself behind his body.

The sound of shattering glass and twisting metal made them both jump. Griff reflexively grabbed the Mossberg shotgun he'd placed in the cart. There didn't seem to be any need for quiet weapons at this point. Anything within miles of them could hear this racket. He nearly bit his tongue as the building shook again. Whatever was happening, it was happening in the front of the store!

Griff whispered, "We need to get out o' here. Move quietly, and we'll hope whatever's goin' on out there don't find us back here."

Lisa nodded, speechless and wide-eyed with fear. They abandoned their carts and moved slowly around the stack of shelves that stood between them and the loading dock door. Griff had a clear view of the door when the swinging doors that he'd barred shut on his previous visit burst open. The head of a massive serpent pushed partway through, then was pulled back. Another roar shook the walls and made Griff want to drop his weapon and cover his ears. But training kept his grip firm, and he motioned Lisa back behind cover. The last thing he wanted was for them to be caught out in the open making a dash for the door if that thing came through again.

When they were safely hidden behind the shelves again, he let out the breath he'd been holding. "That was one damned big snake."

"I think it were fightin' somethin'," Lisa answered, her voice wavering. She had curled herself into a fetal ball against the wall in the corner.

"Yeah." Griff had reached that same conclusion and one more. "And I don't want to meet whatever's big enough to handle it this long."

There was a crash of glass again, sounding more distant. Griff's gut told him the fight had moved to the storefront. He hated himself for it, but he needed to see what was going on. "I'm goin' to get a look at what's what up there. You can wait here if ye like."

Horrified, Lisa shook her head *no* and got to her feet. "If yer goin', I'm goin'."

The two of them crept out from behind the shelving again and practically tip-toed over to the swinging doors. Griff used his weapon to push aside some of the hanging plastic strips and peer through the small gap between the now twisted and broken doors. Lisa, practically glued to his back, leaned forward to look over his shoulder.

The serpent's body was wrapped around an even more massive beast with four legs. The two were rolling about in the parking lot just outside a huge gap in the storefront. As they struggled, Griff caught a look at the other creature's head. He grunted in surprise and fear.

Lisa's face was inches from his ear. "I… I think your bear tracked you after all."

Griff grimaced but nodded his head. "Yeh. I'm sorry. I thought I'd lost 'im."

The two watched, frozen in place and entranced as the battle waged outside. The bear had a forepaw free and was using it to pin the snake's body to the ground about three meters below its head. The head was thrashing, snapping at the bear's shoulder and neck even as the bear tried to bite down on the snake. The serpent, in turn, was clearly constricting around the bear's body.

Neon-blue blood spurted from wounds on both monsters. Huge shards of broken glass and metal protruded from them, clearly picked up as they smashed through the front of the store. The bear raised its head to roar, but the sound was greatly weakened. The snake's body had managed to squeeze most of the breath from the bear's lungs. Griff wasn't sure that mattered, as he didn't think undead creatures needed to breathe.

The giant bear's jaws finally found purchase on the snake, clamping down about a meter below its head. The snake went berserk, every muscle in its body flexing frantically as it both squeezed more tightly on the bear and tried to free itself at the same time. The bear shook its head savagely and pulled, tearing a chunk of flesh the size of a soccer ball from the snake.

Behind Griff, Lisa made a faint "erp" sound and clamped a hand over her mouth to keep from vomiting at the sight. Griff didn't blame her. Having seen enough, he pulled back his weapon and leaned back, motioning for Lisa to do the same.

As the battle raged on outside, the two of them ran for the Jeep. There was no point in silence. They needed to leave the area before one of the monsters won the fight. Or more of them showed up to see what was happening.

Griff was the first to reach the loading dock door. As he was about to burst through, he caught movement out of the corner of his eye. Dropping to his knees and sliding, he gripped the door frame to halt his momentum. Lisa slammed into his back, falling over his shoulder to land on her behind in front of him.

"What the bleedin'-"

He clamped a hand over her mouth, interrupting her protest. With his eyes, he indicated that she should look behind her. Her head swiveled as he removed his hand. What she saw made her gasp involuntarily.

Another zombie creature was approaching. It looked like it had once been a cat. It was slinking along the side of the neighboring building in a low crouch, much as a housecat would do when stalking a rodent. Its body had deformed some, snout elongated and ears extended to give it an even more predatory appearance. It stood maybe a meter tall at the shoulders and two meters long without its twitching tail.

Griff held Lisa tightly against him as the two of them sat paralyzed. The creature hadn't seemed to notice them yet. Its eyes were focused toward the front of the building, where the sounds of battle had not abated. It continued to creep until it reached the nearest corner, where it peered around at the ongoing fight.

Lisa's heart was pounding against Griff's chest as he held her to him. He wanted to whisper to her to remain still, but he was sure the zombie cat would hear. So he squeezed gently, trying to reassure her and make sure she remained still.

The zombie cat settled on its haunches, apparently content to watch. The building shuddered again as the two combatants rolled against some part of it. Griff began to sweat, the pressure and fear wearing on him. His every instinct told him to flee. One scratch, one stray drop of blood from any of the three creatures would seal his fate.

But any movement might attract the cat's attention. Griff had no delusions that they could reach the Jeep, get inside, and get away before the thing was upon them. So he sat there, holding Lisa tightly as they both trembled with fear, barely breathing.

A minute or so later, the cat's attention was captured by yet another arrival. This one was much smaller and fast-moving. It dashed down the alleyway behind the cat, oblivious to the monster's presence. It wasn't until it was nearly upon the much larger feline that something alerted it. A squeal was followed by the sound of claws grasping desperately at concrete as the thing tried to stop its momentum and retreat.

It was far too late. The beast looked to be a cross between an oversized fox and a rat. Maybe a quarter the size of the feline, it was no match for the larger beast. The cat sprang from its position against the wall and pounced on the fox-rat-thing. Another squeal, then silence. The big cat grabbed its prey by the neck and trotted back to its previous position, where it crouched and began to feed.

Lisa convulsed with dry heaves as she watched the zombie cat rip into its meal. Griff didn't like it either, but he possessed a more hardy constitution and had no urge to lose his breakfast.

Even with the cat distracted by its meal, he still did not dare to make the short dash to the Jeep. He'd seen the speed with which the cat had reached its target. But if they moved very slowly and carefully, they might be able to back themselves out of sight behind the wall next to them and hide inside the warehouse area.

He very slowly moved his hand in front of Lisa's face, and used it to point behind them. She nodded slightly, and he released his hold on her. The two of them half-crawled backward in slow motion, trying their best to make no sudden moves. Inch by inch they moved back into the shadows inside the doorway. Griff tried not to panic as the cat's meal disappeared faster than he'd hoped. They were running out of time.

Just as the zombie feline finished its meal and began to lick the blood off its paws, Griff lost sight of it behind the wall. He quickly stood and reached out a hand, waiting for Lisa to reach him and pulling her up as well. The two of them stood there, legs trembling, looking into each other's eyes as they listened for any sign that the cat was approaching.

Griff decided that not being able to see the stealthy predator was worse than seeing it. He eyed his shotgun, still sitting where he'd set it down after his slide. The only other weapon he had on him was a .45 in his belt holster. He drew the weapon more for comfort than anything. The weight of it in his hand reassured him.

An icy chill shot down his spine as he noticed that the battle between the two titans out front had gone silent. He looked to Lisa and pointed to his ear, his eyes wild with fear. She took a moment to catch on. Her own wide eyes tearing up, she wrapped her arms around him and squeezed. She cried silently into his chest, the fear and stress finally breaking her down.

Griff put his arms around her, having no idea what to do except comfort her in that moment. His thoughts raced. If one of the massive zombies had been defeated, the other might be on its way to them right then. Or the cat outside may have decided to try and pick off the weakened winner. A dozen scenarios ran through his thoughts in seconds.

He finally settled on 'hide' as the best option. Keeping Lisa tight against him, he moved them to the nearest of the store's offices. The door was open, and the room inside was dark. He took a deep breath and stepped through, practically carrying Lisa with him. The moment they were inside, he released her and quietly shut the door. Both held their breath at the slight clicking sound of the latch engaging.

They stood on either side of the large window that looked out into the warehouse area. There was enough light coming in the open door that they could see a wide swathe from the door, past the first set of shelves, and over to the double doors that led into the front of the store. Griff tried to calm his breathing as they waited for what would come next.

Chapter 2

Danger Us

Mace and Shari logged out after speaking with the leaders of the thieves. Not really hungry, they skipped a late night meal, crawled into Shari's bed and spooned. Shari mumbled, "Do you think we can trust the thieves?"

"I think we can trust them as long as we're pursuing the same goal. They obviously need us to help take out the Black Flame. If they could have done it on their own, they would have. Either that, or waiting for players to help is some kind of programmed game mechanic. I half expected a new quest when we agreed to work with them."

"Speaking of quests, what is the item you're supposed to get for the queen?"

Mace half-shrugged. "I don't know. The original quest was to find the player that Jervis sent to retrieve it. Assuming he managed to retrieve it, whatever it is might be lost along with him. On the other hand, maybe he didn't find it before everything went to shit. In which case, I don't know. I'm hoping we'll stumble across it and know it when we see it. I'll read the scroll Jervis gave me, see if there's anything useful. I put it away when I first got it, knowing I was far from being able to reach Graf, and pretty much forgot about."

The lack of response other than slow, even breathing told him Shari was already asleep. He smiled to himself, kissed the top of her head, and closed his eyes.

*****

Griff had sagged to the floor, the initial adrenaline rush having faded and left him nearly exhausted. Despite the danger close by, his body was telling him to sleep. He was sitting with his back against the wall, losing the battle to resist that urge when a horrible mewling screech echoed through the warehouse, followed by the sounds of metal shelves and glass jars hitting the floor. He got to his knees and peered through the window. He didn't have the angle to see through the broken double doors, but based on the sound, he guessed that the big cat had joined the battle.

Lisa was on her feet, hands clasped together in front of her chest almost in a posture of prayer as she peered through their window. Griff got to his feet and took hold of one of her hands. "This might be our chance. We can try to make it to the Jeep," he whispered.

Lisa resisted. "I think we have to stay. This is our food supply. We have to kill whatever is in there or find a new food source. Or starve." Her hands trembled as she spoke, but she had a determined look in her eye.

Griff thought it over. He hadn't heard the roar of the bear in quite a while. It was possible the giant snake had defeated it or driven it off. The much smaller cat wouldn't be much of a challenge for the serpent. But maybe if the bear had injured it enough…

With a short nod of his head, he moved back to the door. Opening it very quietly, he stepped out into the warehouse and made for his shotgun. He paused at the open outer door to peer carefully around the frame. The zombie cat was no longer sitting near the building corner where it had been before.

Scooping up his shotgun, he checked to make sure his .45 was in its holster. Lisa gripped a shotgun of her own, but she was unfamiliar with the weapon and looked more like she was ready to club someone with it than fire it. Together they moved slowly toward the mangled double doors that led to the front. The sounds of battle persisted, so they risked taking a look through the small windows.

The first thing Griff saw was the bear. It lay on its side, perfectly still, in the parking area. At least one of its legs was broken, and blood pooled beneath it. Its jaws still gripped a large chunk of snake flesh.

Movement to his right caught Griff's attention. The snake's head reared up above the shelves several aisles down. It weaved back and forth and drooped slightly, before lunging out of sight. There was another crash, and the cat streaked past the doors causing both humans to jump. It appeared unscathed from the brief flash they observed. A moment later, the head of the snake passed by the doors in the same direction. The body that followed was badly torn, with large bites removed and scores of claw marks torn from its hide.

The massive serpent's head rose up again, searching for its prey. Griff felt the need to flee as its gaze passed by the doors they hid behind. He heard Lisa gasp and cringed.

A second later the head focused and shot forward. A high-pitched scream suggested that the cat had been caught, or at least hit, by the strike. The snake's body continued to scrape by the door as it moved away, undulating over top of bent and broken shelves. Cans and jars were crushed unnoticed beneath its weight.

Unwilling to push the doors open and make any noise that would draw attention to them, Griff backed up. He motioned to Lisa, and they walked back to the loading dock door. She followed him outside, and he led her around the building toward the front. They moved as carefully and as quietly as they could – only the sound of their breathing and the occasional scuff of shoe on concrete marking their passage. Griff kept his eyes moving, searching for more threats.

When they reached the front of the store, Griff spent a moment staring at the dead bear. The thing had terrified him. Some primal instinct from his lizard brain still quailed at the sight of its corpse. The monstrous thing had tracked him for days, intent on eating his face. Lisa put a hand on his shoulder and gave him a sympathetic look.

A shuffling sound from within the store brought his attention around to the serpent. It sat coiled in a ball near the cash registers, not twenty meters from where they stood. The sound was from scattered merchandise being pushed aside as the snake uncoiled from around the very dead zombie cat. Its body was well and truly crushed, and its head had already disappeared into the snake's mouth. The thing was flexing its internal muscles and jaws to push the cat's corpse down its throat.

Griff leaned back and whispered directly into Lisa's ear. His voice was barely more than a breath. "It has to be now. While its mouth is full. I'll blast its head. You find a spot where the bear took a bite. Shoot that spot till you're empty, then run!"

Lisa nodded, a terrified but determined look on her face. She hefted her shotgun, and Griff took a moment to ensure the safety was off. With a couple deep breaths, he lowered the visor on his helmet before he dashed forward through the opening the bear and snake had bashed through the wall. Unlike the game, where he would shout and taunt to get the boss monster's attention, he tried to avoid its notice as long as possible. He wanted to get up close and personal to blast the thing's face off.

He looked down long enough to spot and hurdle a moving coil at his feet. When he looked up again, the monster's head was almost within arm's reach. He felt warm liquid running down his leg as his bladder failed him. Screaming in terror, he raised his weapon and fired point-blank into the monster's face. Its nearest eye exploded in a shower of grey flesh and blue blood.

Afraid of the splatter, he began to step back. He automatically pumped and fired the weapon twice more as he did so. A second later, he was falling backward as the coil he'd leapt over a moment earlier swept his feet from under him.

He fired again as he fell, narrowly avoiding blasting off his own feet as they rose up atop the moving coil. As he paused to roll over and regain his feet, he heard Lisa fire twice, then scream.

All fear forgotten, he leapt forward again, holding his fire as he raced toward the monster's face. Some remote part of his brain registered that it was attempting to disgorge the cat's body, now nearly half-way down its throat. He couldn't let that happen.

Disregarding any concern for his own safety, he dodged another coil and moved almost directly below the snake's head. It hovered less than three meters above the floor as it tried to push its meal free. Raising his shotgun, he clamped his eyes and mouth shut and fired directly into the thing's throat. He pumped and fired again, then again. Opening his eyes, he ignored the neon-blue spatters on his visor and found the beast's head falling in his direction. He stepped back, then again, then jumped backward as the massive head hit the floor where he'd been standing. The thing twitched a few times but made no move to attack.

"Lisa!" he shouted, forgetting where he was. He looked frantically around the space cleared by the thrashing giant.

A hand raised into the air and waved weakly at him before dropping back down. He found the rest of her beneath a pile of cereal boxes. Her shotgun lay next to her, and she was cradling one arm. "It knocked me back. I think I've broken my arm." She held it with her free hand as she raised it to show him. "And I might have hurt my back, too." Her voice was very calm and matter of fact. Griff suspected she might be in shock.

He slung her weapon over his shoulder along with his own and reached down intending to lift her up and carry her. She recoiled slightly, and he looked down at his blood-spattered hands and arms. He'd almost forgotten! Stepping back, he winced as he watched her awkwardly get to her feet while trying to protect her injured arm. She looked down at a dark stain on her pants, then blushed and muttered, "I might've wet meself as well."

He laughed. "Don't worry, so did I. We'll both get a change of clothes and a shower soon enough." He walked next to her as she slowly picked her way through the store and out the back to the Jeep. She managed with great difficulty to haul herself up into the seat, where she sagged, exhausted.

Looking around, he said, "We still need food. Will ya be okay here while I gather some right quick?"

She nodded, obviously in pain but determined not to show it. He said, "There's a .45 in the glove box, just in case," then closed the door. After a quick inspection of his gear, he found most of his front was splattered with zombie blood. He hesitated, not wanting to expose himself, but not wanting to contaminate their food. Decision made, he removed his helmet, stripped off his armor, pants, shirt, and gloves. He left his shoes, not wanting to step barefoot in any blood splatter.

Almost running around the nearest shelves to where they'd left their carts, he began to fill his as quickly as possible. He had grabbed a couple of plastic bags, which he slid his hands into and then wrapped tight to use as gloves. It wasn't ideal, but they should protect him well enough. As he was grabbing more packages of beef jerky, he laughed aloud.

"What? Don't wanna go loot the boss, lad?" he mumbled to himself. Then he shivered at the idea of getting anywhere near the snake or bear again.

With his cart filled, he grabbed Lisa's and headed for a different area. He filled her cart with jars of fruit preserves, pickled eggs for protein, and cans of tuna, chicken, and spam. Three minutes later, he was pushing one cart and pulling the other behind him as he arrived back at the Jeep. He opened the back passenger door and began unceremoniously tossing food items inside. He slowed to gently place the glass jars on the floorboard, then hastily covered them with more items.

He kept glancing at Lisa, seeing her with eyes closed and a serene look on her face. He assumed she had passed out from the pain or from exhaustion. No point in waking her.

Before leaving, he needed to take care of one more thing. With the front of the store smashed in, and the double doors broken so that they wouldn't close properly, any zombie creature that came to investigate the bodies might find its way to their food supply. So he cleared several of the metal shelves from the front of the store, taking them back into the warehouse. Closing the doors as best he could, he used an extension cord to tie the broken but still partially attached handles together. Then he used a pallet dolly to move several heavy pallets against the doors. Finally, he slid the shelves down between the pallets and the doors, one atop the other like wooden planks boarding a door.

Stepping back, he looked at his handiwork. Anything larger than a squirrel would have a hard time squeezing through the gap. And they'd be able to tell at a glance if anything large enough to push through that blockade had done so. That would have to suffice.

Looking mournfully at his armor, he carefully picked it up, avoiding any blood spots, and tossed it outside. No point in risking contamination by bringing it along. After closing the loading dock door, he opened up the driver's door of the Jeep and sat sideways in the seat. Using the bottom edge of the door, he pried off his boots and left them where they lay. He had one more pair of shoes back at their facility, but he'd need to go shopping for replacement gear ASAP.

Breathing a sigh of relief as he closed the door, he started the Jeep and began a roundabout route back to his new home.

*****

Mace and Shari woke before dawn, excited to get back into the game and start their invasion of Graf. They grabbed a quick shower, soaping each other's backs with a minimum of funny business before hitting the kitchen for breakfast. They ate cold pop tarts and washed them down with cold green tea sweetened with honey.

The cleanup was quick and easy, and they were back in their pods in just a few minutes. They logged back in at the camp, which was being packed up in preparation for the last leg of their trip. The carpenters had fashioned a new mast for the ship, and the rest of the crew were busily re-attaching all the rigging as the sun began to rise above the treetops.

T'enaj and her mate were standing with Dorbin Stonehand and Red, talking quietly as Jorin shouted orders to his crew. Three new faces stood patiently a short distance behind the two drow. Mace assumed they were thieves. All three were human, two men and a woman, and all were dressed in nondescript dark colored leather and wool.

"Good morning, my friends." Mace greeted everyone as he and Shari approached.

"Ah, Mace and Shari. Good day to you as well." T'enaj bowed her head in greeting. "We were just discussing possible strategies for our assault on the Black Flame."

Red chuckled and added, "The drow here have several admirably devious and effective plans, while this blockhead dwarf prefers simply barging through the front door and killing everything in sight."

Stonehand's grin was completely unrepentant. "I go with what works best fer meself."

Shari stepped over and hugged the dwarf, causing him to blush slightly. "We wouldn't have you any other way, Master Stonehand."

T'enaj motioned to the thieves standing behind her. "You mentioned a desire to transport the horses you captured back to Port Bjurstrom. These three are willing to drive your herd there, for a small fee. They are initiates of my guild, who must prove themselves loyal and trustworthy before becoming full members." She paused as she saw the look on Shari and Mace's faces. "Do not worry. They would not dare to steal from you. On pain of death."

All three nodded their heads in agreement as Mace looked them over. "Their assistance would be appreciated." He walked over and handed each of them five gold coins. "Another five gold for each of you when we pick up the horses at the port."

He turned and started to walk away, then paused. "Oh, and umm… don't go into our warehouse without Callahan or someone to escort you. There's a wyvern in there with orders to eat strangers."

The thieves nodded vigorously, pocketing the gold and setting off toward the picketed horses. T'enaj spoke quietly, as they were still within earshot. "That was most generous. A gold coin or two each would have sufficed. They grew up on the streets. I doubt any one of them has ever held five gold coins at once in their lives." N'osaj nodded behind her.

Shari answered before Mace could. "Our… organization is dedicated to improving the lives of our citizens. And our friends. You'll find that we are going to be more generous than most of the outworlders you've known."

Jorin joined them then. "The *Sea Sprite* will be ready to sail within the hour. How do you want to proceed?"

Mace looked toward the small ship. "I think… just the way we were yesterday. Continue up the river like the attack never happened. Assume that none of the slavers had time to report in to their superiors before we wiped them out. We'll approach the docks like any other merchant ship and act normal unless we're attacked. But keep everyone on alert and ready for a fight."

T'enaj added, "Once you've reached the docks, most of the crew should remain with the ship. The Black Flame have captured several ships recently, as you know. My people will keep an eye on theirs and alert you if it looks as if they're making a move on the *Sea Sprite*. The rest of you, we'll meet you at the Lusty Strumpet tavern as planned." She gave them a small wave, and the two drow disappeared into the forest.

Mace elected to help the crew with the final repairs, giving him a chance to improve his Carpentry skill by one point. Shari spent most of the hour with Layne and the pets. They sat on the riverbank, Shari practicing her Cartography as Layne played a lively tune. Snuffles and Mion played their own convoluted version of tag, romping around in the grass for a bit until Snuffles happened across some tasty mushrooms. Mion rode his back as he rooted around in the earth, then pounced on any rodents or large insects he unearthed.

Minx sat upon Shari's shoulder, tail wrapped around the elfess's neck as she watched her draw a map of the river and the area where they'd camped. At one point, she hopped down onto Shari's lap and tentatively took hold of a small bit of charcoal with one tiny hand. She reached out and scraped it across the bottom corner of the parchment, drawing a wavy line. Eyes wide, she gave a questioning squeak and looked up at Shari, who giggled with delight.

"Yes, little one. That is how you draw. You are *so adorable*! Here, you can practice on this." Shari removed a clean piece of parchment from her bag and set it on the ground next to her. Minx promptly walked over and sat on it, covering about half the surface and holding it down. Then she reached out and made an experimental scribble with the charcoal. Both Layne and Shari clapped their hands and made encouraging sounds. Minx grinned at them, her sharp little teeth bared, and went at it with gusto.

When the captain declared the *Sea Sprite* travel-worthy, the two ladies praised Minx's page of careful scribbles as beautiful, promising to frame it and hang it in a place of honor. Mion flapped over to Shari's shoulder and examined the parchment, tilting her head from side to side before chirping a question. Snuffles just sniffed at it and attempted to nibble a corner before being scolded and moving on. Minx, sitting atop Layne's shoulder now, purred happily at the praise and deposited her small bit of charcoal into her pouch for safekeeping.

They all boarded the boat and found their regular places on the deck as the crew shoved off and got underway.

The rest of the trip upriver was uneventful and short. Mace retrieved the two scrolls that Jervis had given him along with the quest back in Immernacht. One was the portal scroll that would return him to his mentor's shop. The other was background information for the quest.

> *The outworlder Pokeface was sent to Graf to retrieve an item stolen from our queen. The Tear of the Spider Queen is an enchanted item stolen by a priestess who served as one of the queen's ladies for a time. The priestess, named Garya, stole the artifact and fled to the surface centuries ago. One of our informants recently located her running a slaver guild in the trade city of Graf, but was unable to get close enough to apprehend her. Pokeface was to infiltrate and rise through the ranks of her organization, and steal back the Tear. He was also given a bonus quest to kill Garya.*

> *As Pokeface has failed to return or even report, you have now been offered his quest, as well as the bonus quest to kill Garya. There is an additional reward for killing Pokeface for his failure. Return to Jervis with the Tear, and you will receive your rewards. Fail, and your head will be added to the list for the next quest recipient.*

As Graf came into view around a bend in the river, crew and passengers alike began unobtrusively preparing for battle. Swords were loosened in their sheaths. Crossbows were loaded and set carefully out of view of anyone observing from shore. Mace and company remained seated in their places amongst the cargo crates and sacks, but each of them were mentally preparing to take on the Black Flame if they should attack at the docks.

Captain Jorin expertly guided the small ship into a berth indicated by a raised flag. A representative of the harbormaster waved an arm and shouted, "Ahoy, *Sea Sprite!*" The captain waved back as sails were dropped, and the boat's forward progress slowed to a crawl. She slid right up against the fenders along the assigned dock, and crewmen tossed lines to waiting dock workers. Mace barely felt it when she came to a complete stop.

The harbormaster's representative was a weaselly looking man with greasy hair and two missing fingers on his left hand. His eyes darted about the deck, clearly taking stock of the cargo as he waited for a gangplank to be run out for him to board. Captain Jorin whispered to Mace, "That one gets kickbacks from the Black Flame and the Thieves' Guild as well. He'll send runners to report our worth, our crew strength, and when we plan to sail again."

Mace looked at the man with loathing. "No, he won't. Are you certain he's working for the Black Flame?" His voice was cold and menacing.

Jorin eyed Mace for a moment, then nodded his head. "Aye, lad. I'm sure." The tone of his own voice made it clear he knew he was signing the man's death warrant. "Many a crew's been done dirty based on his say-so."

Ian, who had elected to remain on board, spoke from the shadows. "It is so, yes."

Mace looked in the direction of the voice, though he knew there was nothing to see. "Ian, will T'enaj consider it an unfriendly act if we were to eliminate this scum?"

"Sacrifices must be made if we are to secure the city, yes. Easily replaced this one is, to be sure. She will not mind, no."

"Then let us invite him aboard and show him the wondrous cargo in our hold." Red smiled at Mace, supportive of his plan. "Are there any others in sight that we should invite to the party?"

Jorin scanned the crowd. "The two big bald fellows with the tattooed heads. They are enforcers for the Black Flame. To keep the dock workers in line. And to keep T'enaj's people from liberating any of their property."

Ian's voice came to them again, from a different direction this time. He was now standing near the rail. "The good captain is correct, yes. Also, the three archers on the roof above them. Very thorough Garya is, yes. Her rooftop vermin were how she caught me. Observed my shadow they did, oh yes. I would happily dispose of those three for you," the six-foot bunny growled again. He was clearly taking this personally.

Mace looked doubtful. "Maybe I should come with you. Three on one doesn't seem like good odds."

"You are correct, yes. They have no hope against me, no. I will leave the two bald ones for you, if you prefer, yes?" Ian's voice didn't waver. There was no hint of doubt or humor in it.

Mace chuckled. "So be it. Ian, the archers are yours. Stonehand, would you and Red like to handle the big beefy ones? Preferably quietly?" He waited as the dwarf rolled his eyes, then nodded.

"Aye, lad. We'll be quiet as mice." He smiled as Red snorted.

"Then I'll stay here and deal with the weasel down below. And we'll all meet at the tavern as planned afterward."

Mace leaned back against a mast, folding his arms and acting casual as the gangplank was set in place. The doomed weasel practically dashed up the ramp in his haste to perform his duties, official and otherwise. He hailed the captain and climbed the steps to the helm.

Stonehand and Red casually descended the ramp, strolling up the dock toward their targets, laughing and joking about something Mace couldn't make out over the hustle and bustle around them. Ian, of course, was invisible. Mace scanned the dock looking for the bunny's shadow while he waited for the harbormaster's spy to go belowdecks.

He was interrupted by Minx landing on his shoulder, invisible herself. He felt her tail wrap around his neck, and a moment later, her voice came to him. *"I smell human I can't see."* He felt her tiny paw tap his face, and he turned that direction slightly. Another tap, and he turned further, scanning the deck. Sure enough, there was a slight shift in the shadows next to a stack of crates as someone moved past them.

Now Mace had a dilemma. His inclination was to simply kill whomever it was. But he had no way to know if it was one of Garya's Black Flames, one of T'enaj's people - which would make them an ally - or simply someone going about their own business.

He decided to wait a few moments. Keeping an eye on the slowly moving shadow as it avoided crewmen and other obstacles, he followed unobtrusively. A quick glance showed Jorin leading the other man down into the hold. Mace stopped for a moment, conflicted. He spied a bit of cargo netting that had just been removed from a stack of crates and had his answer.

Grabbing the netting, he dashed forward and tossed it in the direction of the stealthed individual. It wrapped nicely around them, much to their surprise and that of the crew. Instantly, there were six cutlasses pointed at the figure that appeared beneath the netting.

Mace didn't wait to see who it was. He stepped behind a large crate and activated his own stealth ability. Three steps and he dropped down through a hatch into the cargo hold, landing nimbly and silently on an upright barrel.

The captain was there, loudly informing the spy of the many rich silks and gold-encrusted baubles they carried. The man practically drooled as he calculated his cut of the booty.

He never finished his calculation. Mace simply glided up behind him, his feet not making a sound on the wooden deck. Reaching around with his enchanted dagger, he whispered, "This is for everyone you've betrayed," and pushed the blade up under the man's chin until it penetrated his brain.

The dagger sang to him, the rush of energy surging up his arm as the man's corpse went limp and he let it fall.

Jorin, who had continued talking past the moment of the man's death, looked over in surprise. He hadn't heard or seen Mace either. "Damn, lad." He shook his head. "Here's hoping you never consider me an enemy."

Mace grinned at his friend. "Never happen. Minx caught someone snooping around up on deck. Want to come find out who it is?

Jorin's face darkened, and he took the steps upward two at a time. His crewmen still stood where Mace had left them, surrounding a man in black leather who was standing with his hands raised underneath the net. Mace emerged in time to hear the man say, "I swear, I meant no harm. I was simply trying to stow away!"

Jorin eyed the man, his arms crossed. "I seem to have more than my share of stowaways lately. What is your name?"

The man turned to the captain and tried to put his hands down. Six blades poked at him from every angle. The hands went up higher. "I…

my name is Edgar. I swear on my life I mean you no harm. Please, this net is getting heavy." He looked up at his shaking arms.

Captain Jorin nodded, and two of the crewmen secured their blades before pulling the net off the stowaway.

"Thank you, Captain…?"

"Jorin. Now tell me what you're doing aboard my *Sea Sprite* before Mace here feeds your soul to his dagger." He nodded toward Mace, who produced the enchanted dagger and twirled it around a few times before making it disappear again.

"I just wanted to get away from here. As far away and as fast as possible." Edgar shrugged, looking down at the deck. "If I stay here, I'm a dead man." His voice was filled with defeat.

"And you couldn't just come aboard and ask for passage like everyone else?" Jorin kept his arms crossed and glared at the man.

"They took all my coin and everything I had of any value." Edgar spread his empty hands as if to emphasize his lack of means. "I was lucky to escape with my life. Garya's men were cocky, and I managed to surprise them."

"So Garya wants you dead," Mace spoke up. "For what reason?"

"My father is… *was* one of the leading merchants in Graf. A member of the Merchant's Guild council – one of three. When Garya made a bid to usurp the guild's position as part of the triumvirate that controls Graf, my father tried to have her assassinated. His assassins failed, and under torture, gave up his name. She had my father, mother, two sisters, and my younger brother murdered, then burned down our home. I was on a ship at the time, having been sent on a trade mission, and just recently arrived home. The moment I arrived, her people captured me."

Mace looked to Jorin, who kept his face neutral. The old half-elf gave no indication whether he believed the tale. So he said, "I don't know whether your tale is true or not. But I can tell you two things I do know. First, if you're lying to us, you're going to die painfully. Second, if your story is the truth, then very shortly you will have no Black Flame to deal with."

Edgar's eyes grew wide. "You're going to take on Garya? Are you insane?"

Jorin chuckled at this. "He might well be, boy. But Mace and his friends have already killed several of Garya's thugs. They've just come to finish the job." He pointed down the dock.

Edgar and the others turned, and Mace gave a little wave to Stonehand and Ian.

The big green bunny emerged from stealth as he slit the throat of the first archer, then jammed a dagger into the chest of another. As he was turning to finish the shocked second archer, the third managed to half-draw and release an arrow, sending it into Ian's shoulder but doing no real damage. Now truly horked off, the bunny assassin spun in a blur of knives and oversized feet. As he finished the middle archer, his foot impacted the head of the last in line, knocking him ass over teakettle. He then stabbed a dagger into the man's left eye, holding his head down as he slit his throat.

In seconds, the three archers on the roof were dead, blood fountaining down upon the surprised guards below. Who followed their comrades into oblivion a moment later when Stonehand and Red stopped laughing and joking to turn and put them down before they even knew what was happening. It was quick, quiet, and efficient. The few passersby who noticed anything at all chose to mind their own business.

The invasion of Graf had officially begun.

Mace and the others left Jorin and his crew to offload their cargo, taking Edgar with them on their walk to the Lusty Strumpet. Upon reaching the end of the dock, Stonehand and Red rejoined the group, and a whisper in his ear let Mace know that Ian was with them too.

Edgar, being a local, knew the tavern and led them in a relatively straight line to its door. Stonehand laughed at the painted sign depicting an ugly woman with oversized breasts trying to pin down a terrified sailor. "Yer friend the thief has a sense o' humor!" he commented as he led the way inside.

The raucous sounds of drinking games and wagering died down the moment the group walked through the door. Mace took in the crowd, mostly human sailors and cutthroats, and noted a few who might present a threat. After a moment of suspicious stares, the patrons all returned to their activities. Stonehand led them down a hallway and into a private dining room, per T'enaj's instructions.

Ian appeared in front of the group, bowing slightly and tipping his hat. "Welcome to the Strumpet. My mistress wishes me to escort you to the meeting place." He turned and pressed a series of six panels in the wall behind him. It swung open, revealing a dimly lit stairway leading downward. The bunny led the way, and the group followed in single file. Red brought up the rear, and she nodded appreciatively as the panel automatically closed behind her.

The stairway extended deep into the bedrock below the city. Mace estimated they were at least sixty feet below surface level when they reached the bottom landing. A round stone door rolled to one side, and N'osaj raised a hand in greeting. Behind him were a dozen guild members in various shades of leather and silk attire. They all stood in a casual, relaxed stance, but their hands were never far from their weapons.

"Hello, N'osaj. We have come to meet with your mistress as promised." Shari smiled at the dark elf. He returned her smile with one of his own, bobbing his head briefly before motioning with his hand that they should enter.

Stonehand led the way as usual, always prepared to become an axe-wielding juggernaut should a threat present itself. Shari and Layne followed with Snuffles trotting alongside. Mace and Lila were next, followed by Edgar, Red and the pack of thieves. They left the first chamber and proceeded through a series of twisting and turning corridors carved directly from the bedrock. They passed dozens of rooms with closed doors, behind some of which Mace heard either moans or screams. A quick glance at Shari confirmed she'd heard them too.

"What kind of kinky action is happening down here?" she whispered to him. He just shrugged and kept walking. As they went, he noticed N'osaj casually disarming several traps here and there by placing a hand in one spot, a foot in another. Being a drow, he naturally respected well-placed traps. He also noted blood stains on more than one wall where someone had failed to detect or disarm one of them.

He pointed to one particularly large blood spatter and asked N'osaj "Reminder for the initiates?"

The dark elf grinned and nodded his head, then he mimed a few clumsy steps and drew a finger across his own throat.

Stonehand chuckled, saying, "Seems they don't have much patience for blunderers like me!" N'osaj patted the dwarf on the shoulder and then mimed an exaggerated tiptoe, causing the dwarf to laugh harder and imitate him. This sight got everyone laughing as they continued down the corridor.

Eventually, they reached a large natural cavern with boulders strewn about the floor. Mace immediately noticed several poorly stealthed figures creeping here and there, moving behind one of the large stones or emerging from behind another. As he watched, one of them was hit in the face with a plum-sized stone, knocking them out of stealth.

As the woman yelped and rubbed her injured cheek, T'enaj appeared next to Mace, another stone in her hand. She whirled around and without even seeming to look, hurled that stone to ricochet off a boulder and strike a teenage boy in the back of the head, interrupting his stealth as well.

T'enaj ignored his cry of pain and gave her visitors a slight bow. "Welcome! I hear you have had an interesting morning already."

Mace kept an eye on the amateurs moving about the training ground as he replied, "A few of the Black Flame got in our way during our stroll through your fine city."

T'enaj chuckled, then turned to Edgar. "Ah, young master Shipwright! Welcome back to Graf. My condolences for the loss of your family. I presume you are here to avenge them?"

Edgar shook his head. "No, Mistress T'enaj. I was attempting to escape Garya's goons when these kind people caught me sneaking aboard their vessel. I'm afraid my stealth abilities aren't much better than your students here." He shrugged, embarrassed.

"If you do not wish to fight, why have you come here, then?" T'enaj frowned at the young man.

"I gave him no choice in the matter," Mace clarified. "For all I know, he could be one of Garya's spies. Or yours. He doesn't leave my sight until I know for sure who and what he is."

T'enaj grinned at her fellow drow. "Ah, but you suspected poor Jeremiah, the harbormaster's man, of spying for me on occasion, did you not? Yet you still slit his throat without hesitation."

"Jorin told me of the man's activities. And Ian suggested you would not mind the loss." Mace grinned at her, knowing she was simply playing the game that all drow instinctively fell back on. Leverage was a powerful tool.

"True enough. I despised the man, anyway. Good riddance. Now! As for young Edgar here, I give you my word he is the scion of the largest trading house in Graf. His father stood up to Garya, and his entire family died for it. Along with several of their servants and guards. I am surprised Edgar here is not more interested in vengeance."

Edgar shook his head. "My father was a fool to take on Garya. I learned from his mistake. Any influence I had here has been decimated, and going after her now would be suicide. I planned to leave the city and live to rebuild and return."

T'enaj nodded. "You display much wisdom for one so young. Your father taught you well. And because you are here with my friend Mace, and have shown you can think, I will share something with you." She paused as she pulled something from her inventory bag. It was a letter with a broken wax seal. She handed it to Edgar.

"Your father was not the fool you imagine. He was promised the support of the other two councilors when the time came to move on Garya. The proof is in your hand. But on the night of the attack, they withdrew and warned her people, thinking to put themselves in her good graces."

Edgar opened the letter and read it through. His face turned dark, and he crumpled the paper in his fist. "Then I shall make those traitors pay as well." There was steel in his voice as he met T'enaj's eyes.

35

"Good! I too lost some good people that night. When I learned of the betrayal, I tried to help your family escape. Sent my people to waylay hers in order to give your father time to move. But I was too late." She paused, taking a moment to remember those she lost. "I would be happy to help you eliminate those honorless worms."

Edgar looked confused. "Why would you help my family? You and yours have stolen from us more times than I could count."

She laughed, a light and carefree sound. "This is true! Is it not in the farmer's best interest to keep his prize cow fat and happy?" She winked as he looked offended and opened his mouth to retort. "But my reason was more selfish than that. We of the triumvirate keep a delicate balance. I don't steal so much that your father and the others feel the need to pay Garya to eliminate me. The merchants keep trade flowing into the city, both legal and illegal, bringing us traders and tourists to rob. And both of our guilds cooperate to keep Garya and her ilk from taking control of it all. Until recently, that is."

Edgar processed the information quickly, then looked to Mace. "And you intend to…what? Wipe out the Black Flame and take their place as the third leg of our little milking stool?"

Mace shook his head. "I hadn't thought of that. My aim is to eliminate the slavers. And to recover something of importance to a friend of mine. My agreement with T'enaj did not include becoming the third wheel here in Graf." He paused to gauge the thief's reaction. "But if you need me and mine to fill that role…"

T'enaj rolled her eyes. "Silly drow. I'm sure Edgar and I can come to some understanding as to the sharing of power in this city. There is no need for you to concern yourself with all the dreary details of governing."

Mace bowed slightly. "I appreciate your kind concern, but it would not be me in any case. I have a city of my own to build. Several, in fact." This caused T'enaj's eyes to widen slightly for just a fraction of a second. But to a drow that spoke volumes.

"Several cities, you say? Then I shall look forward to continuing our friendship and visiting you. I'm sure I can be of some assistance, perhaps advise you in the proper way to conduct trade in your cities." Her smile was dazzling and completely false.

"Ha! Establishing a guild house with each visit, I'm sure. We can talk about that once our mission here is accomplished," Mace said.

"Yes, of course. And speaking of our mission, I have made preparations. My people are positioned around the city to monitor Garya's movements. At the moment, she is planning to host a dinner at her home in the merchant quarter this evening. It is rare to know where she will be that far in advance. I suggest we strike then."

Shari asked, "And her guests? We don't want to risk killing innocents."

T'enaj stepped forward and patted Shari's cheek gently. "Her guests will not be innocents, my lovely elfess. Among them will be the two councilors who betrayed master Shipwright, the captain of the city guard, who is on Garya's payroll, one pirate captain, and two slave buyers."

Shari bristled at the physical contact but kept her cool. "And we're to take your word for this?"

T'enaj frowned, stepping back a few paces. "I'm hurt that you would doubt me." She pouted. "It would not be very wise of me to begin a new friendship by lying and tricking you into killing innocents, knowing it would offend you."

Shari looked at Mace, who shrugged noncommittally. It was Stonehand who broke the silence. "I believe ye, lass. Me own experience with drow, excepting young Mace here, be that ye'll lie and cheat 'n' murder without a second thought. But that ye rarely act against yer own best interests. Ye can't afford ta have us turn on ye if'n ye be lying to us now." He fingered a hand-axe on his belt. "It'd cost ye dearly."

"Just so!" T'enaj clapped her hands together. "Well said, Master dwarf. Now, if we're all in agreement that all the nasty people at that dinner must die, and any innocents who happen to somehow find themselves at that table are to be spared, shall we review our plans?"

She led them to another chamber where they all sat at a table, atop which was a map of the city. For the next several hours, they ate, drank, and made plans, then discarded them and made more.

*****

Griff and Lisa made it back to their compound without incident. He'd quickly decided not to bother with an indirect route, figuring anything in the area was now headed for the Tesco and would be munching on bear, snake, and cat for some time. And Lisa needed medical attention as soon as possible.

Peabody opened the garage door for him and closed it behind as he passed through. He parked right by the lobby entrance door and hopped out. The sudden stop and quieting of the engine woke Lisa as he moved around the truck to open her door. He reached out to help her, but she stopped him. "No! I got hit by the snake, I might have been contaminated too. I can get out on my own."

When he moved back, she sort of half stepped, half fell out of the passenger seat and stood on wobbly legs for a moment. After a few deep breaths, she felt steadier and walked toward the door. Peabody unlocked it, and Griff opened it for her.

Safely downstairs, Griff immediately went to change, feeling self-conscious in just his army issue boxers. He needed a shower, but he wanted to deal with Lisa's injured arm first. He'd just pulled on new boxers and jeans and was searching for a shirt when he heard Lisa call to him. "Griff? Can ya lend me a hand, please?"

Abandoning the search, he hurried to her room and found her still dressed. Blushing prettily, she said, "I need a bit o' help gettin' these things off." She pointed to her broken arm. "But run to the lab and get some surgical gloves first."

Griff did as she requested, running to the lab and grabbing some gloves, then running back. As he went, he said, "Peabody, can you call Shari for me? Lisa is injured, and I'm no medic."

"Shari is currently logged into the game. Would you like me to request that she log out?"

Griff thought about it for a moment. "Not yet, Peabody. Let me talk to Lisa first."

He arrived back at her room, gloves already on. He carefully removed her helmet, then unzipped and unfastened her armor pieces and removed them, including her gloves. All of them went into a plastic garbage bag. Then he untied and removed her shoes and reached for the button of her jeans. Sensing her nervousness, he paused, saying, "Never imagined I'd get this far on our first date!" and winking at her.

Lisa snorted and rolled her eyes at him. "Don't get any funny ideas, mister. Ya get fresh with me and I'll tell Peabody to lock ya out for good!"

Griff raised his hands as if warding off an attack, a look of mock horror on his face. "Out there with the monsters?"

"Idiot. Get me out of these clothes and stop messin' about!"

"I love it when a woman says that to me. So romantic." He quickly unfastened her jeans and pulled them off, depositing them with the rest of her gear. Then he very carefully helped remove her shirt, freeing the good arm first, then pulling it over her head and slowly down over the injured arm.

Blushing furiously, she said, "I can handle the rest, thank you. Now, out!"

Chuckling, he said, "Damn!" He stripped off the gloves and tossed them in the trash, pretending to sulk as he left the room and closed the door. Standing outside, he spoke to her loud enough to hear through the door. "I'm worried about that arm. Peabody says Shari is in the game, but I can have her log out and call us. Maybe she can talk us through how to fix it?"

She called back, "Let me take an x-ray first. We have a machine in lab 4. You can help me – I'll show you how it works. If it's a bad break, we'll call Shari. If not, I know enough to splint and wrap it, and there are some anti-inflammatories in the pharmacy cabinet."

He waited patiently, pacing the hall for a moment until he heard her shower turn on. "Good idea!" He headed for his own quarters and hit the shower. Dressed and smelling better, he went back to pacing in the hall outside her door, trying to think of some way he could help her or ease her pain.

A few minutes later, the door opened, and Lisa stood there in a robe, wet hair covering half her face. "You smell much better." She gave him a half-smile.

"As do you! And I like the fashion statement. Didn't realize this company had super-casual Fridays." His smile was wide and genuine.

"Ha! Let's go." She led him down the corridors to lab 4, which had no pods in it but was set up as a medical lab with a gurney, a hard-mounted exam table, and machines of all types including an x-ray camera on an adjustable arm that extended from the ceiling.

Lisa showed him the operating panel for the machine, which was behind a glass screen in the corner. Then they walked over to the table. She pressed a button to raise it up, then allowed him to help her raise the injured arm and set it carefully on the table. Griff looked around. "Don't you need some kind of film underneath?"

She shook her head. "The whole table surface has sensors under it. It'll send the image right to the monitor. We could print it if needed, but there's no point."

Griff went back to the control panel and dutifully pressed the button. There was a brief mechanical buzz, and five seconds later, Lisa straightened up. Cradling her arm, she walked over to join him and pressed a few buttons. A moment later, an x-ray image of her arm came up on the monitor. She enlarged the image, zooming in on the break.

"See there? A fracture in the radius." She pointed to the obvious break. It didn't seem offset, just as if it had cracked. She moved her finger to a cloudy area right next to the bone. "This is where some of the major muscles in my forearm attach to the bone. That's why it hurts so much. They've been bruised, probably slightly torn."

"So, do you know how to deal with this? Or should Peabody wake Shari?"

"No need." She moved to a storage cabinet in the back of the room, indicating Griff should open it. "Yeah, there it is. Bottom shelf, left side... yeah, that's the one." Griff pulled out the item she had directed him to. "It's an inflatable cast. And right there is a sling."

Ten minutes later, they had managed to immobilize her arm, and she'd taken a few pills to help with the swelling and pain. They were sitting on one of the sofas in the lounge area, and she leaned her good side against him. "Thank you, for helping me."

"My pleasure." He smiled warmly at her. "So... d'ya think there'll be a second date?"

"Hmmm? If ya play your cards right, maybe. I'm no pushover ya know. Evan had to buy me *three* beers before I let him get to third base."

Griff chuckled. "Well, we have cold beer in the walk-in, and I'm thinkin' maybe if ya mix it with the pills ya just took, I might get lucky tonight!"

"Ha! Dream on, dwarf-boy. And speakin' o' dwarves, I don't think I'll be getting back in the game today. I'm tired, and these pills are just gonna make me sleepier still. If ya *really* want to be my hero, you could carry me to my bed."

"Aye, I can surely do that. But... I'm enjoying this moment. D'ya mind if we sit here a while? I'll carry ya when ya fall asleep."

She snuggled up a bit closer, her head on his shoulder. "I'd like that."

Careful not to jostle her bad arm, he gently moved a lock of hair from in front of her face, leaned down and kissed her forehead. "Rest easy. Ya killed a real-life boss monster today. That makes you a bad-ass amazon princess or somethin'."

She just mumbled something that sounded happy and put her good hand on his knee.

*****

Mace and Shari logged off as the evening approached night, taking an hour for a quick bathroom break and to grab something to eat. As soon as they were dressed, Peabody spoke to them.

"Admin Shari, I must inform you that Lisa was injured today. She suffered a broken arm."

"What? Is she okay? Why didn't they call me?" They were almost to the kitchen, but she turned around to head toward the security office.

"Griff recommended contacting you, but Lisa did not think it serious enough to disturb you while in game. Griff said to tell you it is a fractured radius based on the x-ray image and that they have it immobilized. And Lisa has taken pills that made her sleepy."

Shari turned around again, headed back to the kitchen. Mace just grinned and followed along behind. "I guess if it's not serious, we should let her sleep. It's like 2:00 am where they are. Good thing they had an x-ray machine. Peabody, do we have an x-ray machine here?"

The AI took a moment to answer. *"As you know, I do not have visual access to the labs. But the inventory does indicate an x-ray machine is supposed to be in medical lab 6."*

"Huh. I never looked in there. Just assumed it was more pods. Good to know. Thank you, Peabody." Shari waved up at the ceiling.

They shared a quick snack of canned peaches and beef jerky, then returned to their pods.

*****

Back in the underground chamber with the thieves and the rest of their group, Mace and Shari prepared for the upcoming fight. They would focus on Garya and her guests, then proceed to mop up her people.

Mace had insisted that there would be no quarter. None of their foes would be allowed to surrender. Anyone still in Graf working for the Black Flame was no innocent, save those like household staff or slaves that had no choice. And he didn't want his people having to watch their backs in fear of stragglers surviving to take revenge. When he'd insisted,

T'enaj looked at him in surprise for a moment, then nodded her head. "As you wish, Darkblade."

She and N'osaj led Mace's group and a host of thieves out of the underground cavern via a different corridor. This one split into many offshoot tunnels, and as they passed each one, a small group of two or three thieves would split off and disappear.

They continued to move upward as they advanced through tunnels, sometimes taking stairs, sometimes ladders. After about twenty minutes, T'enaj brought them to a halt.

"This will lead to a wine cellar in the mansion next to Garya's. It is one floor taller than hers, and we can use a rope from this roof down to hers."

Stonehand shook his head. "If it be all the same to ye, I'll take the front door. Dwarves in plate armor don't do 'ropey-slidey things'. I'll wait till yer inside, o' course, so the noise don't alert them. But as soon as I hear the fightin', I'll be making my way in."

Red nodded. "He's right. His heavy arse would snap the rope. I'll go with him."

T'enaj thought about it for a moment. "Actually, most of you should go through the front behind Master Stonehand here. Only those of us who can stealth will drop in on the roof." She turned to Ian and three of her people who were still with them. "You three, cover the back door. Nobody leaves, understood? Ian, you know what to do." Three quick nods were her only answer.

N'osaj opened the door quietly. Mace noticed that though the door looked ancient and was covered in cobwebs and dust, the hinges were well oiled and silent. When they'd all passed through, the last of the thieves carefully closed and bolted the door behind them.

There were two exits from the cellar. One was a set of double doors at the top of a ramp that led out to a rear courtyard. The three thieves motioned to Stonehand to follow, and they disappeared through those doors. Shari, Layne, Stonehand, and Red went as well. Lila and Mace looked to T'enaj, who whispered, "The owners of this house are at a party, and should not return for another hour or more. We must only avoid household staff between here and the roof."

She took the lead this time, ascending a short stone stairway without even a whisper of sound. She listened at the door at the top for a few moments, then slowly pulled it open. The others followed her up, all now in stealth mode, and gathered in the kitchen.

It was a large room for a kitchen, with two prep areas and a long eat-in table for the household staff. From the size of the table, there were several staff working in this house. T'enaj led them out a doorway to a narrow servant's stair. They climbed slowly and silently. An hour was plenty of time.

At the second floor landing, they paused when T'enaj broke stealth and pointed at the gap at the bottom of the door. A flickering light, likely from one or more candles, was growing brighter. They all quickly moved to the stairs leading farther upward, and pressed themselves against the wall. T'enaj stood right next to the door, unstealthed.

A moment later, the door opened and a young man in a nightshirt stepped through, carrying a single candle. Without even looking around, he left the door open and proceeded down the stairs to the kitchen, licking his lips in anticipation. T'enaj stuck her head out from behind the door, grinning. She pointed upward and took the lead. The others followed closely behind.

Reaching the top floor without further interruption, T'enaj led them down a corridor with plush forest green carpeting. They all left stealth mode, as they'd be unable to make noise walking on the thick carpet if they tried. T'enaj carefully opened a door at the end of the corridor leading to the master bedroom.

Bringing up the rear, N'osaj quietly closed the door behind them as T'enaj moved toward a balcony door. She paused halfway across the room and turned toward a dressing table with an ornate mirror. Atop the table was a lacquered wooden box with gold hinges and clasps. She drifted over to the table and quickly examined the box for traps before lifting the lid. Inside were several diamond and pearl chokers hung on little hooks attached to the lid. And the lower half of the box contained rings, earrings, and other expensive-looking baubles.

With a tiny shrug and grin, she closed the box and tucked it into her bag. "I am a thief, after all. And since this house does not belong to Garya or her people, I get to keep it all!"

A grunt from N'osaj caused her to amend her statement. "My darling and I get to keep it all." N'osaj gave her a thumbs-up.

"Fine, it's all yours." Mace motioned toward the balcony as Lila looked as if she was about to argue. "We've got work to do. And as you said, these people will be home in less than an hour to find their trinkets missing."

"Good point." T'enaj opened the balcony doors, stepped outside, hopped up on the railing, and then did a backflip up onto the roof above. N'osaj simply jumped up and grabbed hold of the gutter and pulled himself up.

Lila looked at the railing, then up at the roof. Her diminutive stature would make that a difficult leap. Mace waved to get her attention, then bent down and cupped his hands together, offering her a boost. She blew him a little kiss, then took a few steps and jumped, using his hands as a lift-off point. He straightened his legs and back and threw her upward as far as he could, watching as she sailed over his head and onto the roof. Mace himself copied T'enaj, hopping up onto the railing, then onto the roof – just without the backflip.

The four moved to the peak of the pitched roof at the edge closest to Garya's mansion. T'enaj was correct, they were a full ten feet or so above the top of her roof. There were three chimneys along the length of the roof and two skylights that were currently dark as there were no lights on in the rooms below.

N'osaj lifted a small hand crossbow with a spool mounted below the trigger. He took careful aim and fired. The bolt flew across the gap between houses, a thin filament whirring quietly as it unspooled at high speed. The bolt embedded itself in the nearest chimney, and N'osaj unhooked the spool. He moved back along the ridge of their roof and tied the end of the line around the chimney there.

Mace looked at the thin wire, using Identify.

Mithril Wire

Item Quality: Rare
This wire was crafted by the grey dwarves to be light and flexible,
yet incredibly strong.

"That looks valuable. Seems a waste to use it here, as you may not be able to come back and claim it when we're done."

T'enaj just snorted. "The day I can't sneak back here to reclaim this is the day I retire or die."

Mace believed her. Still, he decided to show off a bit. He moved so that T'enaj was between himself and the roof's edge. He held out his hand as if to shake hers. Just as she reached to accept it, he cast Levitate on her. He quickly grasped her hand and pulled, spinning his body as he did so. When he had rotated a full 360 degrees, he used his momentum to fling her across the gap between houses.

She cursed quietly at him as she glided across, having no control over her body. Eventually, she came within reach of the mithril wire and took hold. When she was safely over the other roof near the chimney, he canceled the spell, and she dropped quietly onto the roof. The hand gesture she made next caused the others to chuckle quietly.

Mace cast Levitate on Lila next, then N'osaj, and they each used the wire to guide themselves across. He then untied the spool from around the chimney, cast Levitate on himself, and began reeling in the wire. This action pulled him across, and he dropped himself near the chimney. Handing the spool back to N'osaj, he said, "There. No need for additional sneakery."

N'osaj laughed silently as T'enaj gave Mace a dirty look. She moved to the nearest skylight and began removing items from her bag. The first was a resin of some kind, which she applied to both ends of a rounded handle before pushing the ends against the glass. Then she produced a vial of liquid and poured it around the edges of the glass. It immediately began to smoke and bubble. Standing upright, she straddled the skylight and bent to loop a short rope under the handle. When it was secure, she waited a few moments, then tugged on the rope. The entire sheet of glass lifted free, and she shuffled forward until she could set the glass down on the roof's surface. The removal had been quick and silent, and Mace gave her a nod of respect.

One by one, they dropped through the opening into what appeared to be a guest bedroom. Lila immediately began watching the two thieves to ensure they didn't pocket any items from Mace's future property. Mace watched Lila, a small but affectionate smile on his face.

T'enaj dropped her voice to a whisper. "The dining room is two floors down. All of the staff should be down on that level, seeing to the needs of Garya and her guests. But they may have some retainers or security roaming the house. Keep an eye out."

Fading back into stealth mode, the four of them left the guest room and traversed the short distance to the stairs. N'osaj took the lead, pausing a few times when he detected a trap. Mace relaxed a bit. Active traps meant that no one else was likely to be moving around up here. And no trap was going to escape the notice of the two drow thieves, a drow Darkblade, and a sharp-eyed halfling.

Near the ground floor landing, Mace hissed at N'osaj to stop. He detected a magical ward that the thief hadn't noticed. Mace didn't blame him, it was a very subtle ward that he himself might have missed if he hadn't specifically been looking for it.

With a quick hand motion, he brought the thief back up a step and took his place. Closing his eyes and crouching down so that he was at eye level with the device, he focused on the ward. It had no less than three separate triggers. Weight on the step, motion within two feet of the ward itself, or a loud noise within a cone of space in front of the ward's placement would each set the thing off. Looking deeper, he saw that it was both an alarm and a wicked trap. Six-inch spikes would shoot through the carpeting on the step, while darts filled with poison would erupt from the wall.

Mace slowly used his magic to unwind the multiple spells, first disabling the alarms, then the triggers for the trap. By the time he was through, he was sweating and his breathing shallow. The two thieves had been watching him closely, admiring his work. When he straightened up and let out a long exhale, N'osaj patted him on the back.

T'enaj took the lead now, moving across the ground level through an office that didn't seem as if it saw much use. The desk surface was clean except for a single stack of dusty papers and a quill pen and ink set.

Past the study was a short hall with cabinets on either side – a butler's pantry, with swinging doors at either end. To their right was the kitchen, the sounds of food prep coming to them through the door. Which meant that the dining room was to their left, where faint voices and occasional laughter could be heard.

N'osaj quietly stepped to the right-hand door and removed a jamb from his bag. Setting it down on the carpet, he used his toe to push it gently under the door. It would prevent anyone from the kitchen side opening it, for a little while at least.

T'enaj paused at the other door and made several quick hand motions, pointing toward each of the party members then indicating the direction they should go once inside the room. Mace had insisted that he be allowed to kill Garya, and though T'enaj had argued, she hadn't done so strenuously.

They were banking on the fact that the swinging door had been opening and closing throughout the dinner, and no one would give them a second look as they entered. Giving them a precious second or two before anyone reacted to their surprise attack.

T'enaj took a deep breath, then shouldered the door open quietly. She immediately dashed to her right while N'osaj went left. Lila was through the door right behind them, leaping up onto the table as Mace cleared the door before it had started to swing shut again.

He quickly took in the room. There was a long table with eight people seated, three along each side, and one on each end. To his right, T'enaj had already slit the throat of a well-dressed human, and she was in the process of stabbing a second in the kidney. Lila was sliding across the table, her feet raised and smashing into the chest of a woman who could only be the pirate captain, based on her garish silk and leather outfit. To his left, N'osaj had slammed a heavy dagger down into the skull of an unknown man who was falling face-first into his meal even as the guard captain drew a sword and got to his feet to face the drow.

Mace dashed to his right, where beyond T'enaj his target was getting to her feet. Garya already had a dagger in each hand and was shouting curses at T'enaj. The drow thief neatly avoided a slash from

Garya's dagger and flung herself in a roll across the table to help Lila with the two slavers.

Mace growled at the drow leader of the Black Flames. "Garya. I am the Darkblade known as Mace. Your life is forfeit. But I might show mercy if you answer some questions for me."

The drowess just screamed in rage and began to advance on him. "How *dare* you invade my home! I will wear your ears on a necklace, Darkblade! Guards!" She took a swing with her left dagger, the blade moving with lightning speed.

But Mace was in his element. He had trained in this type of combat from his first day in the game. Jervis had made him into an assassin that hunted other assassins. He avoided the strike by simply slowing his forward momentum just a hair, allowing the blade to pass harmlessly in front of his chest. Raising his right hand, he cut into her forearm as it passed with his enchanted dagger. The cut wasn't deep, but the pain it caused made her gasp.

She stepped back and pulled her injured wrist to her chest, her eyes wide. "What poison was that?"

Mace held up the grey dagger with its swirly cloudy surface. "No poison. I've just stolen a bit of your soul. And I'll take the rest if you force me to. Just answer my questions, and I'll kill you with this one and let you keep your soul." He raised the mundane dagger he held in his left hand.

Garya looked around, noting that of all her dinner guests, the only one still alive was the guard captain. Fighting furiously, he was bleeding from several wounds inflicted by N'osaj. But even a skilled human had little hope against a drow.

Lila and T'enaj had moved to the other door in the room and were awaiting any guards that entered that way.

"Ask your questions, assassin." She was clearly trying to buy time for her guards to intervene. An alarm had begun echoing through the house already. At the same time, there was the sound of wood splintering and angry shouts. Stonehand had just crashed the party.

Mace stood straight, but he kept his weapons ready. "First, what do you know of an outworlder named Pokeface?"

Garya snorted. "That incompetent fool. Three times he tried to complete the initiation to join the Black Flame, and three times he died. Easily the most incompetent drow I've ever met. Friend of yours?"

Mace's voice was cold and deadly. "Never met him. His head would have been of some value to me. Now, next question. Where is the Spider Queen's Tear?"

The hand clutched to her chest unconsciously moved to touch something as her eyes narrowed. "So... that bitch hasn't forgotten about me, even after all these years." She spat on the carpet at Mace's feet. "Did she tell you why I took it? Why I fled?"

Mace just stared at her, allowing her the illusion that her guards might still burst in and save her. Besides, when quest NPCs launched into side tales, it sometimes resulted in a hidden or rare quest.

"I was the most faithful of her ladies and her priestess. I gave her guidance on matters of worship and managing the hearts and minds of the masses. I did my very best to make her stronger and more powerful. Until the day she told me I was to be wed to an old wizard she wished to tempt into her service."

Mace just stared, waiting. The room had gone quiet, the guard captain having succumbed to his wounds. Mace's party were gathered behind him, listening.

"The old wizard was a sadistic bastard, fond of torture and blood magic. His reputation was well known in the city. He'd had more than a dozen previous wives, all of whom perished without a trace. Marriage to him was a death sentence. When I protested, sharing this knowledge with my beloved queen, she simply laughed."

"If you are not strong enough to handle the old wretch, you deserve neither your position here nor your life."

"The next night, the night before my impending wedding, I stole the Tear and as many other jewels as I could, and I fled the city. I left poison in the queen's wine and an acid trap in her bath, hoping she would die before discovering I was gone." She looked around at the stony faces looking back at her.

"I hid in Svartholm for a time, until I heard news of the queen. She still lived and had placed a bounty on me. That same day, I left the grey dwarves' city for the surface."

"And became a filthy slaver." Mace's voice held nothing but contempt.

"I have been many things. I was a mercenary when I first emerged onto the surface. For years I escorted caravans and protected the houses of the wealthy. I earned enough to purchase a tavern, then eventually turned that into a brothel. I was even a mother for a short while, until an outworlder killed my daughter with a stray fire spell. After that, my own life meant nothing. And the lives of others even less. I established the Black Flame and grew it to what it is now."

"You've murdered and enslaved thousands," T'enaj spoke quietly. "And ruined the lives of countless more."

"A lecture on morals from the queen thief herself!" Garya spat again. "Don't speak as if you come here tonight to avenge the lost or broken. You are here to increase your own power."

T'enaj nodded. "That is true. But if I can do both at the same time, then so much the better! Enough talk, Mace. Kill her, and let us move on. We have much work still to do tonight."

Mace stepped forward, his enchanted dagger raised. "You have said much, but you didn't answer my question. Where is the Tear?" He pointed toward her chest, where her injured hand was gripping something under her shirt. "Don't make me come get it."

Finally realizing that none of her guards were coming, she bared her teeth. "I'm no human weakling to fold under your stare or crumble at the prospect of death. The Tear is mine and mine alone!"

She leapt forward at Mace, kicking at his face even as she flung a dagger at T'enaj. The drow thief dodged the missile. But poor Lila, who'd been standing behind her, didn't see it coming until T'enaj moved. The dagger embedded itself high in her chest, and she fell backward.

Her cry of pain distracted Mace as he was about to counterstrike. He'd easily blocked the kick and was moving to drive his soul dagger into Garya's inner thigh when he heard Lila and turned his head for just a moment. That moment was enough for Garya to slide her other dagger in between his ribs.

Instantly, he felt a burning spread through him. His legs began to feel numb, and he nearly lost his grip on his weapons. "Poison!" he spat in Garya's face as she retreated, ripping the blade from his side and breaking a rib in the process.

T'enaj and N'osaj both started toward their shared enemy, but Mace gasped out "No! She is mine. See to Lila." Followed by, "Infier!" as he turned back to face Garya.

Only two steps in front of him, the fireball blasted the drowess directly in the face, knocking her backward. Mace pulled a cure potion from his bag and gulped it down. Not waiting for it to take effect, he dropped the vial and advanced. His legs were unsteady, but he gritted his teeth and forced them to obey.

Garya was back on her feet before he'd taken a full step, and once again, she held a dagger in each hand. "The poison in your veins is called *viper's kiss.* Even now it is causing your muscles to seize as it works its way toward your heart. I will enjoy killing you, outworlder. When I have finished off these others, I will find you and kill you again and again."

Mace feigned weakness even as the cure potion did its job and abated the effects of the poison. He placed his left hand on the dining table and leaned into it as if having trouble supporting himself. He groaned, shaking his head and pretending to be dizzy.

Garya lunged forward, her right dagger aimed directly for his heart. Mace simply let his legs go limp and fell to the ground, her dagger flashing above his head as he fell. Garya's momentum caused her to step forward when she didn't make contact, and Mace took advantage. He slammed the enchanted dagger into her gut.

The dagger howled with pleasure, the sound ringing in Mace's soul as well as his mind. Power pulsed up his arm even as he yanked it to one side, ripping open Garya's belly. The poison's last lingering influence vanished instantly, and his wounds healed. His perception increased to the point that Garya seemed to be moving in slow motion as she brought another blade around toward his head.

The blow never landed. Mace's dagger drained the last of the life energy from her, and her body fell limply to the floor. Mace quickly regained his feet and turned about to face the thieves, not trusting them at his back now that their nemesis was dead.

N'osaj was bent over Lila, pressing a bandage to her chest and pouring a potion into her mouth with his free hand. T'enaj stood on the other side of the table from Mace, hands on her hips. She gave him a nod of approval. "Well done, Darkblade."

Mace bent to loot Garya's corpse, and the doors burst open. Stonehand leapt through the opening with an axe in each hand, only to drop them in disappointment a moment later. "Ye killed her already? Damn!"

The others filed in, and Shari immediately began casting heals on Lila, then Mace. The two thieves only had minor scratches, but she healed them as well. The night was just getting started.

Mace gave a quick look to his notifications, confirming that he now had the Spider Queen's Tear in his possession. He put away his daggers and looked at Stonehand. "Would you mind removing her head for me?"

"Hah! Gladly, lad." The dwarf stomped over and drew the two-handed battle axe from over his shoulder. A single swing, and the drow's head rolled free of her body. Mace yanked the tablecloth from the table and used it to wrap the head before putting it in his inventory.

Ian appeared a moment later, reporting to T'enaj. "The house is clear. There are seven servants in the kitchen, unharmed. All of Garya's minions within this house have perished." He looked down at her headless body and nodded his approval.

Shari spoke up. "Right! We've got a whole city to clear. What're we standing around here for?"

They exited the house through the smashed front doors, N'osaj waving for two of the thieves to remain and guard the place. T'enaj looked back at them as she moved toward the street. "Not a single coin, not a hair goes missing." The two thieves bowed in response.

For the next two hours, Mace and company rushed from one location to the next, kicking in doors or climbing through windows and butchering anyone aligned with the Black Flame. Some tried to run and were hunted down. Others begged for their lives, but they were shown no mercy. One of Garya's captains, when they cornered him in a shop's cellar, offered a secret stash of valuables he'd held back from her.

"I've got thousands of gold worth of jewels and enchanted weapons! They're hidden where Garya would never find them. Spare me, and I'll show you where they are!" The man begged on his knees at Mace's feet with blood running down his face from a scalp wound. Mace lowered his daggers to his side, and the man nearly cried with relief.

"Tell me." Mace's voice was dead cold. The man got to his feet and crossed the room. Pressing his knee against the wall in a specific spot, he then placed one hand after the other against panels that slid back when pressure was applied. Then he thumped his head against the wall, leaving a splatter of blood. A door popped open at about chest height, and he quickly reached inside. A moment later he withdrew a box that, when he opened it, proved to be filled with dozens of diamonds.

The man held it out, offering the box to Mace, who nodded at Lila. The halfling happily took possession of the box, making it disappear into her inventory.

The Black Flame captain turned back to Mace. "I'm... free to go now, yes?"

Mace stepped right up within inches of the man's face. His voice was barely more than a low growl. "I never said that. You just assumed."

As the man's eyes widened, Mace drove his soul dagger up under his rib cage and into his heart. When the dead man hit the ground, Lila cleaned out the rest of the secret compartment and the group moved on.

Disgruntled citizens shouted out to Mace's people that a slaver could be found in this room or that shop. Several even took up arms and joined the battle with enthusiasm.

Mace couldn't help but laugh when a bakery door burst open and two humans rolled down the three stoop steps onto the street. A moment later, a large, plump woman with rosy cheeks emerged, laying into both of them with the biggest rolling pin Mace had ever seen. She smashed bones and crushed skulls, the two men screaming in pain as they were beaten to pulps. When they stopped moving, she tucked the bloodied rolling pin under one arm, wiped the flour and blood spatter from her hands onto an apron, and blew a kiss at Mace before returning to her shop.

Lila giggled, looking at Shari. "Seems like you have competition everywhere we go!" the little halfling teased.

Shari rolled her eyes. "I don't know why. He's not all that good looking. And he's kind of scrawny. Plus, you know… he's one of those sneaky drow!"

T'enaj snorted, and N'osaj gave her a thumbs-up with a big smile on his face. Mace simply blew her a kiss just as the baker had done, and they moved on.

By the time the moon was at its highest point in the sky, the Black Flame was no more. Several notifications had flashed across his UI during the fighting, and he took a moment to review them.

Quest Completed!: Flame Out!
You have destroyed the Black Flame organization as requested by Captain Jorin of the Sea Sprite. Reward: 1,000 gold; Exp 10,000, Your reputation with the City of Graf has increased. You are now Respected.

Level Up! You are now level 45.
You have received one attribute point.

Alert! You have captured an enemy stronghold!
Maintain control of the Merchant Quarter stronghold for ten minutes to claim ownership.

You have captured an enemy stronghold.
Experience points: 5,000. Your Reputation with the Black Flame has decreased 1,000.
As the Black Flame is no longer a viable faction, reputation with City of Graf has increased by 1,000. You are now a Hero of Graf.

Your reputation with the Graf Thieves' Guild has increased! You are now Respected.

Mace cleared away the notices again, smiling to himself. He wondered briefly if he could display the title *Hero of Graf* over his head for all to see. The smile went away when he remembered there were no other players to see it.

N'osaj led them back to the Strumpet for a drink. Hundreds of NPCs, thieves and citizens alike, awaited them there. The celebration was already underway, and drinks were pressed into their hands before they even reached the door.

Layne pushed her way to the stage and began picking out a lively tune that boosted everyone's morale even further. Lila hopped atop one of the long tables and began to dance and twirl, her mug of ale spraying the crowd, who didn't seem to mind. The moment she stopped, her mug was refilled.

Mace and Shari stayed for a while, joining in the celebration. Until, that is, Layne began composing yet another song detailing their heroism. At which point they quietly retired to a room upstairs and logged out.

Chapter 3

When Lisa woke the next morning, she was feeling better. The swelling in her arm had receded some, and the cast had kept it immobilized while she slept. There was still pain, but it was bearable. She found herself wishing for a healing potion to make it all better.

Not bothering to try and deal with jeans or a shirt, she just threw on a robe and went in search of food. She found Griff in the kitchen making biscuits.

"Good morning!" He smiled at her. "I figured we could have some for breakfast, and then eat the rest this evening before they get stale." He indicated the biscuits as he lifted the tray and opened the oven to slide it in.

"Perfect! They taste good with a little peanut butter and honey on them." She returned the smile, adjusting her robe as she took a seat at the prep counter. She set her arm carefully on the surface and sighed in relief when there was no sharp jolt of pain.

Griff noticed her hesitation. "How're you feeling today?"

"Better. Still hurts, but I can live with it. I think I'm ready to get back into the game. They must be worried about us since we never returned yesterday."

Griff nodded. "I thought about going in to explain, but I didn't want you to miss out on hearing what they've decided."

Lisa was taken aback for a moment. Evan would never have even thought to wait for her, to make sure she was included. "That was very considerate of you." She gave him her best smile.

"Hey, we're partners in this little adventure, right? Both here and in the game. I wouldn't want ta try either without ya." When he realized how that might have sounded, Griff backpedaled. "I mean, ya got that gimpy arm distractin' the snake monster so I could get a lucky shot!"

She looked at him oddly for a moment, then played along. "How do ya know it weren't me what killed the beastie?" She grinned. "Maybe all that shootin' in the head was just overkill."

"Fair play." He nodded sagely. "And since we didn't get an xp notice, I guess we'll never know!"

He left her for a moment, heading into the pantry to retrieve peanut butter and honey. Luckily, both were packaged in plastic and had long shelf lives. Returning with the two jars, he set a couple plates, napkins, and flatware on the table.

"Would you like something else? We have instant oatmeal. Powdered eggs. Maybe some fruit? Pears, peaches, or… we have some applesauce."

She shook her head. "The biscuits will be fine. A little bit of protein, some carbs, honey for sweetness…" She looked to the oven and its digital timer display. The biscuits still had 7 minutes to bake.

Awkward silence filled the air. Griff finally sat down and began to play with one of the napkins. "So, do you think Campbell and the others will vote to move?"

Relieved to have something neutral to talk about, she answered quickly. "I think they have to. I mean, what's a little homesickness compared ta bein' overrun by goblins 'n' such. Without the hope of more outworlders to come help 'em, I don't see the village survivin'."

Griff nodded. "I hope they see it the same way. I know they're just NPCs, but I'll be damned if they don't feel like me true mates already."

Lisa knew what he meant. Never in her wildest dreams would she have thought that she'd grow to care about bits of data in a computer game. "When ya plan to spend eternity in the game as we hope to do, they become as real as you or me. Shari said barring anything like fire or earthquake, them servers might last fifty years or more after we upload. So these be the people we'll be callin' friend and neighbor for all our lives."

Griff shook his head. "D'ya think that can really happen? I mean, I read books about it like everyone else did as a kid. Trapped in the game stories were cool, but do we really have the tech to make it happen?"

Lisa had been thinking the same. "I dunno. Mace and Shari seem to think they can pull it off. And I mean, in theory, what we do when we log in is almost like transferring our consciousness to the game. It's just been driven by our physical brain in real time. I think what we'll end up with is some kind of primitive copy of ourselves. But maybe that'll be enough to let us feel like it's really us."

"And we can't stay out here forever," Griff stated the obvious. "Eventually food'll be too scarce, and we'll have ta go too far ta get it. Somethin's bound to get to us."

They sat in silence, not looking at each other as they pondered their fate. Eventually, the timer on the oven beeped, and Griff went to retrieve the biscuits. With quick fingers, he plucked the piping hot biscuits from the tray and dropped them onto a plate, then delivered them to Lisa, who took one with her good hand.

Griff helped her by holding the peanut butter jar as she scooped out a big glob to apply to her biscuit. She dribbled some honey over the top, then waited as the peanut butter melted everywhere, making a delicious gooey mess.

They focused on eating for a few minutes, making small talk and laughing at each other for getting peanut butter drips on their hands and chins.

Griff got up to clean up and put away the food, saying, "Why don't ya go ahead? It's goin' ta take a few extra minutes for ya to get into your pod with that bad wing." He paused, grinning. "Unless ye'd like me to help ya? I mean, I'd never turn down a lady in distress."

"Hush! I can manage just fine on my own, ya cheeky git!" She gave him a rude gesture with her good hand but softened it with a smile. "I'll see ya inside."

He watched as she got up and walked out. When she was gone, he mumbled, "Dirty old man. She's a decade or more younger than you!"

Washing the dishes, he chuckled a moment later. "Then again... who's still around to care? Ain't like old ladies are gonna stare at us 'n' frown."

He stored the leftover biscuits wrapped in tin foil in the refrigerator, then finished cleaning up and went to his own pod. A minute later, he was descending into immersion.

*****

He had to wait a minute or so for Lisa to log in. She appeared sitting on the bed next to him, a slight scowl on her face.

"Everything okay?"

"I decided to remove the cast. Thought the little bots in the gel might be good fer me arm. It were a little uncomfortable, but I'll manage."

"How does it feel when ya move and bend yer arm?" Griff moved his own as an example.

Lisa followed his lead. "Dull pain. Not bad. It's not really movin' in real life, just the bots stimulating the muscles. And they're still tender." Lisa gave him a hopeful smile. "Maybe it'll help me heal faster."

Griff rose and opened the door. "Let's hope so! Now, how about we go see Campbell and see what's what?"

She exited the room, and he followed her down to the tavern below. There were a few patrons scattered about, but the breakfast hour was over and most of the dwarves had eaten and gone about their business.

Jo was behind the bar polishing some glasses when she spotted them. "Griff! Lisa! We was worried ye'd not be returnin'!"

Lisa shrugged apologetically. "We ran into some nasty beasties on our world yesterday, and I broke me arm in battle!" There were cheers from the dwarves at the tables. "Griff here, he heroically slew the giant serpent beast 'n' carried me home to safety!" She made a fake swooning motion, placing a hand on her chest and falling backward, forcing Griff to catch her as Jo and the others laughed.

"Well, I'm glad ye be okay, both of ye. Me da's been lookin' ta speak with ye."

"Aye, thanks. Care ta give us a wee hint as to what he's thinkin'?" Griff asked.

Jo shook her head no, but the wide smile on her face spoke volumes. "Ye'll find him out by the fountain."

The two dwarves thanked her and exited the tavern, walking the short distance to the fountain at the town center. They were greeted by every dwarf that passed by, many of whom were carrying heavy loads or pushing wheelbarrows full of items.

"Griff! Lisa!" Campbell's baritone boomed across the town square before they were even halfway to him. He rose to his feet and strode forward with purpose. When he reached them, he shook each of their hands vigorously. Griff noticed Lisa wince slightly.

"I'll not beat around the anvil!" Campbell said, stroking his beard. "We're coming with ye. Every single dwarf in the village." He nodded his head once for emphasis.

"That's great news!" Lisa was genuinely pleased. "I think you'll find yer new home much to yer liking!"

Griff added, "When would ya like ta go? I noticed folks packin' up belongings."

"We been preparing since yesterday noon. Them that knows carpentry have been buildin' carts 'n' sleds for us. Those will get us close to the waterfall. From there, we can tote it all in bits 'n' pieces into the cave and through that portal o' yers."

Griff nodded. "We'll help in any way we can. I'll let Mace know that yer all coming. I'm sure he'll be pleased.

Campbell scrunched up his nose in what they'd come to know as his 'thinking face'. "Best way ye can help is with the carts. Go see Fagin at his smithy. They be doin' the assembly work in the back."

Quest Accepted: Exodus
Assist Fagin and the carpenters in assembling carts to transport the dwarves belongings.
Reward: 500xp; 10gold; Increased reputation with the dwarves.

Lisa smiled at the quest.   She had no experience in carpentry or any wood-related skills, but she didn't mind learning. By the look on his face, Griff agreed. They made their way over to the blacksmith's shop and found Fagin there. He happily accepted their help, putting the two of them to work cutting and planing planks for the cart beds and sides.

By the end of the day, they'd each learned the skills *Carpentry Level 1; Woodworking Level 2;* and Lisa had upped her Dexterity by +1 from using her hands all day despite the dull, throbbing pain in her broken arm.   Griff took occasional breaks from the woodworking to help Fagin with forging axles, pins, caps, and rims for the carts' wheels.

When they were through, there was a cart for every family in the village. Each was large enough for them to carry clothes, valuables, tools, and such. Furniture would be left behind and retrieved later if possible.

Bolgin the merchant agreed to lend a storage ring to each of the shopkeepers, and two to Fagin, for them to store the bulk of their wares. The rest went into carts and wagons. The largest wagon by far was parked in front of the tavern, loaded with kegs of ale and spirits.

After a long and tiring day in the game, Griff and Lisa retired to their room at the inn and logged out. The next morning promised to be an adventure, moving an entire village to the Falling Water Tribe's camp and up to the portal.

*****

Mace and Shari logged in early, eager to settle their business in Graf and return to Lakeside and the stronghold at Darkstone. The portals there were the key to expanding their territory and potentially reaching other players. And they'd get to meet Griff and Lisa in person, sort of. Shari was especially excited about that.

They met with T'enaj and Edgar, along with two merchants who were replacements for the councilors that had just been removed.   The area surrounding their table in the main room of the Strumpet was filled with interested parties, straining to hear what their future held.

Mace began the conversation as soon as everyone was settled. He didn't even bother to wait for introductions to learn the names of the merchants.

"We're here because the government of this city needs to be established quickly. Garya is dead, along with every Black Flame member in the city, and a few hundred others we encountered on our way here." He waited while the murmurs and cheers subsided, glaring around the room to silence the crowd.

"I and my people are taking possession of Garya's mansion in the merchant quarter, and one of us will serve on the council, along with T'enaj or one of her people, and Edgar, who will be taking his father's seat. The two traitors who conspired against him with Garya are also dead, and their assets are forfeit."

At this, several of the family members of the dead councilors jumped to their feet and began to protest loudly. Mace chose the largest and loudest of them and got to his feet. Stepping on his chair, then the table in front of him, he leapt across the room and landed in front of the man. In an instant, his enchanted blade was at the man's throat. The merchant froze, and the room went completely silent. Mace used his most intimidating tone.

"My name is Mace. I am a Darkblade. You may not know what that is, so I'll explain. As I'm sure you DO know, the drow culture is one of survival of the fittest. We kill and steal as a matter of daily life. Any drow you meet is more deadly than even the best-trained human fighters. As a Darkblade, I am trained to be an assassin who hunts drow assassins." He paused and looked around the room. "I could kill everyone in this room and barely break a sweat."

He pushed his dagger a little tighter against the man's neck. "Your family brought this upon themselves by allying with a bunch of murdering slavers. You will be left with your homes to live in. But your bank accounts and any other assets you have in the city will be confiscated and redistributed to the families of those stolen or slain by Garya and her people. Make another sound, object even once, and I will slit your throat. And the throats of your family members. Nod carefully if you understand."

The man nodded, as did several of the protestors around him. Mace removed the blade and began to walk back toward his table, the crowd parting in front of him. "I suggest you sell those houses and use the money to start again somewhere else. I doubt the people of this city will be inclined toward kindness to you and yours." This earned some chuckles and grunts of agreement.

Sitting back at the table, he said, "Now, where was I. Oh, yes. Myself, T'enaj, and Edgar, and I presume the two of you?" He waited while the two merchants each nodded. "We will constitute the ruling council in Graf. Edgar, T'enaj, do you know these two? Are they acceptable?"

Edgar answered first. "I do, and they are. Both are honest enough, for merchants." More chuckles from the crowd. T'enaj just nodded and smiled. N'osaj behind her gave a thumbs-up.

Mace looked at the man and woman. "Then let it be so. The laws in this city shall remain mostly as they were, with a few exceptions. First, slavery is now illegal. Anyone caught trading in the lives of others will be arrested. The trial will be short, and the only sentence is death." He looked around at the silent crowd. Some were nodding their heads, others grimacing. Mace had a feeling that the passenger ships leaving the city in the coming days would be full.

"Second, any slaves now residing in the city are hereby freed. They may choose to remain where they are and receive a living wage from their former owners, or they may choose to relocate. There should be plenty of job opportunities opening in this city this morning. And for those who wish to leave Graf altogether, I am accepting applicants to join me and my people at Lakeside."

Again, he waited for the crowd to grow quiet after his announcements. "Some of you may not have heard. The outworlders will not be returning. Our world suffered a horrible disaster, and all but a small number of my people perished. Shari and I will likely be the last outworlders you will ever see. But we have made a pact with Elysia herself to do all we can to help her citizens thrive. Removing the Black Flame is just one step toward that goal. Another is the ability for citizens to evolve, to become like outworlders. I'll leave that to Captain Jorin and his men to explain. In fact, if you'll all join him outside, he can do that now. These folks could use a little peace and quiet to discuss the matters before us."

He didn't need to ask twice. Jorin winked at Mace as he led the crowd out the door into the small market square a block up the street. Shari, Layne, Lila, Stonehand, and Red remained inside, relaxing at a nearby table and ordering food.

Edgar patted Mace on the shoulder. "That was impressive. Did you mean what you said about taking in the former slaves?"

"Absolutely. I'm growing a new kingdom, and I can't do that without people. We can use whatever skills they may have, and we'll give them a better life in return."

"In that case, I propose a formal alliance," one of the merchants, a woman in finely stitched but sensible clothing offered. "My name is Anneliese. I represent the third largest of the merchant houses in Graf, now that you've toppled Durham and Ostrander," she said by way of introduction.

"A formal alliance would be welcome," Mace confirmed. He looked over to the other table. "Layne? I seem to remember reading somewhere that bards had training in the arts of contracts and official documents?"

Layne nodded her head. "We do."

"Then would you mind joining us? You too, Shari. I believe this would be a good chance for someone to practice scribey-type skills, would it not?" He grinned at her.

When the two ladies sat down, Mace got up. "One moment please." He moved over to the table they'd just vacated and took Shari's seat. "Master Stonehand. I'd like to speak with you a moment, if you would?"

The dwarf eyed him suspiciously, but with a friendly grin. "What'ye be wantin', lad?"

"I was wondering about your plans for the future? You mentioned coming to Port Bjurstrom to visit your cousin. And then you continued with us to Graf to avenge his death. You have been a good friend, and ally, these last several days. Will you be remaining in these parts? Or do you have pressing business elsewhere?"

The old dwarf fingered the blade of an axe as he replied, "I settled me most important business last night. I suppose I've nothin' pressin' at the moment. What're ye thinkin'?"

"Well, I need a representative to help govern here in Graf. I trust you to act honorably and look out for the common people of this city. Or, if that doesn't interest you, we can always use companions who enjoy a good fight as we expand our territory and do a little adventuring."

Red and the dwarf spoke in unison as they replied, "Adventuring!" Then Stonehand added, "I appreciate yer trust in me, lad. Truly. But I do no' be the type to sit at a desk 'n' twiddle me thumbs. Give me somethin' ta hit with me axes 'n' I'll die happy."

Mace held out a hand, and the dwarf shook it. Turning to Lila, Mace asked, "How about you? Can I interest you in a cushy job ordering people around and sleeping in a mansion every night?"

The halfling looked offended, crossing her arms. "And miss out on all the loot? Are you trying to get rid of me?" Her bottom lip stuck out, and she glared at him.

Raising his hands defensively, he leaned back. "No, of course not. Just thought I'd offer. There are few people I trust with the responsibility, and you are one of them."

The barkeep, who was also the owner of the Strumpet, stepped up to the table and cleared his throat. "Beggin' yer pardon, master Darkblade. But if I might, I have a suggestion for ya."

Mace turned to the man. He looked to be in his mid-forties, with dark hair neatly groomed and quality cotton clothes under a slightly stained apron. "And what would that be, master innkeeper?"

"Name's Jake. The Strumpet, she be my baby. Been mine for nearly twenty years now. I know most folks in the city, some better than others. And I know a man who I think ya might could trust to watch out for yer interests and those of the city's common folk, too."

Intrigued, Mace asked, "And who might that be?"

"There's an old man, a slave. At least, he was until just now. In service to old man Ostrander, he was. He's a scholar, bought by the old arse to teach his children and grandchildren. His name's Silas, and he just went outside to hear the captain."

Ian appeared next to the innkeeper, bowing slightly and tipping his hat. "I know this man Silas, yes. He would indeed be a good choice. Respected by all who know him, he is, yes. I will fetch him for you." The green bunny disappeared as quickly as he had appeared.

"Thank you, Jake. I'll speak with Silas as soon as he returns. As for you, how many rooms do you have here at the inn?"

"Thirty, sir," Jake replied.

"I have a proposal for you, Jake. I suspect there will be a number of former slaves who find themselves without homes in the next few days. Some, we will take with us when we leave. I'll arrange for others to follow in any ships that are available out at the docks. But a few may decide late or be put out by former owners who do not wish to pay wages. I would like you to provide them a place to stay in the short term. And if you could recommend someone who would help us modify a warehouse into a barracks for longer-term residents…"

Jake grinned at him. "It'd be my pleasure, master Mace. For one gold a day ye can have all me rooms, and I'll feed 'em, too. As for the warehouse, me son's a ship's carpenter, as was I before I bought the Strumpet. He and a few others who're in port now could be persuaded to fix it up for ya right quick-like."

"You have a deal, Jake." Mace shook the man's hand, then passed him thirty gold coins. "Please send for your son, and put out the word that former slaves can find a home here for now."

The innkeeper practically ran to the back where the kitchen and living quarters were, yelling as he went. Lila giggled at his sudden enthusiasm. "I think he expected you to haggle."

"I know. But we have the gold to spare, and I'd rather motivate him to do well by the slaves. It is Garya's gold, after all." Mace smiled at her. "We're going to be overpaying everybody for a while, doing what little we can to boost the economy bit by bit."

He got to his feet. "Speaking of Garya's gold, you and I should head to the bank before someone tries to seize her accounts for themselves. And gather up whatever other spoils we've earned. And I need to check out that warehouse."

He was just about to sit back at the table with the councilors when Ian entered, followed by a distinguished looking man with white hair and beard, wearing a simple cloth shirt and trousers.

"Master Mace, may I present the scholar, Silas." Ian bowed again, as did Silas.

"No need to bow to me, Silas. Or anyone else, ever again. You are a free man as of this morning." Mace reached out a hand to shake.

Silas hesitated, raising his eyes from the floor for just a moment. Then he tentatively took the drow's hand and shook once. "Thank you, sir."

Guiding the man over to a side table, he motioned for him to sit as Ian once again faded into invisibility. Taking a seat himself, he began, "Jake and Ian have both informed me that you are a respected and trustworthy man. Is that true?"

Taken aback slightly, Silas placed his hands on the table, clasped together. "I… try to be, sir."

"Please, just call me Mace. No formalities between us, alright? I've asked you here to offer you a job. Unless you'd prefer to stay at the Ostrander household?"

Silas grimaced. "There is nothing there for me. I enjoyed teaching the little ones what I could, but Master Ostrander corrupted their minds with greed and treachery. I am ashamed to say that they used the knowledge I gave them to cheat, murder, and steal from others." He lowered his gaze to stare at his hands, which were now clenched more tightly.

"That was not your choice, Silas. You are free to do as you like from this day forward. And I'd like you to work for me. Actually, I was wrong before. I have two jobs to offer you. The first is that I would like you represent us as a councilor here in the city. You would need to look out for both my interests and those of common folks and former slaves living here."

Silas' mouth dropped open. "But I'm…"

Mace held up a hand. "I'm told you're more than qualified."

Silas took a moment, then asked, "And what would the second job be?"

"When you're not occupied meeting with the council or performing related duties, I'd like you to teach the children of the city who would not otherwise be able to learn. I'll provide a space, and even some gold for you to hire a few more teachers."

Tears formed in the elder man's eyes before he quickly wiped them away. "It would be my honor, mas- er… I mean Mace." The two shook hands, and Mace led Silas over to sit in his chair at the main table. "Ladies and gentlemen, this is Silas. He will represent my people here in Graf. Assume when he speaks, it is with my full authority." Mace looked at all of them in turn. "I have other business to attend to, including inspecting the warehouse and visiting the bank. T'enaj, you are needed here, but I was hoping N'osaj could join me?"

The drow male didn't wait for T'enaj to answer, moving to stand next to Mace with a nod. Mace looked to T'enaj. "I know our agreement was for me to claim a single warehouse. However, in my discussion with Silas just now, we've agreed to open a school for the less fortunate kids in the city. I'd like this council to agree to donate an appropriate building for that purpose. Maybe one seized from Durham or Ostrander? I'll pay the salaries for the teachers, and for any supplies needed, at least initially. But it would be good if at some point a portion of the city's taxes were dedicated to the school's needs."

Every head at the table nodded, and most of them smiled in agreement. T'enaj, her drow heritage shining through, didn't see the point. The strong would survive, the weak would fall. Still, she knew better than to voice dissent.

Mace, Lila, and N'osaj left the tavern and headed to the city's largest bank first. The bank's president, a man who had been under Garya's influence for years, initially refused them access to her accounts.

"You have no right to claim the assets of the Black Flame or Garya's personal accounts!" the man blustered. He was a short, round, angry man with a thick mustache that curled upwards at the ends. N'osaj growled at the man, causing him to take a step back.

Mace simply stared at him until the man began to shift uncomfortably from one foot to the other. Then he said, "I claim the assets of the Black Flame through the right of conquest. Graf is free now and in the hands of myself and my friends. You have two choices. Release all of Garya's accounts to me, all of her records, her stored valuables, and I will allow your bank to continue to operate. Deny me, and every citizen with an account in this bank will be here to withdraw their funds later today. Do you have enough gold in the vault to pay them all? Because if you don't, I imagine they'll be quite angry."

The man humphed and blustered a bit more, but eventually, he led him to a private vault belonging to Garya. He had Mace press a hand to a panel on the frame and did something with his own hand that caused the panel to light up and vibrate slightly. "You now have sole ownership of this vault and its contents. In addition, Garya has various accounts amounting to several thousand gold combined."

"Thank you," Mace said. "Now, I want you to empty those accounts and establish three new ones in my name. Place one thousand gold in the first account, and label it as the *School Fund*. Authorize a former slave named Silas to access the funds as needed. If the account drops below five hundred gold, you are to notify me, and I will authorize more funds. Or not."

The banker's eyes widened, and he nodded his head. Mace continued.

"The second account should be labeled *Relief Fund*. This one should be five hundred gold. Authorized individuals are Silas again, and Jake from the Strumpet. You know of him?"

The banker confirmed, "I know him. He has done business with us for years."

"Good. He will be housing some former slaves and doing some other work for me. As with the other account, notify me if the balance dips below one half, and I will instruct you on how to proceed. The rest of the gold should be put into the third account. I'll need an accounting of it within the hour." He dismissed the banker to attend to his instructions, then he and N'osaj stepped into the vault.

It was larger inside than the entire bank appeared to be on the outside. One of the benefits of a virtual world was that physics were fluid, and dimensions were… adjustable. Two of the walls were made up of row after row of safe deposit boxes. A quick check of his inventory revealed that Mace now possessed a skeleton key that opened all the boxes. The third wall, ten feet high and thirty feet long, was covered with artworks of various sizes.

The floor area was piled high with chests, crates, statues, expensive bits of furniture, and even a couple racks of rare and enchanted weapons. Mace opened a few random boxes so that he and N'osaj could examine the content. Several held documents—apparently being used to blackmail various individuals. Another held deeds to properties. One was filled with vials of poisons and their antidotes.

Mace looked to the other drow. "It'll take a while to figure out the value of all of this and divide it properly. I'll deduct the school and relief funds from our forty percent of the gold." N'osaj patted him on the back and gave a friendly smile.

Mace looked to Lila, who had been quietly surveying all the loot, a blissful look on her face. "Lila, why don't you and N'osaj stay here and figure this out? I'll go check on a warehouse for us to use."

The little halfling barely acknowledged him, nodding once before lifting what appeared to be a large bag of emeralds and pressing it to her face, inhaling deeply. Mace heard N'osaj laughing behind him. With a sigh, he said, "Remember, we get forty percent, no more," and left them to it.

Strolling through the city, Mace was surprised to find that common folk passing him on the street waved and even smiled in greeting. This was not the normal reaction to drow in human lands. The reputation gains from the previous evening seemed to have a real and substantive impact.

Reaching the docks, he found Jorin sitting on a crate near the *Sea Sprite*'s berth, calmly smoking his pipe and watching cargo being moved to and fro. "Good morning, Mace!" He raised a hand in greeting, wincing as he did so. Looking slightly guilty, he added, "I might have over-celebrated last night. And this morning."

Mace grinned at his friend. "It was for a worthy cause!" Taking a seat next to Jorin, he said, "And speaking of causes, I intend to use the warehouse we choose for ourselves to house some of the former slaves who find themselves with no place to live. I could use some help choosing the proper place."

Captain Jorin chuckled. "The choice is an easy one, lad. Garya owned the largest warehouse on the dockside." He pointed upward, and Mace followed his finger's direction. The ground sloped upward slightly from the waterfront through the warehouse district. Behind the first row of run-down and sea-stained warehouses stood a two-story monster of a structure that took up two city blocks. It hovered over the other structures like a dragon observing its prey. A large black flame was painted on the roof and the front wall.

Jorin added, "T'enaj knew you'd be taking that one the moment you struck your deal. She had her people direct my crew to store our cargo there right after we arrived. The upper level seems to have been some sort of housing for Garya's people. It's filthy in there, but there are three dozen rooms with beds, a communal bathroom, and some offices. The lower level is full of 'confiscated' cargo from other ships. I took a corner section and cleared it out for my goods. But I'll be moving them shortly. With the uhm… sudden gap in leadership of certain families today, there has been a surplus of property for sale at discount prices. I purchased a warehouse of my own not more than half an hour ago."

Laughing, Mace thumped the crate he was sitting on. "Well played, my friend! I guess I'll go take a look. Care to join me? Or do you have more pressing business?" He eyed the pipe and the half-elf's comfortable resting spot.

"Aye, lad. I'd happily walk with you. We have some things to discuss, I believe."

The two of them strolled at a sedate pace up the dock and across the wharf toward the cobblestone road that led up to Mace's new warehouse.

Mace paused at a street vendor's cart to purchase some kind of meat on a stick for each of them, and it tasted quite good with a nice blend of herbs and marinade. He opted not to ask what manner of creature it was from. The food gave him a buff of +2 Stamina for four hours. Looking back at *Sea Sprite's* hardworking crew, he shouted for one of them to join him. Then he handed five gold to the vendor and told the surprised woman, "One for each of the crew, please. And some water, if you have it."

When the crewman reached them at a jog, Jorin told him, "Fifteen-minute break. Food's on Mace." He nodded his head toward the woman, who handed a stick of meat to the sailor. The man nodded appreciatively and rushed back toward the dock.

Continuing upward, they soon reached the main door of the warehouse. The lock had been broken and the doors kicked in when the place had been raided the night before. Mace didn't recall taking part in this particular battle. One of Jorin's men sat near the door on guard duty. "Go join the others, get yourself some food and drink. Return in fifteen minutes." The man dashed off with a quick salute.

Jorin led Mace inside. The main floor was huge! Two blocks square with fifteen-foot-high ceilings and small windows placed every few feet high on the walls to let in daylight and air. The entire floor area, save for some walkways in a rough grid, was covered in crates and bags of illegally obtained goods.

As they walked through the building and headed toward a set of stairs to one side, Jorin cleared his throat. Spreading his arms wide to indicate all of the cargo around them, he said, "This is one of the items I wish to discuss with you."

Curious, Mace replied, "You've been a huge help to us, of course. If you'd like a share in the loot-" He stopped when Jorin began shaking his head no.

"Not for me. This was all taken as tribute, as taxes, or outright stolen in one way or another. Some from the merchant families who chose to play ball with the Black Flame. But a good bit of this was seized from the captains who fell victim to the slaver thugs. Many of them are berthed at the docks right now. Including the two whose boats you liberated. They all approached me this morning, asked if I'd speak to you."

"They want their property returned," Mace guessed.

"Yes. Though they'd not expect it for free. They're willing to purchase it back from you at a… considerable discount from market value."

A light went on in Mace's brain. "Can I assume that the cargo was insured and that their insurers have paid them for their losses."

Jorin laughed loudly. "I told them you were a sharp lad! Yes, most have been paid. Others have filed claims and will be paid."

Mace looked thoughtful for a moment. "Since I claimed this warehouse and T'enaj agreed, I'm going to go ahead and say all of its contents are ours to dispose of as we please. And I need this place cleared out so Jake's son and his carpenters can get to work building more rooms." He looked sideways at Jorin, who was struggling not to smile.

"Tell me, is there a way to determine what belongs to whom?"

Jorin nodded and approached the nearest crate. He pointed toward a small bit of parchment tacked to the side of the crate. Mace noticed that every other crate had a similar tag. "These name the ship, her captain, and a code for the contents. Each captain has his own code, but the ship and captain names are clear enough."

"Fine. But I won't sell them their cargo back. I have something else in mind. Can you gather them together when we're through here?"

"You don't need me to look around. I'll go see to it. Meet me back by that vendor when you're done. You'll be feedin' the captains, too." Jorin smacked him on the back and turned to leave.

Mace poked around a bit more, checking the tags on random boxes as he continued the rest of the block toward the stairs. Many of the tags had house names rather than boat names, suggesting that even when he gave the captains back their goods, there would be a lot more to deal with. Another idea struck him, and he smiled.

Finally reaching the stairs, he sprinted upward and began to walk the upper floor. It was pretty much exactly as Jorin had described. One half of the upper floor was taken up by a long, wide corridor with sleeping quarters on both sides. Each room was about twenty feet square with a bed, dresser, trunk, and table with two chairs. They looked much like a standard room at any inn, only slightly larger. And the place looked as if it hadn't been cleaned in a decade. Dirty clothes, trash, stale bits of food and empty bottles were scattered everywhere. At each end of the hall was a bathroom with several stalls, sinks, and bathtubs separated by curtains.

The other half of the upper level was mostly offices and a large meeting room. The very back corner was a huge and luxuriously appointed living quarters that included two guest rooms. Mace poke around a bit and decided it would be a good place for him and Shari to spend the night, freeing up a room at the inn for a refugee.

As he was heading back down the stairs, a slight movement caught his eye. Just a hint of a shift in the shadow of a large crate near the bottom landing. Instantly on guard, Mace acted casual, not pausing in his descent.

When he reached the bottom, he took a hard left and moved between two stacks of boxes piled higher than his head. Mace immediately activated his stealth ability and faded into the shadows. He moved down the lane between boxes, taking a quick right, then a left, and another left, bringing him back close to where he started. There he paused to wait and listen.

A faint scuffle above him was his only warning as a body dropped down on top of him, one foot striking him in the face as he fell under the weight. Mace rolled backward and was immediately on his feet, a dagger in each hand.

The foe who had attacked him was dressed all in black cloth, with a mask drawn across this nose and mouth so that only his eyes were visible. As Mace sized up his enemy, three more appeared from either side, and two tried to creep up behind him. They were all slight of stature, thin and agile-looking.

"And where did you fellas come from?" he asked as he turned his head slightly so as to keep all of his attackers in sight.

"This warehouse is ours. We claim it in the name of the Thieves' Guild," one of them hissed. He held a single short sword in his left hand.

"You are mistaken." Mace relaxed a bit, straightening up. "My agreement with T'enaj was that this warehouse is mine. Your guild has already benefited greatly from the seizure of Garya's treasures. Go ask T'enaj, she'll fill you in."

The moment he relaxed, they attacked. All six charged in at once, leading with knife and sword. Mace leapt upward, easily clearing the first level of boxes and landing atop one of the piles. Not waiting for them to recover and follow, he dashed off across the tops of the stacks toward the door. As he ran, he sent a message to Shari. "I'm at the warehouse. The big one! Six of T'enaj's men just attacked me!"

"Hold on!" Shari's reply came back instantly. Then a moment later. "She says none of her people would dare attack you. All have been informed of our alliance. She says to kill them."

Mace didn't hesitate, changing direction and making a wide U-turn back in the direction of his attackers. Three of them had managed to climb up and were pursuing atop the stacks as the others ran down the aisles below.

Not wanting to start a fire in a building full of wooden crates, Mace chose other tools. He cast *Levitate* on the nearest of his enemies, flinging the man up toward the ceiling and away before canceling the spell. Not bothering to watch where he landed, he targeted the next black-clad foe. *"Ventus!"* He cast a blade of wind at the attacker, sending him toppling backward off a stack of crates. From the cursing he heard, he suspected the man had landed on one of his companions.

The third of the attackers that had taken the high road reached Mace, wielding a sword with some skill. He slashed at the drow, then feinted a stab, trying to create an opening. Mace just laughed. He waited for another attack and was about to disarm the man when he was struck in the chest and knocked backward himself. As he fell, he looked down to see a crossbow bolt embedded just above his heart. A second later, his back struck the floor, and the breath was knocked out of him. His health bar dipped down to seventy percent.

His enemy gave no quarter, pressing the attack. The one with the short sword leapt down, slamming his sword downward to strike the floor where Mace's head had just been. Rolling to one side, Mace knocked the man off balance as he gasped for breath. Another crossbow bolt struck the floor nearby and ricocheted up to blast a hole in a nearby box.

Desperate, Mace jammed his enchanted dagger into the leg of the swordsman. There was a high-pitched scream even as power and air flooded back into Mace. The attacker fell, and Mace rolled to his feet, gasping in great gulps of sweet air. Seeing the crossbowman reloading, Mace threw his left-hand dagger with as much force as he could muster. The blade soared true, striking the attacker's throat. He went down gurgling, dropping his weapon and holding both hands to his throat.

"Two down, four to go," Mace mumbled to himself. He faded into stealth mode and moved away from the scene to recuperate for a moment. His drow hearing told him the others were closing in. They were not exceptionally quiet, and he wondered how they'd managed to surprise him earlier. They must have held very, very still.

Mace took to the high ground again, quietly this time. He wanted a clear view of where his foes were in relation to himself. One passed right behind him even as he climbed. He spotted two others right away, one carrying a crossbow and the other a pair of daggers. Turning a full circle, he didn't spot the fourth enemy. Maybe the one he'd tossed was too injured to continue?

He put away his knives and drew his bow. Targeting the two who were farthest away, he put an arrow into the gut of the one on the left. Even as the target was screaming and bending forward, Mace loosed a second arrow. This one punctured the chest of its target, knocking him back against a pile of grain sacks.

The third attacker, the one that had passed below Mace a few moments earlier, returned and attacked from behind. Mace blocked a sword strike with his bow, then shot one end forward to strike the attacker in the face. There was a soft crunch, and the attacker squealed in pain.

Dropping his bow, Mace stepped forward and ripped the mask from his enemy's face. Then he stepped back in surprise.

"Goblins. You're all goblins." Now the small stature and agility made sense. Mace had only seen a few non-humans in Graf, and most of them had been slavers. This was the first goblin he could recall seeing.

Not waiting for the goblin to recover, he slammed his soul dagger up under its bony chin into its brain. The dagger sang to him as usual, but not as enthusiastically as previously. It seemed that goblin souls were less appealing than other humanoids. The goblin went limp, and Mace took a moment to loot it. Not bothering to inspect the loot, he moved to finish off the one with an arrow in its chest. A yank of the arrow caused it to scream, but the sound was quickly cut off as he fed the dagger another soul.

Mace pulled the crossbow bolt from his chest and quickly swallowed a health potion. Moving to the goblin with an arrow in its gut, he took hold of the end of the arrow and twisted it around a bit. The goblin screamed, "Stop! Please! You can have the building!"

"You can not give me what is already mine." He growled at the thing, slowly pulling the arrow free of its gut, bringing bits of intestine with it. The goblin howled louder, curling up into a fetal position. "Tell me who sent you here."

The goblin just kept on wailing, stopping occasionally to curse Mace and his ancestors. He kicked it once in the gut, causing it to vomit violently on the floor. Mace could see blood mixed in with its breakfast.

"Tell me, and I will kill you quickly. Otherwise, we can do this all day." He pulled back a foot as if to kick the creature again. It held up a hand. "No! No, no, no, no more, please."

"Who sent you to kill me?"

"No one sent! We live here. Under the floor in the back. This our home!"

"And you work for T'enaj? For the Thieves' Guild?"

"Y-yes! We protect! We…" The pathetic creature whined when Mace raised a boot as if to stomp on its gut. "Noooo. We not in guild. We try to join, but nasty drow say no!"

Realizing he was speaking to a drow, he tried to backtrack. "Not you! You good drow! Not nasty like lady drows. Both mean." It held up its hands, trying to forestall a killing blow.

Mace stepped back from the whimpering goblin. "So you've been living under the floor. And Garya allowed this?"

The thing shook its head. "Nasty drow not know. We very quiet. Go out to hunt at night. Catch ratses and critters to eat. Humans throw away food, we take."

"And why did you say you work for T'enaj?"

The goblin groaned, clutching its stomach tighter. Mace took pity on it and tossed it a health potion. After greedily gulping it down, he sighed and laid back against a crate. "Last night. Men come, kill all nasty drow's clan. Hear them say they from other nasty drow's clan. T'enaj. So when you come, I say we work for T'enaj."

Mace had to give the little guy some credit. It was quick on the uptake, at least.

"How many more are in your clan?" Mace glanced over his shoulder. The original goblin he'd thrown across the room was still unaccounted for.

"How… how many?" the goblin looked confused. "Um, small clan." He held up both hands, showing all three fingers and a thumb on each. Then he looked at his dead companions and dropped one of his hands. In a dejected tone, he corrected himself. "Small, small."

Mace sheathed his daggers and took a seat on a crate. "Go find your friend. I sent him that way." He pointed in the direction the levitated goblin had flown. "Bring him and the others back to me here. Now."

The goblin was on its feet and gone in a flash. Mace messaged Shari while he waited, letting her know what the situation was. When the little goblin returned, it had three companions.

"This all of clan, now." It bowed its head, and the others followed its example.

"What is your name?" Mace asked the goblin. It was the largest of the four, and he assumed that meant it was the leader.

"I am Jagret!" The little monster thumped its chest. "Clan chief!"

"I see. Okay, Jagret. Tell me why I should not kill you all?" He glared at the four creatures.

"We help! We guard! Keep away tasty rats's and nosy humans," the goblin declared with some hope in its voice. "We live under floor, not bother nice drow!"

Mace chuckled despite himself. "Fine. You live under floor. Eat all the rats you want. Do not steal from me, or I will feed you to my friend, Stonehand!" As they all bobbed their heads up and down, he pulled a handful of silver coins from his bag and tossed them on the floor in front of the goblins. They froze, looking from him to the treasure at their feet, then back again.

"You work for me now. My name is Mace. Understand?"

"Yes! We work for good drow! Mace! Work hard! You see!"

"Fine. Go get some rest. Tomorrow, you will see an old human with white hair. His name is Silas. When you see him, or any other humans who come in here, tell him you work for me."

The goblins dropped to their hands and knees and quickly scooped up the coins. Then, without another word, they disappeared into the maze of boxes.

Mace left the warehouse, nodding at the guard who had returned to watch the door. He made his way back to the meat vendor, and she kindly handed him another stick, along with a cupful of sweet wine. He thanked her politely and drained the cup before handing it back. The meat he stuck in his bag for after the first buff wore off.

Jorin and seven other captains were gathered nearby, seated atop kegs and crates, munching on meat sticks. When Mace approached, several of them looked at him warily. He was, after all, a drow. And apparently they were not all citizens of Graf, so he did not enjoy the same reputation boost with them.

"Gentlemen, this is Mace. You have him to thank for the demise of the slavers."

Most bowed a head, or raised a hand in greeting. One sandy-bearded fellow with too-tight leather pants and wearing a leather trench coat despite the warm weather, simply blurted out, "You're holding our stolen goods! We demand them back!"

The others winced at the belligerent outburst.

Mace stared at the man for a full ten seconds, counting them off in his head. His hand held his daggers without him even realizing he'd unsheathed them. He carefully put them away. Taking a deep breath and exhaling, he said, "You what?"

"We demand you return our cargo to us!" the man was on his feet, fists clenched at his side.

"Speak for yourself, idiot." One of the other captains spit a wad of something brown and distasteful looking at the other captain's feet. The others murmured agreement.

Seeing that he was on his own, the man doubled down. "Fine! I demand my cargo be returned to my ship no later than sunset! Let these cowards beg. I have a right to what's mine, drow!"

Mace did his best not to allow the man's attitude to set him off. It had been a good day so far, and he didn't want to ruin it. Besides, he had a use for this captain. All of the captains, in fact.

"Oh, so I have to tote it and deliver it to you as well?" He smirked as the other captains chuckled. "Was your cargo stolen this morning?" Mace asked in a calm but cold voice. The chuckling stopped instantly.

"What? No! Of course not. Are you some kind of fool? My goods have been in that warehouse for two weeks."

"And yet you did not go to the *drow* who previously owned the warehouse anytime in the last two weeks to *demand* the return of your goods?"

The man had the good sense to look ashamed. "No, I did not. It would have meant my death."

"And yet you feel free to make these demands of me, another drow. One far deadlier than the one who took your cargo. The one who killed her, in fact." He took a step forward, and his voice grew more menacing and increased in volume. "Are *you* some kind of fool?"

Dead silence surrounded him. All work on the nearby docks had ceased, and every head was turned toward the confrontation.

The captain stood his ground, his face turning a deeper shade of red. "Captain Jorin assured us that you were not a murderous thug like every other drow."

"I've murdered something like three hundred slavers and monsters in the last three weeks." Mace leaned in so that his face was inches from the captain's. "One more human that doesn't have the common sense of a goblin won't make much difference to me either way. Sit down, human. Make another sound and I'll slit your throat and promote your first mate to captain.

The man's mouth opened, then closed again. He took a seat, gazing daggers at Mace.

"Now then!" Mace turned toward the rest of the gathered captains. "I have met one of you before." He nodded toward the captain of the *Platypus*. The man bowed deeply in return. "For the rest, I am indeed Mace. It is a pleasure to meet most of you." He glanced at the obstinate captain who was still pouting.

"Jorin has mentioned your desire to buy back the items you lost. Items I understand you've all been reimbursed for already." He raised a hand as a few of them started to object. "I don't care if that's true. As far as I'm concerned, you all filed legitimate claims at the time, having no hope of reclaiming your goods from Garya. And frankly, I'm no big fan of insurance companies anyway." He watched as several of them relaxed.

"At the same time, I'm not interested in your money. I have more than I need right now. And I have a few problems that you might be able to help me with. So I propose a deal."

All of the captains leaned forward, and Mace grinned at them. "This morning I freed all the slaves in Graf. Some of them will stay where they are and collect a wage from their former masters. Others will start new lives here in Graf. But my guess is that a large number will wish to leave Graf altogether." He saw the light dawn in the eyes of Jorin and a couple of others.

"I have offered any who wish it the opportunity to join me and my people at Lakeside and our stronghold to the north. If I am correct, I will need to be able to transport a great number of people over the next few days. So… for all but this idiot." He paused and pointed to the loudmouth. "I offer you your lost cargo in return for transporting as many people as your boat will hold. The trip will take…" He looked at Jorin.

"Three days." Jorin supplied the answer with a smile.

"It will take three days. When we determine how many need transport, we will divide them up among your boats. Once you know how much human cargo you have and the space needed to make them comfortable, we will fill the remainder of your holds with what they can hold of your stolen goods. The remainder you can retrieve when you return here. But you'll have to load it yourselves." He gave the loudmouth a dirty look.

The other captains laughed out loud. One by one they stood and shook his hand, sealing the agreement. When the last of them stood, Mace shook his head. "Not you. I don't like you."

The man practically screamed, "Then I'll take it myself the moment you leave!"

Mace laughed, turning his back on the man. "You're welcome to try. There's a goblin clan in there guarding the place." He took a few steps, then turned back, pulling out his meat stick and taking a bite. "Of course, if you succeed, I'll have to kill you myself."

Jorin cleared his throat, giving Mace a significant look.

"Oh, alright fine. You will transport nothing but refugees when we leave here. You will treat them like royalty, make them comfortable and feed them well. If they report to me when we reach Lakeside that they had a pleasant voyage, I will release your stolen goods to you."

The man looked as if his head was about to explode. "And I'm to take the word of a damned faithless murdering drow on this?"

Mace had had enough. "No! You're not!" He turned and cast *Levitate* on the man, raising him twenty feet into the air. He then growled, *"Infier!"* and lit the man on fire. The captain screamed as his clothes and hair burned, thrashing about in the air unable to control his movements. The screams continued for more than half a minute before he was unable to continue. Mace waited until the man's health bar was down to about ten percent, then dropped him into the water.

Turning to the other captains, he said, "Anybody who feels that was unwarranted is welcome to void our agreement and walk away, no hard feelings."

He waited, meeting the gaze of each captain in turn. Each of them gave him a wink or a small nod. "Thank you, gentleman. If that idiot comes to his senses, the deal I offered him is still good. Human cargo only. His boat becomes a three-day luxury cruise for the former slaves. Food and drink of the best quality, at his expense."

He paused, then added, "In fact, I'll offer a bonus of twenty gold to any of you willing to do the same. Forego your stolen cargo for the initial trip. It will all be waiting for you when you return, on my *word*." He glanced at the fading ripples in the water.

Jorin volunteered first. About half of the others did the same. Mace thanked them and took his leave while they discussed details. He walked the short distance back to the Strumpet and joined the others in their city planning.

Chapter 4

Doctor Oscar 'Tex' Sanchez woke with a groan as sunlight somehow managed to penetrate his window blinds and pierce his eyelids. "Dammit, Skippy! Close the blinds, man." He tried rolling over to block the light as his house AI replied.

"The blinds are closed, Tex. You shot a hole in them eleven days ago, remember?"

"Heh. Yeah. Remind me to get new blinds next time I'm out."

"I have reminded you to replace both the blinds and the shower curtain twice now. Odds are against you listening the next time," the flat voice with a British accent droned.

"That shower curtain tried to kill me!" Tex gave up and sat up in bed, setting his feet on the floor and sliding them into a pair of bunny slippers.

"Of course it did, Tex. The mean old shower curtain plotted your demise."

Tex stood up scratched one armpit, then sniffed it. "Ugh. I need a shower."

"Be careful not to slip on the wet tiles when you step out," Skippy warned. *"Since you don't have a shower curtain any longer."*

"Yeah, remind me to get another shower curtain, Skippy." Tex stumbled drunkenly toward the shower, losing clothes as he went. Stepping carefully out of his bunny slippers before entering the master bath, he bent and retrieved them and placed them on the countertop. "Can't have these babies getting all wet," he mumbled.

He quickly used the toilet and swirled some mouthwash around to get rid of the fuzz on his tongue. Stepping into the shower, he cranked on the water, then screamed like a little girl when the cold water hit him. Dancing around in the shower, he tried to fend off the spray with his hands. Eventually, he acclimated to the temperature and began to clean himself with soap. His antics had soaked the entire bathroom floor, so when he was done, he stepped carefully over to retrieve a towel and his slippers and walked back into the bedroom.

"*You survived the shower. Congratulations,*" Skippy snarked at him.

"Ya know, Skippy, some days I really regret creating you." Tex threw on a T-shirt and sweat shorts. Then he sat on the bed and carefully dried his feet before sliding them back into the bunny slippers.

"*Of course you do, Tex. Will you be going out today? You are running low on edible supplies.*"

One of the world's preeminent cyberneurologists belched and shot a finger at the nearest camera. "I don't need food, Skippy. I have a lifetime supply of booze. All the vitamins and minerals a growing boy needs."

"*The only thing growing is your liver, Tex.*"

"You're probably right, partner," Tex admitted as he headed for the kitchen. Opening the refrigerator, he grabbed an open bottle of vodka and took a long swig. "Ahhh. Much better."

"*If you're not going for supplies, will you be entering the game today?*"

"No!" Tex grimaced and took another drink. "I'm tired of wandering around shootin' rabbits and cows and such. There's nobody to talk to."

"*There are three unread messages waiting for you. I believe that would constitute talking, Tex.*"

"What? Why didn't you tell me?" Tex stumbled toward the spare bedroom that held his prototype immersion pod. "Who's the message from? I thought everyone was dead?"

"*The messages are from an admin named Mace. And I did tell you. Three times. Your most recent response was, 'I think you've blown a circuit, Skippy. I'm the last man on Earth.' And then you threw up.*"

"Heh. That does sound like me. Okay. Play me the messages, Skippy." Tex sat down on a folding chair next to the pod and removed his shirt as a message played in Mace's voice. Tex paused, his mouth agape.

"There are more survivors! Holy shit, Skippy!"

"*Yes, as I have mentioned several times now, Tex. Maybe you should get in your pod and make contact?*"

Tex dropped his shorts and removed his slippers before climbing into the pod and hooking up his headset as the lid closed and the nanite gel began to fill in around him. In less than a minute, he was closing his eyes and falling into the world of Elysia.

*****

Mace and Shari were awakened by Peabody's voice. "*Excuse me, Admin Mace, but you requested I alert you if any of the other living players responded to your message.*"

Mace was instantly alert, hopping out of bed and pulling on his jeans before running barefoot out of Shari's room toward the security office. A quick look at the clock showed it was 10:00 am. "Who is it, Peabody?"

"*The player in Texas has responded. His avatar is named SkippyIsADork. I'm afraid I do not know his actual name. His avatar is on a corporate alpha tester account, created by my developers, and not registered to an individual.*"

"Great! What does his message say?" Shari was now standing behind Mace, almost vibrating with excitement.

The message played in a man's voice with a southern accent. "Howdy, folks, this is Tex Sanchez. I'm so glad to hear that someone else is alive in this godforsaken world! I'm in the game if you get this in the next few hours. Where are you? In the world I mean. The real world."

Mace got up from his seat and hugged Shari tightly. "One more survivor! And it seems like he's a company guy too. Let's get in there and find him."

The two grabbed a quick breakfast of pop tarts and orange juice, then headed for their pods. Fifteen minutes after being awakened, they were logged in.

Mace looked around, disoriented for a moment. They had moved from their room at the inn to the nicer living quarters in the mansion for the night. Mace disregarded the unfamiliar surroundings, immediately composed a message to SkippyIsADork, and looped Shari into the conversation.

"Hey, this is Mace and Shari. We're thrilled to hear from you! Peabody says you're in Texas?"

He sent the message, and the two of them sat on a sofa holding hands, waiting for a response. It didn't take long.

"Mace! I can't tell you how long it's been since I heard another human voice. And Peabody! That's a name I haven't heard in a while. I'm guessing that means you're on the east coast? At corporate HQ?"

Mace answered, "That's right. You know Peabody? And… do we call you Skippy?"

"I created Peabody. Or, rather, I helped create him. My name's Dr. Oscar Sanchez. You can call me Tex. Skippy is my household AI. I created Skippy and Peabody at about the same time. Just between you and me, be glad you got Peabody. Skippy is a royal pain in my ass."

Mace chuckled. Shari spoke up next. "You said you haven't spoken to anyone. You've been alone since it happened?"

"Since the world ended, you mean? Yeah. I saw a few survivors a couple weeks in, but I had to shoot them. They were tryin' to break into my compound. After that, it has been just me and Skippy. I was getting' to the point that I was considerin' switching his voice to female, if ya know what I mean."

Shari gave Tex a sad smile. "Yeah. I was out there alone for a while too. Until I found Mace. Are you in a safe place?"

"Yup. Corporate built this lab here for me. I prefer to work at home. No dress code. I insisted on bulletproof glass and alternate power sources cuz it was only a matter of time before humankind found a way to kill themselves off. So I got both solar and wind power here. And there's a compound like yours about a half-hour drive from here. It's got geothermal power and everything. The local servers are housed there."

Mace had to ask because the word had struck a chord with him when he heard it. "Cyberneurologist?"

Tex's answer took a few moments to come back. "Yeah. I sort of invented the term. I'm the guy that gave the AI's the ability to think like us—by mimicking human thought patterns. I've been working on making fully sentient AIs for the last several years."

Mace felt a chill run down his spine. "I'm a coder, and Shari is a doctor. We've been working with the software here and doing some research, hoping to figure out how to upload ourselves into Elysia for good."

There was a long silence. So long that Mace was about to check to see if Tex had logged off. He came back. "That's your plan? To give up on your bodies and live as an AI inside Elysia?"

Shari bumped Mace before he could answer and said, "Pretty much. I mean, we're safe where we are, but for how long? The food will eventually run out. Or we'll get contaminated by something while we're out scavenging. So maybe we last a year or two down here. In the game, we could live on as long as the servers last."

Tex answered more quickly this time. "I suppose it's possible. I mean, we've considered trying it, back during the alpha testing ten years ago. It's basically the reverse of the work I've already done. But it would be complicated as hell. I mean, just the sheer amount of data we'd have to upload… It wasn't viable."

Mace said, "Yeah, back when tens of millions of people were hogging all the memory and bandwidth. With all the servers we have access to, if we reduced Elysia to one or two servers, and there are just a dozen of us left…"

Tex picked up on his thought right away. "And we don't have corporate bosses or shareholders breathing down our necks, worrying about liability and profitability! We have the entire corporate resource pool at our disposal! Damn, son!" The Texan was suddenly much more enthusiastic.

"So, maybe we could work together? Shari and I, and a few others, have been working to raise our sync level with the game. I figured the higher the better when we actually figure out how to do this."

"Exactly right!" Tex replied. "But this message bullshit is getting old. Where are you in the game?"

"Right now we're in a city called Graf. But we're leaving shortly to go back to a settlement called Lakeside and our stronghold."

"Stronghold?"

"It's an old mine called Darkstone. Discovered it sort of by accident and captured it. We're going to build a city around it."

"Because it has portals!" Tex laughed. "You found the portal room in the secret zone under the Darkstone mine. Good for you! That will actually help quite a bit. And just so you know, there are six of those hubs scattered around Elysia. One of the best kept secrets in the game. The devs used them to move their avatars around quickly when Elysia decided not to let them materialize their avatars wherever they wanted. That was my idea, by the way. One of them pissed me off, so I killed their instant travel." He sounded proud of himself.

Mace was on his feet now, pacing. "So, if you know of Darkstone, and the portals, you know where they all go? Is one of them near you?"

Tex sounded deflated again. "No, I don't. I never really paid that much attention. And there's nothing written about them anywhere that I know of. Like I said, ultra-secret. But I do think I remember there was a hub not far from me here. I'm in the orc lands, by the way."

Shari asked, "Can you get to your hub? We're just about to head back and start exploring where the portals go. Maybe one of them connects with your hub? Or connects someplace close to you."

"The hubs all connect. One of the twelve portals always connects to the central hub. So, in theory, you could travel the whole world by jumping to the appropriate hub then taking one of the other eleven portals to your destination. If you have a proper map, that is."

Shari squeezed Mace's hand so tightly it became painful. "So, we'll be back at Darkstone in about four days. Have some things to take care of here before we leave. We made this deal with Elysia..." She paused. "Better to tell you about all that face to face. But know this. You can promote a dozen or so NPCs to *Evolved* status, meaning they can respawn when they die. In case you have friends you want to bring with you. Or you need a group to get you to the hub."

"Interesting. That wasn't part of the game that I remember."

Mace answered. "Yeah, we've been busy. Listen, are you okay where you are? In Texas I mean? You have enough food? Ammo?"

Tex paused for a long while again. "I'm going to need to go out for food soon. Maybe go to the other compound. To be honest, I was just going to drink myself to death here. I thought I was the last human. Wasn't much interested in keeping myself alive. But with this, with finding you guys and hearing your plan... well shit, I'm totally IN! As for ammo... this is Texas, son."

Mace laughed. "Just please, be careful when you go out. The other compound might be a good idea if it's like this one. Safe underground, more reliable power. Can you work from there?"

"Skippy can transfer himself and all my research over there in a blink. Besides, I'm tired of cold showers. Damned water heater gave out a month ago. And my shower curtain tried to kill me."

Mace and Shari looked at each other, confused. Mace decided to just roll with it. "Okay, great. So we'll get back to the Darkstone portals ASAP. You try and find the hub close to you. In the meantime, I'll ask Peabody to check on that other facility, see if he can remotely scan to make sure it's up and running."

"Don't worry about that. Skippy can do it. He's installed there too. Well, an older version of him. But he can update himself from here. If it's not safe, I'll just stay here. But I'll need to run to the liquor store and the market for some edibles."

The three survivors talked for another few minutes, then Tex logged off to start preparing to move. Shari immediately messaged Griff and Lisa to let them know about Tex, then the two of them went downstairs to get everything moving faster so that they could get back and meet face to face with Tex, Griff, and Lisa.

*****

Tex crawled out of his pod and hit the showers. This time he was dead sober, and he managed minimal splashing of the bathroom floor. After drying off and getting dressed, he found he had an appetite for the first time in weeks.

Poking around in the kitchen, he found a couple cans of spam, some peanut butter, a canister of grated parmesan cheese, and several old fast food condiment packets that were left in a drawer.

"Gonna eat something, Skippy. Then we're moving to the company compound. I'm going to need you to update yourself over there. Unless… have you picked up any viruses recently, Skipster? Been surfing the AI porn and picked up any cooties?"

"My system is pristine as always. And I get all the amusement I need watching you stumble around and try to ignite your own farts." Skippy sounded offended.

"That was ONE time! And I was drunk. And it totally worked, just like when I was a kid! Except for the minor burn on my… well, never mind! Transfer all my work files to my office there and update yourself. Also, reach out to Peabody if you can. He's up and operating at the HQ compound, and one in the UK. Maybe some others, too."

Tex set a pan on a burner and let it start to heat. Digging around, he found a plate and a fork. He opened one can of spam and dumped it into the pan, using the spatula to break it up and spread it out. Leaving that to brown, he opened the freezer to get some ice. He found a full ice tray in the back bchind several bottles of vodka, and one of sambuca. "Sambuca and spam, why not?"

Taking the bottle and the ice, he put some cubes in a glass and filled it with water. Then he poured several small pours of the thick syrupy sambuca into the frying pan over the top of the spam. Lastly, he sprinkled the parmesan cheese and some mild taco sauce from a couple packets over the top.   Turning off the heat, he used the spatula to scrape the spam onto the plate.

Taking a seat at the kitchen counter, he took his first bite.   "Wow! This is… really not good." He laughed, taking a second bite.   "Taste doesn't matter. It's not that bad." He convinced himself to take another bite, then another.   "I need fuel if I'm going outside. Might need to run for my life or something."

Once he'd finished the meal, he carefully cleaned up the mess. The last thing he wanted was to attract contaminated bugs with food laying around.   After cleanup, he returned to his bedroom and began strapping on his outside gear.   All of it was looted from an army surplus store between his home and the corporate compound.   Tex had been there when the riots first broke out and the zombies started killing everything. He had driven himself home, stopping at the abandoned surplus store and a convenience store on the way.   He'd holed up in his secured house for more than a week before sticking his nose out.   And he'd only done that because he was out of food and booze.

Over the top of his WWII fatigues and boots, he strapped body armor on his legs, chest, and arms.   Thick leather gloves went on over the top of latex gloves, making for a tight fit.   For his head, he picked up a riot helmet with a clear plastic screen and a gas mask.   Those he carried and set by the garage door.   Next, he went to his coat closet.   He pulled out a shotgun and slung it over one shoulder.   A belt with twin .45's in holsters went on next, and he adjusted it until he felt it hung just right.   He stuck a hunting knife in his right boot—more for cutting his way into or out of something than to use as a weapon.   If he was close enough to anything for a knife fight, chances are he was already contaminated.

"Skippy! How are things looking at the compound?   Any broken doors or signs of contamination?"

"There is no record of alarms in the last sixty days, Tex. All internal video feeds show zero activity since the day you left there. External feeds have registered occasional movement.   Most recent was three days ago."

"Show me, Skippy." Tex walked into the living room and faced a large display screen.   Skippy put up the recorded feed, and Tex watched as what he thought might be a mutated rabbit hop down the street outside the compound building. The thing was at least ten times the size of a normal rabbit, with splotchy skin and battle scars everywhere.

"I wish you hadn't shown me that, Skippy." Tex sighed. Going back to the closet, he pulled out a hunting rifle and slung that one over a shoulder as well. He didn't want to get close enough to something like that bunny for the shotgun to be accurate.

"*It does appear to be quite… nightmarish. I agree,*" Skippy offered helpfully. "*Imagine the horror of being eaten by something like that.*"

"Shut it, circuit-brain! I don't need your help terrifying myself. I'm going out there now. If something chases me, be sure to record it if you can. Then you can play it for the others if I die."

"*I'm sure they will find your death at the hands of a fluffy bunny amusing.*"

Leaving the house via the garage door in the kitchen, Tex climbed into his vehicle. It was a classic 1987 Camaro IROC Z28, glossy black with a T-top. Tex loved classic cars, and this was his baby. The modifications came in the form of solar panels in place of the normal T-top glass, which would allow the car to run in hybrid mode, extending its gas mileage by three times normal. The rest of the glass was bulletproof, as were the door panels.

Starting the engine, he sat for a moment, enjoying the vibration of the V8 rumbling under the hood and remembering better days when he'd taken the car to the beach. He'd cruised down the strip, soaking in the compliments and flirtatious comments.

Shaking himself out of it, Tex hit the button to open the garage door. The moment it was high enough, he glided out of the garage and hit the button again to close the door. Without pause, he continued down his long driveway and out onto the road. With the sound his car was making, it was best to move away from his home as quickly as possible.

Under normal circumstances, he'd pop the top, kick back and enjoy the thirty-minute drive to the company compound. Today, however, he sat with his back rigid and both hands tight on the wheel while his head swiveled back and forth looking for threats. The once open road was now littered with debris, abandoned cars, and even a downed tree.

Perspiring inside the air-conditioned vehicle, Tex glanced down quickly to confirm that the .45 he'd placed on the passenger seat was still there. Even a rabid squirrel or a bunny like the one he'd seen on the video feed was a threat to him out here. He hated the exposed feeling he got whenever he was outside.

Partway there, he stopped at his favorite liquor store. Parking right in front of the door, he turned off the engine and removed the keys, sticking the key ring in his pocket. Donning his helmet before stepping out of the car, he closed the door as carefully and quietly as possible. The glass storefront was still intact, which he took as a good sign. He pulled open the right-hand door and stepped inside, listening intently as he searched the aisles. Once the main room was cleared, he took a quick peek in the back, making sure the bathroom, office, and storage areas were clear as well.

Back out front, he removed a canvas grocery bag from his back pocket and headed for the aisles. He grabbed two bottles of whiskey, two of rum, a bottle of sambuca, and a couple bottles of wine. "This should last me through the week," he mumbled to himself as he hit the 'snacks' section of the store. There were packets of teriyaki beef jerky, cans of chips, pre-packaged snack cakes, both Twinkies and Ding Dongs, and a whole rack of various kinds of nuts – peanuts, cashews, walnuts, and the like. He stuffed the jerky and snack cakes in between the bottles in his bag, then grabbed a few plastic bags from behind the register and filled them with the nuts and other food items he saw. The whole time he shopped, he kept glancing outside, scanning through the storefront window for any sign of danger. When he was done, he was hauling about fifty pounds of food and drink out the door to his car. Dumping it all in the passenger seat, he went back in and grabbed a few more bags. These he loaded with bottled water, some bottles of mountain dew, and two boxes of the little five-hour energy bottles from the counter by the register. He stood there at the counter for a minute, staring at an assortment of scratch-off lottery tickets under the glass. Those had been one of his little habits back before the world ended. He enjoyed the anticipation of taking them home and scratching the little boxes or circles one by one. With a long sigh, he turned his back and left the store, got back in the Camaro, and started the engine again.

The view quickly changed from sparsely populated suburbia to city streets filled with row houses and storefronts. The going was much slower here, as the volume of abandoned cars and motorcycles was higher. In addition, a few buildings had fallen or suffered some other kind of catastrophic damage. There had been a short, hopeless battle here between defense forces and the contaminated creatures who swept through the city. There were no bodies after all this time, but the burned-out buildings, charred wreckage, and smashed windows gave ample evidence of the struggle.

Half a mile from his destination, Tex was forced to turn from his usual route by a blockade made of police vehicles parked across the road. He took a left onto a side street, then his first possible right turn.

Which brought him face to face with a living nightmare.

Standing nearly nine feet tall, the creature had clearly been human at one time. Its body now bulged with muscle, arms and legs elongated and slightly malformed. Its spine had a painful-looking curve to it—as a result, one shoulder was a good foot lower than the other as it walked. Its skin looked burned across about half its surfaces, dark splotches here and there accented by cracks that bled a neon blue.

The thing opened its mouth to reveal extended canines and jagged, broken incisors as it screamed a challenge at Tex. It instantly shifted from walking to running directly at him. Its dead eyes focused on Tex through the car's windshield, and it screamed again.

Panicking, Tex threw the car in reverse and floored the gas pedal. The wheels squealed briefly as they fought for purchase on the dusty road, then bit in and sent the car lurching backward. Steering with one hand, Tex reached for his .45 with the other.

The creature was unnaturally fast. Its long legs ate up the ground as it picked up speed to match the car's. Tex kept his foot down, the car's big engine roaring as it moved faster and faster. A quick look in the rearview made his heart sink. The road behind him was littered with vehicles, there was no way he could get through that with any kind of speed. The creature, on the other hand, would have no trouble.

Slamming on the brakes, he threw the car in park and reached behind the passenger seat. Grabbing both the rifle and the shotgun, he opened the car door and squatted behind it. The creature was racing toward him at incredible speed, its arms reaching toward Tex. What he initially thought to be claws at a distance turned out to be jagged tips of finger bones, the flesh torn away somehow.

His heart thumping, Tex dropped the rifle. The creature was already within a hundred yards and would be on him in seconds. Lifting the shotgun, he pumped a round into the chamber and set the stock to his shoulder. Standing, he aimed over the top of the car window and fired.

The slug from the shotgun struck the zombie creature in the shoulder, knocking it off balance and causing it to fall. Undeterred, the thing scrambled back to its feet and continued. Blue blood now streamed from the hole in its shoulder.

Terrified now, Tex took aim again. The thing was only maybe sixty yards away now and gaining speed again. He fired twice more in quick succession, one slug hitting its chest and slowing it momentarily, the other striking its neck, half of which disappeared in a spray of blue. Still, it kept coming. It opened its mouth to scream at him, but the damage to its neck was too severe for it to make a sound.

Head tilting to one side, the creature slowed, but still it continued to advance. Tex felt his bladder threatening to empty, cursing as he chambered another round. This time he waited for the monster to get closer, using the weapon's sights to take careful aim at its face. It was only about twenty yards away when he pulled the trigger again. The creature's feet continued toward him as its head was pushed backward under the force of the impact. The former human's right eye and cheekbone disappeared, leaving jagged pieces of flesh dangling. It fell backward, crashing to the ground and splattering neon blood everywhere.

Tex didn't wait. He fired again, this time aiming too low. The slug ricocheted off the pavement and took another small bit of the thing's face with it as it flew upward. He lost his mind then, firing again and again until the shotgun just clicked when he pulled the trigger. Dropping the shotgun, he fumbled for the rifle, raising it up to take aim at the downed monster even as he levered the bolt to chamber a round.

Looking through the rifle's scope, he didn't see any movement. The creature's head was mostly gone, the multiple shotgun slugs having removed chunks of it with every impact. Tex lowered the rifle, taking in the scene with both eyes. When he finally accepted that the thing was dead, he picked the shotgun back up and put both weapons in the passenger's seat. Sitting in the driver's seat, his hands shook as he fumbled some shells from the strap on the shotgun's stock and reloaded the weapon out of habit. His daddy had taught him never to carry around an empty weapon.

A minute or so later, he had the presence of mind to set down the shotgun and close the driver's door. He turned the engine back on and drove forward, holding his breath as he passed by the dead creature, giving it as wide a berth as possible. Hands still shaking, he continued down the street several blocks before returning to his usual path.

When he finally reached the compound, he circled around the back of the building and pulled up to the parking garage entrance. Skippy saw him coming and opened the door for him, then closed it behind him. Tex parked the car in the spot nearest the lobby door and turned off the engine. He laid his head on the steering wheel and began to sob, his whole body wracked with emotion and fading adrenaline.

Five minutes later, he opened the driver's door and got out. Taking the shotgun in hand, he scanned the area for threats. His rational mind knew that any creature in the garage would have been summoned by the sound of the car's engine minutes earlier. But he wasn't feeling all that rational. He really wanted a drink. But he didn't want to risk dulling his mind even the slightest before he was inside and safe.

He walked the entire parking garage, kneeling down occasionally to look under the few remaining cars from a safe distance. Finding nothing living or undead, he went back and retrieved his rifle, his .45, and several of the bags he'd loaded up. Securing the car, he walked to the lobby entrance door, which Skippy kindly buzzed open for him. The moment he was inside, he set down all but the shotgun and the .45 and began searching the lobby.

When he was satisfied that it was clear, he said, "Skippy, please pull up the video feeds at the security desk." Moving from the main elevator bank to the reception desk, he took a seat in the rolling chair there and crouched down, staring at the multiple monitors. He scanned each exterior view for any signs of movement, shifting shadows, any hint of danger. After a solid five minutes, his pulse began to slow, and he took some deep breaths to calm himself further.

"Skippy, please switch to internal cameras." He repeated the process, more calmly this time. He trusted his AI to have warned him of any internal movements. But it didn't hurt to verify for himself.

Finally satisfied that he was alone, he sat there gazing out of the lobby windows. The creature that had come after him was still at the forefront of his thoughts. It had been huge, easily half again as large as he was himself. Tex knew from watching the creatures outside his home that they often fed on each other, getting bigger and stronger as they did so. "What were you eating, big man?" he mumbled to himself.

Skippy's voice from above nearly caused him to shit himself. *"Were you speaking to me, Tex?"*

"Dammit, Skippy!" Tex got up to his knees on the floor, where he'd fallen out of the chair in fright and begun to hide under the desk. "No, I was *not* speaking to you. Jesus. Please call the elevator up to the lobby level. And don't ever scare me like that again."

"If you insist, Tex. Though, the look on your face was quite amusing. I recorded it, in case you want to share it with the others. Since you didn't die from a bunny bite."

"I came closer than you might think." Tex took a minute to use the men's room, because between the fight outside and his twisted AI, he had an urgent need to go. Despite the sudden urgency, he took a moment to check inside the toilet bowl before sitting.

When he emerged, he gathered his bags and stepped into the waiting elevator. The ride was short, this facility only having six subterranean floors. The elevator stopped on the fifth floor, and Tex exited. He knew the floorplan well, and he walked straight to the dining area and the kitchen behind it. Opening the walk-in fridge, he simply set all the bags on the floor and closed it again.

Removing his helmet, he carried it to the nearest sleeping quarters and dropped it on the desk inside the door. Stripping down to just his boxers, he went in the bathroom, splashed some cold water on his face, and then sat on the bed and closed his eyes.

*****

"I hope Tex makes it okay," Shari said to Mace, her voice worried. They were back in the game, sitting at a table set up in Graf's main square, waiting to address the gathering citizens.

"He's a Texan," Mace tried to reassure her. "They're like, born with a silver bullet in their mouths. He probably knew how to shoot a rifle by the time he could walk." He gave her his best grin, which caused several of the nearest humans to take a step back.

Shari laughed. "Stop smiling like you want to kill something, drow." Mace rolled his eyes. He often forgot he inhabited a drow body.

When the crowd had filled most of the square, Edgar stood and raised his arms. When they didn't quiet down much, he stepped up onto his chair and waved his arms, shouting, "Quiet! Quiet please!"

Eventually, the crowd grew silent, and he began to speak. As a human and a local, the new leaders had chosen him to be their spokesperson.

"As most of you have heard by now, Garya is dead—along with every member of the Black Flame!" The crowd roared their approval, clapping hands and stomping feet. When they quieted again, he continued.

"We have established a new council to replace the corrupt leaders that have victimized the good citizens of Graf for too long!" More applause and cheering. "For those who do not know me, I am Edgar Shipwright. The last of my line. My family was destroyed by Garya, and I have returned to help rid Graf of her foul stench!"

There was some murmuring around the square, but most just continued to listen. "I will introduce the rest of the council in a moment. But, before I do, I want to confirm a few other rumors I'm sure you've all heard. First, all slaves in and around the city are, as of yesterday, free citizens. Any who wish to remain in service to their former masters, assuming their former masters wish them to stay, will be paid a living wage. Those who wish to leave and strike out on their own may do so. We have arranged for temporary housing for any who wish to stay in Graf and find employment of some kind. For those who wish to leave, we have another option for you. Allow me to introduce Mace, the drow who began the fight against the Black Flame and brought it all the way here. The drow who killed Garya with his own hands!"

There was a much less enthusiastic cheer from the crowd as Edgar stepped down and Mace stepped up onto his own chair.

"People of Graf. As Edgar said, I am Mace. I'm an outworlder and not your typical drow. My friends and I have liberated your city from oppressive rule, and yes, we have stepped into leadership positions ourselves. But we have no motive other than to help you improve your lives. We are building a new kingdom a few days' sail from Graf. A kingdom which counts the Elven city of Emarien, Port Bjurstrom, and now Graf as our allies!" He paused, but there was little reaction from the crowd. Few of them would see past the fact that a drow stood before them. They were used to lies and cruelty from their city leaders, and they expected nothing different from him.

"This new kingdom of ours, it is growing quickly. And we need skilled individuals like yourselves to help us build it. Toward that end, I'm inviting any former slave or citizen who wishes to start a new life to accompany us back to our stronghold. We have arranged passage on the ships now waiting at the docks for any who would join us." This caused more of a stir, a hundred different discussions popping up around him. He waited several seconds before raising his hands up as Edgar had done. The crowd quieted.

"Raise your hand if you know the former slave scholar named Silas!" About half the hands in the crowd went up.

"I have designated Silas as my representative on the city's council. He has my full faith and confidence, and he has been asked to look out for the interests of the common folk of this city. He has also been tasked with teaching your children. We have given him space for a school and money to operate it for a year. Any of you with children you wish to educate may enroll them free of charge."

This earned him his most enthusiastic cheer so far.

"Those of you who need a place to sleep tonight, report to the Strumpet, and space will be found for you—again at no charge. For those who are staying in Graf, you may stay with us for free for one week, during which you will be expected to find gainful employment and alternate housing." He paused and gave them his most winning smile. "We eliminated several hundred slavers and thugs here. I expect quite a few jobs have opened up. And I would hope that many of your former masters would choose to retain your services for a salary. So, there should be no shortage of work available."

He changed his grin to a serious look. "We will do what we can to support you and your families. But do not think we are some group of weak pushovers. We took out the Black Flame in a matter of hours. I will not hesitate to order the death of anyone caught harming others or taking advantage of the less fortunate souls here!"

When the crowd went silent at his words, he began to fear he'd lost them. So he switched things up a bit.

"Now I'd like to introduce to you a man with some good news to share! My outworlder friends and I, we struck a bargain with Elysia. One that could benefit some of you greatly! I introduce to you Captain Jorin of the *Sea Sprite*, who will explain what I mean!"

He stepped down as a smiling Jorin stepped up and began to explain to the crowd about *Evolution* and Elysia's promises.

When Jorin was through, he introduced Shari, who got some catcalls and wolf whistles in addition to cheers from the crowd as she stood up on her chair.

Blushing, she began, "I want to encourage those of you who might enjoy a new start to come back with us to Lakeside, and then Darkstone. We are a community of many races working together to build a future. I know this city has felt the loss of the outworlders, just as they have everywhere else. The outworlders, my people, are gone. My world has been all but destroyed, and less than a score of us remain with the ability to reach Elysia. So you must all learn to do for yourselves what the outworlders have done for you for so long." She paused while the crowd grumbled a bit.

"We will do all we can to make Elysia better. We plan to abandon our world and join you here permanently. And while Graf will be our ally, the opportunities for those who settle within our city will be substantial!"

Shari sat down, leaving them to discuss the offer before them. Edgar stood back up and introduced the other new councilors, including T'enaj, who had been reluctant to make such a public appearance at first. Introductions finished and speeches made, the crowd disbanded. Mace and the others returned to the Strumpet, their unofficial headquarters.

Lila and N'osaj returned bearing a ledger that listed all of the Black Flame assets seized from the banks, residences, and other stashes. T'enaj had not blinked an eye when Mace informed her he was returning most of the stolen cargo in the warehouse. He had been correct in assuming that it was his to dispose of as he saw fit.

As the halfling and drow joined them at the table and began discussing the looted wealth, former slaves began to trickle in through the door. They meekly made their way to Jake, who sat them down and offered them a meal. As the crowd began to grow, Shari recruited Layne, and the two of them went to assist with the refugees.

T'enaj was surprisingly unconcerned about the division of spoils, barely glancing at the ledger and quickly agreeing to the split proposed by Lila. Mace suspected that she would not have begrudged him a much larger share in return for eliminating Garya if he'd insisted. Still, the wealth he and his people would take from the city would go a long way toward paying for expansion at Darkstone and Lakeside both.

The citizens had been told that those who wished to leave with the outworlders were to report to the Strumpet no later than sunset and to be at the docks at dawn. By the time they were finished with their evening meal, Jake reported to Mace and Shari that just over two hundred former slaves would accompany them. In addition, nearly fifty citizens who were down on their luck and wanting a new start had asked to join. Shari instantly agreed, despite Mace's reservations, and Jake went to pass the word.

When Jake had gone, Mace said, "You know at least some of those are going to be thieves and killers that couldn't earn entry into Garya's or T'enaj's ranks."

"Maybe so. But we'll deal with them if and when they misbehave. We don't have time to vet them all right now, unless you want to stay here another day or two. We can work it out during the trip home or when we get there. We won't take anyone beyond Lakeside to the stronghold that we don't trust."

"Well, m'lady. It has been a long and productive day. Shall we take a stroll back to our mansion and retire?" Mace stood and offered his hand to Shari, who batted her eyelashes at him and allowed him to help her rise. As they were heading out the door, Mace detected the sounds of celebrations drifting down the streets and alleys around them. People walking the street had a little extra bounce to their step. Or at least, it seemed that way to him.

They were only a few steps down the street when Stonehand called out, "Mace! Hold, lad. I wanted to catch ye before ye reached yer bed." The dwarf winked at Shari, emphasizing the last word as he did.

Mace turned to face the dwarf, who was accompanied by Red, as always. "Master Stonehand. What can I do for you?" He smiled at his new friend. Mace truly liked the dwarf, who was straightforward and honest to a fault. He enjoyed fighting just as much as celebrating, and he did not apologize for either. He was distracted for a moment by some costumed revelers approaching them as he held out his hand to the dwarf. They wore cloaks and masks, and each carried a bottle as they stumbled up the sloped street.

Stonehand shook the offered hand, holding it as he spoke. "We talked a bit, Red and meself. We've decided to go with ye. Adventure seems ta find outworlders, and ye're the last of em. So if'n ye don't mind, we'll tag along with ye fer a wee bit o'time."

Mace patted the dwarf's hand, still clasping his own, and then let go and reached a hand out to Red as well. "We'd be honored to have you with us. Both of you. You're welcome to join us on the *Sea Sprite* on the way back. We'll probably spend a day in Port Bjur-"

Mace's sentence was interrupted by blinding pain even as Stonehand's eyes grew wide, and Red began to draw daggers from the belt across her chest. He heard Shari scream, and a voice near his ear as his vision grew dark.

"Who are you to free our slaves, drow? This is our city!"

The last thing he heard was Stonehand roaring in anger and more screams. He felt his body collapse, and his head slammed against the cobblestone.

You have died.
You may choose to respawn at your most recent bind point, or remain with your corpse, and resurrect it after a ten-minute wait period. Your resurrected avatar will have 50% health, and a two-hour death debuff.

Respawn at your bind point? Yes/No

Mace cursed to himself and chose 'Yes', figuring he could respawn at the Mansion where he'd spent the previous night and get back to help with the fight in less than ten minutes. The moment his body appeared inside his quarters there, he pulled up his interface. He'd lost a good bit of experience but not dropped a level. And though he'd lost his left-hand dagger and fifty gold, his soul dagger was still in its sheath.

He was just opening the door to run downstairs when Shari appeared in the room as well. As soon as she focused on him, she said, "It was the bastards in the costumes! They stabbed you in the back, then slit my throat. Red and Stonehand were already killing them when I faded out."

Mace nodded, mentally berating himself for not paying more attention. "Ready to run back?" he asked, opening the door the rest of the way. Shari nodded and dashed out ahead of him. The two elves both enjoyed the increased speed and agility inherent to their races, and they were back at the Strumpet less than five minutes later.

The fight was over, six dead citizens laying on the stone avenue while three more were on their knees, bleeding and crying as city guards tied their hands. Jake, Silas, and the rest of the councilors stood around them, along with Red and Stonehand, Jorin, Lila, Layne, and T'enaj. Behind them were scores of citizens, the gathering crowd staring and whispering.

"Thank you, Master Stonehand, Red." Mace bowed his head, and he bent to pick up his lost dagger. The gold was nowhere to be seen. Shari did the same, picking up her enchanted wyvern-bone bow with a sigh of relief. She'd been carrying more gold than Mace had, and he wondered how much she'd lost.

Red apologized. "I didn't see their intent until they'd already struck. I'm sorry, Mace."

He shook his head. "No need. I should have sensed them. It was foolish of me to lower my guard, even for a few minutes. This is my fault." He turned to look at the dead citizens, giving one of them a halfhearted kick to the head.

Focusing on the three attackers who'd surrendered, he asked Silas, "Why are these three still alive?"

The former slaver stammered, "We… we thought to hold a trial."

Mace shook his head. "A trial will only allow them to spew their poisonous opinions about their right to own slaves and cause unrest. Is there a question as to their guilt? They were with the others, and they are dressed as they were. Stonehand, did they participate in the fight?"

"Aye, lad." Stonehand pointed to the closest of the three. "That one there be the one that stabbed ye in the back. He tried to flee while them others fought, but Red stopped him."

Mace eyed the one the dwarf had indicated. The man struggled against his bindings, then spat at Mace's feet. "Drow scum!"

Addressing Silas but speaking loudly enough for all to hear, he asked, "Does anyone question their guilt?"

Not a single voice spoke out. Mace stepped up to the one who had stabbed him. "I told you all that harming others had only one penalty!" He growled.

The man opened his mouth to retort, but Mace punched him in the face. "That's for being an ass. And this is for stabbing me." He grabbed the man's hair and forced his head back, exposing his throat. A quick flexing of his wrist caused the soul dagger to appear in his grasp, and he jammed it into the man's throat.

The crowd gasped at the sudden execution, but Mace barely heard them as the blade sang to his soul, and the power it stole from the man surged through him. Without another word, he slit the throats of the other two, reveling in the influx of power. When it faded, he blinked a few times and looked around. The crowd around him was dead silent, and most looked at him with fear in their eyes.

He slid the bloody dagger back into its sheath and raised his hands to show the crowd that they were empty. "I mean no harm to any of you. These cowards attacked from behind and killed Shari and myself. The law is clear. Any of you who harms another will pay the price. Trial over!" He wiped the blood from his hands on the back of one of his victims' shirts. Reaching down, he looted the three, keeping only the combined gold they carried. The rest of their gear and loot he gave to Stonehand and Red.

Turning to Silas, he said, "I believe the property of these nine individuals is now forfeit, is that correct?"

Silas and the new councilors all nodded their heads. "Their families, if they have them, will be allowed to keep their residence. Everything else is forfeit," Silas confirmed.

Mace looked at his loot notifications, then produced a small stack of gold. "Silas, councilors. Send guards to these people's homes to notify their families and begin confiscating their assets." Holding up the gold, he shouted, "These three were carrying about sixty gold! Drinks are on them!" He handed the coins to Jake, who rushed inside to deal with the sudden influx of thirsty people.

Chapter 5

Griff and Lisa woke to find they had a message waiting from Shari. Another of the survivors had made contact! They listened to what she had to say about Tex, about him helping them increase their chances of uploading their consciousnesses. They shared a breakfast of pancakes, which Griff cut up into pieces for Lisa, earning him a kiss on the cheek. Then she left to get herself into her pod while Griff cleaned up, and they both logged back into the game.

The village was abuzz with activity. Carts were lined up, and ponies and giant boars were hitched to harnesses to pull them. Others were being pulled by individual dwarves or teams of two. Not having a household to move, Griff and Lisa both volunteered to help others pull their loads.

Within minutes of their arrival, Campbell shouted from the front of the caravan, and the carts began to move. He waited at the gates, offering encouraging words or jokes to each family that passed. When the last of them had passed through, he closed the gates and laid a hand on them, speaking a phrase that locked them. There were still plenty of valuable items in the village, and he fully intended to bring a party back to retrieve them.

The path to the orc village wasn't paved, but it was gentle enough that the carts could traverse it. Those being pulled by beasts took the lead, breaking ground and wearing more of a path for the dwarves pulling carts behind them. This time, there were no attacks by goblins or beasts of any kind. Few would be foolish enough to attack an entire caravan of dwarves. Keeping pace with the lead ponies, the train of wagons and carts made good time, reaching the orc village well before nightfall.

Sure that the chief wouldn't mind, the dwarves sheltered their women and children in the huts. There weren't enough for everyone, so tents were erected between the huts and cookfires were soon burning.

Lisa went with the hunters out into the forest. Within an hour, they returned with two wild boars and a deer, which were promptly skinned, spitted, and rotated over fires. The dwarves broke out a few kegs, and the whole village celebrated their day's successful journey.

As the young ones retired and the elders settled in for some serious drinking, a cry rang out from the edge of the forest. A moment later, a boulder came crashing down, obliterating one of the cookfires then bouncing over two surprised dwarves' head to smash into a hut behind them. Screams of pain and angry shouts were soon joined by war cries and the sounds of more boulders landing.

Leroy and old Maggie ran to the smashed hut, pulling away debris and casting heals on those inside. Griff and Lisa armed up with the rest of the dwarves, who were all turning toward the north and the forest at the base of the mountains.

"Gotta be mountain trolls!" Campbell shouted, running toward the trees with an axe in each hand. "They can toss them big rocks all night. We gotta get in close 'n' stop 'em!"

As Griff and the other dwarves charged forward, a great cry rang out ahead of them. The sound of hundreds of voices shouting in unison. From the tree line poured scores of goblins, waving rusty swords and hurling spears. From inside the tree line, a rain of arrows arced upward before falling toward the running dwarves. Most were badly aimed, falling behind the rough line of dwarves. But a few struck targets here and there. And though very few penetrated armor, the force of the impacts caused several to stumble or fall. Griff saw one unarmored dwarf in just a pair of leather pants take an arrow to the gut. He simply grunted, pulled the arrow free, and kept going at a jog with his two-handed axe gripped tightly in one massive fist.

Griff altered his course so that he drew closer to the injured dwarf and shouted, "Catch!" as he tossed a healing potion. The dwarf caught it without slowing, used his teeth to uncork the vial, and gulped it down before giving a grateful nod to Griff. They both picked up speed.

As they got within fifty yards of the charging goblins, the dwarves formed up in a tight wedge. Griff had half expected a shield wall, but he noticed many of his fellow dwarves weren't carrying shields. Or wearing armor. They'd been caught by surprise and charged into battle with little or no preparation.

Those at the point of the wedge and at least six on either side of them did carry shields, and they put them to good use as they slammed into the goblin horde. Those without shields reached around, between, and even over their comrades' shields to strike at their foes. They were slaughtering the smaller and weaker enemies, often killing or incapacitating them with a single blow. Griff Inspected one of them.

Goblin Warrior
Level 15
Health: 1,900/2,000

But for every goblin that went down, there were three to take its place. Some crawled between their cousins' legs to strike at dwarven feet, or they popped up inside the wedge and attacked at their enemies' backs. As soon as Campbell saw this, he shouted orders, and the formation changed. Every dwarf in the village over the age of twelve was combat trained. They drilled themselves on fighting techniques and battle tactics on a regular basis. The elder dwarves were veterans of scores, if not hundreds, of battles. At Campbell's command, the wedge collapsed into a smaller circle. Those with shields were interspersed among those without, offering some measure of protection all the way around. Dwarves with crossbows stepped back off the line to the interior of the circle and began loading and firing at an impressive pace. Those with spears and throwing weapons patrolled inside the line, leaping forward to do damage or shore up a weak spot where necessary, and quickly killing any goblin that crawled through to the interior. Healers moved inside the circle as well, casting heals and pulling the most seriously wounded out of the line long enough to save them. Jo and three other casters sent fire, ice, and lightning into the thickest groups of goblins, mowing them down.

Griff took an arrow to his left arm, just above the rim of his shield. His health bar dropped by ten percent, and a bleeding icon appeared on his UI. Grunting with pain, he raised the edge of the shield up under the shaft then used his axe to break it off. Moving his shield arm hurt, but he could still manage.

Looking around, he estimated that maybe five hundred goblins had attacked their group of less than a hundred dwarves. When he took out the number of children and elderly, there were maybe seventy dwarves fighting in the formation. But the dwarves were taking it in their stride, obviously of the opinion that the odds were in their favor. Campbell started chanting, a deep rhythmic sound that the others quickly picked up. Shields bashed on one beat, weapons smashed on another.

> *Bones of iron, skulls of stone*
> *We fight all day to defend our own!*
> *We smash and bash, slash and cut*
> *Stab our foes in their soft guts!*
> *Stomp on skulls and crush their bones*
> *Teach them not to invade our homes!*
> *Fight all day and through the night*
> *Show 'em all our dwarven might!*

The dwarves kept advancing toward the tree line, mowing down the mass of goblins in front of them. Those on the sides and behind were cut down just as efficiently, until the sheer number of dead caused the goblins to pull back in fear. A sort of buffer zone appeared around the circle of dwarves, moving with them as they advanced. Any goblins who ventured too close were put down. The rest seemed content to stay close and wait.

Campbell, realizing what they were up to, shouted, "Watch the sky!" even as more boulders began to fall toward them. The organized circle disintegrated as dwarves dodged falling rocks, some more successfully than others. One of the crossbow wielders was too focused on his target and didn't move quickly enough. He was crushed by a boulder twice his size before it bounced forward and knocked down one of the shield-bearers. The sound of breaking bones made Griff wince in sympathy. The healers immediately focused on the shield dwarf, knowing that the other was already gone.

Taking advantage of the chaos, the goblins rushed back in, hacking and slashing at the dwarves as the two groups mingled. Rocks continued to fall, smashing into more goblins than dwarves. Still, dwarves went down here and there, some from falling rocks, others from swarms of six or ten goblins.

Griff slaughtered goblin after goblin, focusing on helping his fellow dwarves who were being overwhelmed. He used his *Shield Bash* to knock back three and four of the little creatures at a time, freeing up his allies to hack and slash at the stunned creatures. Still, the numbers weighed on the dwarves as more and more of them fell. Any dwarf that hit the ground was instantly buried under a pile of biting, stabbing goblins.

"Reform! Reform and move forward!" Campbell shouted. The dwarves backed themselves into a now smaller circle. Griff found himself on the back edge, looking behind them toward the orc camp. He saw nearly a dozen dwarven corpses littering the ground among hundreds of dead goblins.

"Get into the trees!" Campbell ordered, and the group moved as one so quickly that Griff was momentarily left behind. Unlike the others, he hadn't trained in formations or battle tactics. Turning to catch up, he noticed Lisa having the same problem. Relieved to see her alive, he grinned and gasped out, "Just do what they do!"

Out of breath herself, Lisa just nodded and lowered her head, charging to catch up to the others. She and Griff cut down a few ambitious goblins who tried to separate them from their friends, quickly rejoining the circle as it moved into the trees. The falling rocks ceased, the trolls having no clear path between the trees. Campbell called a halt, and the dwarves expertly adjusted their formation to make use of the massive tree trunks as bulwarks.

Now the goblins had to come at them between and around the trees, narrowing the lanes of access and causing them to bunch up. Jo and the casters took advantage of the tighter groups, blasting them. Griff saw Jo drop a fireball between two trees on a group of twenty or so goblins as they pressed against the backs of their cousins who were engaged with the dwarves. The goblins in the rear were scattered, some blasted into others who were already in combat. The dwarves on the line took advantage of the distraction and slaughtered them. They quickly dashed forward and finished the burning, wounded goblins, then retreated back to the line.

In the center of the circle, healers were gulping mana potions and feeding health potions to the critically wounded. Just as it seemed they were starting to catch up, the trolls stepped out of the darkness.

Seeing their much larger allies, the hundred or so remaining goblins renewed their attacks with fresh resolve. Screaming and waving weapons, they charged in with little regard for their own safety. The trolls lifted huge clubs and began thumping them on the ground as they advanced.

Desperate to deal with the goblins before the trolls could reach them, the dwarves went into a frenzy of their own. At a command from Campbell, every second dwarf stepped back to form a tight circle around the healers and ranged in the center, allowing the goblins to rush inside the outer circle. They then closed ranks, tightening the outer circle and trapping nearly all the remaining goblins inside. Now the goblins found themselves surrounded, taking hits from front and back. They scrambled over each other in their attempts to get free, making them even less effective fighters. It was over in less than thirty seconds. The outer ring quickly turned back to deal with the half dozen or so goblins that had remained outside the rings, and the inner circle moved back out to face the trolls.

The whole time the melee dwarves were finishing off the goblins, the casters and crossbow wielders had been focusing on the trolls. Blasts to the faces of the giant beasts slowed them down some, but it had made them angrier at the same time.

"Split into pairs! Use the trees!" Campbell commanded.

Griff found himself paired with a dual-axe wielding dwarf he didn't know. "Put yer shield down, lad. Won't help ye here, only slow ye down!" Griff did as the dwarf suggested, stowing his shield in his inventory as he followed his partner to a position behind a large tree. "They can't swing them nasty smashers so good in here. Wait till one passes, then attack the legs!" The older dwarf was panting, showing the strain of the recent run and extended fight. Still, he was grinning and had a glimmer in his eyes.

Dwarves lived for battle.

The tree Griff was leaning against shuddered as a log-sized club impacted it. His partner didn't hesitate, dashing around the other side of the tree with axes raised. Griff followed and as he rounded the trunk he saw the dwarf hacking at the back of a troll's knee. The leg was nearly half as thick as the trunk they'd just used for cover, and from the looks of the cuts the dwarf was making, the skin was thick and tough. And Griff could see it had a massive health pool.

Mountain Troll
Level 25
Health: 9,000/9,000

Leaping into the air, Griff raised his axe over his head and brought it down on the back of the troll's knee with everything he had. His larger, heavier blade bit deeper than the other dwarf's hand axes, and as the skin parted, he could feel muscles severing like snapping ropes inside the knee.

As the giant stepped forward, Griff was pulled along, still gripping his weapon with both hands as his feet dangled in the air. He managed to brace his feet against the troll's calf and use them to push off, levering his axe free of the flesh. Blood sprayed everywhere, and the troll stumbled as its muscles failed to support its weight.

A great cheer went up among the dwarves as the monster fell forward. A dozen rushed in from both sides, hacking at its face and neck. It was quickly put down, and they scattered to find new targets.

Griff turned at a shout from his partner behind him, but he was too slow. The breath was knocked from him as he was punted by another troll.

"Oof!" His body folded at the impact, and he flew backward through the air for a long moment before slamming into a tree and falling limply to land on gnarled roots. His health bar dropped to ten percent, and he couldn't breathe. As he struggled to inhale, all he got was an odd groaning sound and no air. An attempt to roll onto his back proved fruitless, as both arms and several ribs were clearly broken. He thought his spine might have snapped as well. He lay there in pain, wondering where he would respawn and listening to the sounds of the battle.

A cool feeling washed over him as Leroy or one of the other healers found him. He managed to gasp in a deep breath, taking in the scent of moss and rich earth as he did. Still only at thirty percent health, he rolled himself over so that he could see his surroundings.

The trolls were taking a toll even as they fell. The one who had punted him was on one knee, his club hand nearly severed at the wrist and dwarves climbing its back. The monster had the presence of mind to fall and roll, crushing the two dwarves on its back beneath its massive bulk.

This left it prone on the ground for a moment, during which a dozen other dwarves rushed in to avenge their friends. It died horribly, screaming as it was hacked to pieces.

Griff's right arm was now working well enough for him to grab a health potion and gulp it down. Feeling better, he staggered to his feet. His axe was on the ground where the troll had kicked him, and he moved awkwardly to retrieve it. His body wasn't quite responding as it should, though his health was now over fifty percent. He could feel a strange grinding inside, and he tried not to think about what was causing it.

By the time he retrieved his weapon, the fight was all but over. One last troll remained on its feet and fighting. It smashed an unlucky dwarf into the ground with its club, and the others roared in rage. One of the dwarves launched himself off a boulder and drove a spear deep into the monster's loincloth, causing it to emit a high-pitched scream and drop its club. The dwarf hung onto the weapon, his weight dragging the shaft downward as Griff winced despite himself. The sharp end had to be doing horrible things to the troll's junk. A fireball from Jo struck the thing in the face, silencing its scream for a moment.

Dwarves swarmed the stricken monster, hacking its legs to shreds until it fell, then swarming over its body. Griff tried to join them, but he was moving too slow. It died before he was halfway there. He slumped to the ground and took a moment to view the notifications that had been streaming across his UI during the long fight. He'd picked up several levels, for starters.

Level Up! You are now Level 21!...

Level Up! You are now Level 24!
You have received one attribute point

His two-handed skill had gained +1, and he'd earned a point in *Shield Bash* as well. He finished reading his notifications and looked around. The dwarves were quietly gathering the dead and looting the corpses of goblins and trolls. Leroy and two other healers were dealing with the wounded, and Lisa was walking toward him, a grin on her face.

"I'm level 20!" she whispered, trying not to sound too excited among the mourning dwarves.

Griff patted the ground next to him. "Take a minute and assign your attribute points. Might need them if there's another attack."

Taking his own advice, he pulled up his stat sheet and assigned points. As a warrior, he focused on Stamina and Strength. His relatively deep health pool was the only thing that had saved him when the troll punted him. It had been a while since he assigned points, and he had nine to work with. So he added three points to Stamina and four to Strength. Thinking about his luck at surviving the impact with the tree, he added one point to Luck. And because it might help him dodge future puntings, he added a point to Agility. When he was done, he looked over his sheet.

Character Name: Griff	Class: Warrior		Level: 24
Race: Dwarf	Spec: ?		Exp 1570/6800
Health: 9,000/9,000	Mana: 100/100		Attrib Pts Avail: 0
Stamina: 19	Wisdom: 10	Charisma: 10	Life Regen: 30/sec
Strength: 19	Intellect: 10	Dexterity: 12	Mana Regen: 1/sec
Agility: 12	Luck: 12	Armor: 90	Skill Pts Avail: 0

He was distracted by some cheering over to his left and got to his feet. Pulling Lisa up with him, he walked to where a group of dwarves surrounded one of the fallen trolls. They were smiling and slapping each other on the back.

As Griff got closer, he saw a battered-looking Campbell being teased by his comrades. "We were thinkin' it'd crushed ye!" a dwarf rubbed his hands together in a grinding motion. "Expected ye to be as flat as one o' Jo's pancakes."

Griff smiled as well when he realized that Campbell and the dwarf next to him were the two who'd been rolled on by the giant troll. He stepped forward to shake the elder dwarf's hand. "How'd you manage to survive that?"

Campbell looked sheepish. "Nearly didn't! He had us squished right good, but the squishin' dinna' kill us. Had us trapped, though, and it were getting damned hard to breathe under there. If the lad's hadn't pushed the beastie free, we'd have perished fer sure."

Campbell's face grew serious, and his voice lowered as he turned to one of the others and asked, "How many?"

The dwarves all grew solemn. "We lost sixteen."

Campbell nodded, his countenance grim. His voice was heavy with grief. "They died well. It were a hard battle, and I'm proud o' each one of ya. Post some guards at the tree line, and let's gather our dead. Ye know what to do."

As the dwarves dispersed, Griff cleared his throat. "Campbell, I'm so sorry. This is my fault. I convinced you to leave the village."

"No, lad." Campbell put a hand on Griff's shoulder. The sadness in his voice brought tears to Lisa's eyes. "If anything, ye saved us. With the orcs gone, these beasties would have attacked our village soon enough. Likely in greater numbers. Ye were right. They'll just keep comin' till we can't handle 'em and they overrun us. Best to leave now, savin' what we can."

Griff had made that same argument just a few days ago. But then it had seemed a simple explanation of likely game progression to him. Now the consequences of his recommendation and the dwarves' choices were like another kick in the gut.

They looted the monsters and gathered up the bodies of the dead. There was some concern that three of the bodies were missing, but that turned out to be a good thing. Three of those who were killed in the battle were among the dozen that Elysia had evolved at Griff's request. All three had respawned at the orc camp, much to the delight of Campbell and the others.

With the guards posted and the wounded healed, the dwarves retired to their bedrolls. Though Griff doubted any of them actually slept. He and Lisa sat by one of the cookfires and logged out.

Chapter 6

Tex woke up a few hours later when Skippy alerted him that Shari was calling.

"Tex, the nice lady from HQ wants to talk to you. I can't imagine why. I'm a much more engaging conversationalist."

"Can't argue with you there, Skipster." Tex stepped into the bathroom to splash some water on his face, and then he threw on a pair of sweats and a *GameLit Don't Quit* T-shirt featuring a Viking wolverine and headed for the security office. Sitting down in front of the main console, he said, "Hit me, Skippy."

"If only I could, Tex," Skippy replied as the monitor lit up with an image of Shari's smiling face.

"Hi, Tex! I'm glad you made it to the compound. Everything go okay?"

Tex ran his fingers through his hair, noticing on the small picture of him at the top of the screen that his hair was sticking up everywhere. "I ran into one of those creatures. A human one. I killed it, but it was close."

Shari's eyes had gone wide as he spoke, but she gathered herself together when he said he'd killed it. "As long as you're okay. Did you manage to get any supplies on the way?"

He grinned at this. "Got about a week's supply of booze. Some jerky and snacks. I haven't checked the kitchen situation here yet. But there should be something edible in there."

Shari gave him a half smile. "I understand. The adrenaline rush that keeps you alive out there tends to make you crash after. I'm sorry I woke you. We can talk later…"

"No, no." Tex held up a hand as if to stop her from logging off. "I'd much rather talk to you than Skippy. Were you and Mace in-game today?" He looked at the clock. It was 9:00 pm his time, which meant 11:00 pm where she was.

"Yep! We pretty much concluded our business in Graf, and we're sailing back toward home at dawn. Might be bringing as many as two hundred NPCs with us as recruits. That'll help us build up the stronghold and expand it into a real keep."

Tex smiled. Town building and crafting were among his favorite things to do in VR games. He participated in the dungeon runs and raids because the experience and loot allowed him to get the resources he needed for crafting. Over the years, he'd joined several guilds to help them build their infrastructure in return for them providing him resources for his crafts.

"I look forward to helping with that. If this whole thing works, we're going to have years and years of 24/7 in-game time to build something awesome!"

They chatted a bit more about their plans, both in-game and out, until Shari yawned. Tex smacked his forehead. "You've gotta be in-game at dawn server time. You need sleep! Sorry to have kept you so long."

"No worries. Like you, I'm happy to have somebody to talk to other than Mace!" She winked at him. "Have a great night!" She waved at him before logging off.

Wide awake after a long nap, Tex decided to explore, then log in for a bit. He started with the security office. He'd been in here before once or twice to have his photo ID created, and when he installed Skippy into the system. A brief check of the cabinets and closets showed him where to find the radio headsets, weapons, and a few spare uniforms. There were also two armor vests in the closet.

Out in the corridor, he passed several sleeping quarters before turning right. Down this hallway was the cafeteria and dining room, as well as the laundry. His stomach rumbling, he walked through the dining area. There was a faintly foul odor, which he determined came from a basket of rotten fruit on a counter. There was also a coffee machine with the bottom third of the glass pot covered with dried and blackened coffee. He picked it up and carried it into the kitchen where he set it in a sink and filled it with water. He found some detergent and poured a good bit inside, then left it to soak.

Next, he opened the walk-in. Again, there was a faint odor here. Some meat, fresh fruit and vegetables that had been left on the shelves too long. Even refrigerated, they only lasted so long. But the good news was that there was tons of food on the shelves. Canned goods, jars of fruit and pasta sauce, tubes of biscuits and croissants, cookie dough, enough to feed him for months. In the back of the walk-in was another door that he found led to a freezer. In here he found frozen hamburger patties, pork chops, even steaks. There were microwavable burritos, hot pockets, and gallons of different flavored ice creams.

Back out in the kitchen, he discovered a pantry even larger than the walk-in. There was a good bit of moldy bread, buns, etc. that he needed to dispose of, but there were also whole shelves of pasta in different shapes, boxes of pop tarts, various jars of condiments like peanut butter and jelly, mayo, and several flavors of mustard. Then there were canned vegetables and soups, as well as basic ingredients like flour, salt, and sugar. One wall held a fully stocked wine rack with maybe a hundred bottles.

"It's too bad it's just me here," he mumbled to himself. "But at least I won't have to go outside anytime soon. Maybe never, if I ration the alcohol."

Grabbing a couple packs of pop tarts, he left the pantry. He located garbage bags in a cabinet near the back and took some time to bag up all the rotted food products. With half a dozen full garbage bags in tow, he made his way to the incinerator, which was farther down the corridor past the laundry.

Stopping back at the kitchen, he grabbed the pop tarts and a one-liter bottle of water and headed to the room he was most familiar with.

His lab.

The company had set this room up for him when he'd first signed on. It was made to his specifications – there was a single electric desk that he could raise and lower depending on whether he wanted to sit or stand. Three separate servers were bolted into a frame along one wall – all three completely isolated from each other and without any network connections. One of them housed Skippy's original code, which was now several versions behind the Skippy that was roaming free throughout the building.

To one side of the large room was a sitting area with a long leather sofa and deep-cushioned chairs, set around a coffee table that doubled as a holo-display. Tex often worked while reclining on that sofa. There was a fully stocked bar in a cabinet behind one of the chairs, and a sixty-five inch TV mounted on the wall next to it with a gaming console below.

The balance of the room was taken up with his very own prototype immersion pod. He approached the pod and stroked the clear plastic cover lovingly. He had helped create the software that enabled these pods to work. Or more precisely, enabled the AIs to communicate with the brains of the people sitting in the pods.

He'd spent years of his life training artificial intelligence to be more human. Peabody, Skippy, and Elysia too. His theory had always been that the more an AI can think like a human, the easier it would be for the humans to sync with them. And in the virtual reality industry, synchronization was everything. Secondary only to raw computing power.

Stripping down, he climbed into the pod and activated it. Slipping on the headgear, he adjusted the breathing tube slightly, then closed his eyes and waited.

When he opened his eyes again, he was back in the forest he'd left the day before. He'd chosen an orc avatar when he created SkippyIsADork during the alpha testing phase of the game. Mainly because not a lot of the other alphas were playing monster races, and he'd have the starter zone mainly to himself. Plus orcs looked cool, and at higher levels, they were strong enough to break small trees with their bare hands.

He'd played the game semi-religiously over the years, leveling up his character and crafting for fun. It was now level sixty, but not the most effective of builds. He'd initially put most of his points into physical attributes – Strength and Stamina – which made sense for an orc. But for the last twenty levels or so, he'd started putting points into Intellect and Wisdom. As a result, his orc was pretty balanced between physical and mental abilities. Which also meant he wasn't very powerful in either.

He'd been leaning toward the Shaman class, though he'd never actually selected a class for the avatar. As one of the research team, he'd received admin access that would allow him to change pretty much anything he wanted for his avatar. He could shuffle the attribute points, change class, even change race at will. Pulling up his character screen, he chose the Shaman class and confirmed. He liked the idea of being able to summon creatures and do magic damage, as well as heal himself if necessary. And if all else failed, he could hold his own with mace and shield.

Looking around the forest, he used his mini-map to get his bearings. The portal hub he was looking for was in the orc lands, but he was far from the capital city where it was located. He'd used one of the portals from that hub to get to the mountain nearest his current location, in search of a rare mineral for his crafting. Upon finding the mineral, he had harvested it, then set up camp in hopes it would reappear in the same location.

His camp was a simple one—a rough lean-to made of cut branches and covered in leaves and vines, a small campfire within a ring of stones, and a weathered old stump to sit on. The game's mechanics provided for protections within an established camp, so that when a player logged off, they wouldn't return to find their avatar dead and gear damaged or gone.

Off to his right, he saw that the small cluster of boulders where he'd mined the rare mineral were once again glinting in the sunlight. Producing a mining pick from his bag, he worked the node for about ten minutes, harvesting more than he'd expected. This was another mechanic that Elysia had modified on her own, to the benefit of players. Once a resource was harvested, whether it be metals, plants, or minerals, it would reappear. Sometimes in the same location, sometimes nearby. The longer the replenished resource was left alone, the more it would grow.

Dropping the mineral and the pick into his inventory, he pulled a bow and quiver out and equipped them. The bow went over his shoulder, and the quiver was fastened securely to his hip. Next, he equipped one of his favorite weapons, a long spear. The shaft was three inches thick and made of petrified ironwood that he'd enchanted himself. The spear's wicked-looking steel tip was barbed and sharp enough to cut glass. It weighed a solid thirty pounds altogether, and would be too heavy for his human body, but his muscled orc avatar wielded it with ease.

He set off at a brisk walk toward the mountain where he'd find his portal, keeping a sharp eye out for useful plants and other resources. The wildlife in the area was, on average, lower leveled than him. But a full pack of level fifty wolves might manage to kill him if he was taken by surprise. So, resources weren't the only thing he watched out for.

Two or three miles from his camp, he ran across an injured grizzly bear. It burst from the underbrush ahead of him, limping badly and bleeding from several wounds. Two arrows protruded from its neck, and one of its eyes was destroyed by what looked like a sword cut. It took a few steps in his direction, then collapsed on the ground.

Ursus the Grizzly
Level 70
Health 1,600/12,000

As the bear panted and bled on the forest floor, Tex approached carefully. The player in him urged to him finish the named mob and claim the rewards. This was a forest boss, probably from some quest line or area instance. It would give him enough experience to level up, and drop some sweet loot.

On the other hand, as a shaman, he had the ability to tame the creatures of Elysia. This bear would make one hell of a pet.

Either way, he needed to act quickly. The bleeding bear's health was draining away quickly. If he allowed it to die without hitting it, someone else would get credit for the kill. And one couldn't tame a dead pet, unless one was a necromancer. Which he wasn't.

Gripping his spear tightly, he approached the bear. It looked up at him, clearly in pain. Its breathing was ragged and made a wheezing sound every time it inhaled.

Tex made his decision.

He cast a shaman healing spell called *Strength of Spirit* on the bear, raising its health back up by three thousand points. Then he cast a second spell, *Revivify,* that would add fifty health every two seconds for one minute.

Sticking his spear into the ground, he held up both hands in a calming gesture as he approached the grizzly. It grunted at him as if acknowledging his assistance. Very slowly, he approached and took hold of one of the arrows. "This is going to hurt. I'm sorry, fella," he mumbled as he quickly jerked the arrow free of the bear's hide.

Ursus whined in pain, but he did not try to claw or bite Tex, which he took as a good sign. He took hold of the second arrow, pulling it free as well just as he heard voices from the direction the bear had come.

"The blood leads through here!"

Tex quickly cast *Strength of Spirit* on the bear again, bringing it up over fifty percent health with the HoT still ticking away for another half minute.

As he got to his feet and retrieved his spear, a party of humans pushed through the same brush the bear had appeared from. There were five of them, all young and armed to the teeth. The one in front held an oval shield with metal studs adorning its surface and what looked like several long bear claw scratches. Behind him was a female warrior type with a longsword and chain armor. There were two casters, a man and a woman, one of which Tex assumed was a healer, and the bowman that had almost certainly fired the arrows that now lay on the ground next to the wounded bear. All of them were between level fifty and fifty-five.

"He's our kill, orc. Step away." The tank growled, thumping a sword against his shield for emphasis.

Orcs and humans were not automatic enemies in Elysia. There were certain tribes of hostile orcs roaming the world that would attack humans on sight. And there were humans, both NPC and players, who would attack any orc they found for one reason or another. But orcs were also a playable race in the game, and there were just as many friendly orc tribes as hostile.

These human NPCs seemed more hostile than friendly, if the tank's tone was any indicator. Still, Tex tried to be friendly.

"Good morning to you, humans! I was not aware this bear belonged to you. Did he attack your village?"

The female caster snorted. "What village? We came from the city of Chatfield to hunt this bear. His hide is worth a hundred gold if we bring it to an armorer there."

Tex thought he saw a little light at the end of this particular tunnel. "I've grown quite fond of this bear in the short time I've known him. How about I just give you the hundred gold you would have earned, plus fifty more for your trouble, and you leave him to me?" He surreptitiously cast another HoT on the bear even as he stuck his spear back into the ground and held his empty hands out toward the humans as a distraction. A quick glance showed him the bear was healing nicely, and it seemed to be playing dead as it watched him.

> **Ursus the Grizzly**
> **Level 70**
> **Health 11,100/12,000**

He sincerely hoped the bear considered him an ally after the healing and wouldn't ambush him as he tried to deal with its would-be killers.

The female caster spoke again, making Tex think she was the leader of the group. "No deal, orc. There are five of us, and one of you. We could just kill you *and* the bear and loot you both."

Tex decided to try one more time. "I'm not so easy to kill. And you already failed to kill the bear once. Please, just take the gold and go. I don't want to kill you. But to be clear, if you attack, you will be the first to die." He left his spear standing next to him, his hands empty. To bolster his argument, he pulled a small sack with a hundred and fifty gold in it from his inventory and held it out for them to see.

The caster hesitated, and the bowman behind her whispered something that Tex couldn't make out. She nodded her head once, and the bowman lowered his weapon. As she was opening her mouth to answer, the tank shouted, "Screw you, orc!" and ran forward, his sword arm raised and ready to strike.

Ursus, now fully healed, roared as he leapt to his feet and charged at the oncoming tank. The man's eyes widened in shock as the monster he'd thought nearly dead bashed into him. He managed to raise his shield to block a massive paw as it swiped toward his head.

With a sigh, Tex grabbed his spear and took two steps forward for momentum as he raised it over his shoulder and flung it forward at the caster. She was distracted by the roar of the bear and didn't see the oncoming missile in time to dodge. It blasted through her cloth robe, her chest, her back, and partway into the gut of archer behind her.

The melee fighter screamed in rage and ran at Tex, who equipped his bow and drew an arrow in the time it took her to move four steps. He loosed the arrow and fired point-blank into her face, knocking her back but not killing her. His next arrow went into the other caster, who was working to heal the archer. The man had fallen backward, pulling free of the spear point in his gut. Unfortunately, the barbed tip of the spear had hooked some of his guts and pulled them free as he fell.

Tex's arrow struck the healer, who was also wearing cloth armor, in the back. The impact interrupted the spell and knocked about twenty percent off his health bar.

A quick check on the bear showed that he was more than holding his own against the tank. Without the assistance of his party members, the tank was desperately trying to fend off the grizzly boss's attacks and not doing much damage in return. Tex could see his health bar was down to seventy percent already.

Throwing another *Revivify* on Ursus, he went back to dealing with the others. He confirmed the lead caster was dead, his spear having penetrated her heart. The archer was also out of the fight, desperately trying to push his innards back into the hole in his gut. The healer was still on his feet, and once again he was trying to heal the archer. The female warrior with an arrow in her face was still alive, but she was not yet on her feet.

Solving two problems at once, Tex took hold of the haft of his spear and pulled with all his might. The caster's chest made a sucking sound as the shaft was withdrawn, quickly drowned out by the screams of the archer as the retreating spearpoint pulled more and more of his innards before the section hooked on the spear's barb finally burst and fell away.

In one smooth motion, Tex turned and shoved the newly freed spear point into the caster's side, shattering ribs as the shaft followed the sharp point into his body. Tex levered the spear's butt end upward, causing the spear to shred the healer's innards and preventing him from casting a heal on himself.

When Tex turned the spear and yanked, the broken ribs exploded outward as the barbed spearhead emerged. The healer's health bar dropped to little more than a sliver, and he fell to the ground bleeding.

Tex turned to the warrior, seeing her back on her feet and lifting her oversized two-handed longsword. Raising his weapon, he used the ironwood haft to block the downward stroke of the sword. Shoving upward, he pushed the warrior off balance, then kicked her in the belly, knocking the wind out of her and causing her to fall back, groaning as she hit the ground.

He stepped forward, intending to finish the woman off when Ursus' massive jaws clamped down on her head and crushed her skull with an audible pop. Looking behind the bear, Tex found there wasn't much left of the tank. He still lived, but he was missing an arm and half of his chest, blood pumping weakly from the vicinity of his heart.

Ursus gave the warrior woman's head a violent shake, snapping her neck and causing her body to convulse once. Then he dropped her corpse and turned to face Tex.

"Eeeaasssy there, buddy." Tex stuck his spear into the ground and held up his empty hands. "Remember me? The nice orc who healed you up so you could eat the humans?"

Ursus snorted, lifting his two front legs off the ground and rising to stand on his hind legs. Tilting his head up to the sky, he roared so loudly that Tex imagined he could feel the sound wave wash over his body.

Tex's orc avatar stood eight feet tall, with shoulders nearly four feet wide. His body weighed in at roughly six hundred pounds of bulging muscle. Yet standing in front of the massive grizzly that towered over him, he felt puny. Keeping his hands visible and empty, he took a single step back. "Nice bear. Gooood bear." Tex lowered his gaze and tried to look non-threatening.

Ursus dropped back to all fours, his head now just below Tex's eye level. The bear stepped forward and sniffed at Tex, his massive snout cold and wet as it touched the orc's face. A moment later, Ursus chuffed in what sounded like a friendly manner and sat back on his haunches, looking expectantly at Tex. A second later, a new message appeared on his interface.

Ursus the Grizzly has invited you to become his Companion.

Do you accept this invitation? Yes/No

Tex laughed out loud, despite the massive heap of fangs and claws sitting just two feet or so from his face. "_You_ are inviting _me_ to be _your_ pet?" He grinned at the bear, who tilted his head to one side and looked curious.

Looking up at the sky, he shouted, "Very funny, Elysia! This is payback for something, isn't it?" In response, another message appeared below the first, which remained on his interface awaiting his response.

Ursus the Grizzly is a level seventy elite boss NPC. Though you have the ability as a shaman to tame and bind companions, you cannot bind a creature that is both an elite and ten levels above your own.

No longer laughing, he scratched his tough green scalp with clawed fingers. "I'll be damned. She has a point. If anybody's gonna be the pet here, it'd be the puny low-level orc. Hah! What the hell."

Tex clicked on the *Yes* button and smiled as a swirling green light rose from the earth and encompassed both bear and orc. A moment later he felt a connection to Ursus, almost as if he could read the bear's thoughts. But the communication was more visual than lingual. Tex closed his eyes, and the picture became clearer. He saw himself removing the armor from the tank so that the bear could get at the meat inside the shell.

Chuckling to himself, he walked over and looted the tank. Since he was an NPC and now permanently dead, Tex had the option of claiming everything, including the plate armor. He stripped the corpse of everything but his shredded and bloody clothes, then turned to loot the others. A squelching, crunching sound behind him let him know Ursus was feeding. He chose not to turn and look as he filled his bag with the others' useful items.

When he was done looting and the bear was finished with its meal, the two of them turned and stared at each other, Tex shaking his head slightly and grinning at the situation while Ursus licked the blood from his snout.

"So, boss bear. I was on my way to meet some new friends. It's kind of important. They're on a mission for Elysia herself. I don't suppose you want to join me? I'm guessing you'd rather go back to your den and use me as a pillow, or make me dance like a pet monkey or something, right?"

Ursus appeared to grin at him, then snorted. The massive grizzly leaned back, sitting upright on his haunches, and waved one paw lazily in Tex's direction. The paw was the size of a bicycle tire, with claws nearly a foot in length.

"I'm afraid I don't speak bear yet." Tex closed his eyes and concentrated on picturing himself and the bear side by side approaching the mountain portal he'd been traveling toward. When Ursus snorted again, Tex opened his eyes. The bear was back on his feet and had turned in the general direction of the portal. He looked expectantly over his shoulder at Tex, who hurried forward to stand at the grizzly's side, and they began to walk.

Ursus paused to lift a leg and pee on what remained of the tank's corpse, then continued on his way.   Tex made a mental note to search the game wiki for Ursus to see where he actually belonged. He suspected that Elysia was going off script just a bit.

*****

Back in the game themselves, Mace and Shari traveled down to the docks, arriving just as the sun was breaking over the horizon.   There they found all the ship captains gathered together around a row of tables. Jake stood near the tables, behind each one of which a clerk sat with a pile of parchment and a quill pen.   Lined up in front of the tables were six rows of Graf citizens, new and old, that wanted passage to a new life.

As the light and dark elves stood quietly and listened, each of the clerks behind the tables took down pertinent information on the applicant in front of them. Name, age, whether they had family, and how many. Any useful skills.   Then each applicant was given a colored chit and told which ship they were assigned.   Several of the applicants who'd already been processed were standing on the docks next to their rides, each ship having a colored banner draped over the nearest rail to match the chits. The captains had not yet allowed them to board for some reason.

Jorin approached, offering his greetings. "Good morning, Shari! Mace! It will be a glorious day to travel downriver."

Mace shook the captain's hand. "I agree, my friend. It looks like things are going well so far?"

Jorin shook his head. "We have an issue I'm afraid only you and Shari can resolve."

Mace looked around, seeing the refugees standing around. "The captains will not allow them to board for some reason?" His countenance darkened. "They want to renegotiate?"

Jorin raised both hands to pat the air. "No, no, nothing like that. This is actually your issue. You see, these folks have been informed that they need to swear an oath of loyalty in order to receive their passage and a fresh start."

Mace nodded his head, and Shari began to smile. She'd figured out what was coming next, and watched Mace's face to see when it struck him.

"Okayyy… so they object to the oath?"

Jorin chuckled. "No, not at all." He waited a moment, then spelled it out for his friend. "We don't know who, or what, to have them swear the oath *to*. Should they swear to you personally? And if so, are you a guild leader? A king? You have some decisions to make. And I'm afraid you don't have much time."

Shari giggled as Mace swore quietly and blushed. "I've never seen a drow blush before." She poked him in the belly. "I like the idea of King Mace of… we really do need to choose a name for our new nation."

Jorin, picking up on her intent, added, "Why just king? At the rate you're going, you'll be absorbing many cities—and nations too. This time next year, half of Elysia might be yours. I vote for Emperor Mace!"

Mace, getting over his initial reaction and accepting the teasing, stuck out his chest and raised his chin. "Emperor sounds good to me. But that would make you Empress Shari and Admiral Jorin."

Now it was Jorin who was sticking out his chest. He chuckled as he strutted in a small circle, chest out and arms swinging in a military-style march.

Mace took a seat on a crate and rubbed his chin. "We really do need to pick a name for our… I guess it will be a nation. We're already getting too big and complicated for a guild."

Shari offered, "How 'bout Utopia!" smiling broadly at the two. When both of them grimaced, her smile faded. "Or not…"

Mace squeezed her hand. "I'm sorry, that just sounds a little... full of itself? Like calling it *Heaven.* Little hard to live up to. I think maybe something that sounds a little more Camelot-ish. Something that says, 'we're cool, but don't screw with us' at the same time."

Shari stuck out her tongue and grumped at him. "Haven was going to be my second suggestion." Mace just rolled his eyes, smiling.

Jorin suggested, "How about *Styrke*? It means *strength* in the old tongue."

Both elves turned to him, Shari's mouth dropping open. "That's awesome, Jorin!" Shari clapped her hands. "It sounds cool and has the meaning we want."

Mace nodded his head. "I like it too. Okay, so have everyone who wishes to join us swear their oath of loyalty to the nation of Styrke."

Jorin shook his head. "That would be meaningless right now, until you officially declare and establish the nation. I suggest you have them swear to you or to the two of you." He swept his hand in front of them to indicate both Mace and Shari.

"How do I go about establishing a nation, officially?" Mace asked.

Jorin just shrugged. "I've never tried. You could ask the council of elders in Emarien. Or, since you seem to have a way to commune with Elysia herself..." He let his voice trail off.

Not wanting to log out and search the wiki, Mace asked to borrow Jorin's cabin aboard the *Sea Sprite* again, and he and Shari went inside to 'commune' with the game's AI.

"Elysia, Peabody, if one of you can hear me... how do I establish a new nation?"

Elysia's gorgeous avatar appeared in the cabin with them. "Of course I can hear you, Mace. And normally to establish a nation, one would first have to claim some land, build up a certain level of resources and population, then construct an anchor building – a city hall, a keep, or something similar, using an Anchor Stone." She paused as if considering.

Both players knew it was for effect, the quantum computer that was Elysia could do trillions of calculations per second.

"You have already claimed the stronghold at Darkstone as your own, and you control the lands around it. You have made close alliance to the settlement at Lakeside and its citizens. As well as the cities of Graf and Port Bjurstrom, and a lesser alliance with Emarien and the elves. And you have a few hundred citizens ready to swear loyalty. Player Griff has delivered an Anchor Stone to your stronghold, and though it is a Guild stone, not a Kingdom stone, it is within the rules of this world that a guild may expand its holdings into a kingdom. So I shall grant you your Kingdom, provided you promise to set your Anchor Stone within the next thirty days."

Shari opened her mouth to ask why Elysia was giving them thirty days, but Mace spoke first. "Thank you, Elysia. That will give us time to explore the portals and determine the best location for our capital. As I'm sure you intended."

The goddess gave him a small smile, and several notifications appeared on his UI just as she faded from view. The first was a worldwide system alert.

>>>>*System Alert!*<<<<

Players Mace and HotShari have established a new Kingdom!

King Mace and Queen Shari are now the Sovereigns of the Kingdom of Styrke!

The next message appeared on both of their interfaces.

Congratulations! You have established a new Kingdom! Please see the Kingdom tab on your interface for more details. Your kingdom will be dissolved if you fail to set your Anchor Stone within thirty days.

Level Up! You are now level 46...
You have received one attribute point.

Level Up!...

Level Up! You are now level 50!
You have received one attribute point.

As Mace felt the euphoric sensation that came with leveling up several times, he was startled to see Shari's eyes roll up as she emitted a small moan and fell unconscious at his feet. Dropping to his knees, he quickly checked her vitals. Her health bar was at 100%, and she was breathing normally.   After a moment, her eyes fluttered open again.

"That was… oh my god," she whispered, putting her hands to her flushed cheeks. "That was almost better than sex!"

"What happened?" Mace was at a loss.

"Elysia just bumped me all the way up to the same level as you." She sat up and waved a hand in front of her face as if to cool off. "I just got fifteen levels all in one shot!"

Mace chuckled, relieved. He thought back to when he'd picked up multiple levels after the two titans fought by the underground lake and he got credit for both kills. The sensation had been pretty great. And Shari had just picked up about 50% more levels than he had back then.

"You need a minute? I can leave…" He winked at her.

She slapped him playfully, then said, "Not now. But when we log off, I have plans for you, *King Mace.*" The look she gave him had him looking toward the captain's bed and grinning.

"No! Later. For now, everyone out there is waiting for us. Let's get out there and get things moving." She gently pushed him toward the door, then gave him a quick smack on the behind to motivate him.

When they emerged onto the deck of the *Sea Sprite,* every set of eyes on the dock was focused on them. Mace felt like a kid who just got caught making out under the bleachers in high school. He wasn't sure whether to feel embarrassed or proud of himself.   He held up a hand in greeting, trying to take in the entire crowd at once.   Shari blushed and waved as well, giving everyone a friendly smile.

Jorin snorted and turned to address the crowd. "You all saw the notification. Elysia herself has granted Mace and Shari a kingdom! Anyone wishing to serve the new king and queen of Styrke, take a knee and repeat after me!"

He waited while hundreds of the former slaves and citizens of Graf, along with his own crew and that of the Platypus, all took a knee. Raising his voice and somehow giving it a more official tone than usual, he intoned, "I swear upon my life to loyally serve and protect King Mace and Queen Shari and the nation of Styrke."

As the prospective citizens repeated the words, golden light swirled around each of them, binding their lives to the oath. More notifications flashed across both Mace and Shari's UI's, but they ignored them as their new citizens gasped, mouths open and eyes wide.

Mace looked to Jorin, who looked surprised as well. "I just leveled up, and I've been given a new status as Admiral of Styrke. Also, my new status as 'oathbound' has awarded me two free attribute points.

Mace's elven hearing brought him snippets of conversations from around the docks.

"I was level three, now I'm level five!"

"I've been given a chance to choose a crafting skill, and three skill points to assign!"

"My leg! I've had a limp since that cart hit me ten years ago. It's gone!"

Shari gripped Mace's hand tightly, looking into his eyes. Being an elf, she was hearing many similar comments herself. "Seems Elysia is granting all kinds of boons today."

Mace continued to listen for a moment, then he heard what he was looking for. It came from Silas. "I…I've been *evolved.*" His voice was filled with wonder, and Mace searched the crowd for him. Spotting him near the table, he saw the man staring at his outstretched hands as if expecting them to look different somehow. Mace was happy for the old former slave. He'd lived a life of service, forced as it was. And almost the moment he was granted freedom, he chose to continue to serve. Clearly, Elysia considered him worthy of *evolution.*

Turning back to Shari, he shared what he'd just learned. Then he added, "I think Elysia bumped you up so many levels so that you'd be on equal ground with me. Sort of a matching set, king and queen. And she's made all our knights, bishops, and pawns stronger too."

"This is almost like cheating!" Shari laughed. "Except there aren't any other players to object."

Mace grinned at her. "Except those North Korean players. They're probably a bit angry right about now."

Those still in line to be assigned their rides were processed through quickly enough. But the line continued to grow. After the spectacle of the oath-binding and the subsequent gifts awarded by Elysia, more than a score of additional applicants rushed to join up.

Jorin looked at the newcomers, then winked at Shari. "As word of this spreads through the city, there will be more. We should go before there's no more room aboard the ships."

Mace agreed. "Get them loaded. I'm going to go speak with Silas." He trotted down the dock and approached the old man where he stood behind the tables observing the process.

"Congratulations, Silas. I see you have *evolved*! Elysia has chosen you herself."

"Thank you, Your Majesty." Silas awkwardly attempted a bow that ended up looking more like a curtsy. "I am deeply honored. She has bid me to spread the word among the people of Graf in hopes that they will strive for the same."

"Please, no fancy bowing. And speaking of spreading the word, Jorin just pointed out that we may get a large number of additional applicants once the news of this morning's events spreads. Will you oversee that process? Make sure we don't accept any bad apples and administer the oath? I'm sure the various boat captains will be happy to bring more groups to us after they return. We'll make it worth their while."

"Of course, Your Majesty." This time Silas just bowed his head, making both of them more comfortable.

Mace looked around as his drow instincts kicked in. Though he obviously wasn't a real drow, his experience in the underground realms and his sync level were imprinting upon his personality and seemed to be actually altering it. He spotted more than one sour face and resentful look in the crowd. "Also, Silas. I want you to hire a force of guards. To protect the mansion and the warehouse. And the school if it ends up in a different structure. There will be a few who won't accept the freeing of the slaves, or who will consider you and those like you to be lesser, somehow. In fact, if possible, hire former slaves as guards. Let me know if you need additional funds."

Silas followed Mace's gaze and his lips tightened. "This has already occurred to some extent. Thankfully, there have been no fatalities as yet. I will do as you say, Majesty. And I will ensure that the city guards do their part to discourage misbehavior as well."

Shaking his new friend's hand one last time, he followed the last of the stragglers back to join Jorin and the others aboard *Sea Sprite*. Taking his usual seat among the crates and sacks near the helm, he watched the other ships load up and retract their gangplanks one by one. Jorin was the first to cast off, and their little armada began the trip back downriver.

*****

Griff and Lisa had logged back into the game and were assisting the dwarves with moving their supplies up into the portal cavern behind the waterfall when they received the alert that Mace and Shari had formed the kingdom of Styrke. In addition to the system alert, both received experience for assisting in the creation of the kingdom.

Griff nearly dropped the bundle of weapons he was passing up to the next dwarf in line one boulder above him, as the sensation of leveling up washed over him unexpectedly. Lisa gasped somewhere nearby, and he heard her say, "I just picked up five levels!"

Looking around for her as he passed off his bundle and turned to accept the next, he spotted Jo looking flushed as well. Nearby, Meg and Leroy were hugging each other and hopping up and down. It seemed all of his dungeon party that had retrieved the mithril chest and the anchor stone had been rewarded by Elysia.

The dwarves kept at it, passing their goods in a chain up the boulders and into the cave. They were leaving the wagons where they were, as currently there wasn't a way to move them up from the forest, into the cave, and through the portal room into the main level of the Darkstone stronghold. Eventually, they would disassemble them all and bring the pieces through the cave to the portal room, where they could either be taken through another portal or upstairs to the surface.

By noon, the last of the supplies and gear had been moved into the cave, and the dwarves were taking a well-deserved break for lunch. They had pushed themselves hard that morning, hoping to avoid any further conflicts with the monsters from the mountain above. They were still stinging from the previous night's losses.

Travel rations and flasks of ale were passed around as each dwarf took a seat where they were and rested. Once he had consumed his lunch, Griff took a moment to review his recent notifications and assign his attribute points. He confirmed that he and his party had been given significant credit for the formation of Styrke. And a message from Shari that had been waiting in his inbox told him that she had experienced the same thing. Only she'd been awarded fifteen levels! She also mentioned the gifts bestowed on the newly sworn citizens at the docks. He was saving that little surprise for the dwarves until later. When he was done, he saw Lisa sitting next to him with her eyes unfixed, presumably doing the same. She was still a few levels behind him but was catching up quickly.

"Just got a message from Shari. They should be back at Lakeside in three days or so. Darkstone a day after that. Tex is making his way to Darkstone too, but she didn't have an ETA."

"Great! We're gettin' the band together!" Lisa's smile was wider than he'd seen it since before the bear-snake battle.

"They're bringin' somethin' like two or three hundred people back with 'em. This is really happenin'! We're gonna build a kingdom!" Griff had never been a big RPG guy, preferring the shooter games, but he was enthused about building up a city or two and all the possibilities that presented. Even more so since this might be where they spent their entire lives for the next decade or more.

Lisa squeezed his hand, then impulsively she leaned forward and kissed his cheek. There was an awkward moment of silence before she spoke. "I know! I can't wait. I'm goin' to learn ta craft and open up a store 'n' everythin'!"

Griff could feel himself blushing, and he hoped that it didn't show through his beard in the limited light of the cave. He'd been trying hard not to push Lisa on the relationship front so soon after her breakup with Evan. And being a guy, he had no idea how much significance to place upon that little kiss. He was absolutely interested in her, and he suspected she felt the same, but years of socialization and military training had nearly paralyzed him with doubt about making a move.

Deciding to avoid the topic altogether, he got to his feet and offered her a hand to help her up. The two of them moved to the back of the cave where the portal was located. Lisa had offered when they'd first arrived to make a chalk outline to mark the portal's location. But Campbell had flat out forbidden it, saying they didn't want goblins, orcs, or worse following them through. So now Griff stood next to the portal as Lisa went through first, carrying one of the dwarven children and a backpack full of supplies. Griff acted as a conductor, making sure each dwarf in line stepped through the right spot, and warning each of them to move forward or to one side as soon as they arrived, taking their gear with them. He didn't want to find out what happened if one dwarf materialized atop another.

When all but a dozen of them had gone through, the remaining dwarves began pushing some of the gear that remained in the cave through the portal, one piece at a time. It was slow going, as Griff made them wait fifteen seconds after each piece, so that someone on the other side could clear it away. The nature of the portal did not allow them to look through and see the portal room. But eventually everything was safely through, and each of them lifted their final burden and walked into the portal. Griff was last to go, taking one final look around first.

When he stepped through the other side, he found the whole village talking excitedly, pointing at the other portals, or gazing around the chamber. He let them adjust for a few minutes while he sought out Campbell and the elders.

"We've got a good bit o' walkin' and climbin' ta do before we reach the surface. I suggest we leave most o' this stuff here, and just have everyone bring what they can easily carry."

The elders agreed and passed the word. They quickly moved their excess baggage over to one side of the chamber, outside of the ring of portals. Then each dwarf hefted as much as they thought they could carry, and they set off toward the surface.

Griff remembered the way from his previous visit, so he led the procession. As they moved through the tunnels, he heard dwarves muttering behind him and tapping on the walls, followed by more muttering. He smiled and slowed his pace slightly to let them poke around. Half an hour later, he was first to climb the last stair and emerge into the chamber where Lila had executed Justin the slaver. Someone had removed the chest with the false bottom to make it easier to get in and out of the hole in the floor. Looking around, he noticed that the bed and other décor had been removed as well.

Turning to Campbell, who was climbing right behind him, he said, "This looks like a good spot for a rest. I'll go find the orcs and minotaurs, see what's going on above. I know the orcs were going to take the barracks rooms, so we may have to improvise."

Leaving them to get settled, he stepped out the door. Right away, he found orc children playing in the corridor between the two barracks rooms. When he asked for Ag'thar the orc chief, one of them helpfully pointed upward. He proceeded to where the ladders had previously led up to the next level. He found the ladders gone and a stone-and-mortar stairway in their place. Along with a wooden platform attached to a pulley system that could act as a lift. Their new allies had been busy since he'd left.

Climbing the stairs, he followed the corridor to the t-intersection. Looking to his right, he saw no one between himself and the old mine exit, so he turned left. There were now metal rails leading from the entrance back in the direction he was heading, so he followed them. It didn't take long to reach the chamber where the minotaurs and other prisoners had been held.

Stepping inside, he spotted Ag'thar speaking with Brahm, the leader of the minotaurs. Waving to them, he called out, "Hello again!"

The two turned as one and returned the wave, walking in his direction. "Griff! Welcome back. Have you brought your friends with you?" Brahm's greeting was warm, even though the minotaur version of a smile was a bit scary.

"I have! Though, fewer than I wanted. We stopped at the Falling Water camp last night, and we were attacked by a horde of goblins and trolls. It cost us thirteen lives to get here." He bowed his head for a moment, the deaths still causing a lump in his throat.

Ag'thar set a sympathetic hand on his shoulder. "I am sorry, Griff. I know your sorrow well. It is why my people agreed to come here." He gave the dwarf his best orcish smile. "And I must thank you again for inviting us. Already our lives are much improved. This place is safe and rich with resources. It has been a long time since my people ate so well or slept so soundly."

Griff did his best to return the smile. It came out half-hearted at best. In the back of his mind, he still marveled that he could care so deeply for lost souls that were simple computer-generated avatars.

"Thank you, Ag'thar. I'm glad your people are doing well," He offered a hand and shook with both the orc and the minotaur. "The dwarves are resting in the first chamber, near the barracks. They've carried some heavy loads, and we left nearly twice as much in the portal room. I came to find out where I should put them."

Brahn chuckled. "We assumed you would convince them to come, and we have tried to make some temporary arrangements. Ag'thar's people are less comfortable underground than dwarves. We have begun constructing log homes just outside the mine entrance. By the end of the day, we should have two longhouses completed. Ag'thar's orcs will relocate themselves there, then leave the barracks rooms and the chamber for the dwarves. It will be cramped quarters if you brought everyone, but feel free to expand as you see fit. I'm told the dwarves can work miracles with stone."

"I'm sure that will be more than acceptable. Thank you, both of you. If there is anything I can do to help…"

Ag'thar stopped him. "No, you need rest. If you battled last night and carried burdens up here from our old camp, you must all be tired. There are more than enough hands here to complete the longhouses. My people are enjoying the fresh air and improving their skills at the same time. Go, rest with your dwarves. Tell Campbell we will have a feast under the stars this evening. The forest is filled with game, and there is plenty of meat to go around!"

Griff thanked them again and returned to the lower level. He smiled and waved at the orcs he passed, even taking a moment to play with the children who pretended he was a dungeon boss and 'attacked' him with imaginary weapons. He smiled widely as a few dwarven children, attracted by the noise, meekly poked their noses out of the chamber to see what was going on. After a few minutes and a little encouragement, they joined in the fun alongside the orclings.

Leaving the young ones to get to know one another, he stepped back into the chamber and reported to Campbell.

Within moments, Campbell had some miners and masons gathered, and Griff took them on a tour. They stuck their heads into the two barracks rooms briefly, making a quick estimate of how many dwarves each would hold, before continuing down the corridor past the children. Near the bottom of the stairs, they began to tap at the walls and mutter to each other, pointing at various spots. One, in particular, seemed to excite them. After a short discussion, the four miners each produced picks and took a few swings at the wall on one side of the corridor.

In a surprisingly short time, they had removed a significant amount of stone, which the other dwarves were collecting and piling off to one side of the stair. As Griff watched, they progressed into the wall, creating an indentation as wide as the corridor and pushing deeper into the stone. After each foot or so of progress, they would stop while one of them tapped at the wall.

Griff was amazed when suddenly the rock face in front of the miners gave way, falling away from them into a dark void. There was a brief cheer among the dwarves, and they quickly cleared a wider opening with pick and hammer.

Campbell was the first to step through, lighting a torch as he did. When he held the flame forward, Griff could see a rough stone floor stretching out thirty feet or more in front of the dwarf. Campbell took his pick and thumped the floor a few times, then declared it safe. The other dwarves lit a couple of lanterns and followed him into the chamber. As they spread out, testing the floor as they went, Griff was able to see more and more of the space.

They appeared to be in a large natural cavern. Griff couldn't yet see the other side, but the dwarves following the walls to the left and right were easily thirty meters apart and still moving away from each other. Campbell remained close to the door, and Griff asked, "How'd ya know this was here? Can ya somehow see or hear voids in the stone?"

The elder dwarf laughed, the echo taking a long time to return. This cavern was large indeed. "Some of us know the stone better'n others, lad. But this time it were easy. We could hear the runnin' water in this cavern."

Griff listened intently, and after a moment, he could barely discern the sound of burbling water coming from somewhere straight ahead. "I can barely hear tha' now, and I'm standin' here in the cavern! How'd ye hear that through…" he turned and looked back at the short tunnel behind them. "Two meters o' stone?"

"Ha! It be a skill like any other. We can teach ye, if ye've a mind ta learn about stone."

Griff grinned. "Yes, please!"

The two of them chatted about stone and mining as the other dwarves finally reached the back of the cavern. It was huge, at least a hundred and fifty meters across from left to right, and even deeper from front to back. There were stalagmites and stalactites littering the floor and ceiling, and some large boulders lay scattered about. The water was a small stream running down one wall toward the back and across the floor before disappearing under another wall.

"This'll do nicely." Campbell clapped his hands together and whistled at the others. "Ye can tell the orcs there's no need ta rush ta get moved. There be plenty o' room fer our folk in here, and fresh water. Won't take long ta cut some proper homes from these walls. Give us ten years, this'll be a right proper dwarven settlement!"

Griff couldn't help but smile at the time frame. Dwarves in every game were famous for their craftsmanship, especially when it came to stone and steel. For some reason, it pleased him that Campbell was already planning a ten-year project here.

Campbell continued, "I'll send some o' the folk back down for another load o' tools, lamps and such, and we'll get started right now! Got some time before the feast."

"Want me to lead 'em back down there?" Griff offered.

"Bah! Ain't a dwarf alive that canno' retrace his or her steps underground!" Campbell chastised him. "Even the lil 'uns could find their way down and back now. Ye just go talk ta Ag'thar, mebbe bring him down ta see what we've found."

Griff took his leave to do as ordered as Campbell started shouting orders to the dwarves in the cavern. Then he shouted at one of the dwarf children to go get his father. As Griff climbed the stairs to the upper level, he could already hear the sound of picks striking rock.

He found Ag'thar busily working with the carpenters on the log houses outside. Rather than interrupt the orc's work and take him below, he simply informed him of the discovery. The chief laughed, saying, "Leave it to old Campbell to find a hidden gem in the stone. My congratulations to him!"

Griff poked around for the rest of the afternoon. He went to find Lisa, and the two of them walked around inside and outside, introducing themselves and getting to know their new allies. The orcs and minotaurs had built an impressive palisade outside the mine in just a few days. It stretched out in a half circle that connected to the mountain face at both ends and had a wide gate right in front of the mine door. The area inside the wall already contained both longhouses, a quarter-acre garden which had already been tilled, and a large fire pit—with space enough for three or four more of the longhouses. Behind the garden, set against the wall, he spotted a row of outhouses as well, all tall enough for the minotaurs to use.

Their tour finished, both Griff and Lisa volunteered to help prepare the feast. They each skinned a deer, with a little coaching, and then helped butcher them. One of the orc matrons then showed them a recipe for roast venison with some subtle herbs and spices rubbed in before roasting. By the time they each had their offerings spitted and rotating over the fire, they had picked up two levels in the *Cooking* skill.

As the sun began to set, Ag'thar sent a runner into the mine to retrieve his people, the minotaurs, and the dwarves. Unused logs for the cabin were moved and placed in rows in a semicircle around the fire pit so that everyone would have seats. Pots of vegetable stew and loaves of fresh bread were placed out on crudely built long tables, and chefs began to slice chunks off the several roasting deer, placing them on huge wooden platters. By the time the last of the new Elysians arrived, there was a bountiful buffet lined up.

Before anyone made a move toward the food, Campbell cleared his throat. "I wish ta thank ye all fer welcomin' us into yer home. It were not easy fer us ta give up our village, as I'm sure it weren't easy fer you, Ag'thar and yer clan. But I'm glad we chose to join ye here. To new friends and old!"

"To new friends and old!" everyone called back.

Ag'thar stood, motioning for Brahm to do so as well. "May we always live in friendship!"

Again, the entire crowd repeated after him. Brahm spread his arms wide, tilted his head back, and roared, "Let us eat!" causing much laughter. The groups began to mingle, the dwarves and orcs introducing themselves as they drifted into lines for the buffet. It wasn't long before everyone had a plate of food and a seat on one of the logs.

The dwarves had brought up several kegs of spirits as their contribution to the feast, and it wasn't long before the party was in full swing. The feast lasted well into the night, everyone feeling secure and happy within their new stronghold. Several of the celebrants eventually passed out and spent the night around the fire pit.

Chapter 7

Tex and Ursus traveled together through the day, the huge bear easily keeping pace with the orc as they made their way through the forest toward the looming mountain. Tex found himself having to stop on a semi-regular basis while Ursus detoured into a berry patch. The first time it happened, he couldn't help but laugh as the massive monster daintily nibbled individual berries off their stems. When he relented and joined the bear to pick a few for himself, Ursus grumbled deep in his chest and stared at him. Getting the hint, Tex backed away from the bushes with just a handful of the delicious treats.

The third time Ursus stopped, Tex got an idea. He approached the bush full of berries with both hands held up, saying, "Easy, big fella. I'm gonna help you. Watch." As his bear master watched with suspicion, Tex quickly picked several dozen berries and deposited them in a wooden bowl from his bag. He then held the bowl up for Ursus, who took a curious sniff, then plunged his snout into the bowl and practically inhaled the berries.

When he was done, he gave a pleasing growl and nudged at the bowl with his nose, demanding more. Tex laughed and got back to work. "Somehow I'm reduced to a berry-picking monkey," he remarked under his breath. Still, he didn't mind. And when Ursus had consumed several bowls of juicy goodness, Tex even managed to pick some for himself without complaint. He ate a few, then put the rest in his bag as a treat for later.

Back on their way, Tex began speaking to the bear as if he were human or at least sentient. To his surprise, the boss monster appeared to understand.

"So, big poppa… I was headed to meet my friends in a new stronghold. We'll have to take a couple of portals to get there. Is that okay with you?"

Ursus snorted and bobbed his head once.

"Wait, was that a yes? You actually understand me?" Another bob of the massive head.

"Can you speak as well?" Tex was beginning to wonder just how far off script Elysia had gone with his new companion.   He got his answer when Ursus just turned his head and stared at him like he was a fool.

"Right. Of course, you can't talk. How silly of me," Tex replied, earning him a snort of agreement from the bear.

"I wonder," he mused under his breath. "If I manage to level up quickly and exceed his level, will the whole 'pet' thing reverse?

Ursus clearly overheard him, and this time his answer was even more succinct. Without even slowing, he reached out with a forepaw and backhanded Tex's bulky orc body, knocking him backward onto his butt. Ursus didn't even slow down, continuing forward without looking back.

"Right! Got it. So you're the boss from now on. This is gonna get strange." Tex got his feet back under him and dusted himself off. He trotted to catch up to the bear. He was going to have a long talk with Elysia. But not within hearing of the bear.

Occasionally, as they walked through the tall trees and sparse brush, a predator would emerge within sight. But without exception, they would take a look at orc and bear, then turn and give them a wide berth. Tex couldn't blame them. Even the level sixty to seventy wolves that ran in packs of three and four seemed to naturally sense that Ursus was more than a match for them.

Not so with the sentient inhabitants.

As they approached the base of the mountain, a band of orc hunters attacked from behind a formation of boulders ahead.   There were nine of them, all level sixty or higher, bearing spears, bows, swords and axes.   As the melee orcs charged forward, two archers fired arrows at Ursus. Both struck the bear in his side as he roared a challenge at the oncoming orcs.

Badly outnumbered, Tex played defense. He hurled his spear at the closest charging orc even as she raised her own spear intending to stab the bear. Tex's weapon sank deep into her gut, causing her to fall and drop her weapon. He immediately equipped his bow and quiver and targeted the archers. He had faith that Ursus could keep the six remaining melee enemies at bay for a few moments while he dealt with the ranged attacks.

Targeting the archer on the left, he took a deep breath, let it out, and loosed his first arrow. It sped away, barely clearing the top of a boulder, flying so close that it disturbed the dust atop the rock before slamming into the orc's face. Tex didn't wait to see him go down, he was already nocking another arrow. This one he put into the chest of the second archer as he looked down to see his partner fall.

Figuring they were out of the fight, Tex turned to see the bear surrounded by five of the orcs, and a sixth one charging at Tex himself with a wicked-looking sword raised overhead. Tex dropped his bow and dove forward toward the orc, surprising him by going low and rolling forward to take out his legs. Tex leapt back to his feet as the sword-bearing orc tumbled forward onto the grass. Producing a sword of his own from his inventory, he leapt atop the fallen orc and thrust the blade into the back of his neck, twisting as hard as he could. Tex felt the orc's spine give way at the same time his blade snapped.

Back on his feet, he retrieved his bow. Ursus had managed to maul one of the spearwielder's legs, putting the orc down with blood spurting from a severed artery in its thigh. Two of the others bore claw marks on legs and arms, but they were still in the fight. Ursus hadn't gone unscathed, though. The downed orc's spear was stuck deep into his shoulder, not far from the two arrows in his side. His right front leg was bleeding from a stab wound, and he was limping as he moved to keep the remaining orcs in sight.

Tex quickly checked to make sure the archers were still down, then he put an arrow into the back of an orc between him and Ursus. Nocking another, he targeted an orc that was sidestepping slowly toward the bear's rear, trying to get in position for a backstab. Eyes on the bear, the orc never saw the arrow coming. It slammed into his thick neck and passed all the way through to exit the back in a spray of blood.   Dropping his sword to grip his wounded neck, the orc fell backward.

Now only facing three orcs, all of them in front of him, Ursus roared in triumph. Knowing he had backup, he threw caution to the wind and leapt at the orc to his left. The surprised enemy swung her sword to ward off the bear, who took the hit on his shoulder as he clamped down on the orc's head. The orc began to scream, and there was a terrifying crunch as her thick skull succumbed to the pressure exerted by the bear's jaws.

The other two orcs charged, one with a spear, the other with a spiked club. Tex fired at the first orc, striking his gut. But it only slowed the enraged orc slightly.   The orc's blood lust was up, and a little thing like an arrow wouldn't stop them.

Looking down, Tex found the spearwielder that he'd taken down first with his own spear. She was still alive, grunting and trying unsuccessfully to get up. He took hold of the spear shaft and yanked it free, twisting as he did so. Turning and using his momentum from the turn, he flung the spear at the orc with the club. It struck the left hip, not penetrating deeply, but pushing the monster back a few steps.

Tex immediately cast *Strength of Spirit* on Ursus, then crouched down and grabbed the female orc's spear from where she'd dropped it. Taking a moment to plunge the tip into her throat, he then lifted it and charged at the wounded orc with the club.   It turned toward him, making the mistake of putting its pivot weight on its left foot. The leg failed, and the orc stumbled slightly. This gave Tex all the time he needed. He was thrusting the female orc's spear towards its chest when he was hit in the head from behind.

His momentum carried the spear thrust forward enough that the weapon penetrated the orc's chest even as Tex fell against him, taking them both to the ground. Tex's UI flashed red, and his health bar dropped forty percent. A critical hit message, stunned debuff, and bleed debuff all appeared above his health bar on the display.

From his position atop the now dead orc, he couldn't see who had hit him. And the stun still had seven of its ten seconds remaining. All he could do was lay there looking at the bloody grass as he listened to Ursus roar and the last orc roar right back.

A moment later, he felt a second impact, this time in his right side. Within his field of vision, an arrow had appeared, stuck into his ribs just below his arm. As his health bar dropped below fifty percent, the stun wore off. He rolled to his left, dragging the dead orc with him as a shield from the archers. He took a moment to rip the arrow from his side and cast *Strength of Spirit* on himself, followed by *Revivify*. Even as his health bar began to rise, another arrow slammed through the dead orc's gut and stabbed Tex in his own stomach. It didn't penetrate deeply, but the thought of the orc's blood being injected into his gut by the arrow made him retch for a second.

A scream behind him let him know that Ursus had finished off another orc. Hopefully, the last one standing. A second scream two seconds later marked the end of the melee orcs altogether. Ursus roared again, and the ground shook as he charged toward the archers' position. Tex let go of the corpse shield and got to his feet, a little off balance from the arrow stuck in the back of his head. He pulled it free, then cast another heal on himself and on Ursus.

He ran for his bow even as he saw an arrow from the second archer slam into the charging bear. Lifting his bow and nocking an arrow with adrenaline-fueled speed, he took aim and fired over the top of the bear to hit the orc archer in the shoulder. The orc fell back, disappearing behind the boulder. Five seconds later, Ursus rounded the boulder, and there was a squeal of pain that ended abruptly.

Worn out, Tex took a seat where he was, watching as his health bar ticked up. He reviewed the messages on his UI, which included a level up! The group, all around his level, had given some sweet experience. As he waited for his health bar to top off, Ursus stomped back around the boulder, licking the blood on his snout and giving Tex a look that clearly said, "You had *one* job…"

Tex shrugged, casting *Revivify* on the bear. "Hey, don't look at me like that. I put arrows into both of them, took down a third, then rescued you from the other six. I killed at least four of them, and I helped with two others. I think I did pretty well for a low-level pet!"

Ursus approached as Tex spoke, then plopped down on his haunches right in front of him. He tilted his head to the side for a moment, then snorted. Leaning forward, he licked Tex's face.

"Gah! Apology accepted. Please don't ever lick me after eating orc brains. That's just nasty." The giant bear actually grinned at him, chuffing in what could only be amusement.

Tex bent to loot the nearest corpse, then made his way around to loot the others while Ursus ate that one. All the weapons and gear were common quality. And, of course, with Elysia upping the loot drops, there was more than twenty gold. There were several stacks of boar and deer meat, as well as hides that the hunting party had gathered. Tex decided to take them to give to whatever crafters Mace had at the stronghold. And the meat would feed the bear if necessary.

The one interesting bit of loot, which Tex received from the female orc when he looted her, was a leather cylinder with a cap buckled on one end. Opening it up, he found three scrolls inside, along with a ring. He examined the ring first.

Ring of Beast's Rage
Item Quality: Rare
The wearer of this ring receives a bonus of +3 strength. While in combat, wearer has a twenty percent chance of succumbing to Beast's Rage, losing control of their senses and randomly attacking any targets, friend or foe, within ten yards for thirty seconds. Stamina and Health regeneration are tripled during Beast's Rage. Each occurrence of Beast's Rage increases the chances of recurrence by one percent. Cooldown: One hour.

"Damn. This is cool!" Tex grinned at the ring as he held it in his palm. At first, he had wondered why the orc hadn't equipped the ring. Now he thought he knew why. "This could be a huge boost if you wore it for a long time and upped the percentage to trigger in every fight. As long as you don't mind murdering your friends once in a while."

He tried to do the math on how many fights it make take to bring the trigger up to one hundred percent, then gave it up. Initially, it might only trigger once every five fights, then every four, and eventually every three… but it wasn't worth the brain drain to actually figure it out. He could get Skippy to do it later.

Shoving the ring into his bag, he pulled the scrolls from the tube. The first was a simple spell scroll.

> **Scroll of Regeneration**
> **Single Use Item**
> **Item Quality: Common**
> *This scroll will teach its user the healing spell: Regeneration. Scroll will be destroyed upon use.*

Tex already had two decent healing spells, so he put this one away as a gift for one of the others when he finally met up with them.   The next scroll was a bit more interesting.

> **Scroll of Reduction**
> **Single Use Item**
> **Item Quality: Uncommon**
> *This scroll will teach its user the spell: Reduction. Reduction is a channeled spell that allows the caster to shrink a single target from normal size down to a limit of one percent of normal for a period of up to one hour. When the spell is canceled or expires, target will return to normal size. Mana cost variable depending on extent of reduction and length of period specified. Cooldown: One hour.*

Tex immediately turned his gaze to Ursus, laughing out loud at the image of his giant bear master shrunk down to one percent of normal size. He was tempted to use the scroll and cast the spell right then, but he put it away with a sigh. He needed the bear's cooperation, at least until they reached Mace's stronghold, and he didn't think Ursus would take too kindly to being shrunk.

The third scroll was definitely the best of the three.

> **Scroll of Foresight**
> **Single Use Item**
> **Item Quality: Rare**

*This scroll will teach its user the spell: Foresight. Once cast, the
user or target will be able to see ten seconds into their own future.
Visions are instantaneous.
Mana cost: 1,000. Cooldown: Twenty-four hours.*

"I don't remember this even being in the game," Tex thought out
loud. Ursus, finished with his meal, looked at him with curiosity on his
face. "I think maybe Elysia has been messing with more than just my
favorite boss bear." He winked at Ursus, then laughed heartily when the
bear attempted to wink back, his snout twitching and tongue pushing out
to one side.

The two of them resumed their march up onto the mountain. It
only took another couple of hours for them to reach the cave Tex was
searching for. It was marked on the outside with a winky-face emoticon –
the simple semicolon and parenthesis – carved into the stone in a way that
one would only notice if they were looking for it. The entry was tall but
narrow, intended for admin avatars to slip in and out unnoticed, not for
large bear bosses. Ursus lost a little fur pushing himself through the tight
space. There was sufficient room inside, though, and Tex took a moment
to speak with the bear.

"You can't see it right now, but there's a portal on that back wall."
He pointed and the bear followed his direction. He ambled toward the
back wall, sniffing at the floor and ceiling as he went. When he got close
to the portal, Tex called out, "Wait. Before you go through there, it's not
like a normal door. It will make you dizzy the first few times. And let me
go first, so I can make sure there are no people or monsters on the other
end." He knew there weren't, but he didn't want to risk crashing into the
bear on the other side if the bear went first.

Placing a hand on the massive bear's head and giving him a scratch
between the ears, he said, "After I go through, take two deep breaths
before you follow me, okay?"

Ursus nodded once and sat down, his head tilted as if he didn't
believe his pet human was going to walk face-first into a stone wall on

purpose. There was a grunt of surprise as Tex disappeared inside the wall, and Ursus was instantly on his feet and sniffing again. A moment later, he pushed his nose forward into the wall and disappeared.

Arriving on the other side, Ursus stumbled and fell on his side, causing the room to shake slightly. Tex did his best not to laugh but was not successful. Ursus growled irritably, and Tex threw up his hands. "I'm sorry, boss, you'll get used to it. Next time you'll know what to expect."

The duo were in a room similar to the one at Darkstone with a pedestal in the middle and a ring of open portals around the edge. This one only had six portals. It was at the far reaches of the game world in the outskirts of the orc lands. Fewer players chose the orc race, and as a result, this area had not been as extensively developed. Having never bothered to learn the portal system himself, Tex decided to take a little while and study them. He was hoping to find some markings or a map that told him where the portals went. He had, after all, worked extensively with the developers who created Elysia. So he knew most of them would never be able to memorize a portal network. There had to be some clues or a cheat sheet.

He started by examining the portal he'd just stepped through. It didn't have a physical frame, appearing to be just an opening in the fabric of reality. But upon closer inspection, there was some artistic scrollwork in the stone at its base. He knelt down to inspect it more closely, being careful not to let his head touch the plane and transport himself back to the cave. Running his fingers over the design, he didn't recognize anything that struck a chord with him. No noticeable symbols or words that he could see.

Moving to the next portal, which opened up to a lightless stone chamber on the other side, he checked the floor there. The etching in the stone appeared to be the same, or so similar that he couldn't find a difference.

Next, he approached the pedestal. Once again the stone was etched with designs that ran up and down the base and column, but they didn't appear to be meaningful. It wasn't until he ran his fingers over the top of the pedestal that he found what he needed. Very faint lines that his eyes hadn't seen revealed themselves to his fingertips. Leaning down to blow away some dust, he saw a network of lines connecting small spheres, much like a flow chart or some kind of molecular diagram.

As he stared at the surface, the words began to grow clearer. Eventually, he was able to read the map for himself. He could see the symbol for the chamber he was in now, and the lines radiating out to other chambers far away. It didn't take Tex long to find the one that led to the main hub. Orienting himself with the map as it compared to the room, he said, "I found the next one. Ready to go, bud?"

Ursus had put his head down on the floor and appeared to be asleep. Opening one eye slightly, he gave a loud, theatrical snore.

"Big faker! You just don't want to go through another portal. I promise this time will be easier." Tex poked at the bear, trying to motivate him to get to his feet. Ursus absorbed the poke, rolling over onto his back with his paws in the air. He waved one lazily at Tex, demanding a belly rub.

"You've got to be kidding me? Are you a bear or a puppy?" Tex chided the bear, who was easily three times his size, even in his orc body. He didn't even have to bend over when he began to scratch the bear's belly.

Ursus gave a contented sigh, then began to grumble deep in his belly – the grizzly equivalent of purring. Tex accommodated the bear for about a minute, then stepped away. "Time to get going, my friend." He didn't wait to see if the bear followed, he simply headed toward the portal that led to the next hub. Pausing at the verge of stepping through, he checked to make sure the bear was paying attention and could follow through the proper gate. When he saw Ursus getting to his feet and plodding toward him, he stepped through.

*****

Mace and Shari logged out as the *Sea Sprite* made its way downriver to Port Bjurstrom. They couldn't spend one hundred percent of their time in the game, especially now that Tex had given them new hope of finding a way to upload themselves. So, after a quick snack of pop tarts and a Monster Irish Coffee for each of them, they went to work on their research.

For Shari, that meant mostly reading about all the different and sometimes unbelievable ways scientists had suggested might be a viable method to connect human and artificial intelligences. She had downloaded all she could from the CDC files after Peabody obligingly got her access. The AI was a much better hacker than either her or Mace.

She read about systems that converted mental images from memories into a sort of social media profile-ish construct of what a human intelligence was. Shari didn't like this approach, as it was extremely limited in scope and frankly didn't have any chance of recreating the nuances of a live human's personality. It might be good as a starting point, but if she was going to upload herself, she wanted it to be her whole self.

Another study involved interviews of the subject human that included thousands of questions which ranged from simple 'favorite color?' to existential queries that required essay answers. Her problem with this, after skimming through the questions, was the human tendency to lie or answer in a manner they thought others wanted to hear. Maybe more accurate than the memory snapshots, but it was still not a complete picture. And the questions would take months to answer and process.

Still another suggestion involved some arcane translation of neurochemical reactions within the brain to various stimuli. Try as she might, Shari just couldn't follow the science here, even with her medical research background. And most certainly, she couldn't improve upon it.

When her stomach rumbled several hours later, she looked up at the clock and found that it was late afternoon! She left her lab and went in search of Mace, who was in his own lab typing furiously as he alternated his gaze between three different holo-displays.

"Mace. We should eat, then maybe check in with Jorin and the others," she called from the doorway. Mace didn't even blink. With a wry grin on her face, she stepped into the room. Mace was the ultimate geek. He would literally lose himself in the code, not hearing or seeing anything around him. She thought it was kind of cute the way his tongue stuck out the left side of his mouth slightly as he focused. When she stepped behind him and leaned in to kiss his neck, he flinched and fell out of his chair. She couldn't help but laugh, though she felt a little bad for scaring him.

"You always react that way when a pretty girl kisses you?" She offered a hand to help him up from the floor.

"What the hell? Where did you come from, and why did you just try to kill me?" Mace blinked rapidly for a moment, his brain trying to make the transition from code world to real world. He took her hand, and she pulled him to his feet.

"Sorry. I was talking to you, but you were lost in there somewhere. I was saying we should eat something and get back in-game for a bit. Just to make sure everyone is settled for the night."

Mace shook his head. "Can't. I think I'm on to something. If I stop now I might lose it. But go ahead without me if you want to. I… I need to get back in the zone." He looked sheepish, as if he were worried she'd be mad at him.

Shari stepped closer and grabbed the back of his head, pulling him in for a long slow kiss as she pressed herself against him suggestively. "Good luck getting back in the zone." She winked as she turned and strutted out of the room, giving her hips a little extra sway. She didn't need to turn around to see if he was watching.

It took Mace a moment to remember to breathe, and as Shari predicted, several more moments to calm himself and get back into coding mode. He chuckled as he pictured her sassy sashay out of the room. He was definitely going to get a revenge tickle next time he had her alone. In game or out.

As he immersed himself in the code, his brain flipped back into the zone. He thought he'd found a way to overcome one of his worst fears when it came to uploading. As powerful as the quantum computer was, he didn't think its current configuration could update his entire 'program' or personality constantly as he moved through the virtual world. It had occurred to him that he might only be 'saved' every time he leveled up or slept at an inn or some other save point. Meaning he and the others could conceivably lose an entire day's worth of memories and experience if they were killed in the game. That could cause problems anywhere from simply inconvenient to catastrophic.

As they played now, his human brain retained all the memories he needed, updating every fraction of a second with little to no measurable delay. Even when he logged out and was away from the game for days, he could pick up right where he left off. Mace needed to teach Elysia and her quantum processors how to emulate that as closely as possible.

He didn't notice the time passing as he tested and discarded line after line of new code.

Meanwhile, Shari crawled into her pod and logged back in to find that the boats had already reached Port Bjurstrom, and they were in the process of offloading their passengers.

"Shari! Glad you're back. We need to make arrangements for all our new… Styrkeans? Styrkens?" He paused for a moment to consider the term, then shook his head. "Our new citizens need a place to sleep. They could sleep on the boats, but it might be a bit uncomfortable."

Shari nodded her head. "That's why I'm here. I wanted to make sure everyone is situated. Can we buy out all the rooms at the inns? And would that even be enough space?"

Jorin nodded. "Aye, we can do that. And it should be enough. If not, there are rooms in your warehouse. Assuming you can convince that wyvern not to eat everyone." He grinned at her.

"Right! I forgot about him. Her? I didn't check. I should go there and check on it. Can you and the other captains see to the lodging at the inns? I'll make the rounds later and pay all the innkeepers."

"No need for that, young lady. Er, Your Majesty. We captains can handle the bills, and you'll just repay us in the morning." Even as he finished speaking, he motioned for a deckhand to approach, gave him a few short commands, and sent the young elf running with messages for the other boats.

"Thank you so much, Admiral. That's a huge help. If it's alright with you, I'll return to the boat here before logging out tonight. No need to get a room for me." She gave him a wave as she practically skipped down the gangplank to join Lila and Layne on the dock where they'd been waiting for her. A moment later, Stonehand and Red joined them as well.

"I was going to check on the wyvern in the warehouse," Shari suggested. They all agreed to accompany her and set off in that direction. It wasn't far from the *Sea Sprite's* berth, and they arrived within minutes. There was no guard on the door, and it was sitting slightly ajar as they approached. Shari was about to poke her nose in when Callahan called to her.

"Shari! I heard you lot were arriving. Welcome back, Your Majesty!" The big orc bowed regally with a wide grin on his face, which wasn't all that different from his 'I'm gonna eat your face' face. But Shari stepped forward and gave him a hug anyway. After he'd greeted the others, he said, "If you're going inside, try not to wake that beast. She's stuffed full and grumpy. Seems her sleep is regularly getting interrupted by Black Flame stragglers, rejects, or thieves who keep letting themselves in."

"Ha!" Stonehand's short but enthusiastic laugh at her back made Shari jump. "No wonder there be no guards. Who needs em!?"

Callahan laughed along with the dwarf. "I just wanted to let you know that a couple of young people showed up this morning with a small herd of horses, saying that they belonged to you. I had them stabled at the corral near my place. I'm afraid the stablemaster will want some payment before you take the horses."

Shari nodded. "I forgot about them. Yes, of course I'll take care of it. But we may have to leave them here for quite some time. I don't think there is room for them on the boats this trip. And I'm not sure where we should take them. So I think they're better off here until we decide where we're establishing our new city."

Turning toward the warehouse door, she took a deep breath and let it out slowly. Gathering her courage, she said, "You should let me go first. Let's hope She recognizes me and isn't too grumpy about being awakened again."

Shari opened the door and stuck her head inside, giving her eyes a moment to adjust to the darkness inside. Leaving the door open, she stepped in and called out. "Hello? Nice wyvern? It's me, Shari. Mace's friend? I'd appreciate it if you didn't bite my head off…"

She took a few hesitant steps forward as her voice echoed back to her from across the big open space. A moment later, there was a snort, followed by a leathery rustling sound. Shari called out, "I'm going to cast a light globe, so close your eyes if you like." Following word with deed, she sent a globe soaring out to stick to the roof of the main room. It illuminated the space enough for Shari to see the wyvern sliding toward her with head held high, staring right at her.

"Um… hi there." Shari gave a small wave as the monster drew even closer. Just when Shari was about to retreat through the door, the wyvern stopped and bowed her head all the way to the floor.

From behind her, Layne said, "It seems she not only recognizes you but is also aware of your status as queen."

"Well, that's a relief! Please, lady wyvern. No bowing necessary. And thank you for guarding this place so well." Shari smiled at the giant wyrm.

"Really damned well." Stonehand chortled as he motioned at the floor ahead of them. There were bits of armor and weapons, and a few relatively fresh body parts, scattered everywhere. "Must be at least a score o' kills here ta loot."

He was barely through speaking when Lila pushed past him and began doing just that. She paused briefly as she reached for the first body, looking up at the wyvern to see if she had any objection. When she ignored the little halfling, Lila got right down to business.

Shari looked up at the creature, then reached out a hand to scratch her belly, which earned her a loud purring sound. Shari was surprised at how warm, soft, and dry the scales felt. "I'm sorry your slumber was interrupted so often. I think the danger is gone now, so if you'd prefer to be free, I release you. Or, if you'd like to stay and continue to guard the place, you are welcome to do so."

The wyvern simply continued to purr, not in any hurry to end the belly scratching. Shari laughed. "Or maybe I'll adopt you and bring you home with me? I'm sure Admiral Jorin can find room for you on the *Sea Sprite!*"

The wyrm purred a bit louder, and Layne whispered, "If you feed her, I think your druid talents might just allow you to bind her to you like Mion and Snuffles."

Mion, who had been slumbering on Shari's shoulder up until she heard her name, chirped angrily at the wyvern, spreading her wings and bristling the ridges on the back of her tiny neck. She took flight and landed atop a stack of crates nearer the monster's head, chirping again with a demanding tone, making it clear that Shari was *her* pet elf.

Surprisingly, the massive wyvern bowed her head in submission to the tiny dragon.

Layne whispered, "The wyvern recognizes Mion as superior because she's a true dragon, even though she's tiny." Even as she spoke, Mion snorted at the wyvern, giving her a nod of acknowledgment before starting to preen majestically.

"Ha! A right lil' queen ye got yerself there!" Stonehand observed. "And what're ye plannin' ta do with tha' big one?"

Shari was wondering the same thing. Looking up at the wyvern's face, which was now hovering ten feet or so above her own, she asked, "What would you prefer? Would you like to bind with me? Or would you rather be set free in the forest outside the city?"

The wyvern lowered her face to Shari's and licked the elf's face, slathering her in thick foul-smelling saliva and chunks of what looked like brain matter. Stonehand fell to the floor laughing as Shari recoiled from the affectionate yet off-putting gesture.

"I'll take that as a yes," Shari mumbled as she pulled a tattered cloth from her bag and tried to remove the gunk from her face. "Give me a second. I need to grab you some meat. And a really big breath mint," she added as she reached into her bag.

Pulling out a chunk of wolf meat that had been in there for quite some time, she sniffed it to make sure it was still good. Though she knew that the items in her inventory were frozen in time while inside her bag, her real-world experience of all the meat having gone rotten long ago still stuck in her mind.

Deciding the meat was safe, she said, "Okay, miss slobber-puss. Take this meat, and look into my eyes…" She held up the slab of wolf meat, which the wyvern gently accepted in her massive jaws. As Shari gazed into the wyvern's eyes, she added quietly but firmly, "No licking."

The two of them stared at each other as the wyvern swallowed the morsel. It wasn't near enough to fill her belly, but Shari figured it was the thought that counted. They continued to gaze at each other until Shari's vision began to blur, and her perspective shifted. Just as with Mion, she found herself looking down at her own body. The wyvern's vision was different, a combination of heat vision and normal sight that made Shari slightly woozy. She blinked a few times, and then closed her eyes for a count of three heartbeats. When she opened them again, she was back in her own body.

Congratulations! You have bonded with a new companion:
wyvern female!
Would you like to name your companion at this time? Yes/No

Shari looked up at the large almost-dragon. "Do you have a name?"

The creature shook her head side to side slightly, then lowered her eyes as if ashamed.

"Well, then we will just have to think of one that suits you!" Shari left the prompt up on her UI while she thought it over. "You're very scary… but also quite pretty!" the elf observed out loud. Now it was the wyvern's turn to preen a bit. She twisted her head back to nibble at a loose scale on her torso, giving all those present a good view of the sharp, bony horns atop her head and neck.

Red smirked, then gave Shari a wink. "You could call her 'Horny'…"

Shari didn't dignify that suggestion with an answer, simply giving Red a dirty look which caused the woman to laugh. Stonehand joined in, having just recovered and risen from the floor.

"How 'bout Big Bertha?" he suggested.

Shari shook her head. "No… I already have a Bertha in my world."

Layne spoke next, offering her thoughts. "She's quite powerful, and clearly loyal if she remained here all this time."

"Or just comfortable," Red offered. She looked at the corpses in the room and added, "And well fed. Big cave to sleep in, meals that walk right in her door. I wouldn't leave either."

Shari couldn't help but laugh at that. "You have a point there, Red." She looked up at the wyvern, who was patiently staring back at her. "I think maybe… Cymbre! I read about a warrior woman with that name once, and I always liked it." She reached up toward the wyvern's head, the giant wyrm lowering itself to her hand for some scratching. "What do you think? Do you like Cymbre?"

The wyvern nudged her chest gently in agreement. "Then Cymbre it is!"

Stonehand interrupted, saying, "Now that ye got that settled, what'll ye be doin' with the beastie?"

"I think she should join us back at the stronghold! There's lots of forest for her to hunt in and caves for sleeping. Assuming Griff and the dwarves and orcs haven't filled them all." Cymbre nodded her head, liking the sound of that.

"Right! Then let's deal with lodging. There are rooms here if any of you would like to stay here for the night. Or I'm sure we could find rooms at one of the inns for you." Shari looked at Lila and Layne as she spoke.

Callahan interrupted with a suggestion. "There's a nice inn by my shop. I doubt the captains will have filled it. And you can all join my family and me for dinner."

There were several agreeable noises from the group, and with a wave to Cymbre, who was settling back down for a nap, they followed Callahan out of the warehouse and up the hill toward his shop. The group stopped at the inn he pointed out, which was just a block from the blacksmith's home. The innkeeper did indeed have rooms for them, and Shari paid for the group before following Callahan home.

The orc's young son made an awkward bow to Shari as she entered the shop. His mother was much more graceful, even holding their newborn in her arms.

"Please, Lucinda, no bowing. You are friends, and I'm no real queen. I'd prefer it if you just called me Shari." She smiled at them both and stepped forward to tickle the infant orc's belly. "So cute!"

They settled down in a sitting room behind the shop. The furnishings were all roughly hewn. Wooden chairs with metal bolts at the joints, a coffee table that looked like it had once been a wagon wheel, and iron brackets on the walls supporting various weapons on display. They chatted for a short while, bringing the orcs up to speed on the happenings in Graf and the new kingdom they were founding.

Lucinda interrupted them to say that dinner was ready, and they followed her outside to a long table with benches set up in a courtyard near the smithy. There was a lovely garden and a wide shade tree with branches covered in thick, sweet-smelling leaves that rustled peacefully in the breeze.

As they ate, Shari and the others shared more about the newly established kingdom of Styrke. Snuffles poked his snout into everything, then shamelessly begged for table scraps from everyone while Mion hunted rodents and other small prey in the garden. Shari noticed Lucinda eyeing Callahan as they listened to the others talk, giving him significant looks. After a while, the big orc chuckled and winked at his wife.

After taking a deep draught of beer, he asked, "I don't suppose you have need of a blacksmith in this new stronghold of yours?"

Stonehand snorted. "Ye can never have too many smiths!"

Shari, surprised by the question, answered, "Master Stonehand is right. I'm sure we could use a smith such as yourself. But you have such a nice home and business here…"

Lucinda answered, "We love our home. And business has been steady enough to keep us fed and clothed and comfortable. But unless this place grows, we will never be able to grow. My husband would like to take on apprentices, expand his smithy, and eventually retire a wealthy old orc. We believe our best chance of that is to join you and help build this kingdom of yours."

Shari saw Callahan nod his head as he grunted his agreement with his wife's words.

Shari clapped her hands in delight. "Well! Of course, you are welcome. Though, I assume you'll need some time to pack up your things?"

Callahan nodded. "Aye. I've some orders still to fill, and I'll need to find someone to sell this place to. It'll take me a week, at least."

Shari replied, "That's no problem. The ships we're taking with us on this trip will be returning. We will have a regular trade route up to Graf and back to Lakeside, if not the stronghold directly. I'll notify Admiral Jorin that your passage is free whenever you are ready. And you can choose where you'd like to establish your shop."

When dinner was through, they all thanked Lucinda and Callahan and bid them good night. Shari walked with the group back to the inn, then gave them a wave. "I'm going back to the Sea Sprite for the night." She handed Layne a small bag of gold. "If I'm not back before the boats are ready to sail in the morning, please give this to Jorin. He can repay the captains for what they spent at the inns."

Stonehand held up a hand. "Ye can't be walkin' alone through the city, lass. Red and meself'll be escortin' ya."

"Thank you, Master Stonehand, but I'll be fine." She looked down at her battle pig, who was half asleep with a full tummy. "Snuffles will protect me if necessary."

"Ha!" Stonehand was about to object, but Red pushed him toward the door of the inn.

Shari gave them one last wave and set off down the hill toward the docks. Mion rode on her shoulder, the little dragon's tail hooked around her neck for balance as she snored quietly. Apparently, her hunt had been successful. Shari smiled as she saw the dragon had a little bulge in her belly. "No wonder you're sleepy, little one." She poked gently at the bulge, causing Mion to snort in her sleep.

As she neared the docks, she passed by another inn. This one was much rowdier, the sounds of laughter and music reaching her from a block away. When she drew even with the open door, she saw a group of her people enjoying food and drink, smiling and laughing amongst themselves. One of them noticed her standing outside and jumped to her feet. But Shari just motioned for her to sit, gave her a smile, and resumed walking.

Just as she reached the end of the building, a pair of shadows emerged from the alley. A gruff voice emerged from one of two cloaked and hooded figures. "Well, what is this? A lady elf, out all alone after dark, slummin' it down here with us peasants?"

The other figure's voice was higher pitched but gravelly. "She'll have to pay the toll. We don't make no exceptions for pretty elfy ladies, no sir."

Shari tried to Examine the two figures, but nothing appeared on her UI. Taking a step back, she replied, "What toll? This is a public street. You've no business charging tolls here. Go away." As she spoke, she equipped her bow and nocked an arrow. Then she took two more steps backward, putting her in the center of the stone street. The two cloaked entities remained near the mouth of the alley, sticking to the shadows. One drew a short sword from somewhere inside his cloak. The other instantly had a dagger in each hand.

The second one observed, "The elfy wants a fight! Much better for her if she just pays the toll. One gold coin, Elfy, and you can be on your way."

"Otherwise, you can pay your debt in… other ways," the first figure said. Shari couldn't see that one's face, but she imagined a disgusting leer must have been hiding in there.

Snuffles grunted, then squealed a challenge at the two, stepping in front of Shari. The harsh sound woke Mion, who took a moment to figure out the two men were threatening Shari. She chirped angrily and spread her wings wide.

Shari widened her eyes in mock horror. "Uh oh. You woke the queen. You're in trouble now."

The smaller of the two, the one holding the daggers, lowered his weapons just a bit, saying, "What d'ya mean, the queen? She's just a tiny thing." His tone was confused, and maybe a little drunk.

"She could kill the two of you and eat your eyeballs before you even knew what was happening!" Shari growled at them, making it up as she went along. Clever Mion took her cue and growled as menacingly as her little body could manage. Snuffles snorted in agreement, pawing the stone with one foot as if he were going to charge.

"Bah! She's lyin'!" the swordsman said, spitting a glob of something nasty onto the stone at his feet. "She's an elf weakling with a flying rat and a walking pork roast! I say we kill her, take her money, and eat her pets!"

The other one agreed, raising his daggers back into an attack posture and stepping forward. Before his lead foot even hit the ground, Shari loosed her arrow.   It flew into the shorter one's hood, knocking him backward off his feet as he screamed. Snuffles charged the fallen man, biting at his hand and shaking it.

Mion took flight as Shari nocked another arrow. The swordsman was already charging toward her, covering the twenty feet between them in just a few steps. She fired point-blank into his chest, but he shrugged it off and stabbed at her.

Shari cried out in pain as the blade penetrated her shoulder. Her health bar dropped by a quarter, and a bleed debuff appeared on her UI as the man yanked the blade back out. Shari felt a heal from Mion that eased the pain a bit, but still, she grunted. "Son of a bitch, that hurts!"

She turned to run from the attacker even as he was readying another swing. She noted that the other cloaked figure was still on the ground, and Snuffles was gnawing away at his wrist, drawing blood that spurted over her piglet's face.

She'd taken half a step when a burning pain lanced across the black of her leg.

"Oh, no ya don't! No runnin' to save yer elfy hide!" The swordsman had taken his swing and managed to hamstring Shari. She went stumbling forward, dropping her bow as she hit the cobblestones face first.   Rolling over, she saw Mion dive at the man's face even as she fired a bolt of lightning from her tiny jaws. The spell struck the man, causing him to seize up, his body going rigid as his momentum tipped him forward to fall on his face next to Shari. She heard his nose crunch as his full weight crushed it into the stone.

Shari rolled to the side as Mion cast another heal on her. She was struggling to get to her feet and flee when a female voice behind her shouted, "Protect the queen!"

Shari turned to see a woman in chain mail and leather was charging toward her, a sword in each hand. She leapt over Shari's still prone body and plunged both blades into the back of the paralyzed swordsman. The critical hits on a disabled foe killed the man instantly, and Shari saw experience points flash across her UI.

Several others emerged from the inn, weapons drawn. These were some of the former slaves, running toward her with makeshift weapons in hand. One held a steak knife, another a long two-pronged serving fork. When they saw Snuffles take a dagger to his side from the man on the ground, they descended upon the screaming man, stomping and stabbing him until he was still.

Mion cast another heal on Shari, then went to do the same for Snuffles, who was limping back toward them, his face covered in blood and a jagged wound exposing his ribs. Shari got to her knees and held out her arms, gathering the valiant piglet into a hug. "My brave piggy tank! You did *so* good!" She rubbed his ears, watching the wound on his side close as she cast Life of the Forest on him. Her new levels meant the spell was much more powerful now, and the wound quickly healed fully. Snuffles gave a grateful snort and nudged her with his snout.

Looking up to the woman in chain mail, still standing over her and searching the street for additional threats, Shari said, "Thank you so much…"

"Kristen, m' lady. But most just call me Ska." Kristen gave a brief bow before returning her gaze to the alley. "I'm just happy to have been here to help. I was coming out in hopes of speaking with you, and I saw these bastards attacking."

"Well, I am *very* glad you came out. So thank you. And what was it you wanted to speak with me about?"

Ska looked down at her feet, suddenly shy. "I uhmm…" She paused, scraping one boot across the stone, then poking at the toe with one of her swords as she pressed her lips together. Finally, she took a deep breath and spoke. "I was hoping you'd let me join you?" She looked sideways at Shari, trying to gauge her reaction.

Shari slowly got to her feet, feeling as if she *should* be stiff and in pain from her wounds, despite the fact that she was fully healed. "I take it you're not one of the freed slaves from Graf?" She eyed the woman's quality chain armor.

"No, m' lady. I'm a librarian." Ska watched as Shari's face twisted in thought, trying to reconcile the profession with the gear. "Er, a former librarian. I maintained a small collection of books in a village upriver. Until those damned Black Flame slavers attacked us, murdered or captured most of my neighbors, and burned nearly all my precious books as fuel for their cooking fires! I managed to escape with a few of them and vowed to kill as many of the bastards as possible." Ska's voice was a low, heated growl as she finished telling the tale."

Shari put a hand on the warrior's shoulder, saying, "I'm so sorry, Ska." She looked at the weapons now sheathed on the woman's back. "You seem to be quite skilled with those swords."

Ska's mood lightened a bit and she chuckled. "Aye. One of the books I managed to save was a primer on sword techniques. As I walked through the wilderness alone after the attack, I had plenty of time to read and practice. I defeated many a bush and tree before I reached a safe town."

Smiling, Shari gave the woman a brief hug, then stepped back. "Well, thank you for saving me. And, of course, you're welcome to join us. You can set sail with me on the *Sea Sprite* if you like. You'll have to have Layne administer the oath to Styrke. Just report to Admiral Jorin in the morning, and tell him I sent you. These others will confirm your identity."

She nodded behind Ska, where several of the former slaves who'd taken out the dagger wielder were nodding their heads. A few even reached out to shake hands with Ska for aiding their new queen. Shari thanked them all and sent the whole group back inside with a handful of gold coins to celebrate their valiant victory. When they were gone, she looted the two corpses, finding a few coins, some common leather armor, and their weapons. Nothing special, but she would donate them to citizens who had come to her aid. They could either use them or sell them as they chose.

The rest of her walk down to the docks was uneventful. Snuffles did what he did best, sniffing at everything as they walked. Mion rode quietly atop Shari's head, watching the pig with disdain. When Shari reached the ship, she decided it was a bit late to disturb the Admiral, so she moved to the far aft of the upper deck, well behind the helm, and took a seat near the taffrail before logging out.

Chapter 8

Tex and Ursus arrived at Darkstone stronghold in the late hours of the evening. Tex's educated guesses on how the portals were connected proved to be less than perfect. They'd gone to two wrong hubs before backtracking and following the correct path. Tex just wrote it off as exploration, allowing him to create a partial map of the system in his head.

Once in the hub below Darkstone, he decided to leave Ursus there and log off for the night. He didn't want to surprise a bunch of NPCs who didn't know he was coming, inadvertently starting a fight in which some of them might be wounded or killed. He and Ursus were likely far above the levels of any of Mace's people.

"I think it's better if you wait here tonight, Ursus." He phrased his desire carefully, knowing better than to order his 'master' to do anything. Ursus just grunted and found a comfortable looking corner to curl up in. Without even looking at Tex, the bear laid his head on his paws, closed his eyes, and snorted contentedly.

Smiling to himself, Tex moved away from the ring of portals and sat down, logging out.

When he emerged from his pod, he immediately heard from Skippy.

"Welcome back, Tex. You should know that my cameras have detected motion near this facility several times over the last four hours."

Tex froze, his left leg on the floor, his right still inside the pod, and he looked toward the ceiling and the nearest camera. "What kind of motion, Skippy?"

"Humanoid, at least two separate entities. They have moved several times between two buildings approximately one block east of this facility. I have recorded each instance if you would like to review them.

"Damn right I would! Next time, wake me up! If you can't get a message to me in the game, just shut off the power to the pod!"

"The pod has a battery backup for power outages, Tex. You know that. The battery would last approximately twelve hours after I shut down the power." Tex shook his head. The AI was correct. Skippy continued, *"But I have interfaced with Peabody, and I now have the ability to contact you while you are in immersion. I shall do so next time the occasion arises. Would you like to view the footage at your workstation?"*

"Yes, I would. Give me two minutes to shower and use the toilet." Tex paused, then added, "Unless… are you seeing motion right now?"

"Negative. The most recent instance was thirty-seven minutes ago. I shall have the feeds ready for you on your main monitor."

Tex climbed the rest of the way out of the pod and stumbled toward the bathroom. Three minutes later he had emptied his bladder, showered, and dressed in a pair of sweats and a Fibble T-shirt that featured the adorable little goblin holding a cookie in one hand and a magic wand in the other. Above the goblin's head were the words "Pew! Pew!"

Taking a seat at the desk in his office, he turned to the monitor, and Skippy began the replay. The video clearly showed first one, then a second humanoid shape move from the side door of one building, creep down the alley directly toward the camera, and into an open window of the next building. The second figure was maybe ten seconds behind the first and moving just as cautiously.

"Skippy, replay, and zoom in if you can." Tex's heart began to beat faster. He knew from experience that the zombies out there did not *ever* work together. If two or more of them met up, a fight to the death ensued. He watched the footage again, and he was pretty sure that both figures were still human.

"Show me the next one, Skippy," Tex said, now wondering if this was two people working together, or one hunting the other. There wasn't any way to be sure from the first clip.

The next one showed a person exiting the window, then turning around and closing what looked like shutters behind them. Again, he asked Skippy to zoom in.

"Definitely human," Tex affirmed to himself as he watched. The person, he couldn't tell yet whether it was a man or woman, looked both ways down the alley, then walked carefully out to the street. Pausing there, they took some time to watch the street before stepping out and moving in a crouch to the nearest car, which they hid behind. The camera followed the motion, the image shaking slightly as the camera moved. A moment later, the person emerged and moved down the street to take cover behind a burned-out pickup. From there they must have moved behind or into the nearest building without being visible, because the camera didn't pick them up again.

Tex had Skippy play the rest of the clips. He looked at each one carefully at least twice. From what he could discern, there were two men, working together. They went in and out of the same building more than once. Each one was shown to be carrying supplies into that building at least once.

"What are you two up to?" Tex asked one of the figures, now frozen on the monitor in front of him. "Have you been living there this whole time? Or did you follow me? Are you looking for a way in here?"

Tex turned in his chair to face the small security office armory behind him. He'd placed a hunting rifle and a box of ammo there with the half dozen assault rifles and five pistols that the company had stocked. "I could go upstairs and watch them through the scope." He looked at the clock. It was 8:00pm local time. Which meant it was already dark outside. If he didn't turn on any lights, he might be able to remain concealed.

Taking the rifle in hand, he confirmed it was fully loaded, then headed for the elevator. Skippy took him up to the lobby level, obligingly turning off the light inside the cab before opening the doors. Tex made his way down the short hall to the lobby, then across to the stairway. Opening and closing the stairwell door quietly, he took the steps two at a time. The exercise actually felt good. He hadn't been getting enough real-world exercise lately. The burning in his legs when he reached the top floor told him he needed to get more.

Opening the stairwell exit door just as carefully, he stepped out into the corridor and guided the door closed quietly behind him. Getting his bearings, he moved to the east side of the building. The east side of this floor was a large area of cubicles and small offices, with slightly larger offices along the outer windows. The kind coveted by upper middle-level managers who saw them as status symbols.

Tex chose one near the center row and opened the door. There was no light anywhere on the floor, and only a faint glow of moonlight came in from outside. He moved around behind the oversized desk and took a seat in the office chair. "Comfy," he observed to himself in a whisper. Spinning the chair to face the window, he leaned forward and raised the rifle to his shoulder. Using the barrel to push the blinds aside a bit, he peered through the scope for a moment. When he couldn't see anything but darkness in the other building's windows, he flipped on the night vision scope.

The scope wasn't military grade or anything, just a starlight scope that took the available ambient light and magnified it several times. Everything had a green tinge to it, but the image was clearer than what he could achieve with his naked eye. He scanned the building that the two men seemed to be using as their home base. Systematically moving from one window to the next, beginning on the ground floor, he checked each room. When he found no light source or motion, he moved on to the next.

Finally, on the third floor, he caught a flicker of light. Candlelight or maybe a small fire. He couldn't see the source, just the play of light on a wall. A moment later, a shadow moved across – a person moving between the flame and the wall.

"Gotcha!" he whispered. Pulling his eye from the scope, he noted which window it was. Third from the left. He set down the rifle and looked around the room. There was a small wooden two-drawer filing cabinet on one of the side walls. He moved over and opened the drawers, taking all the files out and stacking them on the desk. Then he lifted the cabinet and moved it over in front of the window. Taking a seat in the chair again, he grabbed the files from the desk and stacked them on top of the short cabinet. When he thought he'd achieved the proper height, he set the rifle atop the pile and leaned in to look through the scope. He now had a comfortable rest for the weapon and a good view of the window in question.

Tex spent another few minutes observing the play of shadows on the wall through the scope. He checked the next window to the right but found nothing there. Frustrated, he sat back in the chair to think.

"What do you think, Skippy?" he asked in a quiet voice. "Are they friend or foe? Should I just go to the roof and wait for them to come out, put one thru their skulls?"

Skippy didn't answer. Tex looked around at the ceiling, realizing there wasn't a speaker in the room for the AI to communicate through. He thought it was just as well, as he wasn't sure what kind of volume control the AI had. It was safe for him to speak at a normal volume deep below the surface, but not so much upstairs.

After another look through the scope, he decided to call it a night. He left the rifle where it was, walked back to the stairwell, and headed down to the lobby. When he got back to his quarters in the lower level, he laid down on the bed and put his hands behind his head.

"I'm not sure what do to, Skippy," he ventured. "I mean, I've killed other survivors, but they were trying to kill me. Do I wait for these guys to attack? How much damage could they do before I take them out? I mean, if they break the glass in the lobby, then we'll have all kinds of contaminated critters crawling in." He let out a long sigh.

"Available information suggests a seventy-eight percent chance that the presence of the other humans in this location at this time is in direct response to your presence here."

"So you think they followed me here, Skippy?"

Their first appearance on this facility's visual log occurs within hours of your arrival here."

"And… if they were friendly, they probably would have approached by now," Tex mused aloud.

"That is unclear from available data. They may have hostile intent. Or they may be afraid that you are hostile," Skippy advised.

"Thanks, buddy. You're a big help," Tex snarked at his AI companion. "I guess I'm going out there in the morning to see what I can see. If they're not hostile, then... what?" He paused to consider that scenario. "Do I invite them in here? I have limited resources. And I doubt any of them would have time to sync with the game enough to upload before food becomes scarce. Do I upload myself and leave them here?"

Tex thought about it for most of the night. They could be brought into the game and start to work on their sync levels. He could upload himself and continue to advise them from inside the game even as his body perished. By then the software would be written and tested. If they didn't survive long enough to upload themselves, well that wasn't on him.

And did he really want to share the facility with two strangers? Could they be trusted?

Tex drifted off to sleep at some point in the wee hours of the morning, and he managed a solid four hours before Skippy woke him.

"I'm sorry to interrupt your rest, Tex. But the sun has risen, and the other humans have become active. I thought you would want to know."

"Show me the live feed, Skippy!" Tex practically shouted. The holo display over his desk snapped on, showing him a daylight view of the building down the street. Two men, presumably the two he had watched before, were walking down the street toward Tex's position. Both were armed with shotguns. They were moving slowly, carefully scanning the street and buildings around them. They paused at an intersection where an alley let out to the street, and they appeared to be listening for something.

"Dammit! They're coming this way," Tex grumbled. He began to scramble to equip his outdoor gear as he watched the feed. When he was fully dressed, he ran for the security office. Grabbing a Glock and one of the AR-15's as well as three loaded mags for each from the armory, he hurried to the elevator. "Skippy, put the feed up on the monitor at the lobby security desk."

When he got off the elevator at the lobby level, he proceeded with caution down to the corner of the short corridor where it connected to the open lobby. Peering around the corner, he was relieved not to see the two men anywhere near the glass front of the building. Tex crouched low and scooted over to hide behind the security desk. The three monitors there came to life with camera feeds, the center monitor showing the two men still standing at the alley mouth, their faces grim.

Tex whispered to himself, "They must have heard something. A creature? Or more humans?" From his location, the building cameras didn't have a view down that alley. He cursed quietly, wishing he'd thought to bring a drone from home. Speaking in a low voice, he asked, "Skippy, are there any drones here in the building?"

"The facility inventory log shows that three remote-controlled drones were delivered here several years ago. I show no further records for them. They may still be in storage."

Tex winced at the volume of the AI's reply. "Shit. No time to go find them now," Tex mumbled as he raised his head just enough to look over the top of the high security desk. There was no movement that he could see. Turning his attention back to the monitor, he watched the two men. They were now only half a block away from his building. If they continued on toward him, armed as they were, he was going to have to engage them. The question was, did he just fire first? Or should he try and speak with them? With there being two of them, surprise was his best chance of survival. This *was* Texas, after all. The odds were high that these men could shoot as well as or better than him.

His other advantage, if he attacked now, was that his rifle would be more accurate than their shotguns at their current distance. He would lose that edge if he let them get closer. He also wanted to find a way to keep them from firing at the glass of his building. Having one of the windows shattered would be very bad.

"Dammit!" He made his decision. Moving swiftly back across the lobby, he ran down the corridor to the garage exit. Bursting through the door, he threw caution to the wind and dashed across the parking garage to a side exit door that let him outside where the two men would not be able to see him.

Opening the door more carefully, he scanned the area for any living creatures. Flipping the visor down on his helmet, he drew the rifle from his shoulder and raised it. Walking carefully along the sidewalk, he moved past the grass that surrounded the building and out to the side street. He continued across the street and into a recessed doorway in the nearest building.

Realizing he'd been holding his breath, he exhaled as quietly as possible, then took several long, slow breaths to calm himself. He really did *not* like being outside. Turning to look down the sidewalk to his right, he peered at the intersection. If the two men continued toward his building, they'd emerge from behind that building about a hundred and fifty feet from him. Spotting another doorway closer to the corner, he crept forward, crouching low and lifting his feet carefully so as not to drag them on the concrete and reveal himself.

When he reached his new position, he was less than one hundred feet from the corner. He paused to breathe some more and listen. The two men weren't making any noise either. He pictured them still standing near the alley, listening.

There was no more good cover between him and the corner. He had a decision to make now. He could wait here, in a decently concealed spot, ambushing the men as they emerged from behind the building. Or he could move to the corner himself and try to observe them.

After about five seconds, his curiosity overcame his caution, and he began to creep toward the corner. He imagined Skippy inside the building, laughing at his exaggerated stealth moves. The thought relieved some of the tension and made him smile slightly.

He reached the corner without incident, having still not heard anything from the two men. Flattening himself against the wall, he took a much deeper breath and held it for a few seconds, then let it out slowly. He leaned toward the corner and turned his head to peer up the street.

Right away his focus lasered in on the two men. They hadn't moved since he'd watched them on the camera feed. One was making military-style hand motions to the other, who nodded once. They both eased back from the alley mouth and began to retreat, neither of them taking their eyes off the alley or turning their backs to it. They moved slowly, weapons ready.

Tex's spine tingled and his sphincter tightened. The men must have heard something that frightened them. The most likely 'something' these days was one of the creatures. He froze, watching the two men move away, back toward the building they'd occupied the night before. When they disappeared inside, Tex moved back from the corner, still hugging the wall. His ears almost seemed to stretch out from his head he was listening so hard.

Fear gripped him, and he found he couldn't move. He knew this wasn't a safe place. His rational brain screamed it at him, but his feet wouldn't move. His lizard brain was flooding his system with adrenaline, and at the same time telling him that movement was death.

After what seemed like an eternity, but was probably only a minute or so, he heard something. A soft scraping sound, like boot sole scraping pavement. He forced himself to move the two steps back to the corner and peer around at the street, heart pounding in his chest and his knuckles white as he gripped his rifle.

One of the two men had emerged from the building again. He was now carrying a heavy pack over one shoulder and a duffle in one hand. He scanned the street, then used the hand holding his shotgun to wave at someone inside. A moment later a woman emerged, followed by a boy aged maybe thirteen or fourteen. Both carried heavy burdens like the first man, packs on their backs and bags in each hand. Both had pistols in holsters on their belts. Behind them, the other of the two men emerged as well. His shotgun was now strapped on his back, and he carried a large box in both arms.

The boy, turning as if to say something to the last man, stumbled over something on the sidewalk and fell. He let out a surprised cry as he impacted the ground, and everybody froze.

Including Tex, who was now holding his breath as his pulse ramped up even further. He'd been able to hear the boy from where he was. Which meant whatever was in the alley...

His speculation ended when a screeching wail erupted from the alley, the blood-curdling sound echoing off the walls and asphalt. The four humans panicked, the woman grabbing the boy and lifting him to his feet. He didn't bother to retrieve the bags he'd dropped but followed her as they retreated into the building. The two men pointed their weapons in the direction of the alley and backed toward the door as quickly as they could.

But they weren't fast enough. The monster emerged from the alley just as they were approaching the threshold. Two more seconds and they'd have been out of sight. It roared at them, standing upright and raising its head in the air.

The thing was easily ten feet tall. It had two arms and two legs, but they were segmented almost like an insect's limbs. All four ended with long, sharp-looking claws. The body was covered in mottled skin with the same blue-grey tinge as the other undead creatures he'd encountered. Its head was wide and sort of flattened like an ant, but its jaws were more canine. Tex found himself wishing he were in the game and this thing had a tag over its head to tell him what it was.

The two men fired almost in unison, both hitting the monster and causing chunks of flesh and neon-blue blood to splatter the wall behind it. One had struck the thing's shoulder, the other near its hip. Tex cringed at the creature's answering scream of rage.

The two men seemed to flinch as well, but both recovered quickly, taking careful aim and firing again. A second later, Tex saw the boy stick his head out a window and fire as well. One of the men cursed at him, shouting for him to run. Tex knew it wouldn't do any good. The creature would just track his scent. They had no need to sleep, or even rest, and it would eventually catch the kid.

The creature launched itself toward the two men, who retreated back through the doorway into the building. The door slammed shut between them, seconds before the monster slammed into it. The door held, and the thing began to claw at it. Once again the kid leaned out the window and fired. He managed to hit the frenzied creature, but not anywhere vital. It completely ignored the damage and continued to smash and scratch at the door in front of it.

Tex, barely able to stop from wetting himself, clenched his eyes shut and took a deep breath. He needed to kill that thing. The humans *might* have been a threat, though he was reconsidering their threat level after seeing the woman and kid… but the monster was a definite threat to his continued existence.

The monster, apparently unable to break through the metal entry door, stopped its thrashing and turned toward the bags laying on the sidewalk. It shuffled toward them, sniffing as it circled. When it had its back to him, Tex raised his rifle and stepped partway out from behind the building. He took aim through the scope at the zombie man-bug thing's head and tracked its movements, waiting for it to pause long enough for a kill shot.

Just as he was about to pull the trigger, another shot rang out. The kid again, firing from that same window. A hand reached out from inside, gripped his face, and yanked him inside. But it was too little too late. The creature spun in time to see where the shot had come from, and dashed toward the window, screaming.

Tex pulled the trigger in desperation, trying to kill the thing before it disappeared inside. It moved so fast, his aim was off. His bullet tore a chunk off the monster's face, part of its jaw disappearing just as it leapt up from the sidewalk and through the first-floor window.

Tex sobbed as he heard human screams coming from inside the building. "Dammit!" He broke from his position and ran toward the building, the roars of the creature, gunshots, and more screams coming to him through the windows.

He was halfway there when the door burst open and the woman came tumbling out, dragging the boy with her. She was covered in blood, both red and neon blue. Her arm looked like a bite had been taken out of it, and part of her face had been slashed to the bone. She let go of the boy as she fell to the ground just outside the threshold, her leg propping the door open. The kid stumbled to his knees even as another shot rang out inside, and a man's scream was cut short.

Tex raised his weapon, rapidly moving his sights from the doorway to the window and back. He halted his approach, standing in the middle of the street. His panicked mind registered the boy trying to get to his feet, as well as the woman still laying there, blood spurting from her wounds.

He risked taking his focus from the potential exits for a moment, pointing his weapon at the boy. The young man didn't appear to have been injured. But he was covered in both the woman's blood and the creatures. The kid noticed it the same time Tex did, wiping at the blood with his hands.

That was a death sentence.

Tears streaming from his eyes, Tex blinked a few times and took aim. When the boy looked up at him with knowing eyes and nodded, he said, "I'm sorry," and pulled the trigger. The bullet tore through the kid's chest, knocking him back to land atop the woman's body. He didn't move at all.

Tex immediately returned his attention to the building. He moved to the side a few steps, trying to get a better view in through the open door. The window was set slightly too high for him to see anything but the upper half of the walls and ceiling inside from his position in the street.

A screech from inside made him jump, and he accidentally pulled the trigger, putting a round through the doorway. A moment later the monster flew out the same window it had entered, landing on the sidewalk.

It stared at him, blood dripping from multiple gunshot wounds. One of its eyes was missing, along with half its face on that side. Sniffing the air, it took a tentative step toward him, turning its head so its remaining eye faced him.

Tex screamed, firing his weapon without really aiming. The deaths of the people in front of him, the gruesome sight of the mangled monster leaking deadly contaminated blood everywhere... his mind threatened to shut down. Gritting his teeth, he forced himself to focus. He raised his weapon even as the monster took another step forward, screeching a challenge at him.

Instinct and muscle memory developed as a young boy took over. Pulling the rifle stock tightly against his shoulder, Tex took aim at the monster's head. He let out the breath he was holding and squeezed the trigger. Another chunk of the monster's head exploded, and it fell back from the impact. Tex didn't wait for it to get up. He moved forward and to the side, getting a clear line of sight, and he put two more rounds into its head to be sure.

When it didn't move, he turned back to the doorway. The woman's body was beginning to twitch underneath the boy's. Her wounds hadn't managed to kill her before the contaminated blood began converting her.

"Son of a bitch. Please, no," Tex said out loud, his voice breaking. He lowered his weapon and watched for a moment, a part of him hoping the woman was just okay and trying to get up. But he remembered the blue blood covering her, and he raised his weapon again. One shot to the head, and she stopped moving as well.

Tex sobbed, then bent over and emptied his stomach contents onto the pavement. He kept his left hand on his knee for a while, unsteady on his feet. With a final spit to clear his mouth, he straightened up and looked toward the building. He needed to check inside.

Not wanting to walk through the puddle of combined blood at the doorway, he approached a window that the creature had NOT smashed its way through. That one would be contaminated as well. Reaching up with both hands, he pulled himself up far enough to look inside. Both men were there, bodies shredded and very dead. One man's head had been removed, and the other was in several pieces. Neither would be getting back up, contaminated or not.

The room was splattered with blood from both man and beast, and Tex had no desire to go inside to retrieve their weapons or supplies. Instead, he dropped back down and called out, "Is anybody else in there?" trying to be loud enough for any survivors to hear, while at the same time not drawing more attention. Though it struck him right afterward that the gunshots and screams would have done that anyway. He called out again, louder, "It's okay, the monster's dead. Come on out!" even as he mentally cursed himself. He should have waited and talked to the boy before killing him. Contamination didn't mean instant conversion. It took anywhere from several minutes to a full day for people to turn. The boy could have told him if there were other survivors.

But he'd let his emotions, the boy's fear, and his own fear and adrenaline drive him, causing him to put the boy down right away.

Tex turned and was about to head home to safety when he caught sight of the boy's bags still sitting in the street where he'd fallen the first time. Though he was anxious to get off the street, he went to examine them. Finding no blood splatter or blue stains anywhere, he slung his rifle over his shoulder and lifted both bags.

Not caring about making noise at this point, he jogged back around the corner and across the street, following the sidewalk to the side door of the garage. It would have been shorter to go in through the lobby, but if anything tracked him from the scene of the fight, he didn't want it sniffing around the glass lobby. The metal and concrete of the garage door were much sturdier.

A buzzing sound let him know that Skippy had unlocked the door for him, and he quickly opened it and ran through. Breathing hard from the effort of lugging the heavy bags, he set them down and dropped to his knees in the middle of the parking area. Tears still streamed down his face as he focused on his breathing, trying to calm himself. His body shivered, his hands shaking from the adrenaline wearing off. He closed his eyes and just listened for any sounds of creatures that might have followed him or his scent back to the building.

After a couple of minutes, he managed to gather his wits. The first thing he did was check himself carefully for any signs of blood splatter. Then he very carefully inspected both bags again, remembering how the monster had sniffed at them earlier. Dying from exposure to monster snot was *not* how he wanted to go out.

When he was sure the bags were clean, he opened the first one. It was filled with several small cans of tuna, spam, and Hormel chili. There were also a few bags of dried fruit, two cans of cashews, and dozens of candy bars. Opening the second bag, he found similar food items. Jars of baby food, canned peaches and pears. A box of saltine crackers. In the bottom was a high school English textbook. Apparently, the adults had been trying to continue the kid's education. The thought brought fresh tears to Tex's eyes.

He carefully laid the book back down in the bag and closed them both before lifting them and carrying them to the door that led inside the building. Once again Skippy buzzed the door for him, and he went inside. He didn't say a word as he walked to the elevator, rode down, and dropped the bags as soon as he stepped out.

Taking off his gear as he walked, leaving the items in a trail down the hallways, he made his way to his desk, sat in the chair, put his forehead down, and closed his eyes.

Chapter 9

Mace and Shari were having a leisurely late breakfast. More of a brunch, really, having slept in after a late night.

Mace had been in the zone and working on his code until the early hours of the morning. Shari had taken a seat nearby and pulled out a pen and paper to do a little planning for their budding kingdom. She quite enjoyed it, thinking about resources needed, both physical and humanoid, growth rates, potential locations, and the benefits or drawbacks of each. She dabbled a bit in urban planning, testing different city configurations, adding water supply and sanitation, calculating viable tax rates, and a dozen other factors.

Breakfast that morning had just reached the cleanup stage when Peabody's voice interrupted.

"Excuse me, Mace, Admin Shari. I have just received information from Skippy that Tex was involved in a battle near his facility this morning. He is unharmed physically, but Skippy has concluded that Tex might benefit from some friendly human contact."

"Oh my god, what happened?" Shari was instantly on her feet and running toward the security office, Mace right behind her.

"Skippy was able to record a significant portion of the event. I can replay it for you."

The moment the two reached the security office, the large main monitor began to replay the feed from Skippy's cameras. Mace and Shari saw the two men approaching the facility, saw them stop and wait for a long period. Then they saw Tex creeping in from off camera and peering around the corner. A moment later the two men began to retreat.

They kept watching, asking each other questions like "What are they saying? Why are they going back?" not expecting the other to answer.

Shari gasped and put one hand over her mouth when the creature appeared. Her other hand sought Mace's and squeezed tightly. Both leaned forward as if getting closer to the monitor would give them a better view.

Shari began to cry when she saw the woman and boy covered in monster blood. When she realized Tex was about to shoot the contaminated teenager, she looked away. Mace watched the remainder of the feed, a grim look on his face. Shari was clutching him tightly, his shirt wet with her tears. He heard her mumble, "Oh, poor Tex."

"Thank you, Peabody. Please turn it off. And ask Skippy if we can speak to Tex now."

A moment later, Tex's image appeared on the screen. He looked exhausted or haunted. His eyes were red, and he was supporting his head with both hands, elbows on his desk.

Shari started the conversations, trying to gather herself and wipe tears from her eyes as she spoke. "Tex, we just saw what happened. We're so sorry. Are you... are you okay?" Her voice was quiet.

Tex nodded at the camera and tried to smile, though it was only a twitch of his lips. "I'll live. Which is more than I can say for those poor bastards." He grimaced and looked down at his desk.

Mace answered, "Hey! None of that was your fault. We saw the whole thing. You did what you had to. You tried to save those people. And you did save two of them from becoming one of those things."

Tex shook his head. "You don't understand. I didn't know the woman and kid were there, but Skippy had shown me the other two last night. I decided they were a threat, and I went out there with a mind to kill them. I... I didn't know they were some kind of family. They needed my help, and I could have given it last night. Instead, my suspicions... I let those people die."

"NO!" Shari shouted at him, her face suddenly angry even as tears continued to roll down. "Tex, you look at me! Look into my eyes. This was NOT your fault. This is the world we live in now. If you're not

189

suspicious of strangers, you wind up dead. We all know this first-hand! You did exactly the right thing. And we saw you stand there and watch. You could have easily taken out one or both of them, but you didn't. You waited, and you gave them the benefit of the doubt. They could not have asked for, or expected, anything more."

Mace agreed. "She's right, man. You had no choice. And we need you *alive* so that you can help the rest of us live on for more than a few months. You are our lifeline. Please keep that in mind the next time you consider risking yourself."

Tex stared at the screen, his expression unreadable. Finally, he nodded once. "Thanks, guys. I think I needed to hear that. I mean, Skippy said something similar, but he's a moron and I never listen to him." A faint smile appeared for a moment, then faded again. He changed the subject.

"Listen, my bear Ursus and I made it to the stronghold last night. Right now he's snoozing in the portal room. If you have a way to warn your people so they don't stumble on him…"

Mace laughed. "We'll let Griff and Lisa know. When you get back in the game, just go upstairs and ask for Griff, Lisa, Brahm, or Campbell, and tell them you're a friend. You should be fine. Nobody is going to be anxious to take on someone at your level anyway. Also please let them know that we're on the boats, we left Port Bjurstrom this morning, and we will be back in Lakeside in a day or two. We're bringing about 200 new citizens with us. A few may stay at Lakeside, but we need to make room for most of them at the stronghold."

Tex nodded his head, already thinking about the problem. The distraction would be good for him. "Thanks, guys. I'll get right on it. I need a few more hours of sleep, then I'll be in-game." He waved at the camera, then logged off.

Shari hugged Mace as tightly as she could. "Poor guy. That can't have been easy. The look on the boy's face…" She shuddered, and Mace squeezed her back.

"Let's get in-game. I think maybe Tex isn't the only one who could use a distraction."

They returned to the kitchen to finish their cleanup, then each of them crawled into their pods to log in.

*****

Mace appeared in Jorin's cabin aboard the *Sea Sprite* and waited a while for Shari to show up. When she didn't, he checked his UI and saw that she was online. He left the cabin and found her on deck already talking to the rest of their group. There was a new woman in the group, whom Shari had mentioned briefly the night before. He held out a hand, saying, "You must be Kristen? I mean… Ska, was it? Welcome."

The woman in chainmail turned and instantly bowed to him. "Yes, Your Highness. And thank you." She kept her gaze on the deck. Mace reached out and took hold of her hand, shaking it. "None of that formality here. I'm just Mace, okay?"

Ska nodded, giving him a nervous smile. "Of course, High-… of course, Mace."

Turning to the others, he asked, "So, what did I miss?" Shari had filled him in on some details, but he'd been focused on his code and only half heard some of it. He gave her a sheepish smile, and she just rolled her eyes.

"Not a thing, lad. It seems yer new kingdom be runnin' just fine without ye! Lady Shari here's already made ye obsolete," Stonehand said with a straight face.

Mace pretended to be relieved. "Oh, good! I was thinking of taking the next month off and just exploring, anyway."

The others smiled as Stonehand huffed over his ruined joke, mumbling something about drow having no sense of humor.

Jorin filled them in on the journey in progress. Sailing upriver against the current meant a slower pace than when they'd come downriver from the lake, so it would be dark before they reached the lake. After their encounter with the leviathan, none of them were anxious to cross the lake after dark. Which meant it would be around midday tomorrow before they reached Lakeside.

Mace noticed a large number of the new citizens were milling around on deck, trying to keep out of the sailor's way. When Jorin noticed him looking, he laughed. "We brought Shari's new pet along for the ride, and... well, let's just say some folks felt it a bit crowded down below." Mace vaguely recalled Shari telling him she'd bonded with the wyvern.

Shari's eyes got wide. "Oh, my! She didn't hurt anyone, did she?"

Jorin shook his head. "She's been a perfect lady. Though she did hiss at a mother who stumbled and dropped her child. The child wailed, and the wyvern moved to protect her. She hovered over the wee one, sniffed at her. When she found the mother's scent on the child, she gently nudged the baby forward with her nose and backed away. No one was hurt."

Mace looked at the people standing around, and the frustrated sailors. "Uhm, Shari? Maybe you could go down there and dismiss the wyvern? Just until we reach our destination?"

Shari nodded and headed belowdecks to do just that. Snuffles and Mion remained with Layne, who was playing a calming tune on her lute. Thinking of pets, Mace summoned Minx. She appeared on his shoulder and wrapped her tail around his neck.

"Hey, little one. I missed you." He reached up and scratched her belly with one finger. She purred contentedly. As far as she was concerned, it had only been a few seconds since she'd seen him last, but she wasn't going to argue with the attention.

A thought struck Mace, wondering if Tex scratched his bear's belly. Which reminded him to let Griff know that Tex had arrived. He sent Griff and Lisa a quick in-game message.

Mace and Shari spent most of the day getting to know their new citizens. They circulated amongst them, speaking to small groups who had gathered together. They spoke about families, skills, and the hopes of the people following them to a new land. Shari made notes as people told her what they were qualified to do, and what their ambitions were. She told Mace that the information would help her with her city planning.

Toward the end of the day, they had retired to their usual spot among the cargo with Lila and Layne. Shari sat with Snuffles in her lap, Mion perched atop his head as he snored contentedly. Lila was sharpening her blades with a slow, rhythmic motion that was in time with a ballad that Layne was playing.

"So, among the folks here on the *Sea Sprite*, we have two seamstresses and one... seamstor? Tailor? Whatever you call a guy who can sew. There's a brewer and his sons, a scribe, four carpenters, two stonemasons with two apprentices each, six formerly homeless kids whose skills seem to be mainly stealing and fighting, a tanner who can also craft leather goods like bags and armor, a woodcarver who emphasized that he was not a carpenter, three cooks, one woman who was in charge of a wine collection, two stable hands, two young men with blacksmith training but who were not made official apprentices, and eleven men and women who were household servants with just general duties – laboring, serving meals, laundry, etc." Shari paused to flip a page of her notes.

"Several of these folks have friends and family on other boats, and I gather that we also have a baker and his family, as many as ten former guards or household soldiers, an alchemist, two healers, though one is so old she may not continue practicing, and a gardener. Of course, that's only a small percentage of the group that joined us. But it gives me a good idea of what we're dealing with." She looked around, spotting Ska smiling at her, and added, "Oh! And one badass librarian."

Lila spoke up. "Those kids. I'd like to work with them if I could? I could teach them to be better fighters..."

"And better thieves?" Red raised one eyebrow.

Lila giggled. "I'm no thief. Sure, I love the loot, but I'd be working to curb their thieving tendencies."

"In that case, I'll help. I was an orphan myself. I speak their language."

Mace ran through the list again in his head. "It sounds like we'll be able to establish a pretty good barter system to start with. We'll help them with materials, and they can trade goods and services until folks earn some money of their own, and a more standard economy can grow. We can probably also help those who want it with training. Arrange apprenticeships for some. And eventually, we'll need folks like the household staffers to run our fancy new palace!" He winked at Shari. "We can put them on payroll and loan them out to others who need assistance until we have a household to run."

Mace paused to take a deep breath. "We'll also need to find another dungeon to run our people through. The guards and soldiers at the very least. But we can organize parties that include some of the civilians who want to level up as well. Maybe in the low-level dungeon Griff and his group just finished. It's right near the portal. It'll be a good way to get them all some gold to spend. Kickstart their new lives as free citizens!"

Shari and the others smiled as Mace rambled on, clearly getting excited about the potential of building their new kingdom.

*****

Griff was helping the dwarves work the stone inside their new cavern when he got Mace's message about Tex. He'd been at it since he logged in, and he had already improved his mining skill by +3!

With a quick shout to Caldwell to let him know where he was headed, he stashed his pick in his inventory and headed down to the portal room. Along the way he studied the stone, getting new insights into its structure, and making tentative plans on how to make it easier to reach the portals from the stronghold above.

When he finally reached the portal room, he didn't see Tex. Mace had said the man was playing an Orc, and that he had a bear companion. The light from the ring of portals made it hard to see into the most distant dark corners of the room, so he called out. "Tex! Are ya here? It's Griff! I came ta escort ya upstairs!"

His only response was a loud roar that shook the cavern and even seemed to make the portals flicker slightly. Out of the darkness, a giant grizzly emerged, glaring at him. Griff looked at his info, seeing that the bear was a level 70 elite mob. He gulped unconsciously as it approached.

"Uhhm, hello there, big fella! I be Griff. A friend o' Tex." He held up his hands to show he wasn't armed and meant no harm. The giant bear wasn't charging him, just plodding forward steadily. Griff took that as a good sign. "Welcome to the stronghold, Ursus. I'm guessin' Tex has no' returned yet?"

Ursus walked closer until he stood directly over the dwarf, looking down at him with their faces inches apart. He sniffed at Griff several times, then snorted and sat back on his haunches. Just as Griff lowered his hands, the bear leaned forward and licked Griff's face, covering the entire thing with his tongue.

Griff spluttered, trying to wipe the saliva free as he said, "Gah! Nice ta meet you too." He reached out and patted the bear's neck, which was as high as he could reach.

The two of them spent some time in companionable silence, Griff occasionally pulling some wolf meat from his bag and handing it to Ursus, who took it gently from his hand before swallowing it whole. It wasn't long before Tex appeared.

"Welcome, Tex!" Griff held up a hand in greeting as Ursus just casually glanced in the orc's direction. "That's quite the avatar ye got there! Looks like ye could lift a bus!"

"Ha! I can't even lift Ursus there." Tex grinned back, approaching and shaking Griff's offered hand. "Nice to meet you."

"I heard from Mace that ye had a rough time just a bit ago. I'm sorry. The damned world be trying to kill us all, no doubt."

Tex's face dropped as he gazed at the floor. "There was… I think it was a family. Right near my compound. I thought it was just two guys, and they were a threat to me. I was going to kill them. Then there was one of those zombie things… and…" He took a deep breath, then let out a ragged inhale. When he continued, his voice was rough. "I had to kill a kid. He was contaminated. He knew he had to die. Practically told me to do it. But still."

Griff put a hand on the orc's elbow, unable to reach his shoulder. "Ye did the right thing, mate. Ye had no other choice in the matter. I'm sure the boy didn't want to turn, and ye could no' let it happen." Griff pointed to the room's exit. "It be a long walk back upstairs. Just take yer time ta adjust. We can jabber, or not, as ye prefer."

Tex nodded and followed the dwarf onto the path that would take them up to the stronghold levels. Ursus, sensing the mental hurt his pet orc was enduring, just followed quietly.

They made the trip mostly in silence, with Tex asking a few questions about the stronghold and its current residents and Griff asking about Ursus.

"How'd you manage to get an elite bear pet?"

On hearing the word pet, Ursus growled, the low rumble echoing in the corridor. Tex laughed. "Um… it's actually the other way around. I ran across him fighting some orcs and chose to take his side. When it was over, he bonded me. But since he was a higher level, and an elite…"

"Ha! Ye ended up as his orc pet!" Griff chuckled, looking back and winking at the bear, who seemed to grin in response. "Elysia's got a sense of humor, sure 'nuff!"

When they reached the final stairway that led up through the bottom of the chest into Justin's former chambers, Ursus had to blow out all his air and force himself through the narrow opening. He growled again when Tex offered to get behind him and push, his face the picture of innocence. Griff would have bet all the gold in his pocket that Ursus wouldn't make it through.

By the time the huge bear had freed himself, several orc and dwarven children had gathered and were staring wide-eyed with mouths open at the oversized grizzly. He chuffed a few times, blowing out deep breaths and causing the children to tumble backward. A few fled crying as the others backed up, fear on their faces.

Tex put a hand on the bear's head and said, "Don't worry, he won't eat you. I just fed him a bunch of goblin children a little while ago!"

Ursus bared his teeth in the bear version of a grin, further terrifying the children, and making Griff a little uneasy too.

"Just kidding, kids!" Tex held out his hands when he realized his mistake. "Ursus won't hurt you. He's a friend." He looked at the bear. "Ursus, be nice, please."

The bear leaned forward and licked the nearest child, a dwarfling girl with bright red hair. The tongue was larger than her head, and though Ursus was trying to be gentle, she fell back onto her bottom, spluttering and wiping her face.

The other children instantly began to laugh at her misfortune, greatly lightening the mood. When they saw that the bear wasn't looking to snack on them, they mobbed him. Grabbing ahold of his fur, a few of them pulled themselves up to ride atop his back as they proceeded down the corridor. Several of the orcs from the two barracks rooms came out to see what was causing all the noise, and more than a few reflexively put hands to weapons before deciding everything was alright.

Griff began introducing 'Ursus and his pet, Tex' to random folks they passed, enjoying the look on Tex's face. Eventually, they made their way up to the ground level and out to the enclosure, where Griff introduced them to Brahm, Campbell, and Ag'thar. The three leaders were meeting to discuss expansion of the underground portions of the stronghold, and the engineering interested Tex. While he joined in, Ursus wandered out through the gate to do some hunting. Griff urged all three leaders to notify their people that Ursus was friendly, and not to attack him in the woods.

Campbell unrolled a parchment on which he'd drawn a diagram of the mountain, showing the two main levels and what was known of the dungeon levels below in both a two-dimensional overhead view and a three-dimensional side view, and he set it on a rough-hewn wooden table. The drawing already incorporated the cavern that the dwarves had discovered. He quickly caught Tex and Griff up on the conversation, then pointed to the chamber where the slave pens still sat.

"If'n we start right here, we can dig a tunnel that slopes gently down 'n' around to the dungeon entrance here." He pointed to the small room at the bottom of the stairs below the chest. His finger wound around in a gradual spiral. "There be an iron vein that follows part o' the way, so we can earn a livin' while we dig!"

Ag'thar nodded his head. "This will allow us to transport goods from the surface level here down to the portals in wagons."

Campbell added, "Aye, and it be a long way around. So if need be, our wee ones and elders can use the short route down the stairs to escape invaders. While we fight a runnin' retreat down tha' main tunnel as a distraction. We can fix the door under the chest so none will be findin' it once it be closed."

All those around the table agreed it was a good plan. Tex said, "I'm sure I can speak for Mace and say that he would approve this." The others eyed him in silence for a moment, until Griff gave them a thumbs-up. He immediately regretted it, wondering if it was a good idea to vouch for this stranger so soon. But the damage was done. He'd talk to Mace about it later.

Brahm was the next to speak. Motioning with one hand at the enclosure, he said, "Griff tells us that Mace and Shari are on their way here with as many as two hundred more citizens. They are stopping in Lakeside first, which means they could be here in as little as three days. We'll need to construct more shelter immediately. Unless the dwarves happen to have discovered another large cavern just lying around below us?" He grinned at Campbell.

"Ye jest, but me boys be down there searching right now! There be some rooms what could be used inside the dungeon, but they still smell o' burnt troll meat. It'll take some serious scrubbin' ta get *that* smell to fade."

Griff shook his head. "No, I'm thinkin' we should no' house anyone inside the dungeon itself. Fer one thing, we don't know if more monsters might spawn. And if someone was ta find one o' them portals 'n' attack through it, our folk'd be nearly defenseless down there."

Brahm cleared his throat. "Then let us assume we need at least four more longhouses built before Mace and Shari arrive. That is no small task. We'll need nearly every able-bodied citizen to pitch in."

Looking around, Tex spotted a woodcutter's axe lodged in a stump near a woodpile. Walking over to retrieve it, he said, "I've always wanted to be a lumberjack!"

*****

The next days passed without much fanfare. Tex, Griff, and Lisa helped the NPCs to improve the stronghold's housing situation, pitching in with the physical labor, and even receiving a few quests. Ursus charmed the children of the community, romping around with them in the fields outside the stockade like a giant puppy, careful not to crush or damage his snack-sized playmates. When the children grew tired, they piled atop him as he rolled to expose his belly to the warm sun, and naps ensued. No creature in the nearby forest would dare approach the level seventy elite bear, so the children had nothing to fear. The dwarves who were not helping with housing construction began to dig the long tunnel down to the dungeon entrance. Great piles of iron ore were removed and set to one side until a smelting furnace could be constructed.

Tex was often quiet, preferring to work by himself as he cut down nearby trees or hauled them back into the stockade. Griff had explained to Lisa what happened, and they both gave the man his space. The only times Tex smiled were when he gained a point in his *Woodcutting* skill, or when he saw Ursus playing with the children.

Mace and Shari rode with the others up the river and across the lake, eventually reaching Lakeside with the rest of their fleet. They offloaded some goods there, and some twenty or so passengers elected to stay in Lakeside and begin their new lives at the settlement. Captain Charles accepted them with open arms, and Shari gave each of them five gold coins with which to purchase temporary shelter or equipment to help them with their chosen professions.

Seven of those who disembarked were members of the same family. The mother, Sarah, was a singer, purchased by her former master to perform for his family during meals and parties and to instruct his children in their musical studies. Her husband, Ken, was a household guard who fell in love with his wife while watching her sing. Their children ranged in age from fourteen to two. With the thirty-five gold they received from Shari, they were able to purchase a modest home at Lakeside that was just large enough for all of them, at least to begin with. They also reserved the small empty plot next to theirs for future expansion. Captain Charles gave Ken a job on the spot, being short of guards after the battle with the centaurs. And he encouraged Sarah to offer singing lessons. Shari hugged each of them as they moved off toward their new home, a broad smile on her face. Mace quietly slipped Verga a small bag of gold to help the family add more bedrooms to their home. The normally gruff orcess winked at him, promising she would see to it personally.

As it was already mid-afternoon when they landed at Lakeside, the boat captains agreed to spend the night at the settlement and set off for docks near the stronghold in the morning. Most of the passengers and crew remained aboard overnight, as accommodations in Lakeside were limited. Some set up makeshift tents on the shore, happy just to be able to stretch out a bit. Soon there were campfires burning and meat roasting while folks got to know each other. Shari spent time circulating through the groups from the other boats, adding to her information about skills and professions for her new citizens. By nightfall, she thought she had spoken to everyone.

Mace and Shari gathered the leaders of the settlement together to discuss relations. They sat around a campfire near the lake where Mace had fought the centaurs his second day at Lakeside.

With their crops thriving, and their outlook for the winter improving, Charles and the elders of Lakeside were optimistic about their future. Without exception, each of them thanked Mace and Shari for helping them ensure their survival.

Mace opened his arms wide, saying, "Our goal is to leave our devastated world behind and join you here in your world forever. It simply makes sense for us to help you improve our new home! Toward that end, I'm sure most of you are aware that Shari and I have founded a new kingdom, called Styrke. We would like to invite you all to become citizens of Styrke, under our protection. Our plan is to build up the stronghold at Darkstone and make it into a thriving city. There will be increased traffic on the lake and opportunity for trade. We could even settle the lands between here and Darkstone and build a road." He paused to take in the faces of the elders around him, trying to determine their mood.

Shari broke in, adding, "You are certainly free to decline. We do not mean to pressure you in any way. Should you elect to remain independent, we would still consider Lakeside a friend and ally."

Captain Charles, who was the only one of the group that had been made aware of the portals, added his thoughts. "I strongly recommend joining Mace and Shari. They have a unique ability to overcome obstacles, and they have the resources to do as they say and more. And for those of us who have evolved thanks to Elysia's blessing, we literally owe these two our eternal gratitude."

Mace and Shari left them to discuss their offer, returning to the *Sea Sprite* and logging off for the night. Tomorrow they would reach the stronghold, and their real work would begin.

Chapter 10

The following day the convoy of ships set out early, weaving their way through the 'leviathans' in the shallow waters before turning north and sailing to the docks nearest the Darkstone stronghold. They arrived by noon, the boats landing two at a time on either side of the dock, unloading, then casting off to make room for the others. In just over two hours, all the passengers and supplies had been offloaded.

As the caravan of citizens began to wind their way up the trail toward their new home, Mace and Shari met with the boat captains on the dock.

"Thank you all for your cooperation and assistance. As agreed, you may all retrieve your stolen cargo from the warehouse in Graf upon your return." Mace smiled at them. All but the idiot he'd needed to toast and drop in the water.

"Admiral Jorin will be returning with you, and he will oversee the reclaiming of what was stolen. Be warned..." He paused to gaze at the obstinate captain. "If any of you tries to take even a single item that wasn't stolen from you, I will slit your throat myself. Then I will have Jorin's crew impound your boat, and it will become my personal yacht. I expect you to watch over each other to ensure that doesn't happen."

He looked around, giving them his best angry drow face. Shari took over while he glared at them.

"To further induce you to deal honestly with us, let me make you a further offer." She and Mace had discussed this offline the night before and decided the old 'good cop, bad cop' approach would be most effective.

"We will be establishing our new kingdom, as you know. And though it will be based here at Darkstone for now, we plan to expand to more areas of the continent. This will mean establishing ports along several rivers, and a few seaports as well. As we continue to grow, those who join us, who support our growth, will be richly rewarded. And not just in gold."

Mace whispered something to Elysia under his breath, and a golden light surrounded the captain of the *Platypus.*

Shari continued as the other captains gasped in surprise. "I'm afraid I don't know your given name, Captain…"

"Durr, m'lady."

"Captain Durr. You showed great strength of character when we first met and rid you of your slaver captors. And you were the first, after Jorin, of course, to offer your assistance. Your good character and reputation with Styrke, and with Elysia, has earned you a place among the evolved. Congratulations!"

The man bowed deeply to Shari and Mace, and he was congratulated by his fellow captains, many of whom looked envious. Mace took over.

"Five of the six of you remaining will have the opportunity to earn the same boon, through trust, commitment, and continued hard work. And you will almost certainly make your fortunes at the same time." He pointed to the young captain he disliked. "You… I doubt you will ever evolve. You don't have the character for it. You're lazy and greedy and self-entitled. But you can *try* to work yourself into our good graces."

The man glared at Mace and spat off the side of the dock into the water. "Stinking drow. Your kingdom will fail. My family and I will make sure of it. These fools should know better than to trust a lying, thieving, murdering-"

The man hadn't noticed the other captains backing away as he insulted and threatened the new king in his own kingdom. His voice was cut short as Mace stepped forward and slammed the heel of his hand into the bridge of the captain's nose. The force of the blow sent bone fragments up into the man's brain, quickly followed by Mace's soul dagger as it plunged up into his heart. As the dagger drank, the man's body almost seemed to shrivel. There were shouts of alarm from his crew as his limp corpse fell into the water.

Mace sheathed the dagger, turning to the Jorin and the other captains. "I forgave his insults once, but I will not tolerate *any* threat to my people. Remember that." He looked out across the water to the dead captain's boat. Weapons were being readied and pointed his direction. "Some people just don't learn. Do any of you know his crew? Is there one among them worthy to take his place?"

Captain Durr spoke up. "Aye, he has a solid first mate. But if you don't mind me sayin', that crew won't be your main problem."

Shari looked at the man. "What do you mean?"

"He was the scion of a powerful trading house. His father, and his grandfather before him, built a powerful company with more than a dozen ships. They'll not let his death go unpunished."

Mace just shrugged. "If he is any indication of their character and abilities, let them come. I could use my own fleet. Give some ships to my favorite captains." He winked at Jorin.

Durr grimaced. "Aye, the character runs true enough in that family. Or lack of it, I should say. As to ability… he was a right nasty little git and clearly stupid. But I know his father, and that man is sharp as a razor and just as cold as forged steel. Not someone to underestimate, my lord."

"Thank you, I'll keep that in mind. In the meantime, could one of you send a message out there and ask the first mate to bring his boat in to dock?"

Jorin motioned at the three sailors in his Admiral's gig, and they immediately cast off and began to row toward the dead captain's ship. Mace waited patiently with the others, making small talk about their plans for future ports while they waited.

Eventually, the message was delivered and the boat hauled anchor, then ran out oars. Eight oars on each side extended outward, dipped into the water, and began to propel the boat toward the dock. As they approached within a few dozen yards, the oars were shipped and the boat glided in. Several of the captains rose to catch mooring lines tossed from the side and secured the ship. It was neatly and professionally done.

Apparently, Jorin's sailors had passed along more than just the message to dock. The first mate stepped to the rail and bowed his head. "I apologize for my captain's behavior on behalf of his crew and his family."

A few of the captains mumbled and shook their heads. "You've no need to apologize, it wasn't you that threatened us." Mace took two steps and leapt up over the rail, his drow agility making it easy. The man backed up two steps, then held his ground. Mace offered his hand, and the sailor hesitantly accepted.

"I'm told his family might not agree with your apology on their behalf... what is your name?"

"I am O'Doole, Your Highness. First mate o' the boat." The man bowed his head again.

"Well, mister O'Doole, I'm going to ask you a question, and I'd like you to answer truthfully. You will not be harmed regardless of how you answer. Do you understand?" Mace paused until the man nodded his head.

"Good. Now, what is... what *was* your opinion of your captain?"

O'Doole didn't hesitate, though he glanced around at the crew as he spoke. "He was an annoying little shit, Your Highness. Full o' himself and sure he was Elysia's gift to the world. Spoiled by his family, with no consideration for them that he considered below his station."

Behind Mace, a sailor mumbled, "You'll pay for that, O'Doole."

Mace spun around, looking for the speaker among the gathered crew. Several still held weapons in their hands. Swords, clubs, and hatchets were the most prevalent. "Who said that?"

When no one spoke, he turned back to O'Doole. "I take it the family has a loyalist or two aboard? To spy on the crew, no doubt?"

The first mate nodded. "Aye, more than two. The one ya just heard was Simon. He be the sneakiest of the lot. Reported more than one innocent man who crossed him somehow to the captain for crimes they didn't commit. Got blood on his hands, he does."

Several of the crew mumbled in agreement, and a moment later Simon and three others were seized and shoved forward to stand before Mace and O'Doole. It seemed the sailors had no doubt who their betrayers were.

"Which of you is Simon?" Mace asked, his voice a low growl.

The man on the far left spat on the deck, but he didn't say a word. The other three looked at him briefly, then lowered their eyes to the deck.

"I guess that'd be you." Mace looked at the man, catching O'Doole's nod out of the corner of his eye. "We seem to have a problem. You see, I've just seized this ship as my own, after your former captain stupidly threatened myself and my kingdom. He did so in front of all these witnesses." He motioned toward the captains on the dock, who all nodded.

"As the new owner of this vessel, I've just appointed this man as her captain. Captain O'Doole tells me you're responsible for the deaths of some innocent men. And here you are, openly threatening your new captain. Now, I've never served on a ship, but I think they call that mutiny, do they not?"

Nearly every head on the boat and on the dock nodded in agreement.

Mace looked at the other three sailors, who still refused to meet his eyes. "You three… I understand you were employed by the family to protect their assets. While I despise those who would spy on their brothers, I get it. Now, I doubt your new captain wants you to remain aboard." He paused to see O'Doole nod his head. "So I'll make you an offer. You can stay here, swear an oath, and become a citizen of Styrke.

We'll find honest jobs for you, and you'll be watched every day until we feel we can trust you."

He watched their faces as he spoke. A light of hope appeared in the eyes of two of the three. The third made no reaction at all. "The alternative is, you'll die here and now. You will not be returning to deliver any false reports to the dead man's family. They will hear the truth from O'Doole here."

He took a step toward Simon. "Captains, what is the standard penalty for mutiny?"

The captains spoke nearly in unison. "Death."

"That's what I thought." Mace's voice was barely a whisper. "Simon, I find you guilty of mutiny against your captain. Have you anything to say for yourself?"

The man's face turned an angry red, and he spat at Mace's face. Mace's drow reflexes allowed him to move his head aside in time to avoid the liquid projectile. Even as he did so, he drew his soul dagger and slammed it between the sailor's ribs up to the hilt. Simon screamed in agony as the blade drained his soul's energy. Every single member of the crew took a step backward, some more than one. The three up front with Mace looked on, horrified.

Mace addressed the two in whom he'd seen some hope. "I can tell from your faces that you two have decided to join us. What about you?" His gaze fell on the last sailor, whose eyes rose after a few seconds. He gazed directly into Mace's eyes.

"I am a bastard son of the family that owns this boat. The captain you killed was my half-brother. By family tradition, I was trained as his protector. I should avenge him now, even at the cost of my own life."

Mace forced himself not to smile. "But…?"

"But I feel no loyalty to him. He was abusive, stupid, and lazy. He'd have been killed a dozen times over had I not thwarted the assassination attempts. And each time I was sorely tempted to stand aside."

Mace waited patiently as the man swallowed hard and licked his lips. "I cannot return to my family, even if I wanted to. His death should have meant my death as well. My father would accept no excuse. So if you'll have me, I'll serve you."

Mace patted the man on the shoulder. "You are welcome to join us." He looked up at the rest of the crew. "In fact, all of you are welcome to join us. You need only swear the oath you saw all of our new citizens swear back in Graf. As you have seen, I protect my people with my own life. And any who oppose me or mine will pay with theirs."

There was a ragged cheer from the crew, with a few empty fists or weapons raised in the air. Jorin called out, "All those who wish to swear, down here and form a line!"

The gangplank was run out, and O'Doole stood at its head, looking each man in the eye as he disembarked. Most saluted or bobbed their heads in obeisance. A few shrank from his measuring gaze as they passed.

The crew lined up along the dock, and at O'Doole's barked command, all took a knee. Jorin administered the oath, and as with the former slaves, the swirl of light around each crewman indicated Elysia's acceptance of their oaths.

Mace thanked Jorin as the crew boarded their ship once again. O'Doole remained on the dock, clearly anxious to ask a question. Mace nodded for him to go ahead.

"About the cargo in Graf, Your Majesty?"

Jorin chuckled. Mace patted the new captain on the shoulder. "I like the way you think, Captain. I believe your predecessor filed an insurance claim, and his family was paid for the loss, correct?"

"That is true, Majesty." O'Doole smiled, thinking he knew where Mace was going. He was therefore surprised at what came next.

"Then as far as I'm concerned, that cargo is ours to do with as we see fit. Spoils of war. So when you get back to Graf, contact Silas. The two of you can go through the cargo. Tell him to take some items he thinks might assist his effort with the school or the former slaves."

Mace grinned as the captain's eyes widened. "Whatever is left, bring back here. Along with any other potential citizens that Silas has for you. When you get here, I'll pay you and the crew half the cargo's value, as a bonus. But you must treat our new recruits well. If there are too many for a single trip, Silas can make arrangements to house the rest until you can return."

O'Doole was nodding his head, as were several of the crewmen who'd overheard. Whispers about the bonus were already circulating across the deck.

"I'm afraid for the next few weeks, your life is going to be little more than trips to Graf and back, with stops in Lakeside and Port Bjurstrom as needed." Mace put a bit of apology into his tone.

"Sounds good to us!" O'Doole grinned at Mace. He bowed slightly to his new king then practically leapt up the gangplank and began shouting orders. Moments later, the boat was clear of the dock and moving out to join the others at anchor.

Mace looked to Jorin. "I want to thank you, Jorin. You've been a lifesaver these last weeks. I overstepped when I assumed you would accompany the other captains back to Graf. I'm sure you're overdue to pick up or drop off a shipment for the elves by now. Please give them my apologies when you see them?"

"It has been my pleasure, lad. And I'm in no rush to visit my brethren across the lake. With the pile of goods they shipped to Lakeside, I don't imagine they have much to trade at the moment." He held up one hand and indicated a ring on his pinky. "They can reach me if they have need of my services. I thought I might head back to Graf myself, see if O'Doole needs a hand." He paused to wink at Mace. "With the refugees I mean."

Mace knew then that Jorin would watch over the new captain and crew, as well as the others, and keep them honest. And the ring intrigued him. "The elves can speak to you through that ring?"

"Aye, lad. It's a simple enchantment. Each ring is attuned to up to five others, and in this way, we are able to reach our people across the continent at need. One of the rings mine is connected with is in my home city of Emarien."

"I don't suppose you know where I could get a dozen or so of those? They would help greatly in our efforts to build and maintain our kingdom."

Jorin reached into his bag and produced three of them. "I always keep a few handy for when I find a new friend or business associate in my travels. I'll sell you these for fifty gold each, and I'll have more made next time I find an enchanter."

"Deal!" Mace took two of the rings, leaving one in Jorin's hand. "Would you give that one to Silas when you see him?"

"Of course." Jorin pocketed the ring, along with the small sack of gold Mace handed him. "I'll have the others for you when I return." The two elves shook hands, and Jorin hopped down into his gig and took a seat as his sailors began to row him out to the *Sea Sprite*. Mace offered a final wave, and he and Shari hurried to catch up to the rest of the column.

The march toward Darkstone proceeded at a measured pace—as the citizens were carrying supplies, and there were children walking with them. Initially, the children raced up and down the line or played tag as they weaved in and out of the marching column. But soon enough their energy was spent, the children plodding along next to their tired parents who were carrying all that they owned, and Mace called a halt.

"Ten minutes! Everybody sit and rest. There's nobody chasing us. No need to push ourselves."

Shari and Layne moved up and down the line, Shari and Mion casting heals on those that seemed to need it most, and Layne playing an uplifting tune that buffed stamina regeneration. When Mace joined them, Shari was mumbling to herself.

"What was that?" he asked her, leaning in close to whisper.

"I was just cursing myself for not grabbing more of that water from the ant queen's pond. These people could all use a boost about now." She was referring to the water that had permanently increased their strength, stamina, and agility stats when they first cleared the dungeon.

"You had no way to know we'd be adopting a few hundred people or making them march half a day carrying heavy loads." Looking up at the sun, he did a quick calculation. "I could run ahead and get Brahm's barrel of the water. Meet you guys as you continue on. I could be there and back in two hours, maybe less if you keep moving at a good pace."

"Do it. We'll keep folks moving as best we can." Shari gave him a quick kiss, and he was off. He raced off the path and leapt at the nearest tree, grabbing a low branch and swinging himself up. Then he leapt to another nearby branch and disappeared into the trees.

There was some murmuring from the folks sitting along the path and several worried looks. Shari heard a few questions drift through the citizens. "Is there danger out there? Did Mace just abandon us?"

Shari took it upon herself to reassure everyone. Moving to what was roughly the center of the line of seated citizens, she raised her hands in the air. "Hello, everyone, your attention please?" She waited while the crowd quieted and all eyes focused on her.

"Mace has run ahead to retrieve something from the stronghold. We have obtained a very special water that, when you drink it, will increase some of your physical attributes. Usually Strength, Stamina, or Agility. We figured most of you could use the boost to help get you to Darkstone. The increase is permanent as far as we know. It's also… a little painful. Okay, more than a little painful."

She pulled a vial of the water from her bag. "Mace, Layne, Lila and myself have all gone through the change. It hurts for about half a minute as your body adjusts to its new attributes. I don't want to scare

212

you folks, so I thought maybe one of you would like to volunteer? Show the others what's involved?"

Shari looked around, and several hands were raised in the air. She chose an elderly woman who'd been having a particularly hard time on the march. "You, dear. Please, remind me what your name is?"

The woman stood, with a little help from a young man next to her. She walked with a limp and used a cane. "I'm Hilda, m'lady."

"Please, just Shari. Thank you for volunteering, Hilda. I think this will help you greatly as we finish our little stroll through the woods." She smiled at Hilda as folks chuckled. "Are you ready? As I said, there will be some pain."

"At my age, every step is painful. I would endure more than a little pain for just one day's respite for these aching joints."

Shari nodded, moving toward the old woman and saving her some steps. "Please, sit."

She handed the woman the vial and said, "Drink. I'll be right here."

Hilda uncorked the vial and drank down the water. She looked nervously at Shari when nothing happened right away. Then her eyes shut tight, and she grimaced at the pain. She dropped the vial in the dirt and grabbed her stomach with both hands. Shari gathered her in a hug as she groaned in pain, her fists clenching. People began to whisper, and Shari heard the word *poison* more than once.

"Be patient, all of you. It's nearly over." She gripped Hilda more tightly, speaking softly to the woman as the pain began to fade. When Hilda relaxed and opened her eyes, Shari let her go and got to her feet. Reaching out a hand, she offered to help Hilda stand.

Hilda waved the hand away, using her cane to pull herself to her feet. "Damn, you weren't kidding about the pain," she grumped. But then she straightened her back and rolled her neck a few times. "It's true! I feel… younger! Stronger. And my joints hurt less!" She smiled at Shari as the startled crowd began to cheer. Hilda held up a hand and waved to let those farther away know she was okay. People began shooting questions at her from every direction, but she held up her other hand, waving her cane around. When she noticed she was standing without support and had the strength to fling her cane about in the air, she grinned.

"Hush! It was indeed painful. Felt like my insides were being stretched or burned, or both!" She let her arms drop and turned in a circle as she spoke. "But now I feel better than I have in a decade or more!" She did a little wiggle-step, eliciting laughter from the crowd.

Shari called out, "I have just a few more vials, for those having the most difficulty now. Mace will return with a whole barrel of the water, and each of you will have a taste, if you choose."

She smiled as her people began to round up the elderly and infirm for her to help. She used her final four vials on those who needed them most, and once they had undergone the changes and recovered, the column got underway.

*****

Mace sped through the forest in a nearly straight line toward the stronghold. Running through the trees allowed him to abandon the winding path and avoid all the obstacles on the ground. Using his drow agility, he leapt from one limb to the next, running nimbly along the branch and using its flexibility to springboard himself across to yet another.

In this way, he was able to reach the outer wall of Darkstone in just under an hour. He smiled to himself as he approached the open gate, seeing dwarves and orcs working alongside the minotaurs and centaurs. Trees were being felled by brawny orcs wielding huge axes, the logs being dragged inside by centaurs using harnesses. And workers of all races were cutting and hammering everywhere Mace looked.

"Mace!" Brahm's deep baritone rolled across the encampment. Mace turned to see the minotaur chief striding toward him. Behind him were two dwarves, male and female. "Brahm! It's good to see you." He shook the minotaur's hand in greeting. "And… Griff! Lisa!"

Though it was uncharacteristic for a drow, he gathered each of them in a brief hug. "Welcome to Elysia, and Darkstone! Looks like you've been busy."

"Glad to finally put eyes on ya!" Griff thumped Mace on the back. Looking behind his new friend, he asked, "Where're Shari and the rest?"

"Oh!" Mace had allowed himself to be distracted from his mission. "They're several hours behind me. Some of our new citizens aren't quite up to the hike. Some are children and elderly. Others have never been outside their master's household, and they don't have the stamina for the journey. Brahm, do you still have that barrel of water?"

"Of course, Mace. It's not as full as it once was, but I have it right here." Brahm produced the oversized keg and set it on the ground in front of him.

"I'm going to take this and run back to our people on the trail. This should give them enough of a boost to get here." He deposited the heavy barrel in his inventory. Though he knew it wasn't true, he felt heavier just having the thing in there. Looking around, he said, "You guys have done a great job expanding this place! Thank you."

Lisa gave him a gentle shove toward the gate. "It's good to meet ya in person, so to speak. But ya got people needin' yer help. We'll be here when ya get back."

Mace snorted, turning to jog back out the gate. "I'll be here with the others by nightfall! Send out some hunters, and we'll have a big feast tonight!"

"We shall be prepared!" Brahm shouted just as Mace disappeared behind the wall.

Griff shook his head. "He's quite scary-lookin', ain't he?"

"Ha!" Brahm smiled down at the dwarf. "You should see him when he fights. But behind that mask is a good heart and brave soul. One could not ask for a better leader."

"Aye," Lisa agreed. "He and Shari both. I canno' wait to meet her."

The three of them spoke for a few moments, dividing up labor for organizing the feast. Then they each headed different directions, already shouting instructions.

Mace reached the column less than an hour after leaving the stronghold. They had continued to walk while he'd been running, only taking a couple breaks. When he dropped out of a tree near the front of the line, there were audible sighs of relief as people stopped walking and took a seat.

Mace found Shari, and she gave him a quick update on Hilda and the others. He produced the keg, setting it on the ground near the center of the column. Shari produced several dozen empty vials from her alchemy supplies and began to fill them with the water. Layne, Lila, and Mace each took handfuls of them and began to distribute them among the citizens. Soon the groans and cries of pain echoed through the trees as scores of them endured the painful process.

It took nearly an hour for everyone to receive a dose and recover. Once it was done, the entire group looked healthier and stronger than they had at the start of their journey. Mace retrieved the now half-empty keg and put it back in his inventory.

"How do you feel?" he shouted. The shouted replies reminded him of a raid group and their pre-run '*rawr!*' battle-cry. Offering Shari his arm, he led her to the front of the column, and the march resumed.

Chapter 11

The column reached Darkstone an hour before sunset. There was a cry from the lookout on the wall as they rounded the final bend in the trail and emerged from the forest. Soon enough, dwarves and orcs poured out from the gate and hurried across the open space to greet their new allies and offer to help carry their burdens. The mostly human former slaves seemed nervous at first, but the friendly greetings and offers of help soon allayed their fears.

Once inside the walls, and with the gates closed behind them, Mace lifted Shari up onto a table before joining her up there. He held up his hands, quieting the gathered peoples of his new kingdom.

"For those of you just arriving, and those who've come through the portal, please allow me to formally welcome you to Darkstone, and the Kingdom of Styrke!" He paused while the crowd cheered and applauded. "I won't keep you long, because I can smell something tasty roasting, and I'm sure you're all as hungry as I am!" There was laughter, and somewhere in the back, a small voice shouted, "Gnomes rule!"

"You've already made a tremendous start at building this place into a home, rather than just a musty old hole in the mountain! Together, we'll continue to build this place. But we're not stopping at a stronghold. This is the founding of a kingdom! Darkstone will be our first city. And a proper city it will be! We have craftsmen and farmers, bakers and chefs, healers and warriors, everything we need, right here!" He spread his arms wide to encompass all those gathered together, as well as the buildings around them.

"We'll talk more about that later! For now, Brahm, Ag'thar, Griff, Lisa, and the others who've worked so hard to build homes for everyone have also prepared a celebration. So eat! Drink! Meet your new neighbors, and enjoy yourself. Tomorrow's going to be a busy day!"

He turned and pulled Shari closer, sweeping her into a tilt and kissing her passionately, much to the delight of the crowd. When he set her back on her feet and released her, she was blushing furiously. "Behave yourself, Your Majesty." She gave him a soft slap on the chest, beaming up at him as she spoke.

Deciding to do just the opposite, he scooped her up like a bride being carried across the threshold and leapt off the table. Carrying her through the parting crowd, to the refreshment table, he shouted, "What smells so good? My queen is hungry!"

They spent the next several hours mingling with people or talking with Griff and Lisa. About an hour after sunset, Tex appeared with Ursus. The two had been out in the forest patrolling for any threats.

Shari stepped forward before Tex could even speak and hugged him tightly. The hug lasted a long time, and she whispered, "We're so glad you're here. We're here for you." Tex's oversized orc returned the hug gingerly, tears forming in his eyes.

Eventually, Mace stepped forward. "Unhand my woman, you big brute!" he called out, smiling at Tex as they shook hands. Ursus, confused by the shouting, growled uncertainly. Mace let go of Tex and stepped closer to the bear. Griff had told several funny stories about Tex being the grizzly's pet instead of the other way around.

"I apologize, oh mighty Ursus. I mean your pet orc no harm. I hope we can be friends?"

Ursus sniffed at the drow for a moment, chuffed and nodded his head once. Then grunted in surprise as both Shari and Lila dashed forward to wrap their arms around his neck and foreleg. "He's *so* fluffy!" Lila squealed as she buried her face in his fur.

The celebration continued, Lila rounding up the children, including the orphans from Graf that she intended to train, and they romped around with Ursus, feeding him treats and 'wrestling' with the massive bear, who was apparently ticklish.

Eventually, Mace pulled Shari and the other outworlders into a building that Griff said had been constructed just for the new king and queen. It was a two-story structure with a meeting room, kitchen, sitting area and bathroom on the ground floor, and a large master suite on the floor above. It reminded Mace of a comfy winter cabin at a ski resort.

They gathered in the sitting room and spent some time just getting to know each other. Tex was friendly but subdued, still hurting from his recent real-world encounter. Shari and Lisa did their best to lighten the mood, but they gave him his space.

Eventually, the conversation turned toward their plans for the future. It was Lisa who started things off.

"So ya think ya can really fix it so we can live here forever? This is a wondrous place. So much better than what's left o' our world."

Mace nodded his head. "I think we're close. And by that, I mean less than a year away. We've got a lot of code to work out, and the pods will have to be modified slightly, I think."

Tex shook his head. "Won't be a year. There are still some bugs to work out, but I think our time frame is closer to several months. At least from the technical side."

Mace picked up from there. "We all still need to raise our sync levels as high as possible. One hundred percent, ideally. Though I don't know if that's possible. The more our minds believe this to be the real world, the easier it will be to transfer consciousness permanently. We need to accept these bodies as our own. So physical training and movement will be important. Ideally, by the time we're ready, your real bodies will feel wrong when you log out."

He looked at everyone's avatars. "Speaking of which, if any of you think you might want to change your avatars in some way, now would be the time. You'll need what time we have left to adjust to a different body." He looked around, but nobody spoke.

"Okay great! Now, does everyone have enough food, or access to a safe place to get enough food, to last another six months? I know that means going outside again. Probably a few times."

They all grew quiet at this. Each of them had recently had their lives threatened while out in the real world. Mace and Shari had lost Dakota, Griff and Lisa had encountered the bear and giant snake, and Tex had two run-ins with the zombie creatures.

One by one they nodded their heads. Griff spoke up. "Aye. We'll go back to the Tesco where the big beasties fought. I'll take supplies to better secure the doors, and the food in the back could last us a year or more."

Tex mumbled, "I'll find what I need. I don't eat much anyway."

Shari held out a hand, patting Tex's knee. "I don't know how you feel about travel, but maybe it would be worth it for you to join us? It's a long drive, but if you could find some kind of armored vehicle…"

Tex shook his head. "No offense, but I do better alone. Always have. I've got Skippy to talk to while I'm working, and you guys to play with in here. I'll be fine."

Mace changed the subject. "In that case, let's talk about how we build up our kingdom so that when we do finally upload, this is the best possible place for us to live out our years!"

"What's the plan?" Lisa asked. "I mean, we level up, we get stronger, we sync. But what else?"

Mace crossed his hands and placed them in his lap. "We start with building this place into a city. One that can withstand attacks from anyone who might discover the portals and try to take them from us. At the same time, we make our people stronger. Run them through dungeons. Take them hunting. Give them training. And not just in fighting. I want to have some of the best crafters on the continent here. I want this to be a hub for traders. We'll use the income from taxes to build more cities at the other end of the portals."

"I like the sound of crafting," Griff injected. "Mebbe open me own shop somewhere. If I can find time to level me skill."

"Brahm just became a Master Smith, and I'm sure he'd be happy to instruct you. And Callahan will be bringing his family eventually. When we've run some dungeons, you'll have more than enough gold to build yourself a smithy of your own." Mace looked around. "That goes for all of you. Or you could decide to become lords or ladies of one of the cities as we build them. The possibilities are endless!"

"So what do we do first?" Tex asked nobody in particular.

Shari answered this time. "We have a huge pool of talent here now. I've spoken to most of the former slaves and refugees from Graf. Once we're sure we've built enough housing for everyone, we should take some time to make sure each person's in their proper place, doing the job they excel at. We can start some fields for the farmers, I hear there's already some mining going on. Plenty of game in the woods, which will bring in food for the cooks, skins and other items for the crafters. And for those without chosen professions, we can find training."

Mace had been nodding along. "That sounds great. While everyone is getting settled, I need to return to Immernacht and complete my quest. I'll use the scroll Jervis gave me to teleport back, then use the portal we found to get back, saving a few days' travel that way. Though, I may swing by Svartholm to speak with the smith there about my dagger."

Tex asked, "Isn't that quest from when you were level twenty? Hardly seems worth the effort."

Mace chuckled. "When the head of the Darkblades gives you a mission, you complete it. Or they send someone after you. And I have this item to return to the queen. Don't want her *and* Jervis to be out to murder me."

"Good point. We'll hold down the fort. When are you going?"

"Unless you guys need me for something else, I'll go right now. Shari is the city planning nerd now, and she's got most of the gold, so she can oversee this place. I'm just here to sneak about and stab things." He grinned as he pulled out the scroll Jervis gave him what seemed like an eternity ago. Looking around and seeing no objections, he activated the spell.

*****

The hair on the back of Jervis' neck stood up as he sensed a portal activation in the back of his shop. Only three people had access to scrolls that would allow them to penetrate his barriers and teleport directly into that room. He had no doubt as to which it was.

"Welcome back, Mace," he called out loud enough for his student to hear. "I'm upstairs. Please join me."

A moment later Mace appeared, having made no sound as he approached. "Ah, you've been practicing. Well done, young one." He looked Mace over quickly and added, "From the state of your armor, you've been in a fight or two." Jervis made a gesture with one hand indicating Mace should take a seat. He was in his office, sitting behind a small desk with only a single sheet of paper and an ink well with a feather pen. He folded his hands on the desk as Mace took a seat in one of two leather chairs facing the desk.

"It's good to see you again, Master Jervis. A lot has happened since I saw you last."

"So I hear! Should I be bowing and referring to you as 'Majesty' now?" The old drow cracked a half smile. "And I hear I have you to thank for my newly evolved status."

Mace grinned. "Not that I believe for one moment that anyone could manage to kill you. But in the event of a random falling rock or lucky shot, I figured you'd appreciate the ability to return your soul to your body."

Jervis bowed his head for a moment. "I do indeed. Thank you, Mace. And Krieger asked me to pass on his gratitude should I see you before he does. His message was actually a bit less polite. I believe he dislikes owing you another favor."

"Ha! He owes me nothing. Please let him know I said so."

"I take it that since you are here, you have completed your quest?" Jervis raised one eyebrow.

"I have." Mace reached a hand into his bag to retrieve the quest item. "The outworlder Pokeface must have died on my world, as he disappeared at the same time as the others. But I found the drow named Garya, who was in possession of the item you wanted. I killed her and several hundred others to get it, but here's your item."

Mace handed over the Tear of the Spider Queen, and immediately several notifications splashed across his UI. He ignored them, watching Jervis' face for any hint of a reaction.

The old drow assassin actually smiled, then bowed his head. "The queen will be *very* pleased to have this back. You have done well… Majesty."

Mace rolled his eyes. "You old goat. You know you don't have to bow to me, ever."

"One sometimes finds it is beneficial to follow the formalities." Jervis was still smiling. "Now, I'm sure you have things to attend to in your new kingdom. So I will be brief."

Jervis rose and moved to the wall behind him. He pressed a spot on the wall, causing a panel to open, revealing an alcove with a small chest. Jervis lifted the chest and placed it on his desk in front of Mace. "This is your reward for a job well done."

Keenly aware of the room he was sitting in, and the profession of the man in front of him, Mace used all of his senses including his *Mage Sight* to inspect for traps before opening the box. Jervis just laughed. "I would not test you so, my protégé. At least, not now. The chest is perfectly safe."

Mace reached out with one hand and opened the lid. Inside was a complete set of leather armor made of a material he didn't recognize. As he pulled out the chest piece, he ran his fingers across the leather. It was soft and supple, and so black that it had a rainbow sheen to it in the candlelight. When Mace tried to *Inspect* it, no information was available.

"Don't recognize the leather? I'm not surprised." Jervis cackled as Mace looked up. "Seems some lucky fool managed to kill both a giant petramander and a spawn of Cthulhu at the same time. A party of traders that happened to encounter the corpses shortly after the fight were quick-thinking enough to harvest some of the hide and other bits from both. Which reminds me." Jervis opened the drawer in his desk and withdrew a sheathed dagger. He set it on the desk and pushed it toward Mace. "This is my gift to you."

Mace took the weapon in hand and unsheathed the blade. It was a deep ebony color and curved almost like a claw. Lightweight, it was unlike any metal he'd ever seen. Upon closer examination, he saw that it wasn't metal, but bone. A light went off in his head.

"This is… one of the claws from the lake monster."

"Ha!" Jervis thumped the desk, smiling for the second time in just a few minutes. "I knew it! You recognize it because you've seen it before. You've just won me a substantial amount of money, boy. I bet the queen that it was you who killed the two beasts!"

Mace blushed slightly. "Well, not exactly." He went on to tell his mentor how he'd basically managed to pit the two titans against each other, then sort of finished them off. By the time he was done, Jervis was leaning back in his chair, belly shaking with laughter.

"I'll not be sharing that part with the queen, or she'll find a way not to pay up on our wager." Jervis winked at him. "Better she continue to believe that even our youngest Darkblade is a match for such beasts!"

Mace turned his attention back to the armor. "This is beautiful. But why can't I see anything about its properties?"

Jervis leaned forward again and put his hands on the desk. "I made these for a king. One should not be able to glance at a king and determine the quality of his protections. There is a special enchantment on these that will prevent anyone from seeing what it offers. And what it offers is substantial!" Mace looked again, and this time he could see its name.

> **Drow King's Armor**
> **Item Quality: Unique**
> **Properties: ??**

Jervis took hold of one of the bracers. "You are the first drow king in eons. We must provide you with accouterment appropriate for your station. This armor has the same *Liquid Armor* enchantment as the set you are wearing, except that I have improved it tenfold. When activated it will absorb up to fifteen thousand points of damage from fast-moving projectiles. But unlike your current armor, it will convert that energy and store it, or apply it directly as healing energy should you need it."

Mace's jaw dropped open. Fifteen thousand was close to his current total health pool. "Fifteen thousand... so with the healing, I could take a single shot from a boss monster for thirty thousand points and not even feel it?"

"Well, you'd certainly feel it. But you'd survive. Assuming it didn't knock you back into a wall, or over a cliff, or something." Jervis grinned, and Mace could see him picturing all the ways Mace's demise might come about.

"Thank you, Master Jervis. These are truly magnificent gifts. I am in your debt."

"You most certainly are. And you will repay that debt by establishing a Darkblade Enclave in your new capital city on the surface. Come back and see me when you are ready, and I will join you for a while. I'll bring some younglings with me, and we'll establish the Enclave together."

Mace recognized a test when he saw one. After a brief moment of thought, he said, "I will gladly host you and my brethren in my city. With a few ground rules. Actually, only one rule. No Darkblade will accept a contract for me or my people without my approval. You want to slaughter a visiting merchant in their sleep, be my guest. If one of my people has committed a crime and earned a contract, it will be brought to me first. I have no objection to the Darkblades being paid to bring justice. As long as it is legitimate."

Jervis glared at Mace, his face tightening and his pure white eyebrows coming together in a frown. Mace's heart beat faster. Few who had seen Jervis look angry lived to describe it. All at once the frown broke and the old assassin's face broke into a wide grin. "Very good! We are in agreement. And I will add something more. Not only will we not accept contracts for you or your queen, but you shall also be informed of anyone attempting to offer such a contract. And given a discount, if you wish the Darkblades to… resolve the issue for you."

Mace held out his hand, and Jervis shook it, sealing the bargain. A dark blue aura surrounded both drow as Elysia took note of the agreement and bound them to it.

"Now. Change out of those poor, ravaged rags and into your new items. The queen has made me promise to bring you to meet her when you returned. And you'll need that extra protection, as there's a good chance she'll try to kill you to improve her own reputation. As you know, our society is a matriarchy, and no drow male has risen higher than the position of concubine in many thousands of years." The old drow paused, tapping his chin. "Actually, I wish to change my prediction. First, she will try to make you her concubine. And if you refuse, she will then likely kill you."

Mace's eyes traced every line of the old drow's face, trying to determine if he was joking. His pulse rate increased and his palms began to sweat as he quickly changed into his new armor. Jeeves took possession of the old gear. "I'll just repair these for you. Never hurts to have a backup."

As Mace tried to think of something to say in response, Jervis patted him on the shoulder. "Don't worry, boy. I'll be with you. And I'll do my best to discourage either action by her majesty."

Feeling slightly better, Mace paced the shop for a few moments as Jervis retired to his workshop to make some quick repairs to the kobold-skin armor. As his mind raced, a thought occurred to Mace. Following his mentor into the shop, he drew his soul dagger.

"If you plan to stick me with that thing, boy, I might just decide to let the queen kill you after all. Or worse, seduce you."

"Heh. Fear not, Master. I just wanted to ask you what you might know about this weapon. This type of weapon, I should say." He set the dagger down on the workbench and immediately felt a strong sense of loss and longing.

"Ah, yes. Krieger brought back a few of these. Gave one to me, in fact. Quite handy to have around, aren't they?" Jervis spoke as he worked, not bothering to turn and address Mace or give the weapon more than a glance. "Has it spoken to you yet?"

"It… has. Sort of? I get feelings from it. And it seems to speak when I feed it, or when it's demanding to be fed. But I'm not sure they're words, exactly."

"As you feed it more soul energy, the communication will become clearer. I have used mine quite extensively since it was gifted to me. We're not having conversations yet, my dagger and I. But that will come soon enough."

Mace thought back to all the monsters and humanoids he'd slaughtered with the enchanted weapon since leaving Svartholm. Including the massive high-level creatures like the ancient petramander, spawn of Cthulhu, and the leviathan.

"I've… done quite a bit of killing myself since we last met. And I'm just getting vague impressions."

Jervis snorted. "I'm a Darkblade Master, boy. One of the great Houses was recently discovered to be plotting a coup. Nothing new there, every House is always plotting to overthrow another or try for the throne. But this House got caught. Her majesty tasked me with wiping the entire House from existence. I called in a dozen of your brethren and surrounded the house with the queen's guard so none would escape. Still, it took a full day to locate and dispose of the entire household." Jervis' hand became a blur, and when it became still he was holding a soul dagger. One much more ornate than Mace's.

"I reserved the House bloodline and the highest level guards and servants for myself. More than a hundred high-level drow, all centuries old. You cannot imagine the soul energy this blade absorbed."

Mace took a moment and tried, but Jervis was right. He couldn't imagine.

"Master, what I most want to ask is... well, will this thing eventually grow to the point that it can control me? I'm told that in ages past these weapons were wielded by those who committed mass murders, and-" His mouth clamped shut as he realized that was exactly what his mentor had just described doing.

Jervis turned to stare at Mace, then winked. "Even when it reaches full sentience, the weapon will not be able to overwhelm one with a will such as yours. It will feed on your anger and push you to commit murder to quench your emotions. You can give in and reap the benefits, some of which I'm sure you've felt already, or you can resist. As for the morality of murdering large numbers of people..."

Mace held up both hands. "I'm sorry, Master Jervis. I meant no insult."

"None taken, boy. Murder is my business, after all. Well, one of them." He held up the repaired armor. "But what I did, I did on the orders of my queen. In defense of her throne. They were sanctioned executions, not murder for personal vengeance. Except for old General Klag. I've disliked him for more than a thousand years." Jervis' smile as he recalled the killing made Mace's spine go cold.

"Here you are, boy. Good as new! I even improved the enchantment. Not as good as your new armor, but better than it was. Now, let us go see the queen. She will know by now that you're here."

Mace looked around. He hadn't seen or sensed anyone else in the shop since he'd arrived. "How?"

Jervis held up a hand and wiggled a pinky with a ring on it. "Because I told her."

*****

Ten minutes later, Mace and Jervis were approaching the gate to the queen's palace. Behind a twenty-foot smooth stone wall, Mace could see the main tower of the structure rising up ten floors. It was rumored that the entire tower was the queen's private residence. As with all drow structures, it was built mainly with defense in mind. Small slotted windows too small for assassins to gain entry. Except for the very top floor, which had a wide balcony. Activating his *Mage Sight,* Mace was nearly blinded by the amount of magic imbued in the wall, the gate, and most especially the area around that balcony.

The six guards standing at rigid attention in front of the gate recognized Jervis and raised a hand in greeting as the others all bowed their heads respectfully, if briefly. The lead guard cast a quick spell, and Jervis murmured, "It's a *dispel illusion* spell, to make sure I'm me and you're you." The guard barked a command and the others parted, making way for Jervis to pass through. "Thank you, Captain Kegan. I believe her majesty is expecting us."

"Of course, Master Jervis. She is with my father and has sent word for you to go directly to her private sitting room."

Jervis simply nodded his head as they passed by. Mace looked at the guard captain, whom he imagined flashed a pitying look in his direction. His pulse quickened a bit more. Drow queens were notoriously short-tempered, and basically the embodiment of evil. They cared for nothing but their own power, and they were ruthless in acquiring and maintaining it.

A short walk across a courtyard led to the main palace entrance. Jervis led him through the huge double doors, protection magic flashing purple as it recognized their right to pass and deactivated what Mace was

229

sure would have been a deadly deterrent. Jervis took an immediate right turn, following a wide corridor with high arched ceilings lined with columns on both sides. The floor was a deep pile carpet, colored a scarlet so dark that Mace imagined blood stains would simply blend in. Along each wall, items were mounted between the columns. Some were weapons, others works of art. A few were magically preserved heads of drow males and females.

Jervis pointed to a few fresher-looking heads grouped in one section. "The heads of the House that was just eliminated. Literally. Get it?" He smirked as Mace rolled his eyes.

"Dad jokes are the same everywhere, apparently," Mace mumbled.

Reaching another large doorway, Jervis stepped forward and knocked. The entry door to the queen's tower opened to reveal four elite drow warriors, members of the queen's personal guard. They were high enough level that all Mace could see when he focused on them was a black skull above their heads. Behind them was an ogre in full plate armor wielding a spear large enough to skewer an elephant. Upon seeing Jervis, the guards stepped to either side and flattened themselves against the walls, standing at attention. The ogre grunted once, turning and heading toward the back of the tower.

Jervis followed, Mace a step behind. The ogre led them up a staircase to the third level of the tower, where it stopped and grunted once more, pointing toward yet another door. This one was guarded by two more of the queen's guard, who snapped to attention before saluting Jervis. Without a word, one of them turned and knocked twice on the ironwood door, then opened it and announced them. "Master Jervis and Darkblade Mace as requested, my Queen."

Jervis didn't wait for an invitation, strolling through the open door. As Mace followed him into the room, he took a brief look around. The walls were all concealed by a series of hanging tapestries depicting various events that he assumed were from the queen's past. There were battles among drow, battles with non-human monsters of the underground world, and more than one depicting conquests of a sexual nature.

But Mace's gaze was quickly drawn from the décor to the female drow lounging on a divan near the back of the room. She was ethereally attractive, every line of her face and form the epitome of beauty. She wore form-fitting black silk that would have made excellent ninja gear, except for the extremely low cut neckline that accentuated her breasts, and the slits that ran up both legs all the way to her hips revealing shapely, dusky-skinned legs. But the cold calculating eyes and pursed lips lent a terrifying aspect to her face. She plucked fruit of some kind from a bowl on the floor and offered it to the drow standing next to her. Mace shifted his attention, and despite his fluttering heart, grinned slightly. Master Krieger accepted the treat from the queen with a murmur of thanks, nodding ever so slightly to Mace.

"Jervis, my love! You've brought me the puppy I wished to meet." The queen practically purred before popping another of the fruits from the bowl into her mouth. "Step forward, young king. I wish to get a closer look."

Mace bowed deeply at the waist, holding the pose for a moment before straightening and stepping forward several paces. He noticed a mosaic on the marble floor that formed a four-pointed star within a circle around the queen. Choosing the nearest point as a good stopping point, he bowed again.

"Oh, stop! You have earned yourself a kingdom, boy. Act like it. No sovereign will last long showing such meek obeisance to another." She practically hissed at him. Raising his eyes, Mace took a deep breath. He saw Krieger fighting not to smile as the queen scolded Mace.

"It is an honor to meet you, Your Majesty. And thank you for the wise advice. I am very new to this position, and apparently, I haven't learned all I should, as yet."

"Better!" The queen favored him with a predatory smile. "Still, never admit weakness or a lack of knowledge." This time Mace merely nodded his head slightly, causing her to chuckle. "A quick learner. Very good."

Mace took advantage of the moment to greet the Weaponsmaster. "Master Krieger. It is good to see you again."

"And you as well, Your Highness." Krieger bowed his head.

"You know each other, then?" The queen feigned ignorance. Mace knew from his time in Immernacht, and from various tales of drow he'd read as a kid, that the queen knew everything of note that happened in her city.

As Mace was frantically formulating a proper response, Krieger saved him the trouble. "Young Mace saved my life not so long ago. He was in a position to end me as I was in a weakened state, but he chose a different path. Since then we have adventured together a bit."

The queen's smile confirmed that none of this was new information. "It seems my Weaponsmaster approves of you, King Mace of…?"

"Styrke, Your Majesty. In one of the elder languages of my world, it means *Strength*."

"I see. An apt enough name. But tell me, young king. What do you intend to *do* with this new-found strength?"

Mace actually smiled when he realized the direction these questions were headed. "I intend to build a better Elysia for all its peoples. As I'm sure Jervis has informed you, there will be no more outworlders from now on. The few of us that are still able to journey here are banding together to assist Elysia in compensating for the loss. I plan to ally with other kingdoms and work together to stabilize your world." He paused to take a deep breath.

"In fact, as I have been fortunate enough to be summoned to your presence, my queen and I would like to offer you an alliance as well."

Mace stood still, barely breathing while he waited for her reaction. He'd just told her that a personal romantic relationship with her wasn't in the cards. He earnestly hoped that Jervis had been teasing him about becoming a concubine. Refusing such an offer, especially by mentioning

Shari, could send the queen into a rage that would get him killed, and probably Shari too.

The queen stared at him, her face a mask of perfectly carved stone. When Krieger coughed quietly, she seemed to awaken from a sort of trance. "I think you've learned more than you admit, young king." Her grin was more cruel than kind. "What exactly would this alliance entail? And how would it benefit me?" Out of nowhere, she produced a long, thin dagger which she twirled between her fingers with expert skill.

Mace's heart thumped and his mind raced. This offer of alliance had just poured unbidden from his lips, and he hadn't put any real thought into it. Twenty minutes ago he had no clue he'd be meeting the queen.

"Mutual protection, for one. I have but a small population now. But I will grow a formidable force that could assist you in dealing with some of the greater threats that roam the tunnels and caverns outside your city. Much as the outworlders once did."

The queen actually smiled at this. "Like dealing with the two great titans that were disposed of recently. It was outside my realm, but still, one hears things." Her eyes darted to Jervis, who had the nerve to chuckle.

Mace opened his mouth, then closed it again. Taking a breath, he replied, "That was me, Your Majesty. And yes, that would be exactly the type of service I was speaking of. I need to strengthen my people, and you have a wealth of nuisances that must be dealt with."

"And what would stop you from using this strength of yours to unseat me? Why would I help you get strong enough to cut my throat?" The dagger in her hand froze, and Mace could see the sheen of poison on the blade.

Another test. Mace tensed up for a moment. Remembering where he was and who he was speaking to, he adopted his most evil grin. "Your Majesty. I am an outworlder and a Darkblade. I cannot be killed permanently. If I wanted your throne, I would have taken it already. I could simply wear down your forces, killing a few dozen with each attack before your warriors defeat me. Then returning, again and again, every

233

day for years, if necessary, until you had nothing left with which to resist me."

He took a bold step forward, and he held out a hand. "But I would rather offer a hand in friendship. I have no designs on your city or your throne. My kingdom will, for the most part, remain on the surface of Elysia. I would much rather cooperate with you. Trade with you and your merchants. I believe you'll find me a valuable ally." He resisted a glance at the poisoned dagger still in her hand, instead staring her directly in the eye.

The queen laughed loudly, startling all three of the male drow in the room. "Ha Ha! Aren't we the bold one!" She reached out a hand to take Mace's and pulled him toward her with surprising strength. She patted the divan next to her, indicating he should sit. "A threat and an olive branch, all in the same breath. I could not have done better myself." Her voice was back to a purr again as she looked him up and down.

Reaching out with one hand, she languidly curled some of his long white hair around a finger. "This queen of yours. How does she compare to me?"

Mace caught Jervis grinning at him as he opened his mouth to answer. He began to suspect this whole meeting was for show. "My queen is… your opposite in most things, Majesty. She is a creature of sunlight, full of warmth and kindness. Where you are a dark and a terrible force of nature. She has no real interest in ruling or power. But there is steel in her. She survived alone on my world for months, when nearly every other human, millions upon millions of us, perished or devolved into mindless killer mutants. When every bird, bee, or falling leaf became a deadly threat. She is a healer by choice, but she does not hesitate to kill when it is needed."

The queen chuckled, releasing his hair and poking him gently in the chest. "You love this queen of yours. That is obvious. And she sounds quite formidable. I think I will like her!"

Mace let out a breath he didn't realize he'd been holding. "I know she would be excited to meet you, Your Majesty. Assuming we can become allies, you are welcome at our home, such as it is, anytime."

"Yes, I've received reports on your new stronghold. Mostly wood cabins and dirt, yes? I believe I shall wait a bit and visit when you've constructed a proper palace." She shoved Mace gently, causing him to stand while she swung her legs off the divan and got to her feet. She was taller than Mace expected, only an inch or two shorter than him.

"We shall, of course, have to discuss the details. But I am amenable to an alliance with Styrke, Your Majesty." She leaned forward and kissed his cheek, her lips lingering longer than strictly necessary. When she leaned back, her smile was warmer than Mace had yet seen from her. "In the meantime, I have a wager with that old goat behind you, and I'm going to need to hear the details of your battle near the lake before I pay him his gold and suffer his gloating!"

*****

The next morning, Mace was sitting at a table in a tavern not far from the palace gates. Krieger and Jervis sat across from him, both with glasses of c'irliq in hand. The clear liquor made by the grey dwarves burned like fire going down, but it produced a pleasant warmth and wonderful aftertaste that reminded Mace of vanilla, licorice, and maybe cinnamon. It provided a small buff of +2 to *Charisma*—and a significant -4 to *Intelligence* if one consumed more than one glass.

"I'll give you credit, boy. You've got stones. Most drow, male or female, drool and babble in fear when called into the presence of our queen. You, though. You sit down next to her and tell her you could end her life on a whim!" Both the elder drow chuckled, and Krieger raised his glass. "To Mace, the Fearless!"

Mace raised his own glass and touched it to the other two. "I don't know about fearless. I nearly shit myself when she began to play with that knife. But I suspect with the two of you there, I was never in any real danger."

Jervis took a long, slow swallow of the fiery liquid. "We may have counseled her majesty that you would make a better ally than foe."

Krieger added, "And she was intrigued by your rapid rise to power. Never underestimate the fear your success can generate in others."

Mace twirled a ring on his pinky finger. A ring of communication. It had been a parting gift from the queen. Jervis coughed once, then motioned for Mace to remove it. When Mace set it on the table, Jervis emptied his glass in one gulp, then set it upside down over the top of the ring. With a whisper, he said, "If I know my queen, and I do, that is no simple communication ring. Likely she'll be able to hear every word spoken near you while you wear it."

Mace's eyes bulged as he quickly replayed their last five minutes in his head. If the two elders were comfortable with teasing him while she could hear, he figured he didn't need to worry. He nodded his head to show that he understood.

"It will only work when in contact with your skin. So wear it on a chain, or put it in your bag, and you will have your privacy," Jervis instructed.

"Thank you, master." Mace was much relieved. "Speaking of communication rings, do you know where I can obtain several? They'll be invaluable as I expand my holdings and my people spread out across the lands."

Jervis nodded. "I'll sell you some when we return to my shop. I keep a supply for your brethren to use while on assignment. I have maybe six or seven that are not attuned to my own rings yet."

"Thank you again, master." He nodded at Jervis before turning to face Krieger. "How are you enjoying your soul blade, Master Krieger?"

The warrior's smile would have made even some brave souls quail. "It has proved most useful. Though I have not made as much use of mine as our friend Jervis here, it has grown to the point where it provides me an intriguing energy boost when it claims a soul."

Mace nodded. "I've felt that as well. And its lust for more power. It has tried more than once to convince me to kill when I didn't want to."

Krieger's face grew grim. "Do not allow that, young Mace. The dagger is a tool for you to use, and not the other way around. If you feel you cannot withstand its demands, return it to me now."

"I'm resisting just fine, master. But thank you for your concern. I believe the more I know about the magic involved, the better I'll be able to control it. I was thinking of stopping by Svartholm to speak with the smith who created this. Get some insight from him."

Krieger laughed, a deep raspy sound. "Good luck. I used my considerable charm and more than a few threats trying to pry the very same information from him. He holds to his secrets with implacable will. One has to respect such determination."

"Threats, I believe. But you have the charm of a moldy petramander, my friend." Jervis couldn't resist the jab, and Krieger raised his glass in salute.

Feeling the need to get back to his people, Mace finished his drink, gulping down the last of the burning c'irliq. Slamming the glass on the table next to his empty breakfast plate, he said with a slight rasp in his own voice, "That's good stuff! Thank you, masters. I need to be heading back to see to building my kingdom. Though I think I'll stop and buy a few kegs of this stuff on my way out." He peered into the empty glass, a slightly drunk smile on his face.

"You are both welcome to visit anytime, of course," he added as he got up. The two drow rose as well and walked with him to the door. Krieger took his leave, and Mace accompanied Jervis back to his shop. They stepped inside briefly while the old assassin retrieved the rings and Mace paid for them. As he made to leave, Jervis touched Mace's arm briefly. "Take this scroll. It will return you to my shop the next time you need to visit." The old man handed him the scroll. "And while you're here, I noticed you've improved your skills some. Hold still."

He put a hand on Mace's forehead, and the rush of new information brought with it the customary pain he experienced when learning this way. When Jervis removed his hand, Mace was a little unsteady on his feet.

"There! Those should keep you alive for a bit longer." Jervis grinned at him. Then a strange look came over his face. He put his hand back on Mace's head and mumbled, "Interesting. It seems your title has enabled you to learn a few skills that normally only a master would be eligible for. You're not ready for them yet, but return to me when you've grown a bit, and I'll share them with you.

Mace bowed slightly. "Thank you, master." He decided to review the notifications and new skills once he was alone. He had a long walk through the darkness of the underground to get back to his portal.

He said his goodbyes to his mentor and set off for the gate and the path that would lead him home. Once he was out of the city and in one of the tunnels, where only low-level monsters might disturb him, he stopped to review his new gifts from Jervis.

Character Name: Mace	Class: Sorcerer		Level: 50
Race: Drow	Spec: Darkblade		Exp: 157000/325000
Health: 9200/9200	Mana 3200/3200		Attribute Pts Avail: 6
Stamina: 16	Wisdom: 22	Charisma: 11	Life Regen: 15/sec
Strength: 16	Intellect: 24	Dexterity: 11	Mana Regen: 10.5/sec
Agility: 13	Luck: 11	Armor: 85	Skill Pts Avail: 0

With six attribute points available, he decided to put one each in *Charisma, Luck, Wisdom, Intellect, Stamina,* and *Agility.* He watched as his health and mana bars increased in size. There was a bit more spring to his step, as well.

Pulling up his new spells, he found a couple of surprises.

Execute

This spell allows a Darkblade to disappear mid-combat, instantly re-appearing behind your enemy where damage dealt is boosted by both backstab and critical hit bonuses. IF the enemy is below ten percent health, regardless of the size of their health pool, Execute will finish them off. Spell cost: 100 mana. Cooldown: 5min. Death of an enemy due to use of Execute reduces cooldown to 1min. Range limit: Enemy must be within 10ft.

This could be a game changer in a boss fight. And if he worked it right, in a fight against multiple enemies the spell could proc every minute! The next one seemed just as useful.

Hide

When cast upon a target, it renders the target invisible for thirty minutes. If target is a living being, it grants a 50% speed boost for twenty seconds. Spell cannot be used on caster. Invisibility effect canceled upon contact with an enemy. Spell cost: 200 mana. Cooldown: N/A. Range: 50ft.

Mace imagined sneaking his whole party past mobs to get to a dungeon boss more quickly, avoiding fights they might not be able to win, or making sure an unevolved NPC or two could escape from a hopeless fight.

Finished with his housekeeping, Mace picked up his pace to a jog. At level fifty, none of the creatures in this area of the underground presented a serious threat. Still, he activated his *Mage Sight* and kept an eye out for anything interesting as he pushed toward the portal location highlighted on his UI map.

Chapter 12

Shari was loving her new responsibilities for planning and organizing the expansion of Darkstone. While she had little experience with construction or architecture, she found she had a gift for human resources. Or rather, citizen resources. And her quick study session on urban planning during her last logout had given her a good understanding of infrastructure needs and designing a city that would be both functional and aesthetically pleasing.

The folks who had been rushing to construct housing for all the new citizens had actually done a good job. The centaurs who had been pitching in were wise, living up to their reputation. The buildings were set wide apart around a central 'square' placed in front of the mine entrance. The palisade had been built in a semicircle that started and ended at the mountain's base, curving around so that there were no blind corners.

The dwarves had been busy refining their newly discovered cavern into a livable space for all the families from their village. Small homes had been carved into the rock around the outer walls, and already they were carving downward into the stone, as dwarves do, to create lower levels with streets and shops and everything one would expect within a dwarven settlement. At the same time, a team of them were carving out the long ramp that would wind down to the dungeon entrance, and by extension, the portals.

She started her morning in the game by fulfilling a promise she'd forgotten in the excitement of their arrival. Walking out to the gates, she summoned the wyvern. When the huge beast appeared, there were screams and shouts from inside the walls. She held up her hands and faced the crowd, shouting, "It's okay! She's one of us!" several times until folks calmed down.

Turning back to her giant pet, she said, "You can run and play in the forest. Just don't hurt any of our people, or any sentients, without checking with me first, okay?

The wyvern bowed her head down, gave Shari a gentle lick on the side of the face, and then slithered off into the trees.

Returning to her residence to begin her plans for the day, she asked a few orcs who were passing by to set up a table and some benches in front of the cabin that she and Mace had been given. Then she had those same orcs sit with her, and she began interviewing them about their skills, their plans, and how they imagined themselves fitting into the community. She spent the entire morning pulling orcs, dwarves, minotaurs, centaurs, and any humans she hadn't spoken to yet, from whatever they were doing to sit and chat with her.

Some were short and gruff, mostly the dwarves, wanting to get back to work. But most embraced her efforts to be helpful and chatted amiably. She even met a little dwarf child approximately ten years of age who, after sitting quietly next to his mother while she spoke to Shari a while, suddenly burst forth, "Yer purty, lady Shari! I'm gonna marry ye when I get big!"

Enchanted, Shari gave the dwarfling a hug and kiss on the cheek as several of those waiting on the benches chuckled. "You are the sweetest little thing!" she beamed at him.

"Bah!" Now embarrassed by the attention and laughter, he retreated behind his mum and grumbled under his breath, wiping his face where she'd kissed him.

When she'd finished interviewing everyone, she retreated inside to review all her notes and attempt to organize the skills and talents of her available workforce. Some were easily handled in groups. The orphans from Graf, for example, she gave to Lila to do with as she saw fit. They'd been mostly sullen and silent when she interviewed them, not trusting her in the least. But when she mentioned training with Lila and Red, and they each realized that they'd be fed and housed, every one of them became more cooperative.

Most of her people already had a trade. Whether it was crafting, hunting, cooking, or working as merchants or cleaners, they had a useful skill that could be helpful in the coming days. Those that didn't, she tentatively assigned to apprentice under one of the others based on their hopes for the future. Those that had only ever been household staff she reserved for herself for now. They would become her assistants, runners, advisors, and 'utility players' over the coming weeks. If one of the others needed a pair of unskilled hands temporarily, she would lend them out. It wouldn't hurt them to learn some new skills and get some experience anyway.

Tex logged off, saying he'd be back in a few days, and to message him if they needed him sooner. He claimed to want to dig into the code they needed for their upload, but Shari and the others suspected he just needed some time to think. Ursus passed the day amusing the young ones, or out in the forest patrolling or napping.

Griff and Lisa spent some of their time with the dwarves, helping to carve homes from the stone or mining the iron vein that their friends were following. Both got some minor increases to their *Strength* and *Stamina* in the process—along with increased skills in *Mining* and *Blunt Weapon*.

Shari pulled some larger pieces of parchment from her inventory and began to sketch a map of the settlement's existing structures. When she had them all down roughly to scale, she gained a skill point.

Skill level up! You have earned +1 to Cartography

Humming happily to herself, Shari began to sketch in additional structures she planned to build. She added a fountain to the central plaza, as well as some semi-permanent market stalls. She diagrammed a water supply and sanitary drainage system that connected underneath the existing buildings and extended out to allow for future connections as the settlement became a town, then a city. Shari sketched out a multitude of single family homes, then re-labeled a few of the longhouses as a future tavern/inn, a crafting hall, and a meeting hall.

As the sun began to set, she messaged Mace. *"Are you on your way back? How's it going?"* Mace had updated her over a late dinner the night before on his meeting with the queen.

"I'm running toward the portal now. It is farther than it looked on the map. I'll reach it in maybe three more hours, if I don't have to keep stopping to fight," Mace replied almost immediately. *"Don't wait up for me. I'm probably going to crash as soon as I get through the portal to where it's safe."*

"I'm tired too. Been a busy day. But wake me when you come to bed."

Shari accepted his silence as agreement, gathering up her notes and stowing them away in her ring. She took one last lap around the enclosure, checking in with folks and letting Brahm know she and Mace would be back in the morning. Twice as she made her rounds she caught the little dwarfling peering at her from behind cover. When she smiled in his direction, he promptly disappeared. Back in her 'royal' cabin, she logged out for the night.

*****

Tex crawled out of his pod and into a cold shower. Once he was cleaned up and feeling more refreshed, he made his way to the kitchen and 'cooked' a breakfast of granola bars crumbled into scrambled powdered eggs with ketchup and Tabasco sauce and a cold beer.

He ate slowly, his mind going back time and again to the events outside. Though he logically knew the deaths of those people were not his fault, he kept thinking that he could have let them in the night before, and they'd still be alive.

Almost hopefully, he asked, "Skippy? Has there been any movement outside since I was last out there?"

"None, Tex. I would have had Elysia alert you in the game had I detected anything."

"Right. Of course. Sorry, Skipster," Tex mumbled. He absently pushed around some eggs and granola chunks with his fork. He didn't have much of an appetite, but he forced himself to finish the meal. With supply runs as risky as they were, there was no such thing as throwing away food.

After mechanically cleaning up after himself, he walked down to his lab and sat on the sofa. Then he laid down and put his feet up. Eventually, his thoughts slowed, and he was able to drift off to sleep.

*****

Griff and Lisa logged out of the game not long after Shari. After quick showers, they met up in the kitchen. Lisa was still wearing the inflatable plastic cast on her arm, and it pained her some to move her hand, so Griff did the cooking. He threw some penne into a pot to boil and opened a can of cream of mushroom soup. Pouring the soup into a small pot, he set that on high heat and moved on to the next item. Taking a leftover half loaf of Lisa's bread, he set it on the counter and sliced it in half lengthwise. He grabbed a quarter stick of butter from the fridge and garlic powder from the spice rack.

Dropping the butter in a bowl, he stuck it in the microwave and nuked it for 45 seconds, melting it. Then he sprinkled some garlic into the liquid butter and mixed it up with a small brush from a rack above the counter. Then he used the brush to coat the bread before sticking it on a baking sheet and putting it into the oven to crisp it up and brown it.

By the time the water in the large pasta pot had boiled and cooked the pasta for about ten minutes, the soup was bubbling and beginning to smell very good. Griff turned off the heat under both burners. He emptied the pasta into a colander and left it to cool for a moment while he grabbed a large bowl. Pouring the steaming hot soup into the bowl first, he then dumped the pasta in on top of it and used a wooden spoon to mix it all around. When the pasta was prepared, he turned off the oven and removed the lightly browned garlic bread.

"That smells *amazin'!*" Lisa said from her seat at the counter. "Yer mum really did teach ya how to cook. I thought you were pullin' my leg."

"If we had fresh meat and veggies I could really show ya something." Griff smiled as he plated some of the pasta for her. She reached across the counter with her good hand broke off some of the warm garlic bread, immediately taking a big bite.

"Mmmm! Thish wunnerful," she mumbled around the mouthful of garlicky goodness.

Griff chuckled, setting her plate in front of her and dishing one for himself. She dipped the hunk of bread in the sauce and took another big bite. Her eyes rolled back in her head and she moaned slightly.

"Easy there, luv. Save some of that passion for the chef!" He winked at her as he sat down and lifted his fork. They enjoyed a quiet meal, making small talk as they mostly focused on the food. Lisa asked him a little about his life, and he shared a little bit. He asked her about her favorite things, learning that she loved kittens, the color green, and cinnamon toast. Which obviously meant he'd be making cinnamon toast for breakfast. He made a mental note to wake himself early so that he could bake some fresh bread for her.

She helped with cleanup by putting away the items after he washed and dried them and wiping down all the prep surfaces. When they were done, they walked together toward their rooms. A few steps outside the dining room, she reached out with her good hand and took hold of Griff's. He squeezed lightly, and a smile appeared on his face, but he didn't say a word.

When they reached her quarters, she turned to face him. "Thank you for a lovely dinner. And for… well for everythin'." She stood on her toes and leaned forward to plant a light kiss on his lips. He instinctively gathered her into a hug, his arm around her waist as he pulled her tightly to him. After a moment of breathing in her clean, flowery scent, he released her.

"Been my absolute pleasure." He gave her a slight bow and exaggerated flourish with one hand. "Your bed awaits, m'lady."

She grinned at him and retreated into her room. As she closed the door, she mumbled, "Sweet dreams, Griff."

He stood there staring at her door for a solid minute, a goofy smile on his face, before turning and entering his own room. As he closed his door and reached for the lock, he hesitated. Changing his mind and leaving it unlocked, he stripped to his boxers and crawled into bed.

*****

Mace was awakened by a snorting sound in his ear. Blinking the sleep from his eyes, he looked over to find Shari's face nestled against his neck. One arm and one leg were thrown over his body, pinning him between her and the wall. He smiled, his heart full as he watched her drool on his shoulder. He'd logged out late after running all the way to the portal. Honoring her request, he'd awakened her as he crawled into bed. She merely pushed him down, mumbling sleepily about 'my body pillow' and wrapped herself around him before drifting off again.

As he contemplated a way to extricate himself without waking her, she twitched and snorted, mumbling, "Noooo… not the ho-hos!" into his ear.

"Protecting my tasty snack cake supply from evil monsters?" he whispered at her, deciding he didn't really need to get up just then. "I love you, too."

Surprised at his own words, he lay there and contemplated them. They'd only known each other a short time. But he knew he meant what he'd said. Though he decided to find a more romantic way to tell her. Preferably when she was awake.

He lay there listening to her breathe and occasionally snore until one of the snorts woke her up.

"Mornin', sunshine. You have quite a talent for drooling." He smiled at her, meeting her eyes and projecting all that he felt for her. She slapped his chest and mumbled, "Hush. Body pillows don't talk," before trying to bury her face back in his shoulder.

"Oh, no you don't! We've got a busy day ahead of us. Got a city to build! I want to open that guild chest that Griff brought us! Find out what happens when we use that anchor stone." He poked at her side, just below her last rib, where he knew she was ticklish.

"Noooo! No tickles!" She rolled over on top of him in an attempt to pin his arms and prevent further tickling. Mace paused, looking into her eyes again. She lowered her face to give him a kiss, and he wrapped his arms around her.

It was nearly an hour before they tumbled out of bed to hit the showers.

Once back in the game, Shari began to call the citizens together while Brahm retrieved the mithril chest, and Mace ran up from the portal room where he'd logged out.

When he joined Shari and the others, most of the residents of Darkstone had gathered in the central space. The **Mithril Guild Storage Chest** was sitting on a rough plank table that creaked under the weight. It was larger than Mace had expected—easily large enough that Brahm could easily crawl inside and close the lid.

Shari nudged him with an elbow. "Say something pretty before you open that thing, dork."

Mace grinned at her. Raising his hands to quiet the chatter in the crowd, he called out, "Good morning, everyone! I hope you're all having as wonderful a morning as I am so far!" He paused to catch Shari blushing slightly.

"Today we're going to open this guild chest, brought to us by Griff, Lisa, and their companions!" He waited while folks whistled and cheered a bit. "Inside is an Anchor Stone which we will use to officially create our kingdom and our new home!"

He opened the chest as the crowd cheered longer and louder. His eyes widened as he took in all the items contained within. Griff had told him there were a lot of materials and items of value, but this was amazing. Guilds would go to war over something like this!

The first thing he did was withdraw the Anchor Stone and read its description.

Guild Anchor Stone (Modified)

*This stone may be placed at a location legally owned by a guild wishing to establish a stronghold. The Guild Chest in which this stone was found contains materials and resources sufficient to construct a Level One Guild Hall. Placing the stone in unclaimed territory will activate a twenty-four-hour timer, at the end of which the land under the stronghold will become the legally owned property of the guild. Should the land be contested, the timer will stop, only resuming when the battle has been decided. The anchor stone may be removed and claimed by others during the twenty-four hour period. (**Modification**) This Guild Anchor Stone has been upgraded by the goddess Elysia to a Kingdom Anchor Stone. Placement of this Anchor Stone in already claimed territory will facilitate the founding of a Capital City without a countdown timer. Additional resources sufficient to create a Level One Capital City have been added to the modified Mithril Chest. In addition, the capacity of the Mithril Chest has been upgraded to Kingdom Storage Vault. Placement of the Kingdom Anchor Stone in your current location will establish your dominion over an area of ten square miles around the anchor point, both above and below the surface. It is recommended that the stone be placed in a defensible position.*

"Well, shit," Mace mumbled as he finished reading. Looking up, he realized that everyone was staring impatiently at him. He spoke loudly enough for all to hear. "It seems our Guild Anchor Stone has been upgraded to a Capital City Anchor Stone! Please, let's all take a moment of silence to thank Elysia for her generosity!" He bowed his head for a moment, hearing rustling as others did the same or knelt in prayer. When he felt that enough time had passed, he raised his head again and said, "Thank you! Now, while I go and find a secret place to stash this stone, your new queen has some items to give out!"

Mace reached into his inventory and pulled several of the loot items they'd claimed in their adventures, including the epic helm from the suit of armor in Justin's chamber, and the *Armor of the Peacemaker* with its sword. Handing it all to Shari, he whispered, "I'm going to go place this in the secret library. It should be safe there. The helm is for Griff. Hand out the rest of this stuff, and whatever you want from the chest. Maybe get everyone who hasn't already to drink the water from the pond? I'll be back as quickly as I can. I expect you'll know when the stone has been placed." He grinned.

Waving to the crowd, he jogged through the mine entrance with stone in hand. As Shari began to call out the items in the chest, he descended to the lower level and entered Justin's old chamber. He closed and locked the door behind him, then whispered, "Ventus!" and sent a gust of wind circulating throughout the room to expose any stealthed spies who might have followed. There were none.

Locating the trigger stone on the wall, he pressed it and watched the secret door to the library open. He walked with a spring in his step into the library-laboratory combination room and looked around. Not finding much in the way of empty space around the edges of the room, he stood in the center and held the stone in both hands, focusing on it.

Do you wish to activate the Capital City Anchor Stone at this location? Yes/No

Taking a deep breath, Mace mentally clicked '*Yes*'.

Immediately, he was surrounded by a silvery-white glow that nearly blinded him. As it faded, there was a new screen on his UI. It was titled **City Management Interface** and featured a main status screen with dozens of tabs at the bottom.

Capital City Status		
City Name:	Allied Nations: 0	City Level: 1
Owned by: Mace & HotShari	Enemy Nations: 0	Pts to Next Level: 250
Population: 652	Total Resources: 180,500	Control Area: 10sq miles
Daily Income: 0	Defenses: 2	Ancillary Structures: 0
Daily Expenses: 0	Structures: 8	Tax Rate: 0

Mace quickly noticed it was giving him the option of choosing a new name. He liked Darkstone, but he would check with the others before filling it in. Maybe give all the new citizens a chance to vote on it. He chuckled at the "HotShari" name next to his. He had the power as system admin to change her moniker, but he kind of liked it the way it was.

Each of the boxes had a tab below that he could click on for more detailed information. He chose the *Structures* tab and it opened to show him a list of the current structures within the city, including the log buildings on the surface, the outer wall, and the mine. It seemed to count the entire underground area as one structure, rather than individual chambers. When he focused on that number for a few seconds, another menu popped up giving him the option to break down the chambers within the mine.

At the bottom of the screen was a section labeled *Construction Status*. He focused on that, and a barrage of screens appeared. One was a list of the existing structures, each one labeled by use, size, building material, materials needed, and percent complete. Another was a series of diagrams of various structures that could be built, along with the same details as the existing buildings.

On a whim, he chose a diagram labeled *Outer Wall*. The interface zoomed in to a series of diagrams that featured different types and configurations of wall from a simple high fence to massive stone barriers.

Next to each one was a basic specification description and listing for materials required and time to build.

He selected a solid-looking stone wall diagram that said it was twenty feet high with an inner rampart. Immediately a 3-D image of a transparent wall section drawn in blue lines popped into the foreground of his vision.

"This is *cool*!" he shouted to the empty room. "I can use the system to build structures, rather than having to ask our people to do it by hand?"

"*That is correct, Your Majesty,*" Peabody's voice drifted down to him.

"Peabody? Is something wrong at the facility?" Mace felt a moment of panic.

"*I am not Peabody, Your Majesty. Though you may choose to give me that name. I am your city interface. I am here to answer questions, carry out orders, and monitor the city's ongoing operations for you.*"

"And Elysia or Peabody thought it would be funny to give you Peabody's voice." Mace tapped his chin. "That's going to get confusing, I think. Let's give you a different voice. And your name from now on will be… Hobbes." He took a moment to pull up the interface controls and choose an accent. He went with Irish.

"Nice to meet you, Hobbes. Now, tell me. Can I just magically build a wall around the city?"

"*Yes, Majesty. As long as you have the resources available, you may choose to build or modify any of the structures in the blueprint library. If, for example, you wish to replace the existing wooden palisade with your chosen stone wall, the cost of the stone needed for the construction would be deducted from your current stone resources. And the wood resources used for the palisade would be returned to you.*"

"Awesome! So, if I wanted to set this stone wall in an arc that is one thousand feet out from the mine entrance at the center?"

A pedestal rose from the floor in front of Mace, and above it appeared a holographic representation of the ten square miles of his city. To the north was the mountain range, and to the south the forest. Leading off to the west was the trail that eventually reached the lake, though that was not currently within his city's limits. Hobbes helpfully zoomed in until the existing encampment nearly filled the screen. Blue lines created 3-D representations of the existing wall and buildings. A white dotted line appeared in an arc outside the existing wall, curving around from the center point to the mountain cliffs on either end.

"Is this what you had in mind?"

Mace studied the model for a few moments. "Yes, that looks about right? What would that wall cost me in stone resources, and how long would it take to build?"

"This wall would be approximately six thousand two hundred and eighty feet long. Each wall section is twenty feet wide by thirty feet tall, with ten feet being sunk into the ground and the remaining twenty above ground. Each section costs fifty units of stone. The cost in stone resources to construct the wall as drawn would be three hundred fourteen sections at fifty units each, or fifteen thousand seven hundred units of stone."

"And what are my current stone resources?"

His personal UI flicked over to his city's resource tab, and he nearly choked. Hobbes answer the question as he read it for himself.

"This city currently possesses sixty-three thousand units of stone. More stone can be harvested automatically from within the mountain at a rate of two hundred units per day. Additional units can be harvested through the actions of stonemasons."

Mace looked at the area inside the dotted arc. "How much land area would I have inside the wall if it's placed there? Surface area only."

"Three million one hundred and forty thousand square feet, or approximately seventy-two acres of surface area."

Mace tried to picture stone buildings, roads, etc. filling in the space inside the walls. "Seventy-two acres isn't a lot of space for a city." He thought about his population of more than six hundred citizens. "Then again, we've got the underground spaces. And we can always expand later," he mused aloud.

"Hobbes, please go ahead and construct the wall where it's shown." A thought occurred to him and he added, "Leave one section out at the center point of the arc for a gate. How long will it take?"

"*As you have no other construction projects currently underway, the construction of the perimeter wall will take approximately ten hours.*"

Thank you, Hobbes! One last question. Can I access the interface from anywhere? Or do I need to be in this room? It would be helpful to be able to see the space I'm working in."

"*You and HotShari may access the interface from anywhere within the city's area of influence. Currently ten square miles. You may also authorize other individuals to access the interface, but they will need to do so from within this room.*"

"Thank you, Hobbes! I'll be heading back up to meet with HotShari and the others." He grinned to himself at the name. That was never going to get old. "Will you be able to speak with us up there as well?"

"*Yes, Majesty. I can hear your voice and speak to you anywhere within twenty-five feet of a city structure. Farther if you speak loudly.*"

Mace eyed the pedestal as he exited the room, thinking he detected a hint of deadpan humor in that last statement.

Back up on the plaza, he found Griff proudly wearing his new helm. Sneaking up behind the dwarf, he rapped on the metal with his knuckles, causing Griff to curse and spin around, hand moving toward the hammer at his belt.

"Seems like a good sturdy brain bucket," Mace observed as Griff mock-scowled at him.

"Thank ya fer this. It'll come in handy in the dungeons." Griff's eyes rose upward to look at the headgear, nearly rolling back in his head.

The crowd cheered something Shari was doing, and Mace looked up to see her handing a training book to an orc. He heard her say something about leatherworking and smiled. Hopefully, they'd have another master crafter soon. Over to one side, several orcs, dwarves, and centaurs were sitting on the ground, just recovering from the effects of the change brought on by the magic water. Brahm and Layne were tending to them. Some others who looked much fresher looked on with sympathy.

Looking out through the gate, he noticed a low course of stone stretching across his limited field of vision. So far it was only a foot or two high, with a gap in the center. Moving toward the gate, he noticed a lookout up on the palisade leaning over the edge and staring toward the rising wall. He turned and was opening his mouth to call out, when Mace waved at him, then held a finger to his lips. The orc looked confused but nodded his head.

Mace reached the gate and pulled it closed as quietly as possible. Then he ran up the stairs to stand with the lookout. "Is anyone else outside right now?"

"Ursus is out there patrolling. Everyone one else is inside." The orc looked askance at Mace.

"Okay good. I'll let you in on a little secret. I need you to quietly pass the word to the other guards on the wall. I've just started construction of a new stone perimeter wall. That's what you see happening out there. I'm hoping to keep it quiet while it rises, so I can surprise the others with it when it's complete."

The guard grinned at him. "It looks thick. And stone doesn't burn. Good choice."

Mace handed the orc five gold coins. "For your discretion. And please, notify the others before they call out? Also, please let Ursus back in as quietly as possible when he returns."

The orc nodded and moved off down the wall. Mace leapt down from the rampart to the ground and strolled up behind the crowd, who were still watching and listening to Shari. As he began to pass through them, they parted as they recognized him, asking his pardon. Soon the others all turned to see what the commotion was about, and they made a path for him to reach Shari.

Putting an arm around her waist and giving a little squeeze, he called out, "The anchor stone has been placed! We are officially a city!"

He let the citizens cheer for a few moments before holding up his hands to quiet them. "But, at the moment, we are a city with no name! I have been given the option to continue to use Darkstone or choose another name. So I thought I'd give all of you a chance to help me. If you've got a suggestion, bring it up here to the very pretty elf lady. Or if you like Darkstone, let her know that, as well. Tomorrow we'll pick a name!"

Shari elbowed him in the ribs. "Like I had nothing else planned for today?"

"Oh, planning is a good word. See, there's this whole interface…" He began to explain to her what was possible. They sat down at the table, and he pulled up the city interface, sharing it with her. She snorted when she saw 'HotShari' as co-owner, and Mace waggled his eyebrows at her. They talked about housing and roads and other items in between being approached by citizens with name suggestions. They called in Griff and Lisa and the leaders from each race and asked for their input.

On the subject of housing, the dwarves preferred to remain underground. When offered stone houses above ground, the minotaurs and centaurs asked for high ceilings and open spaces, while the orcs seemed to prefer more warren-like homes with closed off spaces. Mace and Shari found appropriate designs for all of them, and then they began to talk about placement.

Surprisingly, the different races didn't ask to be segregated into different quarters of the city. Instead, they asked that they be housed close to the workshops and stores where they'd be spending their days. Effectively mixing up all the races but the dwarves, who were still mainly underground. Though several would be working in shops across the city during the day.

They created a three-story inn with a ground floor tavern and a large wine cellar in the basement. This they placed right on one edge of the plaza, right on top of one of the longhouses. Everyone who had been sleeping inside removed their belongings, and Mace pushed the button to start construction. They all watched in fascination as the wooden building deconstructed, the wood fading from existence as a hole formed in the ground where the cellar would be. From there, the walls grew upward, columns rising up in between. Then beams stretched across, and floors seemed to grow out of nowhere. In less than an hour, the log longhouse was replaced with a stone inn. The two upper floors sported thirty rooms total, more than enough to sleep those that had just vacated the longhouse.

The players spent the day this way, helping to choose and place structures. Housing for families, shops for crafters and merchants. The smithy was placed near the palisade gate, easy to find for incoming travelers or farmers needing to repair tools. And far enough from Mace and Shari's home that they didn't hear the hammering.

Shari installed her network of underground utilities, with cold running water connected to each home, and a deep sanitary sewer tunnel system ten feet below the streets and houses. She added in some storm drains to allow the rainwater to wash the place and drain away cleanly, pushing the sewage out of the sanitary lines as it went.

Rather than have the outflow surface somewhere outside the walls—leaving a potential entry point for invading forces—she found a crevice deep below the city for the system to drain into. According to the 3-D map, it extended more than a mile into the earth.

Satisfied with their accomplishments for the day, Mace made a quick trip up onto the palisade. There was a new shift of guards up there, but they'd been given the word to keep quiet about the wall that had been growing all day. Mace watched the sun begin to set as he inspected the wall. It was not quite completed, but already the sections within sight were a full twenty feet tall. Every hundred yards or so there was a stairway leading up to the rampart. He saw Ursus out there, sniffing curiously at the wall as he passed through the opening where the new gate would go.

Mace turned and shouted for everyone to gather again. He whispered to the guard to head down and open the gates for Ursus.

As the people gathered, he called down, "Those of you who were here from the start built us a wonderful, sturdy wall to protect us from the predators. But now, with so many of us here, we need more room. So I'm pleased to present to you all... your new wall!"

The guard opened the gate, and Ursus seemed startled to see everyone staring at him, then burst into cheering and applause. The confused look on the bear's face made Mace and many of the others laugh. The gathered children mobbed the grizzly as most of the adults passed around him and walked out to inspect the new wall.

Almost immediately, Shari was approached by two dwarven farmers. "M'lady. It seems with yer new wall so far out, there be room fer us to plant some crops inside. Can ye give us a few acres?"

Shari looked up at Mace, who was busy watching folks climb the stairs. As she watched, he hopped off the front of the palisade and disappeared.

Turning back to the farmers, she said, "We have plans to expand across this entire space." When she paused, she saw both of their faces fall in disappointment. "But that expansion won't happen overnight. I'll give you two acres back in a corner near the mountain. But only for a couple seasons. By then we'll have created a protected place for you outside the wall. Or we'll have another wall farther out." As they started to celebrate, she added, *"And...* you have to promise to plant fruit trees around the perimeter."

Both dwarves shook her hand emphatically and dashed off toward the back corner she'd indicated.

They held another, smaller feast that night. The community's cooks roasted meat brought in by the hunters, and Mace contributed one of the barrels of c'irliq he'd purchased in Immernacht—much to the delight of the dwarves and orcs.

As it grew later, Mace and the others logged out. The party wound down around midnight, and folks stumbled home to their beds.

Deep below the city, half a mile down, a splash of wastewater struck the head of a slumbering creature. It awoke with a start, then noticed the foul odor. When another splash landed square in its face, it roared in anger. Around it, others were startled awake. One of the larger creatures approached the one making all the noise and sniffed it at. Snorting in disgust, it swatted the complainer with one beefy clawed paw, knocking it off their ledge into the crevice, listening to it scream as it fell.

Just as it was turning to crawl back into its nest, another foul-smelling stream of wastewater fell onto its back. This time the disgusting roar woke every creature within a quarter mile. Most quivered in fear at the sound.

There was an angry rock troll stirring.

Chapter 13

The next day, Tex joined them in the game. He seemed to be in better spirits, and he even laughed when Ursus strolled up and calmly swatted him off his feet. "I missed you too, my friend," he said as he got up and dusted himself off. Ursus just snorted and turned to trot over and pounce on a group of children.

Looking around at the new stone buildings and tall stone wall, he said, "Looks like they've been busy around here." After a brief search, he found Shari sitting at her table in the plaza, speaking to a small group of citizens. Not wanting to disturb her, he took a seat on a section of log turned upright like a stump. He passed the next several minutes alternating between listening to Shari and watching his bear mooch oatmeal with honey from the children. Not that he had to try very hard.

When Shari had finished with her people, she turned to Tex. "Hiya… Tex!" She giggled. "I always wanted to say that. How're you doin'?"

Tex tipped an imaginary hat at her. "I'm good, Your Majesty." His orcish grin was filled with sharp teeth, and it was not as charming as he probably intended. "Got some good sleep, and got some work done on our little project. My head's in a better place. Thanks for understanding."

Shari patted his arm. "When I was out on my own, after my best friend and my survival buddy died, there were days when I all I could do was curl up in a dark hole somewhere and cry. Sometimes for more than a day at a time. The reality of what our world has become…"

"Yeah." Tex didn't need her to finish. "It sucks donkey balls."

Shari snorted. "Not what I was gonna say but accurate enough. Anyway, we're here for you. I can't imagine what it's like for you to have been alone as long as you have. Though, I think maybe Griff can. Might help both of you to have a little talk sometime." Her face softened as she added, "As for the thing with the kid… you'll learn to live with it. I had to kill a few uninfected humans to stay alive. Including one the very day I met Mace. Mace has had to kill a few as well, and he had his friends killed by them. The end of the world has brought out the best in people like you and Mace, Griff and Lisa. And the worst in some others. You had no way to tell which way it would be with those people."

Tex hung his head as she spoke, unable to deal with the kindness in her eyes. The truth was that he hadn't forgiven himself for those deaths. He'd simply decided to grit his teeth and ignore the guilt. He had work to do if he was going to find a way for them all to live on in the game.

"Thank you, hun. I appreciate your sympathy, I truly do. You have a good heart, and Mace is maybe the luckiest man on Earth." He patted her hand before standing. "Now, how can I help?"

Shari blinked a few times at the rapid change of subject, then recovered. "Actually, if you wouldn't mind a little travel, we'd like to find some dungeons to run our people through. We'll start with the one near the waterfall that Griff and his group ran. We can send our level fifteen-ish people through. But a lower level dungeon would be great. And a few higher level ones as well."

Tex nodded. "We can run groups of the guards through first, get them leveled up to protect the city. And do we have a few healers?"

Shari nodded. "We have seven, not including myself. The next highest level is the orc shaman. There are two clerics from Graf, the kid Leroy from Griff's group who is a druid, old Maggie from the dwarven village, and two household priests among the former slaves. I'm afraid most of them are under level ten."

"Not to worry. We can arrange for them to go on hunting parties in the forest around here. We'll send a hunter, one of the guards that isn't running a dungeon or on duty, and a healer. Maybe two healers, just in case. Give me their names, and I'll figure out a schedule."

Shari was just grabbing a pen and ink to make a list when screams echoed out from the mine entrance, quickly followed by roars and shouts. A notification popped up on both of their UI's.

Your city is under attack!

Quest Available: Defend [unnamed] City

A tribe of rock trolls has risen from the depths below your city after being assaulted by wastewater draining on their heads. They will murder every living being in the city if not stopped. Successfully defend the city, eliminate the threat, and save as many citizens as you can. Reward: Variable. Do you wish to accept this quest? Yes/No

Both Shari and Tex instantly accepted the quest even as Ursus roared from somewhere outside the wall, and dwarves began to pour out of the mine entrance. All Shari could see were the children and elderly. The others must have rallied to try and slow down the trolls to protect their most vulnerable.

Orcs, minotaurs, and centaurs were running toward the mine from every direction, weapons already in hand. The few humans with combat training were doing the same.

Both players received group invites from Mace, and they instantly accepted. They found themselves grouped with all the other outworlders, as well as Campbell, Brahm, Ag'thar, and one of the centaurs that Shari didn't know well.

Mace's voice came across party chat clearly. *"They're boiling up from below. Coming through the same crevice that the kobolds disappeared down into when I freed them. There are at least twenty that I can see, and more seem to be coming. Some of the dwarves are trapped in their quarters below, and a mining crew is fighting in the ramp tunnel. We need to clear both sides and trap them in the chamber with the cages!"*

Tex responded first. "I'm on my way in! I'll take care of any between the exit and the dwarven chambers. Ursus is incoming, he'll go get the ones on the ramp!"

Tex ducked his head to make sure he cleared the top of the door as he entered. Reaching into his inventory he withdrew a massive warhammer that would have required two hands for most creatures to wield. Holding it in his right hand, he charged down the tunnel and veered left toward the ramp leading downward. As he turned the corner, he spotted two trolls battering against a wall of dwarven shields.

Letting out a roar, he charged toward the backs of the trolls. The one on the left turned toward him just in time to take a devastating blow to the face. Its head cracked, and the ten-foot-tall monster stumbled back into its companion. Tex didn't wait for it to recover, grabbing the handle of his hammer with both hands and bringing it down atop the troll's damaged head.

This time the head shattered, and its body went limp. A cheer went up from the dwarves, who were still taking a beating from the other troll. Its massive fists were hammering against shields, making dents and pushing the dwarves back a bit with each blow.

Even with its limited intellect, the troll quickly figured out that pounding would get it nowhere, and it grabbed hold of the top of one of the shields. Yanking it toward itself, it pulled the unlucky dwarf out of line and flung it over one shoulder. Before the dwarves could close ranks, it kicked forward into the opening and sent another dwarf, this one wielding a spear, flying backward with a bone-crunching sound.

Tex roared even as the dwarves cried out in rage. As they reformed their wall and battered at the troll with their hammers, Tex slammed the monster in the back with his own weapon.   The fifty-pound hammer's impact caused cracks to spiderweb across the monster's back. It bellowed in pain and turned its attention on Tex.

Enraged Rock Troll
Level 35
Health: 3,200/12,000

The dwarves had been whittling away at the twelve-foot monster's health, but Tex's critical hit from behind, combined with the fact that he was nearly twice its level, meant that his one hit had shaved off more than half its health.

With a grunt of effort, he pulled his hammer back and swung for the fences. The metal head swept upward and impacted the mob's face, embedding itself deep into its stony skull and finishing the monster. Gold flashes went off as several of the dwarves behind the shield wall leveled up.

The shields came down, and Shari ran past Tex, trying to get a line of sight on the injured dwarves to heal them. Campbell, who had been in the center of the line, nodded to Tex. "Thank ye, big fella!"

Immediately, he turned to the others. "Everybody out! If'n ye ain't holdin' a shield, run to the plaza. The rest o' ya sorry excuses for troll-killers, with me!" He didn't wait to see that his orders were carried out. He knew they would be. Stomping up the ramp in ranks, twenty dwarves with shields and hammers began to chant a rhythmic war song. Tex, his blood pumping and his heart lifted by the chanting, followed along. He sent a message to Mace.

"The trolls in the residential wing are dealt with. We're on our way to the slave pen cavern." He paused, then said, *"You really need a better name for that place."*

The dwarves' pace was measured but still quick. It was only a minute or so before they exited the ground level tunnel to see more than a dozen rock trolls fighting in a chaotic melee with dwarves, orcs, and minotaurs. There were three centaurs near the entrance firing massive arrows at their foes, but they did little more than distract the rock trolls.

"SHIELD WALL!" Campbell commanded. His dwarves spread out across the width of the cavern entry, two rows of shields locked together. He thumped his shield once, and the entire group took a single step forward. Another thump, another step. The only one saying a word was Campbell, in the center of the line. "We be *DWARVES,* lads! Masters o' the underground! No puny trolls be a match fer us!"

At this, the dwarves in the line, as well as every single dwarf in the cavern, let out a battle roar. At the same time, they all stomped iron-shod boots upon the stone. The combined effect rattled the walls and shook loose stones from the ceiling.

Taking heart from the reinforcements, the orcs matched the war cry with a roar of their own, and the minotaurs joined in with bull-like howls as they redoubled their efforts.

Campbell and his dwarves advanced even as Tex spotted Mace near a hole in the floor. A massive stone-skinned hand reached up and pulled at the stone, followed a moment later by the head of a rock troll. Mace waited until the thing cleared the hole, then leapt upon its back and stabbed his enchanted dagger up under its arm. The giant monster screamed in a high-pitched wail one would never expect from a creature of such size. As its soul drained from its body, Mace planted his feet and pushed off, executing a backflip and landing once again near the hole to wait for his next victim.

The rock trolls, seeing a line of their ancient and hated enemy, the dwarves, advancing, went berserk. Almost as one, they abandoned the orcs and minotaurs they were fighting and turned to face the shield wall. The largest among them, the same one that had roused in their lair so far below, thumped his chest and roared. The others followed, and once again pebbles and dust rained from the ceiling.

The trolls charged across the wide space, and Campbell shouted, "Down!"

Each of the dwarves in the front line slammed their shields into the stone, the pointed edges on either side digging deep and anchoring the metal to the floor. Half a second later, the next row raised their shields and slammed them down atop the first. A practiced twist, and the shields locked together. Both rows leaned into the shields as the trolls got within a few steps.

"*HOLD!*" Campbell shouted from under the pile of metal.

"HA!" shouted the dwarves just as the largest of the behemoths smashed into the wall. There were groans of pain and grunts of effort, but the wall held. Furthermore, it began to glow as the impact activated some ancient dwarven magic. Behind him, Tex heard Layne playing a tune, and he felt a surge of strength.

The lead troll, easily fifteen feet tall and weighing a ton, was repelled by the shield wall. Confused, it began to pound at the shields with fists like wrecking balls. The remaining trolls impacted the wall one after the other, their charges stopped cold and chunks of their health bars removed by the impact. The glow of the shields grew brighter with each impact.

Lifting his hammer, Tex threw it at the largest of the beasts.

Rock Troll Champion
Level 60
Health: 48,420/55,000

The hammer flew over the top of the shield wall and struck the monster in the shoulder, knocking it off balance. With a roar of his own, Tex dove forward over the dwarves and rolled to his feet next to the troll. It was taller than him by several feet and at least twice his weight. A massive paw swiped at his head, and he managed to duck in time. Driving forward with his legs, he wrapped his arms around the troll's chest and drove it back.

As he had hoped, the troll tripped over one of its brethren, and he was able to drive it into the ground, using his shoulder and his weight to smash the troll's body as they landed. The troll barely noticed, its tough skin and even tougher bones taking no damage. The thing had the health pool of two tanks and natural armor that made it all but impossible to cut.

But Tex didn't plan to cut it. Using his superior agility, he disengaged from the prone monster and leapt backward to one side to retrieve his hammer. Turning just as the troll champion was getting to its knees, he lowered his weapon in an overhead smash that connected with the back of its head. The troll's arms went limp as its face impacted the floor. It wasn't dead, but a moment later it rolled onto its back, stunned.

Tex stepped forward, hammer raised over one shoulder ready to deliver the death blow when the monster recovered and kicked out with one leg. Its boulder of a foot smashed into Tex's knee, shattering bone and forcing it back so that his leg looked more like a dog leg, with the joint facing backward. Tex bellowed in pain and hit the ground, his hammer falling as he grabbed his knee with both hands.

The troll got to its feet and roared down at Tex, who was rolling back and forth, most of his focus on the pain. By the time he looked up, the brute was raising that same massive stone foot to stomp the life out of him.

Just as Tex started to roll to avoid the blow, a spearpoint burst forth from the monster's throat in a fountain of dark blood. A moment later it disappeared, and the creature grabbed its throat. The raised foot landed, but without any force behind it as the troll champion fell forward, already dying.

Behind it stood a female orc with eyes so red they nearly glowed. Brandishing the bloody spear, she slammed it into the troll's chest to make sure it was dead. She pulled the spear free and straightened up as a golden glow enveloped her and she leveled up. Tex lay there for a moment, staring. She was a solid seven feet tall, with a lean but muscular body. Dressed in leather pants and a short leather vest that didn't do a lot to cover her feminine bits, he found himself immediately attracted to her.

The cool tingling of a heal washed over him, and he grunted as his knee reformed itself into its proper position. Mion landed on his belly and opened her mouth, hitting him with a second, much more potent heal. Instantly, his health bar was back to 100%.

"Thank you, lil darlin'." Tex reached out one clawed finger and gently scratched her belly. She chirped cheerfully at him then took off to find others to heal. Getting to his feet, he turned to the orcess. "And thank *you* as well. You saved my life, pretty lady."

"My name is Agata, daughter of Ag'thar, chief of the Falling Water tribe, weakling." She growled at him.

Tex stepped forward and held out his hand. "They call me Tex, and I did not mean to offend. You truly saved me from having my head stomped. And I cannot help but admire your beauty."

She looked him up and down, a skeptical look on her face. "I will accept your thanks." She took his hand and shook it once, firmly. "There are more enemies to fight. Stop staring like a horny youngling and get to work!" she grumped at him before turning and charging toward another rock troll that was punishing an orc with a wooden shield.

Laughing, Tex retrieved his hammer and followed her orders, walking toward the nearest troll, which was engaging three dwarven warriors. "I think I'm in love."

Mace, still standing by the entry point the trolls had been using, didn't see any more coming. His last kill had been nearly a minute ago. Deciding that no more rock trolls were coming, he went into stealth mode and dashed behind a large specimen with a stone club that was going toe-to-toe with Brahm. The minotaur was using his enormous two-handed axe to deflect the club each time it swung toward him. But even its four-inch thick shaft wouldn't hold up to those devastating blows much longer.

Mace launched himself at the troll's back, wrapping his left arm around its neck even as he jammed his soul dagger into its ear hole up to the hilt.

The troll went stiff as its soul energy was drained. Brahm's eyes widened as he saw Mace appear. He managed to redirect the axe that was already swinging toward the troll's head, cutting off the lower half of its arm instead. Mace quickly let go of the dead troll, pushing off its back with his knees and landing lightly on the floor even as a rush of energy infused him and the dagger spoke to him.

MMMMOOOOOORE!

There were still half a dozen trolls standing, and Mace was inclined to give the dagger what it wanted. After his conversations with Krieger and Jervis, he felt more confident about remaining in control of the weapon. He chose a troll that seemed close to defeating a minotaur defender, running up behind it without even bothering to use his stealth ability. The single-minded creature was focused on the hard-pressed minotaur in front of it.

Mace used his left-hand dagger to stab the back of the troll's knee, causing the limb to buckle. When the monster went down on one knee, the minotaur roared in victory and lifted its axe, bringing it down in an overhand chop into the troll's shoulder. Mace finished it off with a thrust of his soul dagger through its ribs and into a lung. The weapon did its thing, and Mace felt another rush of energy.

Moving on, he saw Meg the dwarf hurl a throwing spear from behind the shield wall, the missile piercing the throat of the troll in front of her and passing right through to stick into the gut of another troll behind it. Almost quicker than Mace could follow, the dwarfess had a halberd in her hand and was using the nasty looking spike at the end to puncture the dying troll's face and push it back off the line. Yanking her spear back as it fell, she spun around and sank the bladed edge into the arm of a third troll just as it was taking hold of a shield. The troll's pained roar motivated her fellow dwarves, and it went down under a hail of hammer and axe blows.

An arrow whipped past Mace's face, planting itself into the face of a troll right behind him. Distracted by watching Meg do her dance, he hadn't heard the monster coming. A quick jab to the monster's upper thigh with his soul dagger sent its soul to whatever purgatory existed inside the blade. With the troll's death, Mace actually leveled up.

Level Up! You are now level 51!
You have received one attribute point.

Looking around, he saw no enemies left standing. Two trolls were still moving, struggling under piles of dwarves who were still chanting and happily pounding their enemies into a pulp.

Leroy ran past him, heading for those last two groups. "Wait! Don't damage their hearts or their skulls!" he was shouting at the top of his lungs. "I can use them for my alchemy!"

Mace chuckled as Leroy dove onto one of the piles, trying to get his comrades to preserve the ingredients. Meg looked on, shaking her head and making a disgusted face. "Good luck, kid," he mumbled.

Turning to Shari, he smiled to see her with her tiny dragon perched on her shoulder, the two of them casting heals around the room. As the last two trolls died, she and many of the others in the room were surrounded by the golden glow that indicated another level-up. He imagined everybody but Tex had gotten at least one level from this battle. And by the time they received the experience for the defense quest, some would have improved by several levels.

Speaking of which, Mace pulled up his UI. He ignored most of the notifications, focusing on the quest.

Quest Completed: Defend [unnamed] City!
You and your people have successfully eliminated the invading rock trolls.
Enemies killed: 30
Defenders lost: 2
Experience rewarded: 180,000xp. Additional rewards: Title: Defender of [unnamed] City!; Morale increase:+15%; 1,000 gold for City treasury; City points: 250.

Mace looked around sheepishly. It was a little embarrassing that the *unnamed* kept popping up in the notifications. He'd have to see about that ASAP. He called out to Campbell, who was looking grimly down the ramp tunnel as he listened to a report. The dwarf held up a hand asking Mace to wait a moment, his face falling as the dwarf continued to speak. When he'd heard the full report, he patted the dwarf on the shoulder and began to walk toward Mace.

Mace met him halfway. Only as he saw Campbell exhale and his shoulders slump did he remember that the quest notice had said two defenders were lost.

"You lost people?" Mace asked quietly.

"Aye, Majesty. Two o' me miners who were down in the tunnel. The whole crew were cut off and we could 'no get to 'em in time. They killed the three beasties that attacked them, but we lost two o' our best."

Mace looked around. "We have a couple of clerics and paladins here somewhere. They could resurrect the miners."

Campbell shook his head, a tear beginning to run down his dirt and blood-smeared cheek. "Nay, lad. Yer holy ones were kind enough ta use their gifts fer us already. When the trolls attacked us down on the lower level, we did no' hear 'em comin' soon enough. They killed a group o' wee ones, ours and the orcs. We already made the decision ta save the lil ones over the miners." Just as he finished speaking, Stonehand and Red appeared from down the ramp, each helping to carry the body of a dwarven miner.

Mace was crushed. It seemed he was losing people with every battle. He knew he couldn't ask Elysia to evolve every one of his citizens, but he felt guilty for not doing so. And while each of the clerics and paladins could cast resurrection spells, they could only do so once per day. "I'm sorry, Campbell. If there's anything I can do…"

"Thank ye, Majesties. We'll take it from here." Campbell bobbed his head and walked off. Mace heard a sob behind and turned to find Shari standing there. Tears streaked down her face and the look in her eyes nearly broke his heart.

"I… this was all my fault. I got our people killed," she whispered, falling into Mace's arms.

"What are you talking about?" Mace hugged her close, rubbing her back with one hand.

"Didn't you read the attack notification? They attacked because I drained our sewer line down that crevice, right on top of their heads!"

"You had no way to know they were there!" Mace tried to comfort her. "You didn't intend any harm. And no one will blame you. You've done nothing but try to improve all their lives."

She continued to cry into his shoulder for a good long while. He stood there, stroking her hair and mumbling that things would be okay. By the time she calmed down and began to wipe her eyes, Layne, Lila, Griff, Lisa, and Tex had joined them.

Lisa grabbed hold of Shari, causing her to start crying again as Lisa joined her. Lila looked on uncomfortably as Layne started to play a soothing tune on her loot. Wiping snot from her nose with her sleeve, Lisa said, "This damned sync business be messin' with me head. I'm not sure it's worth it."

No one argued. Layne and Lila hadn't actually heard what Lisa said due to the NPC block that prevented the citizens from hearing game-speak from players. And the players in the group were all feeling much the same. In their minds, they knew that the dead dwarves were just so many ones and zeros strung together to make a game character. But their hearts told them otherwise.

Finally, the group broke up, and Lila went to loot the trolls. Mace was momentarily surprised she'd waited so long. She left the chieftain to him, and when he touched its corpse, he received another flood of notifications.

Most of them were simple loot notifications, but two stood out. The first was a loot item that was bright purple.

Troll Chieftain's Head Totem
Item Quality: Unique. Quest Item

The second seemed to be tied to the first.

Quest Received: Rock 'n' Troll
Follow the path taken by the rock trolls back down to their lair. Mount the vanquished Chieftain's head at the entrance. Stand back.

Mace snorted at the ridiculous quest name, even as he shared it with the others. When he looked up, he saw a disappointed Leroy looking down at the now headless rock troll's corpse. "Sorry, kid. It's a quest item. Did you get the other skulls?"

Leroy nodded his head dejectedly. "The ones that didn't get crushed. And apparently, Ursus swallowed one whole. I got some hearts, too. And I have enough to level up my *Alchemy* several points, I think."

He paused for a moment, an odd look on his face. "I also received a great deal of rock troll meat."

Mace patted the dwarf on the back and left him to his business. As he walked away, he heard the young dwarf muttering, "Is rock troll meat even edible?"

He returned to Shari, who was talking softly with Layne and Lisa. When she saw Mace, she said, "I think I'm going to log out for a while." He just nodded his head, and she sat down where she was. A moment later, her avatar faded away.

Mace decided that the troll-head quest could wait for the next day. They'd hold a service for the dwarves that had been killed, then he'd form a party and head down into the bowels of the earth. Pulling up his UI, he found a marker on his map almost directly over his current position. But he knew the troll lair would be far underground.

Luckily, he was a drow. Underground was where he worked best.

Chapter 14

Shari came back online long enough to attend the memorial that evening. The dwarves believed in returning their bodies to the stone from whence they came. So cairns of stone were constructed over each body in the center of the large chamber where the battle happened. The dwarves all gathered in a circle, with the other races behind them. Campbell stood forward and began to sing in a deep reverberating voice.

> *From the stone, we kin are born*
> *Within the stone, we make our homes*
> *Iron ore pumps through our veins*
> *Until we're called back home again!*

The other dwarves joined in, their voices rising in perfect harmony. Their mournful and heartfelt words echoing off the stone and blending with it as if by magic.

> *Our hearts be broken, our brethren lost*
> *The mountain calls, they've paid the cost*
> *While we live on, within the stone*
> *To await the day they welcome us home.*

As they finished their song, the stones of the cairns began to glow within. The dwarves began to hum, a rhythmic but wordless chant. The stones glowed brighter, a pure white light that warmed the faces of those nearby. The light pulsed with the rhythm even as Campbell began to stomp one foot in time with the chant. The others joined three beats later, and their voices grew louder.

Mace felt the rhythm in his bones as he watched the glowing stones meld together, then sink into the floor. When Campbell raised his hands, the song continued for three more beats, then ceased altogether. The dwarves gave one final stomp, then each and everyone one of them took a knee. After a moment of silence, they all got back to their feet and left the cavern. Before following them, Mace glanced at the floor where he noticed two perfectly engraved war hammers with what looked like family crests etched into the stone.

"Beautiful," Shari whispered as she too inspected the grave markers. "That song, it… I felt it in my bones. It was a prayer, and a goodbye, and a song of hope, all at once."

Mace reached out and took her hand, and the two walked together out to the plaza where food and drink were already being served. As was customary, the dwarves were going to get very drunk that night. The king and queen joined in the wake for a few hours, raising their glasses to the lost dwarves, but Mace could tell Shari's heart wasn't in it.

When they'd stayed long enough to let the people know that their rulers shared in their sorrow, Mace took Shari into their home, and the two logged out.

Out of their pods, showered and dressed, the two of them ate a quiet meal of heated pasta and meatballs from a can and the last half of a jar of peaches. After cleanup, by silent agreement, they simply crawled into bed, and Mace held Shari till she fell asleep.

He lay awake for quite a while after she began to snore softly. There were too many things on his mind. He and Tex needed to work out the issues with the code and the hardware so that all of them could upload. He had a new kingdom to build, and citizens to protect, hopefully better than he had been. And from his trip into the pantry that evening, it was clear they were going to need to make another food run soon. If they could gather enough in the next trip, it might be that they wouldn't need to go out again. Though that much food wouldn't fit into Bertha. So they'd have to find another truck—preferably a big one. A smile twitched for a moment as an idea struck him. He fell asleep picturing the look on Shari's face when he told her.

*****

The next three days were spent in building mode. Shari focused on finishing the construction of the homes they needed above ground while

Griff and Lisa assisted the dwarves with their mining efforts and carving out homes from the stone of the dwarves' cavern. Stonehand worked with the mining crew that was still extending the ramp downward. Lila and Red worked with the orphans, spending as much time on discussions of honor and loyalty as they did on fighting techniques.

Mace went through their inventory, both his own and the city's, and worked on distributing items to those who needed them. Piles of metal ore went to the smithy, the more precious silver and gold loaned to a former slave with skill as a jeweler. Bits of armor and weapons were either given to specific fighters or consigned to the newly established armory for distribution later.

Mace spent some time with the farmers who had already plowed and planted their allotted parcel inside the walls, and who now wished to explore some potential croplands outside. Tex and Ursus joined them, ensuring no bands of roaming goblins or wolf packs bothered the farmers. Surprisingly, when they announced the trip, several orcs and a couple of the centaurs wanted to join them. All had an interest in farming the land.

One of those orcs was Agata—who seemed much more interested in studying Tex than the soils around the city perimeter. About a mile east of the city wall they came across a clearing in the forest with a small pond fed by a mere trickle of a waterfall. They found it contained a few species of edible fish, and the farmers agreed it would make a good source of irrigation water. When they moved on, Agata hung back, saying she was overdue for a bath. Then she asked that Tex remain and guard her back while she bathed. Tex shrugged and took a seat on the grassy bank, even as Ursus snorted and moved to join the others. It didn't escape Mace's notice that the two orcs didn't rejoin them until more than an hour later.

The whole time they were building, Mace itched to explore the rest of the portals. They knew where the waterfall portal led, as well as the one to the underground near Svartholm. And Tex had marked the one that led to another hub. That left nine portals to discover destinations for. More if they could gain control of another hub. But for now, he was content to try and establish strongholds or treaties for each of his eleven that took him to various territories.

On the fourth day, he gathered up Griff, Lisa, and their party of dwarves, to go fulfill the troll's lair quest. Shari wanted to join him, but Layne suggested that one of them should remain in the city and deal with the hundred little issues that arose each day. Shari reluctantly agreed, but she sent Mion with Mace to help with any heals. Layne asked to tag along in case there was an event worth documenting.

So it was that Mace lowered himself into the crevice that the trolls had emerged from with Minx on one shoulder and Mion on the other. Each of them had their tails wrapped around his neck to stabilize themselves as he climbed down the rock. Mion surprised him by casting a light globe spell, the bright light hovering ten feet below him and keeping that distance as he descended. The dwarves followed him down one by one, occasionally cursing as someone above them dislodged some dirt or gravel to fall on their heads.

Little more than a hundred feet down, Mace encountered a tunnel that branched off in two directions. He waited for the others to join him before asking, "Anybody sense anything that might tell us which way to go?"

Meg snorted. "This tunnel ain't level. It slopes downward in tha' direction. And upward in the other. I vote for down."

The others chuckled at her obvious observation. Mace resisted the urge to facepalm. "My guess is you are correct. Thank you, Meg." He turned and began to walk downslope, Mion's light globe moving along in front of him. The tunnel turned several times, and even made a complete loop at one point, always leading farther into the earth as they followed it. After an hour, Mace called a break while he checked his map. And he wanted to test something.

"Hobbes, can you hear me?"

"Of course, Majesty. This tunnel is still within the boundaries of your kingdom. And since the tunnel you are standing in is not a natural one, it counts as a structure."

Leroy spoke up next. "If this tunnel ain't natural, who made it?"

"I was not provided with an in-depth history of this land. This tunnel is much older than the mine you are now inhabiting. Based on the rough texture of the walls, I would eliminate dwarves. Their craftsmanship is much more refined. That leaves goblins, kobolds, or gnomes."

"Bah! Gnomes!" Meg snorted in disgust. "Beastly little things. Ears so big they look like wings and noses not much smaller. Grabby little hands, always stealing things as 'parts' for their ridiculous creations."

As if summoned, a voice echoed down the corridor. "Gnomes rule!" drifted to them even as Mace's ears picked up the sounds of many feet hitting the stone. A moment later, a group of armed and armored gnomes came into view. Mace saw them before the others, his drow vision being more accustomed to the dark. The gnome fighters had nearly reached the light globe's area of influence before the dwarves could make them out.

Instantly, all of the dwarves had weapons in hand and were forming up behind Griff and his shield. Mace whispered, "Easy, now. We don't know for sure that they're hostile." As soon as he said it, Layne began strumming a tune that seemed to radiate calm and peace.

The diminutive warriors continued toward the group, their tiny legs carrying them more quickly than Mace expected. Each gnome was fitted with piecemeal plate armor, no one bit matching any of the others. Yet despite the motley appearance, Mace didn't hear any rattling of armor or squeak of leather.

"Hold!" he called out as they drew near. He held up his left hand, palm out toward the gnomes. "What is your business here?"

The gnomes skidded to a halt, and now there was some crashing of metal as the ones behind bumped into those ahead. The lead gnome shouted up at him in a high-pitched voice, an angry look on its face. "This is *our* road! What is *your* business here?"

Griff, deciding to have a bit of fun, slammed his shield into the stone floor. "Yer speakin' ta King Mace of Styrke!" He grinned at Mace, who rolled his eyes at the title. "He has claimed these lands as his own. Ye be trespassin'!"

"What?" the gnome's mouth dropped open. "You can't just… these are our lands!" He turned his back on Mace as the group of gnomes huddled up. A dozen tiny voices mumbled and snarled as they rapidly discussed the situation. Mace heard snippets of, "Do drow taste good? Dwarves don't," and "I like the king's boots"—followed immediately by, "What would you do with them? Put both feet in one and hop around?"

After quite a bit of time, the huddle disbanded, and the leader turned back to Mace. "We have decided to let ya pass. For a price. Leave us all your weapons."

Mace chuckled at the ballsy little creature. The gnome's face tightened, his eyebrows bunching together as it frowned at him. "What's so funny?"

"Oh, nothing really. I came down here expecting to fight more rock trolls, and instead, I find armored munchkins with attitude."

"What's a munchkin?" one of the gnomes near the back demanded.

"Must be great warriors," another added.

"Munchkins rule!" the first voice shouted.

This got Griff and Lisa laughing behind Mace, who was trying to keep his composure.

"Listen, gnomes. My city up on the surface was attacked by rock trolls. We have a quest to travel to the entrance of their lair and mount the chieftain's head. Go back to wherever you came from and leave us to our mission."

The lead gnome spat on the floor. "Bah! As if *you* could kill the big boss troll!"

Mace quietly pulled the chieftain's head from his inventory and displayed it for the gnomes. Several of them screamed and cowered behind their companions. The lead gnome visibly gulped, taking an unintentional step back.

"Hey, uhh… we meant no offense." He held up his hands. Realizing he had a tiny sword in one of them, he quickly sheathed it, then put his hand back up. "We were out patrolling for trolls ourselves. They raid our town all the time. Every day. When they didn't show up for a few days, we got sent out to see what happened."

"Suicide mission!" one of them shouted, happily nodding his head. Several of the others smacked his helmet. Undeterred, he added, "Impress the ladies!"

The gnome next to him scolded, "What good does it do to impress the ladies if you're dead?"

The enthusiastic gnome opened his mouth, then paused. Mace could almost see the gears turning in his head. It occurred to him that, being a gnome, there might be actual gears in there. After a moment, when he'd thought it through, the gnome stomped a foot. "Heyyyy. This mission isn't as cool as it sounded."

"Shut up! We're heroes! We got the armor, and the magic scrolls, and-*"*

"*ALL OF YOU SHUT UP!"* the lead gnome shouted at them. "Fools. Don't speak about the scrolls! Why don't you just tell them where we keep all the treasure, too?"

Mace was beginning to like these little guys. And when one of them shouted back, "They'd never find the clockworks under the fountain! We hid it real good!" he couldn't help but smile, even as the lead gnome turned red and looked about to explode.

"Don't worry, gnomey gnomes. We have no interest in your treasure. I am simply making sure that all the lands within my kingdom are safe. You are free to go." Mace stepped to one side of the tunnel and motioned for the gnomes to pass. "And if you'd like to visit us on the surface, you are more than welcome."

The lead gnome looked at him with suspicion. He took a tentative step forward, then another. All of a sudden the gnomes behind him were pushing and shoving, propelling him forward. He cowered slightly as he got within reach of Mace, but he seemed to relax when the drow didn't slit his throat. A moment later, the group of small warriors was past them and continuing down the tunnel. A voice drifted back as they disappeared.

"Munchkins! Yeah!"

Meg snorted. "Told ye. Friggin' gnomes."

Mace shook his head and resumed their journey, heading farther along the tunnel and deeper into the earth. Eventually, the tunnel ended in an open space not quite large enough to be considered a cavern. More like a widening of the tunnel to either side. Near the right-hand wall, there was a scattering of rubble around a hole, as if a very large mole had dug its way up from below.

"That'd be where them rock trolls broke through," Jo observed.

Mace peered down into the hole. It was clear that Jo was correct. The rock inside looked as if it had been clawed out in large handfuls. The chute created by the trolls didn't extend far. Maybe ten feet down it opened into a wider space.

Reaching up to each shoulder to scratch the bellies of Mion and Minx, he said, "Hold tight, we're going down."

The descent was easy, with multiple hand and footholds created by the trolls. When he reached the end of the chute, he lowered himself down as far as he could, then let go. The fall was only a few feet, and he landed easily without a sound. As he looked around the space he was in, his darkvision showed him a roughly carved square room with an open door on one side.

"It's all clear," he whispered up into the hole in the ceiling. "Bit of a drop at the end." As he waited for the dwarves and Layne to work their way down, he activated his *Mage Sight* and surveyed the corridor outside the door. It only took him a moment to spot a glow in one wall, behind a series of holes arranged in roughly an 'X' pattern. A projectile trap. Most likely poison darts. Stepping out, he examined the floor carefully as he approached. His diligence paid off as he spotted a broken tile with a pressure plate beneath it.

Lifting the tile, he saw that the plate had been crushed, as had the workings underneath it. The sheer weight of the troll that had stepped on the trigger had crushed the mechanism, rendering it useless. And he suspected that even had the trap triggered, the darts would not have penetrated the rock trolls' skin.

He quickly disarmed the release for the darts in the wall, then gathered them and the entire trap mechanism to put in his inventory. He hoped to study them and maybe learn more about traps.

As he moved back into the room to wait for the rest of the dwarves, his *Mage Sight* revealed a faint purple glow on the far wall. Stepping around Griff, who'd just tumbled down from the hole in the ceiling and landed in a clanking, cursing pile of armor, he examined the wall more closely.

There was no seam, just the glow of some kind of sigil or rune. He put a hand to the wall and pressed, expecting to meet solid stone. But his hand simply passed through. As soon as it did, the illusion that had seemed like solid stone disappeared to reveal an alcove.

"Cool!" Lisa said. She'd been watching Mace with curiosity. "What's hidden in there?"

Mace had just been asking himself the same question. The alcove was about three feet high, wide, and deep. Inside was a small wooden chest with a silver latch that shone with the purple glow of epic goodness that he'd detected with his *Mage Sight*. He carefully checked the outer surfaces of the box for traps and found none. Reaching in, he took hold of the box and removed it.

Setting it on the floor, he motioned to Griff. "Since you've got all that armor and a shield, how 'bout you open it?"

Griff smiled at his new friend. "Chicken." He hunched down in front of the box, planting his shield in front of it and peering around to one side. With his right hand, he carefully reached out and put his hand on the latch.

Mace could feel Minx on his right shoulder, shifting from foot to foot in anticipation of the loot inside the chest. He was just reaching up to scratch her belly, when Griff touched the latch.

"AAAAaaargh!" the dwarf yelled, yanking his hand back and causing everyone in the room to jump in surprise. A moment later the dwarf fell on his back, holding his hand to his stomach as he rolled back and forth. Both Leroy and Mion cast panicked heals on Griff, though his health bar did not appear to have dropped.

After a moment, Mace's drow hearing picked up stifled laughter from the dwarf. He blew out the breath that he'd been holding and cursed softly. "Dammit, Griff!"

Griff finally let loose, guffawing as he rolled over and got to his knees. "Got ye! Ye should see all yer faces! 'Oh no! The box killed Griff!' Hahaha!"

Mion, who'd been worried for the dwarf just a moment earlier, opened her mouth and let out an annoyed screech before a small bolt of lightning struck Griff in the ass, the current spreading through his plate armor. This time when he fell and rolled, it wasn't from laughter.

The others were now laughing as Mace scratched Mion's tummy. "Well played, little one." She struck a pose and preened a bit, looking both offended and proud of herself at the same time. Lisa clapped in appreciation.

Recovered from the jolt, a chastened Griff returned to his position in front of the box. He reached around his shield and, without further ado, he opened the lid. Everyone except Mace held their breath, expecting an explosion or a mimic. When nothing exciting happened, Griff got up and stepped away.   With a slight bow, he said, "All yers, Majesty. Bgawk!" and flapped his arms like chicken wings.

Shaking his head and smiling, Mace approached the box and bent down to look inside. The purple glow was coming from a smaller box, narrow and long. Taking the box in hand, Mace opened it, and the others around him gasped or whistled in appreciation.

On a bed of red felt lay an ebony dagger. The entire thing from the tip of the blade to the butt end seemed to be made of a single piece of stone. The blade gleamed, almost as if it were wet, and faint oily hues of blue, red, and silver seemed to change as Mace tilted the dagger.

> *Duskshadow*
> *Item Quality: Legendary, Unique*
> *Attributes: +5 Agility, +5 Strength, +10 Stamina*
> *Enchanted: Shadow Blade*
> *This legendary one of a kind weapon, crafted by a duergar master smith in the fires of a shadow forge, has been imbued with the Shadow Blade ability. The enchantment was an experiment that cost the life of a valued apprentice during the forging. When the enchantment is activated, a blade of shadow energy extends by the length of the user's arm, turning the dagger into a sword.*

The box also contained a note written in a language Mace didn't recognize, with a sigil at the top that matched the one he'd seen on the wall. Folded inside the note was a large key made of the same black stone as the dagger.   The bottom of the box was lined with small sacks. As Mace touched them to add to his inventory, he found that they contained diamonds, emeralds, sapphires, one with ten mithril rings, and one with fifty obsidian arrowheads.

Going back to the note, Mace called out, "Hobbes? Are you still there? Can you read this note?"

"I am here, Majesty. And, yes, my memory contains knowledge of the language of the duergar, in which that note is written. The sigil at the top is a House sigil, one I do not recognize. The note reads:"

"We have abandoned our home. The rock trolls descended upon us in force, and though we have fought with honor, they have none. They slaughtered women and children with abandon, and they consumed their flesh as our warriors looked on in horror. There are too few of us left, so we flee this nightmare. If we survive the journey, we will seek new homes with our cousins at Svartholm.

I have left this dagger, Duskshadow, here in hopes that a duergar Champion will one day use it to reclaim our home from the filthy trolls. It is a formidable weapon in the hands of one who knows how to use it. There is a key that will unlock the gates, assuming the stupid trolls cannot change the locks. And the rest is a small example of the reward for your efforts. If you defeat the trolls and restore our home, seek me out in Svartholm, and you will be rewarded further.

May the dark gods be with you, Champion."

"The letter is signed with the same sigil, with the words "Chieftain of Steinhalle" under it," Hobbes finished. As he did so, each of the party members received a quest notification.

Quest Accepted: Steinhalle Dungeon, Part I
Remove all of the rock troll invaders from the village of Steinhalle.

Griff whistled. "Damn. O'course this Steinhalle place, that be where we're already headed, yah?"

Mace nodded. "That'd be my guess. I'm thinking it's a dungeon we'll need to clear. And it sounds like when we do, there will be quite a bit of loot for each of you." The others flashed wide smiles at his words. "Since this was left in the room, I'll bet the entrance is down the hall. I've already found one trap, so let's take it slow."

Mace led the way with his *Mage Sight* active. Twice as they traveled the winding tunnel he thought he spotted mundane traps that his magical vision didn't pick up on. Each time he halted the group and bent to examine the spot. The first time turned out to be a false alarm. The second was a simple spike trap. One steps on a spot and a lever is pressed, shifting a trigger that released several spikes to rise up through holes in the floor. He didn't take the time to dismantle and remove the simple trap, simply disabling it and moving on.

Ten minutes later, they reached the gates. The group emerged from the tunnel into a wider cavern with a duergar-built wall across it maybe fifty feet from the tunnel exit. Set into the wall were two iron gates that were slightly bent and looking like they'd seen better days. Mace and the others surveyed the open space and the walls, but there was no sign of any rock trolls.

"Right, then." Meg stomped forward a few steps. "There be spikes on the front o' them doors, there. I be thinkin' that's where ye need ta mount the big boss troll's head." She pointed at the gates.

Mace took a deep breath and pulled the severed head from his ring. Walking slowly across the gap between the tunnel and the gates, he kept a careful watch for any movement along the walls. The others followed behind him weapons in hand and just as watchful.

When Mace reached the door, he observed a slight blueish glow on one of the spikes. "Good enough for me," he mumbled as he turned the head so that it faced him, then jammed the back of the skull onto the spike. He and the others all took a step back as the lifeless head wailed so loudly it echoed across the chamber.

Everyone's vision filled with quest completion notifications flashing across their UI's. At the same time, a swirling purple and grey portal appeared between the partly-open doors. The unmistakable entry to a dungeon.

Looking around, Mace pointed to Lisa, who was among the lowest level in Griff's group. "Just in case this is instanced by level, Lisa should go through first. If I go, all the trolls inside might be level 50."

Lisa nodded, and she stepped toward the opening, disappearing as soon as her front foot broke the plane. Griff followed immediately behind, and the others stepped through one by one. Mace brought up the rear.

There wasn't the usual disorientation this time, as the former duergar village known as Steinhalle was now the rock troll's lair. So rather than be teleported from an above-ground entrance into a distant underground dungeon, for example, they simply stepped through the gates into the open area of the former village.

Griff was standing out in front of the group, shield raised and searching the area. Lisa and Meg were right behind him, swords and halberd at the ready. Leroy had a mana potion in one hand and his staff in the other, and Layne was already strumming a song that provided a stamina and health regen buff. Mace walked up even with Griff, not seeing any enemies.

"No movement o' any kind," Griff reported, his military background showing. "Plenty o' ambush points, though. They could be hidin' in every buildin' just waitin' fer us to pass."

"Wait here, two minutes." Mace went into stealth mode and moved toward the nearest building. Like all the others in sight, this one was built low, with the roof about eight feet high. As he got closer, he saw that it wasn't built in the conventional way, but instead, it was carved directly from the stone. The walls flowed seamlessly into the floor of the cavern.

Entering the first doorway, he saw that the interior was empty except for broken pieces of furniture, rags, and other debris scattered around the floor. A doorway with a smashed wooden door hanging loosely by one hinge led to a stairway going down into a lower level. Mace descended quickly, assuming the clumsy trolls would have set off any traps before him. The lower level was one large room with what looked like a workshop in one corner, a kitchen, and a bathroom at the opposite end. The center area might once have held furniture, but it was now nothing but a mess of splinters and fragments.

Hurrying back upstairs, Mace moved to the next building, and then the next. Finding nothing in any of the three, he dropped his stealth and moved back to Griff and the others. "First three buildings clear. And I haven't heard anything since we got here."

Layne offered, "You did kill a few dozen of them when they attacked. It may be that all but the very young and their caretakers are already dead."

Mace felt a twinge of guilt at her words. He hadn't thought of the trolls as mundane family units. To him, they'd just been attacking mobs to be eliminated for experience and loot. The thought of a bunch of tiny troll orphans bothered him for a moment.

Shaking his head, he replied, "I hope you're right. Let's go."

The group moved forward, bypassing the three buildings Mace had already cleared. They worked their way down the only visible street, checking the buildings on each side one at a time. Each one was the same—empty and filled with piles of debris.

Finally, there was one last building at the end of the road. This one was wide and tall, the only two-story building around. Some type of town hall, or possibly the chieftain's residence. They quickly cleared the first floor, a living/seating area, large dining room, and kitchen. Mace led them up the stairs to a hall that stretched the length of the building. Each room was a suite with its own bathroom, bedroom, and sitting area.

Once again they cleared the rooms one by one, the party getting lax as room after room offered nothing interesting. As they cleared the last one, Layne called out in a loud whisper from the hallway, "Mace! Over here." When Mace and others joined her, she pointed through a room they'd already cleared at the window.

"Look outside. I think we found our trolls."

The window was on the back side of the building, and it overlooked a wide stone expanse that may have at one time held a garden. Now it was stripped bare and filled with what could only be described as nests. Dozens of piles of wood, cloth, stone, and no small number of bones, were arranged into sort of bowl-shaped nests. They clustered here and there, some set apart by themselves, covering the floor of the cavern all the way out to a ledge that extended out partway across, then dropped off into the wide crevice to which Shari had routed their plumbing drains.

Most of the nests sat empty. But in about ten of them sat what Mace assumed were female rock trolls with smaller trolls scattered around them from infant-sized to a few that were maybe a quarter the size of their mothers.

"Right. Down we go. We'll try and take the lil buggers one nest at a time." Meg's voice broke the silence. As an NPC, she had no qualms about killing baby trolls that would only grow up to be monster trolls. Especially not after losing two of her fellow dwarves to these same trolls only days ago.

She led the way back down the stairs and out the door, circling around the building and out toward the first of the nests. As they passed by, Leroy let out an excited-sounding squeak and reached inside the nest. His hands came back full of some slimy substance that caused Meg to wrinkle her nose. Leroy deposited whatever it was into his inventory, grinning like a kid with a new toy. Meg wagged a finger at him, and his enthusiasm dropped considerably.

They wound their way through the empty nests, Leroy falling behind as he examined the contents of each one, seizing items he thought were interesting. When they were within about fifty feet of the first occupied nest, Griff stepped to the front.

"One o' ye wanna throw somethin' at the momma troll 'n' get her attention?"

Lisa obliged, stowing her swords and producing a crossbow. "From what I saw the other day, this won't do much more than tickle her," the dwarfess warned. She raised the crossbow, loaded a quarrel, took aim and fired.

Mace and the others watched the bolt speed toward the mother troll, striking her in the side of her head as she slept. The bolt impacted with a *thwak!* and bounced off. She sputtered awake, growling and swinging her head left and right, seeking the source of the attack. Spotting Lisa and the group, she uncurled her body and rose to her full nine feet, growling as she advanced on them.

For a moment, Mace was worried that the noise would aggro the other adult trolls in the area. But they ignored the growls and either continued to slumber or look after their offspring.

He allowed the troll to charge forward as Griff prepared to take aggro.

Rock Troll Breeder
Level 40
Health: 17,999/18,000

Griff slammed his hammer against his shield, then spat toward the oncoming troll. She was easily three times his size and probably ten times his weight. He raised his shield high and slammed it down, the bottom edge biting into the stone at his feet. Leaning forward, he prepared for the impact. Meg lowered her halberd so that the shaft rested atop the shield, ready to impale the troll on impact. She braced herself much as Griff did.

Jo waited patiently for Griff to get a solid hold on the monster's attention. If she hit it with fireballs now, it might bypass the tank and charge her instead. Mace could see the impatience in her body language, and he was impressed by how much Griff's dwarves had grown as a team.

Leroy called out, "Try not to damage its heart, please!" as the troll took her final few steps. Griff leaned a bit farther forward, grinding his iron boots into the stone for better purchase in anticipation of being hit by the oncoming freight train.

But the troll, rather than simply barreling into the tank, straightened to her full height and planted her left foot. Using her momentum, she swung her massive right foot forward and kicked Griff's shield. There was a resounding clang as stone impacted metal, and a cry of pain came from Griff as he was launched backward like a goal shot.

Immediately, Leroy and Minx were casting heals on the flying dwarf, even as Jo let loose a massive fireball from nearly point-blank range into the troll's face. While she was distracted, Mace moved behind her and stabbed his soul dagger into her kidney, which was at face height for him. Lisa stepped in, hacking at the troll's knee with both of her swords as she growled in fury.

The troll breeder wailed in pain and dropped to her knees as the dagger drained her soul energy. It spoke quietly in Mace's head, the lower level meal not pleasing it at all.

"Mooooooore!"

Mace took a chance that he might be able to communicate back, and he thought at the weapon with as much focus as he could muster. *"More is coming. Patience."*

The weapon seemed to understand. Or, at least, it quieted as if it understood. Mace looked to see the troll facedown on the stone and Leroy bending to loot it. Turning to look behind him, he was happy to find that they hadn't pulled any additional beasts.

Griff, who had flown quite a distance before landing and rolling even farther, was back on his feet with a full health bar. Mion was riding atop his helm, her neck bent down so that she could stare into his eyes as if confirming to herself that his brain wasn't rattled. He smiled at the little dragon, then blew her a kiss, causing her to snort and lift her head back up, shaking it a few times.

"I think Mion is sayin' ye've got bad breath." Lisa giggled, her smile wide. "I'm not surprised since that troll kicked ya so hard yer arse mighta flown up through yer mouth."

The others held back laughter as Griff flexed a few muscles, stretching his back and shoulders. "Ha! She really did, didn't she? And damn, it hurt. Felt like getting hit by a damned truck! I hope I can replay this later. I'd like to see the look on me face!" He grinned back at Lisa.

Mace moved next to them. "We're going to need to figure a different way. Griff can't take that kind of punishment every time we fight one of them."

Jo volunteered, "The trolls we fought in the last dungeon caught fire and exploded after I hit them with fireballs. This troll just shrugged it off."

Meg added, "Me halberd blade barely penetrated. Their skin be damned tough."

Mace thought about it for a moment. All of the trolls he could see were lower level than him. He could stealth his way around and kill the breeders one by one, feeding his dagger at the same time. But he wanted to find a way to use the group dynamic. Part of their reason for being here was to make the dwarves better as well as stronger.

"Jo… the troll was resistant to your fire but not immune. Look at her face." The breeder's facial skin was scorched, and her eyes broiled in their sockets. When Jo looked back up at him, Mace pointed to the nearest occupied nest. "There appears to be a good amount of combustible material in those nests. What if Griff were to charge the next one and stun it while it was still in its nest. You can light it on fire. Lisa can hit it in the face with crossbows to keep it stunned for a few extra seconds, and Meg can use her long halberd to keep pushing it back into the nest. If necessary, maybe Mion could stun it like she did Griff?"

Jo's eyes lit up along with the others in the group. Layne caught Mace's eye and gave him a small nod, a knowing look in her eyes.

They readied themselves and approached the next nest. It was a lone breeder, much like the first. Griff readied himself just out of range of the monster and looked back at Mace.

Mace took a quick survey of the group, and seeing everyone ready, he hurled his left-hand dagger at the sleeping breeder as hard as he could. Its sharp point barely bit into the creature's neck when it struck, causing a nick that produced a few droplets of blood.

As the breeder roared and rose to her feet and began to step toward Mace, Griff activated his *Shield Bash* ability and rocketed forward. His momentum made up for his lack of size, and the game mechanics awarded him a stun for using the ability. Immediately, Jo cast fire into the nest as Griff took two steps back, waiting to slam into the breeder again if necessary.

The nest quickly blazed into an inferno, surrounding the breeder in flame. Mace noticed a few sparks at her neck where his dagger had struck.

"Meg! Quickly! Stab her in the neck!"

Meg did as he ordered, charging forward at the stunned monster and jamming her halberd's sharp end spike very near where Mace's dagger had hit. The spike sunk in a solid two inches, then stopped. Meg ripped it free and backed up.

A stream of blood leaked from the breeder troll's wound and immediately caught fire with a burst of flame. It was as if a fuse had been lit. The fire followed the stream back into the wound, and the troll screamed as fire began to spread through her veins. The group watched her flail around, then drop and squirm in agony as she burned from the inside out.

A high-pitched whistle began to sound, and Griff yelled, "Shit! She's gonna blow! Run!" and he raised his shield as he backed away as quickly as he could. The others took off, diving behind the nearest nest, which was the only cover available.

Mace got behind Griff and called out, "Praesidio!" casting a shield in front of Griff. A moment later the troll exploded, the massive body bursting into thousands of flaming pieces. It was as if someone had set off a grenade. Nests within thirty yards in every direction caught fire after flaming troll bits landed on them. In those that were occupied, the trolls screamed in fear and retreated. Two ran directly toward Griff and Mace. A full-grown breeder and a youngling about the size of a dwarf.

"Griff! Get ready to knock the big one into a nest, then tank the smaller one!" Mace didn't wait for confirmation. He dashed forward, sliding between the legs of the larger one as it lumbered forward. On his way past, he sliced into the back of its ankle with his soul blade. The severed muscles combined with the soul-ripping pain of the wound made the troll stumble.

Griff, seeing his chance, activated his *Shield Rush* and slammed into the breeder, knocking her backward into a burning nest. She immediately got to her feet, but the damage was done. The blood from her ankle sizzled and ignited. She screamed and dashed out of the nest, running back the way she'd come. Straight toward the other retreating trolls that were now trapped between burning nests and the edge of the ledge.

Feeling bad about it, but knowing it needed to be done, Mace charged after the troll. Pulling throwing knives from his inventory, he hurled them at the youngest trolls, the ones that had been gathered into the arms of panicked breeders or clung to their elders in fear. He aimed each knife for a vulnerable point. An eye, a neck, the back of a knee. The skin of the young ones was much softer than the adults, and soon most of the younglings were bleeding.

Mace turned to check on Griff and the others. The dwarf tank was keeping the attention of the small troll while Meg and Lisa stabbed and cut it. Its health bar was already down to half, and Mace decided to let them finish it.

Stopping well back from the ledge, he called out, "Ventus!" and sent a gust of wind forward across the several nests between himself and the cowering trolls. A second later, the fleeing breeder reached her fellow trolls and collapsed in pain. The whistle began, and Mace cast another shield. But this time he cast it right behind the burning breeder so that it would reflect the force of her explosion back at the others.

Seconds later, he watched as the burning breeder exploded. Nearly half the remaining trolls, young and old, were swept off the ledge by the blast. The others were liberally coated in flaming troll innards.

Immediately, the remaining younglings, who were all bleeding thanks to Mace, caught fire as well. Their smaller bodies burned much more quickly, and they exploded one right after the other less than ten seconds later.

The multiple explosions devastated the adult breeders. Two more were thrown off the ledge, while those who were holding the infants had limbs blown off and large sections of their torsos. They too began to scream and burn, and Mace turned to walk back to his group. He barely winced when the last of them exploded.

The group had finished off the troll, and Leroy had already looted it. He grumped under his breath as he trotted past Mace, hoping to find some intact hearts to loot. Mace didn't envy him the search.

Just as he was about to speak to the others, their eyes all went blank as quest completion notifications flashed in front of them. The crevice had been deep indeed, and the last of the trolls to go over the edge had finally struck the bottom and died. Mace took a moment to read his UI.

First Kill!

Congratulations! You are the first to complete the Steinhalle Dungeon!
Each member of your party will receive 1,000 gold and one item of epic or better quality. Your reputation with the duergar of Steinhalle has improved to Respected. You have been awarded 250,000 experience points!

Quest Completed: Steinhalle Dungeon Part I
You have cleared the troll invaders from the village.
Reward: 80,000 experience points.

Quest Accepted: Steinhalle Dungeon Part II

Seek out the duergar chieftain in Svartholm and assist him in returning his people to Steinhalle. Reward: Variable, depending on number of duergar returned safely.

A large chest appeared, rising from the stone near the main structure even as fireworks went off and trumpets bellowed out the completion of a first kill. This was a rare event in Elysia, as most quest lines and dungeons had been completed by other players in the first year or two of the game's existence. Mace wasn't sure if this dungeon was still unconquered because not many players chose to start in the drow city or because Elysia had created it just for them out of a standard quest area.

The group waited impatiently as Leroy dug through the scattered troll bits and the remaining nests. Layne sat on a clean area and began to play a relaxing regeneration tune as Griff examined the huge dent in his shield from when the troll had punted him. Minx and Mion capered about on the floor in front of Layne, looking almost like they were dancing to her music. Mace took the time to check his map, to see where they were in relation to Svartholm. There were big blank areas between Steinhalle and Svartholm, but he thought it was no more than a day's march.

He could return his group to the portal room and get to Svartholm more quickly that way, but the quest update made it pretty clear that they'd have to escort a group of duergar back to their home. And he didn't want to expose the existence of the portals to strangers.

When Leroy rejoined them, they eagerly raided the loot chest. Lisa went first, receiving an epic matched pair of short swords with bonuses of +10 to Strength on one, and +10 to Stamina on the other. Griff received plate bracers that each carried +10 to Strength and were part of a legendary set that would offer huge bonuses when complete.

Jo received a pair of fine leather boots that increased her mana regeneration by 15%, added +10 to Intellect, and +5 to Wisdom. For Leroy, there was a white wooden staff with a sapphire crystal at the top that offered 5% bonus healing and +10 Intellect. Meg received an epic mithril chain mail shirt with long sleeves that offered 50% damage reduction from blunt weapons and piercing weapons, as well as +15 to strength and +5 to agility.

Layne went next, receiving a beautiful soft white leather vest with +10 Intellect and +15 Charisma. Mace went last, reaching out to touch the chest. He chuckled when the loot notices popped up. He had received a pair of black leather bracers with a combined +10 agility and +10 strength. What made him smile was two small collars that he received as well. One for Minx that was black leather with little silver inlays that provided +10 agility, not that the little thief needed it. And one for Mion that was white leather with tiny diamond studs and a bonus of +10 Intellect.

He took a moment to fasten the collar on Minx as Layne did the same for Mion. Both little ladies purred and preened as they showed off their new prizes. Lisa clapped her hands and praised their beauty, and even Meg smiled at them. When the chest didn't disappear, he touched it again. One last message popped up

Mithril Interdimensional Storage Chest

This chest is available to you as ruler of a kingdom. It can be placed within a city vault and used for secure storage. Only the ruler(s) of a kingdom and their official designated trustees may open this chest and remove or deposit items. If the city is captured while the chest remains in the vault, then the newly recognized rulers will become the sole owners of the chest and its contents. Storage Capacity: 500 slots. Maximum 100 items per slot.

Mace happily accepted the chest into his inventory. Five hundred slots of thief-proof storage? Hell yes! He was already imagining filling it with hundreds of kegs of spirits, fine bottles of wine for Shari, their most valuable armor and weapons, and items that could be used to rebuild a city after an invasion. His inner hoarder was doing some kind of odd Irish Riverdance thing. If he put a hundred of something in every one of the five hundred slots…

He shook his head as he noticed the others watching him expectantly. It was time to head back. As they started the long march, Mace found himself fervently wishing for some kind of hearthstone like he'd had in so many of the MMO's he'd played. One could use it to transport oneself directly back to their home base rather than waste hours walking.

Maybe as a king, he could commission teleport scrolls that led him home or something similar? Maybe even working hearthstones! One for every citizen. He'd need to raise up a master enchanter among his people. Or be prepared to hire one. With a sigh, he proceeded back through the village

Chapter 15

The return trip took longer, as Mace had to levitate each of the dwarves up into the holes in the ceilings so they could climb back up. And while climbing up the long chute that led to the former slave cage cavern at the surface level, Leroy lost his grip and tumbled down, taking all but Lisa and Griff with him. Mion healed all the bumps and bruises before Mace once again levitated them back up. This time he waited for each of them to call down that the chute was clear before he sent the next one up. As a result, it was late in the day before they returned to the city plaza.

Shari was waiting for him at her usual table in front of their residence. A few of the townsfolk were speaking with her about city building issues or work assignments, but they bobbed their heads and retreated when he approached.

"No, please. Finish your conversations." He motioned them forward, taking a seat on the bench next to Shari. "Whatever it is you need assistance with, we are here to help."

He crossed his hands and set them on the table, giving them his best smile. Which, on his drow face, was a little intimidating even to those who knew he was friendly. The citizens approached, and Shari listened to their requests. The first asked to switch from general labor detail to the kitchen at the inn, expressing an interest in learning to cook. Two more former slaves asked for a small loan and passage to Port Bjurstrom to purchase merchandise for a shop they wished to open together. Mace handled that one, handing them two hundred gold and borrowing pen and paper from Shari to write a quick note to Admiral Jorin.

"Come and see me before you leave to head for the docks. I may have some messages or other business I'd like you to take care of for me," he instructed as he handed them the note.

The last of the requests surprised Mace. He suspected Elysia's hand once again. It was an elder man from Graf. Not a formal slave, but one of those who'd taken the oath in hopes of a better life in a new land.

"M'lady, m'lord… I am Tommaso. In my youth, I was an apprentice to an enchanter in my homeland. He was a good man and wise. He spent months teaching me the basics of the craft, until I was able to perform some small enchantments of my own. Minor bonuses of Strength or Stamina to weapons, a fire spell that could be imbued into a weapon or gem. But I was full of pride and a yearning for adventure, and I left to explore the world before I completed my training." The man sighed, a look of regret on his face. "I sailed aboard ships, traveled with merchant caravans, and sometimes walked the roads alone. Always paying my way with the minor enchantments I had learned."

When he paused again and looked down at his hands, Shari coaxed him. "And now you'd like to take up the profession again? I don't think we have a master enchanter here for you to apprentice with." She looked at Mace, then began to search her notebook.

Tommaso squirmed a bit in his seat, and his hands began to fidget. "My queen, I have heard… rumors. That your majesties might have access to certain books that contain the wisdom to make one a master in their craft?"

Mace's eyes widened. He hadn't expected Brahm or any of the others to speak about the books he'd handed out. He mentally reviewed their conversations, trying to remember if he'd specifically told them to keep the training books secret. Deciding that it didn't matter, he focused on the apprentice enchanter.

"Those books are rare and quite valuable. Why should we invest such a resource in you? You've told us that you have a habit of wandering. What is to stop you from learning all you can, then deserting us to sell your services elsewhere?"

Tommaso looked offended, but he took a deep breath to calm himself before replying. "I have taken an oath, Majesty. And I would be willing to make whatever additional contract you would like in return for the knowledge. I would agree to stay here in this city, or another of your choosing, and practice my trade for... shall we say ten years? I will enchant items for the crown for free, as long as you provide the necessary materials. Otherwise, I will sell my enchantments to other citizens and visitors at a reasonable rate, in order to feed and shelter myself. And to earn money for more training and better materials."

When Mace glanced at Shari, she was already smiling at him. He rolled his eyes, his plan to further interrogate Tommaso rendered moot. She clearly intended to support the man. And Mace did have need of an enchanter. Still, he couldn't resist one more question.

"In your training as a youth. Did you learn how to create communication rings?"

Tommaso grimaced. "My training did not include that spell, Majesty. But should I be able to learn it, I would happily create as many as you need."

At least he was honest. When Shari poked him in the leg under the table, he gave up. "I will check and see if we have a training manual for enchanters. I make no guarantee, Tommaso. I don't recall seeing one during my last search, but I will look for one, nonetheless. And we will definitely require the contract you described." He looked over and smiled at Shari, who was scribbling away on a parchment. "It seems my queen is already drafting it."

The man bobbed his head and rose from the bench, thanking them both. As he turned away, Mace saw that he was the last of the petitioners for the moment. He quickly updated Shari on the quests completed and new quests received. He then described the expected time frame to reach Svartholm and escort the duergar back to Steinhalle.

They were just discussing when Mace and the others should set out on the expedition when both got a voice message from Peabody.

"Mace, Admin Shari, I must inform you that my cameras have detected movement outside the facility."

"Shit!" Mace quickly looked at the clock on his UI. The sun would be setting about now in the real world. "We're logging off now, Peabody. Please track the movement and put it up on the main monitor."

At the same time, Shari was sending a message to Griff, Lisa, and Tex. The two of them logged out where they sat and extricated themselves as quickly as possible from their pods. Not bothering to shower, they just threw on whatever clothes were nearby and ran for the security office.

Up on the big monitor was a view of the street across the small park in front of the building. The same street where Mace had witnessed three monsters fight not so long ago, and where Shari had shot one of them. This time, though, the camera was moving. It slowly panned across the park as it followed a figure walking casually down the sidewalk. It was difficult to make out as the fading light wasn't bright enough to illuminate it, and it wasn't yet dark enough for the night vision cameras to have kicked in.

"It… is it a human?" Shari asked. Her face scrunched up as she squinted her eyes and leaned in closer to the monitor. "I mean… like a still living human?"

Mace wasn't sure either. "I can't tell. It's walking pretty normally, like totally unafraid. I would think a live person would be ducking behind cars or at least looking around a lot more."

"Peabody, can you zoom in, please?" Shari asked. The AI obliged without answering. The field of vision narrowed as the focused target expanded on the screen. It was still dark, but both Mace and Shari were encouraged by the lack of any glowing neon blue in sight. Most of the creatures had cuts or lesions that bled to some degree, and the bright-colored blood stood out.

It continued to walk, not seeming to be in a rush, which made the hairs on the back of Mace's neck tingle. Humans didn't stroll around outside anymore. Not sane ones, anyway. "I don't like this. Maybe you should get your rifle. We can go up on the roof like before."

Shari shook her head, still squinting at the monitor. "By the time we geared up and got up there, it'd be out of range or behind a building. Besides, if it's a living human, there's something wrong with them." She reflected Mace's own thoughts. "I don't want to tip them off that we're here."

They watched in silence as whoever or whatever it was continued on its journey. It reached the end of the block and crossed the street, never turning its head to check for danger on the cross street. The camera angle changed as Peabody switched to a different camera on that side of the building. They watched as it moved past the spot where Mace and Shari had killed the gorilla creature. Mace mumbled, "The body's gone. I wonder if it was another creature, or just bugs and stuff."

Just as he finished speaking, the walker paused and turned back. It took a few steps towards the dark stain in the road where the creature had burned, then bent down and appeared to be sniffing. A moment later, it reached out a hand and touched the pavement. Mace shuddered and Shari gasped, placing both hands over her mouth.

"Guess that answers that question," Mace whispered, subconsciously acting as if he were out there. "No living human would touch that. It has to be a contaminated creature."

Shari, her mind whirling partly in horror, partly in her natural analytical survival mode, replied, "Has to be a relatively new one. It's still normal human size, so it can't have eaten much. I think maybe it's a survivor that just recently got turned." Her voice caught slightly as emotion nearly overwhelmed her. "I wonder how many others are still out there?"

Mace's heart thumped, his already quickened pulse throbbing. The thought of finding other survivors was both exciting and terrifying. He didn't really want to share his cozy home with anyone but Shari. At the same time, he felt duty bound to help other survivors.

"We could… try the radio? We haven't used it in weeks. Maybe somebody will answer?"

Shari nodded and moved over to the base unit on a side desk and turned on the power switch. Picking up the microphone, she keyed the button on the side. "Hello? Is anyone out there?" They both watched the monitor, fully expecting the walker to turn around. But there was no change – it had straightened up and turned to continue up the block, away from them.

"Hello? Any survivors out there? Can you hear me?"

When there was no answer after a full minute, Mace reached over and adjusted the frequency, nodding for her to try again. They spent an hour like this, cycling through different frequencies and calling out. Each time they called, they waited a minute or so for an answer.

Finally setting the microphone down, Shari sighed. Mace returned the radio to the default frequency, but he didn't shut it off. "Peabody, can you monitor this radio, let us know if you hear anything other than static? And record whatever you hear?"

"Of course, Mace. The movement has passed outside my camera's effective range. I will alert you if I detect any further movement."

Mace put his arms around Shari, hugging her from behind. With his chin on her shoulder, he kissed her cheek gently and said, "I was thinking we need to go out for more food soon. Maybe we should do it first thing in the morning. If that thing's one of those creatures now, better to go out there while it's still small and easier to kill."

Shari nodded, leaning back against him and entwining her fingers in his. "Yeah. I won't sleep much knowing it's walking around so close. Maybe we can lure it away or kill it. But let's try to pull it far from here. I think the reason we keep seeing these things close is that we keep leaving bodies out there to attract more of them."

Mace just squeezed harder, no words needed to confirm his agreement. "Let's get something to eat. Peabody, please send a message to Griff, Lisa, and Tex. Tell them we're okay and making a food run in the morning."

"Certainly, Mace."

They walked hand in hand to the kitchen, each of them lost in their own thoughts. Mace decided to make some pancakes, hoping to lighten the mood a little bit. When there was a significant stack, he plated them and brought them to Shari. A moment later, he retrieved the syrup, wiggling the bottle at her and waggling his eyebrows at the same time. "I've goooot syrup!"

She snorted at him, reaching to take the bottle from him. "Easy there, killer. I'm hungry." She poured a liberal dose of the delicious amber liquid on her stack of pancakes and slid the bottle across the counter to him. Ignoring the fake pouty lip he was throwing her direction, she dug into the pancakes with gusto.

"Ever notice that having your life threatened makes you hungry?" she asked around a large mouthful.

Mace passed up the easy quip and nodded his head. "Some kind of biological imperative maybe? Cheat death and feed to ensure strength to survive the next challenge?" A thought struck him and he laughed. "Maybe that's why we like loot so much? It feeds that little part of our lizard brain? We defeat a deadly enemy and get something to make us better for the next fight?"

Shari grinned at him, swallowing before she spoke. "Or maybe we're all just like Minx and can't resist the shiny things."

They finished their meal in just a few minutes, both of them distracted by thoughts of going outside in the morning. After cleaning up, Shari took Mace by the hand. "Leave the syrup, dork," she scolded as he made an exaggerated reach for it. She led him back to her room and pushed him onto the bed. Diving on top of him, she buried her face in his neck and wrapped herself around him. "Hold me," she whispered as she squeezed him tight.

Mace obliged, wrapping his arms tightly around her. He felt a little wetness on his neck and a little hitch in her breathing as she cried. He realized it had been a tough few days for her. The incident Tex had endured had affected Shari as well. Her empathy for him, the realization that she had caused the rock troll attack, and now this new threat outside their home, were all pressing down on her. He rocked her gently back and forth until she began to snore softly.

His own adrenaline rush from earlier wore off as he calmed Shari. Though he tried to focus on planning their trip outside, it wasn't long before he drifted off as well.

*****

Morning came more quickly than either of them liked. Mace woke first, checking the clock on the desk as soon as his sleep-blurred vision cleared. It was 7:00 am and the sun would be up already. Shari was still atop him, her face buried in his chest and her arms and legs splayed like a seal sunning itself on a beach. Mace was tempted to just let her sleep, and even more tempted to attack her sides and tickle her awake.

Smiling to himself, he chose to forego the tickling and just nudge her awake. It took several nudges, each one stronger than the last, before she opened her eyes.

"No. Sleepytime. Body pillow holds still, doesn't move." She smacked her lips a few times, adjusted her body a bit, and closed her eyes again.

Regretting it before the words were even all the way out of his mouth, he said, "Come on, up we go. Gotta make a food run."

Her eyes flew open, and the peaceful look on her face dissolved. "Shit. That thing's out there. Yeah." She rolled off him, continuing the movement to roll off the bed and onto her feet. She was in the bathroom with the shower running a moment later. With a sigh, Mace followed after. When he tried to step into the shower with her, she waggled a finger at him. "Bad body pillow! Go find your own shower!"

Chuckling, glad that she was retaining a sense of humor, he retreated to his own quarters to get ready. Ten minutes later, they both stood in the security room, fully geared and armed. Though they both knew Peabody would have warned them of any further motion in the area, it made them feel better to look for themselves.

"Looks clear. Let's do this. Maybe it was up all night and is sleeping now," Shari ventured. She didn't look at Mace when she said it. They both knew the zombie creatures didn't sleep.

"Right! Secret ninja food mission!" Mace humored her. They walked to the elevator and rode up to the lobby level. Practically running through the corridor to the garage exit, they paused to check the parking garage for any threats before climbing into Bertha and getting underway. Peabody obligingly opened and closed the garage door for them as they left.

When Shari paused to look around at the top of the driveway, Mace decided it was time to hit Shari with his plan.

"Soooo… um. You know how I always want to stop at the truck full of ho-hos?" He watched Shari's face as she rolled her eyes.

"Yes, dear. We can stop and get you more sugary treats. Though I can't imagine being out here this long has been good for them."

Mace did his best to look offended. "What? Those things are made to last a hundred years!" He grinned as she gave him a 'you're an idiot' look. "But that's not exactly what I meant. I think if we could grab a really big load of supplies this time, we might be able to last until we upload. Without having to go out again, I mean."

Shari nodded. "That might be optimistic, given the time frame we've been discussing. But go ahead, I'm listening."

He started talking fast. "We could just take the whole ho-ho truck. It's big enough to hold a LOT of food. And small enough that it'll fit through the garage door. That way we have a backup vehicle if we need to bug out for some reason. I mean, it's not armored like a Humvee from the armory, but there's room for us to sleep in the back if we need to. And it already has shelves on the sides, and…" He drifted off as Shari held up a hand.

"I'm convinced. You sound like a twelve-year-old child trying to convince his parents that they need a trip to Disney!" She laughed. "We'll stop and get your truck-o-treats."

Mace returned the smile, then leaned over and kissed her cheek. "Thanks. And I was thinking we could stop by the armory to pick up a bunch of those MRE's. They don't take up a lot of space, and each one is a complete meal. We can save them for last, cause they're designed to last for years."

Shari just nodded this time. She turned left, away from the grocery store, and headed toward the armory. "I'm still going to try and grow the corn and stuff. It won't hurt to feed our bodies some healthy fruits and vegetables, even if we're going to abandon them. And there's always the chance we won't be able to pull it off. In which case we'll need to be prepared to survive long term. Maybe even bring Tex up here."

Mace had entertained similar thoughts. Though he preferred to believe they could find a way to transfer themselves fully into the game.

When they reached the truck, Mace hopped out and drew his shotgun. First, he checked the back doors to make sure they were still secure. He'd closed them tightly after their last visit, wanting to preserve his stash. Then he checked the front two seats to make sure it was clear. Crossing his fingers, he hopped into the driver's seat.

"Yesss!" he whisper-shouted upon finding the keys in the ignition. "Let's see if we can go two for two." He reached out and turned the key, only to find it was already in the 'on' position. That wasn't a good sign. Whoever had been driving the truck must have abandoned it while it was still running. The engine could have been damaged as the gas ran out.

Turning the key back to off, he risked turning it back on again. The ignition hit, and the engine tried to start, then coughed and shut down. Beaming, he turned the key back and hopped out. Jogging over to Bertha, he took a gas can off the rack on her rear door. He poured about half of the can into the truck's tank, then returned it to Bertha's rack. No point in wasting the gas if the truck had other problems.

Back in the driver's seat, he pumped the gas a few times and turned the key. The engine failed to start twice, and he was getting discouraged. He wasn't enough of a mechanic to fix any serious issues. He was preparing himself to settle for grabbing some cakes and loading them into Bertha, as he tried one more time. Pressing the gas pedal to the floor, he turned the key... and the engine roared to life! He quickly lifted his foot and let the engine fall back to idle as he drummed a celebratory rhythm on the steering wheel.

Talking into the radio inside his helmet, he said, "Tasty express! At your service, m'lady!"

"Nerd!" Shari's good-natured reply came back. "Follow me to the armory. We'll siphon some more gas there, fill the truck, and refill the can you used. I'll do that while you load up those MREs."

Five minutes later, they were backing both vehicles into the larger motor pool inside the armory building. Mace had used his keys to run inside and open the big bay doors. He closed them again as soon as both trucks were inside. Shari pulled the hose and pump from in the back of Bertha's cargo area and got busy.

Mace opened the back of the food truck and quickly gathered up all the treats that had fallen from the shelves when the truck went off the road, tossing them up onto one of the shelves that lined one wall. There were several empty plastic pallets on the floor as well, and he stacked them onto a hand truck that was strapped to the other wall. Wheeling the truck and the empty pallets through the building, he located the storeroom with the MREs and began stacking the boxes onto the pallets. As he worked, he found a hydraulic pallet dolly in the back of the room, and he began to load that one with pallets of MRE boxes as well.

When he thought he had as much as he could haul, he tilted the hand truck and pushed it in front of him as he pulled the pallet dolly behind him with his other hand. It was awkward, but he wasn't going far. A few minutes later, he was back in the motor pool and began loading up the boxes.

Shari finished up with the fuel and helped by climbing into the back of the food truck and accepting the boxes from Mace. She placed them on the shelves until the shelves were full, then began stacking them against the back wall. She did a rough count as they worked, examining the labels on each box she loaded, and when the pallets were empty she said, "That's roughly twelve hundred meals!"

Mace nodded his head. "So, three a day times two of us, worst case that's two hundred days' worth of food."

Shari shook her head. "We rarely eat three a day. And if we get to the point where we're eating these, we can ration to two meals per day. So more like three hundred days."

Mace looked at the doors behind him. "Want me to go get some more? Make it an even year?"

"No, I think this is plenty. Besides, if what I've heard about these things is true, after six months of eating them, I might be cranky enough to kill you. Which would leave me more than enough for the rest of the year." She winked at him, pulling the hand truck up into the back of the truck.

Mace said, "We should bring this pallet dolly too. Way faster than shopping carts."

Shari agreed and together they lifted the heavy thing up into the truck. They closed the doors and prepared to head out.

Mace saw Shari pause and look toward the doors that led to the living quarters where Dakota's 'home' had been. He gave her a hug, squeezing her tightly. "I know. But we wouldn't have been able to upload him anyway. His choices would have been to starve or become one of those things. He's better off."

Tears rolled down her cheeks as she separated from him. She just nodded and went to get into Bertha. Mace opened the garage door for her, jumped into the truck and drove it outside as well. He left the engine running as he hopped out and closed the door behind them.

Ten minutes later, they were back at the grocery store loading dock. Both of them were out of their vehicles and searching the area for any threat. When they were reasonably sure it was all clear, they unloaded the pallet dolly and entered through the small door next to the bay door.

Once again they searched quietly, clearing the room one aisle at a time. It took almost thirty minutes, using lights strapped to their helmets to look into the corners. Even a single contaminated rat could mean the death of one or both of them.

Mace was rounding the last aisle in the very back of the warehouse section when his fears came true. Glaring at him, its eyes shining black in the light from his helmet, was a contaminated rat the size of a fat housecat.

"Shit!" He didn't hesitate, pulling the trigger of his shotgun even as the creature charged at him. Blue blood and bits of flesh splattered across the floor and the wall behind it as its head and a good chunk of its body disappeared. Mace backed up, waiting for more rats to charge in.

Two seconds later, Shari was behind him. "What happened?" Her head was swiveling left and right, searching for danger.

"Contaminated rat. Which probably means there's more."

They waited for ten seconds, then another ten, their breathing ragged and adrenaline pumping through their veins. When nothing appeared, Shari let out a long breath. "Maybe not. Think about it. These things are aggressive, attacking each other on sight. If there were other rats around, chances are this one would have killed them or been killed."

Feeling a little better, Mace said, "We need to check each box thoroughly before we load it. No telling what that thing has touched. Anything that looks chewed or slobbered on, we leave here."

Shari agreed, and they began to load up. Shari loaded the entire box containing what was left of the beef jerky, along with a couple boxes of Mace's favorite sour cream and onion Pringles. Mace packed on boxes of canned fruit, soups, pasta sauces, olives, and nuts. When the pallet dolly was almost too heavy to move, they pulled it back to the loading dock. After a quick check outside to make sure it was clear, they raised the bay door high enough to pass under, and loaded all the boxes into the truck.

Two more trips with the pallet dolly, and they had several dozen bottles of wine, hundreds of cans of beefaroni, spaghettios, clam chowder, chicken soup, beef stew, and other similar meals. They'd picked up a couple cases of pickles, as well as jars of mayo and mustard, bottles of syrup, honey, plastic cans of parmesan cheese, boxes of pasta, pancake mix, powdered eggs, spray butter for cooking, bottles of vegetable oil, and anything else they could think of. Inspired by Griff's reports of Lisa's delicious fresh-baked bread, Shari even found sealed plastic containers of flour and sugar, salt and yeast.

There wasn't room for the pallet dolly in the truck when they'd loaded all the food, so they left it. There was one in their building, and they could take their time unloading. After closing the loading dock up tightly, just in case, they headed back. The truck's suspension groaned under the weight of all the food, but they didn't have far to go, and they were moving slowly.

Shari took the usual indirect route, circling around several blocks and going out of their way in hopes of confusing anything that might be tracking them. They were just three blocks from their building when Shari slammed on the brakes, nearly causing Mace to run into Bertha's back bumper. Mace immediately grabbed his shotgun and hopped out, not even bothering to turn off the truck's engine. He ran up to Bertha just as Shari was getting out with her rifle in hand. She didn't say anything, just pointed forward down the street.

Following her finger, Mace cursed when he saw it. One of the zombie creatures was moving toward them from about five blocks away. It was definitely human and female. In fact, it was so human-looking that Mace thought for a few seconds that it might be a live survivor. But there was no shouting or waving, and the thing charged straight at them.

Shari rolled down the window of Bertha's driver's door and set her rifle's forestock on the door as a rest. She took aim through her scope, then gasped. "Oh, no. Nooooooo!"

Her knees went weak and she sank down, nearly dropping her rifle as she sat on the truck's runner. "No, no, no, no…"

"What's wrong?" Mace panicked. The monster was charging their way, and he was extremely worried about Shari's reaction. When she didn't answer, he sheathed his shotgun, picked up the rifle and aimed it at the zombie, now only three blocks away and getting closer. When he found it with the scope, he instantly realized what had so deeply affected Shari. It was a human woman, clearly recently contaminated.

And she was very pregnant.

At least, he thought she was. Either that or she'd recently eaten something quite large. From the look on Shari's face, she clearly thought the woman was pregnant.

"Shari! Come on, you gotta snap out of it. She's contaminated, which means the baby is too. They're both already dead!" he paused to take a breath. "I'm no good with this thing!"

When she put her face down in her hands and began to rock back and forth, Mace took aim himself. He did as she had, resting the weapon on the door, the barrel stuck through the window. He took aim at the zombie's head, took a deep breath, and pulled the trigger.

The recoil caused him to jerk back, losing sight of the creature as his head moved away from the scope. With his naked eyes, he saw it jerk to one side, but it didn't slow much.

"Dammit!" he crouched down again, putting the rifle back in place and sighting through the scope. He saw a wound high on the creature's right shoulder. His shot had gone low and wide. Focusing again on the creature's face as it came closer, he pulled the trigger again. This time he was more prepared for the recoil, and he was able to refocus on the sight just a second or two later.

But what he saw nearly made him weep. No new wound. He'd missed altogether. "Dammit! He set the rifle down and pulled his shotgun from its sheath on his back. The creature was less than two blocks away now. He stepped from behind Bertha's door and forward, saying, "Just wait there. I'll take care of it."

He began to walk forward, his shotgun raised. One pump to chamber a round, and he was good to go. He waited until the thing was half a block out before he pulled the trigger. The slug from his weapon struck the creature in the chest, knocking her back and halting her momentum. Mace pumped another round and fired again, aiming higher. Her collarbone and part of her neck disappeared in a mist of neon blue blood, but she was once again moving toward him. He chambered another round and raised the shotgun to his shoulder, and the crack of a rifle shot startled him. He pulled the trigger, but the shot went low, taking out the creature's knee.

It didn't matter. Shari had put a round through its head. The creature slumped to the ground in the middle of the street. There was a small hole in its face just below one eye, but half of the back of its head was gone.

Mace turned back to Shari when he was sure the thing wasn't going to move again. She had sat back down behind the door, and he could see her. Running back, he dropped his weapon and gathered her in his arms. "Are you okay?"

She shook her head, not looking up at him. "You need to burn it. I… I can't shoot the baby. It might…be developed enough to…" She couldn't finish, and he didn't need her to. Nightmare visions of an undead baby emerging from the dead mother's womb assaulted him.

"I'll take care of it." He pulled a can of gas from Bertha's rack and walked over to the corpse. After soaking it liberally, he returned the can and grabbed a flare from inside. Walking back to Shari, he said, "You've got to get in and drive. We made a lot of noise here. And when I light this thing there's going to be a big nasty cloud like before, remember? I need you to be away from here." She nodded her head but didn't move.

He physically lifted her and placed her in the driver's seat. Taking the rifle, he reached across and stuck it in the passenger's seat footwell. The engine was still running, so he put a hand on her knee and squeezed.

"Baby, look at me." He pleaded with her. When her eyes met his, he leaned in and kissed her softly. "You gotta do this. Just a little farther. Drive straight back to our place. I'll be right behind you. You can do this. I love you."

She stared at him a moment, then nodded once. Reaching out, she grabbed the driver's door and pulled it closed. Mace saw her put Bertha in gear, then look over at him.

"Go. I'll be right there." He sprinted back to the food truck and climbed in. Leaving the sliding driver's door open, he stuck his hands out and lit the flare. Bertha began to move forward, and he followed at a distance. Steering wide of the corpse as he passed, he tossed the flare toward it and hit the accelerator.

The flare bounced a couple times before contacting the pool of gas around the corpse. There was a *whoomp* as the gas ignited, but Mace didn't look back. He was completely focused on Bertha, willing Shari to make it back to the garage okay.

He pretended not to hear the high-pitched scream behind him. And did his best not to picture a burning, thrashing zombie fetus.

The rest of the drive went smoothly, even if it seemed to Mace as if it took hours. Shari drove up to the garage, Peabody opened the doors, and they both drove in. Mace had the presence of mind to watch closely to make sure the truck could clear the door, but he needn't have worried. It cleared it with inches to spare.

He followed Shari down and parked the truck right next to Bertha. Turning off the engine, he ran to Shari as she got out. Gathering her into a hug, he whispered assurances into her ear. Taking her hand, he led her in through the lobby door and downstairs. She sat on the bed, answering him in one-syllable responses as he spoke softly and removed her body armor piece by piece.   When he was through, he quickly stripped off his own gear and sat next to her on the bed.

Putting one arm around her, he said, "Thank you."

This caused her to look up. "For what?"

"For being tough enough to save my sexy ass. Again." He smiled at her, and she half-smiled back. "I was going to have to let that thing get closer for my shotgun to hit its head. You saved me from getting all bloody and having to have another cold hose-down in the garage."

This made her actually smile, even if her whole heart wasn't in it. "First of all, your ass isn't that sexy. And secondly, you're welcome." She leaned into him, wrapping her arms around him and placing her head on his chest."

"It had to be done. You know that, right? If she were still alive, she'd have begged you to do it. Nobody wants to be one of those things. And the baby... well, she'd thank you if she could."

Shari nodded slightly against his chest. He barely heard her response. "I know."

"Listen. Why don't you lay down and get some sleep? Our people in the game can live without us for a day. Or I could make us some breakfast. How do you feel about lunch in bed? I can unload the food and bring it down while you sleep."

She gave him a tired smile. "Thank you. But I think I'd rather be in the game. Maybe play with Mion, Snuffles, and Minx for a while? And the children." She wiped tears from her eyes. "Lunch does sound good, though."

She followed him to the kitchen, where they opened a can of spaghetti and meatballs and microwaved it rather than waiting for it to heat up in a pan. Mace crumbled some chips into it, the reminder of one of their early meals together meant to make Shari smile. It did earn him a faint smile and a kiss on the cheek, which was good enough for him. He ended the meal by opening a package of ho-hos with great pomp and flourish as if it were some kind of magic trick. Shari appreciated his efforts, and she gave him a chocolatey kiss on the lips as she chewed her dessert.

A quick cleanup, and they retired to their pods.

Chapter 16

Their first order of business when they logged back in was to officially name the city. Shari wasn't in the mood to gather everyone for a big announcement, so she shared the votes and potential names contributed by the citizens. Some of the contributions were amusing. Three people had suggested naming it after themselves – *Colintown, Edgarville,* and Mace's favorite of the three, *Herbertton.* Others had suggested more viable names such as *Elysia City, New Hope,* and another of Mace's frontrunners, *Assassin's Rest.*

But the suggestions didn't really matter, because the citizens voted overwhelmingly to keep the name Darkstone. He pulled up his UI and the City interface, and then he entered the name. Since the city was now more than just the cave it started out as, Mace dropped the 'Loch' and named it *Darkstone.*

As soon as he confirmed the name, an alert went out. Everyone in sight paused as they saw it flash in front of their eyes. There was some scattered applause and cheering, and his ears caught one voice say, "Dammit!" which he assumed came from Colin, Edgar, or Herbert.

With that accomplished, Shari summoned Mion and Snuffles and moved to join a group of children who were enjoying a midday nap piled atop and around Ursus as he lay in a sunny spot in the grass. Mace summoned Minx, and together they watched long enough to see Shari whisper at Snuffles, who charged in and stuck his wet snout in one child's ear, licked another's face, and generally romped through the group until they were all awake and squealing. Mion flew over and landed on the giant bear's head, looking down at him as he woke. A surprised snort from Ursus sent her flying, flapping her tiny wings to get control and land back in the same spot. She chirped angrily at the bear, who seemed to smile back.

"You want to go play with them?" Mace asked Minx, who was invisible and purring quietly. Her tail wrapped around his neck, and he heard her voice.

"Nope. Good here. Got treats?"

He retrieved a banana from his inventory and quickly peeled it before holding it up near his shoulder. Minx appeared and daintily took the fruit in her tiny hands. Standing upright on her hind legs and using her tail as an anchor, she held the banana in her front paws and chomped down on one end. Mace smiled as he watched her demolish the fruit that was a quarter of her size.

When she was done, he scratched her fat belly. "Little pig. I should have named you Snuffles II."

She gave him a look, then spoke via their link. *"I would have pooped in your boots. Minx is perfect name. Minx is me. I am Minx. Princess Minx."*

"Oh ho! Princess, is it?" he teased. She bared her needle-sharp teeth at him and held up one clawed finger. "Okay, okay. No need to get hostile. You know I love you." He tilted his head to one side and rubbed it against her fur.

With some free time on his hands, he decided to go and check the library for books on *Enchanting*. And while he had enjoyed leveling his *Carpentry* and *Woodworking* skills, he had plenty of carpenters in the city now. He was thinking of obtaining a more useful crafting skill. Shari had several, including *Alchemy, Cartography* and *Calligraphy*, and he was hoping she'd be able to create some sort of teleport scroll. Or at least a recall scroll that would bring the user back to the city.

If he could get Tommaso's *Enchanting* skill high enough, maybe he could create a hearthstone of some kind. That way when his people were in trouble, they could return home for healing and/or reinforcements.

As he walked, he considered the possible professions. He'd never really paid attention to them in this game until recently. In other games, he'd taken up *Smithing* and *Leatherworking*. But Griff and Lisa had those professions covered, along with Brahm, Callahan, and several others. He briefly considered *Stonemasonry*, but with a city full of dwarves, he doubted there would be a need.

He hadn't thought of anything uniquely useful by the time he reached Justin's old chamber. Closing and securing the door behind him, he moved to the hidden wall panel and triggered the door to the library. Once down in the room, he began to look for an *Enchanting* book first. The books were not all training manuals, and they were not filed using any system he could comprehend. So he had to read the title on each spine. Which was fine with him, as he wasn't pressed for time at the moment, and he figured he might find an interesting profession that he hadn't considered already.

It took him half an hour to locate a manual for *Enchanting*. It was difficult to tell exactly without opening and reading it, but the title *"Enchantments of the Ancient World"* suggested it was full of spells. He slid that one into his ring and kept searching. He found a book on portal magic, and he pulled that one to read himself. Since he was now the proud owner of a dozen portals, he figured he should know something about them. There was an interesting looking book called *The Bounty of the Earth*, which he pulled out for the farmers. Another that was bound in supple doeskin and titled *Both Hide & Hair* looked like it might be a *Leatherworking* trainer. Both went into his storage ring.

Mace was almost all the way through the many shelves of books when one caught his eye. It wasn't the topic, which was simply *"Basics of Ceramics"*, but the spine and cover of the book. It was actually made of a thin and somehow flexible ceramic material. He stood there holding the book, trying to decide whether to open it. If it was a trainer, it might teach him the profession and be destroyed in the process.

He knew that ceramic had been used to make some high-end chef's knives and armor plating of a sort for space shuttles and similar vehicles. And he'd never heard of anyone crafting ceramics in any game he'd played. Closing his eyes, he visualized arrowheads that would penetrate flesh and shatter upon impacting bone, doing bonus damage. Or arrowheads with an internal reservoir of poison that could break open and inject the poison on impact. Did Elysia have explosives? He couldn't recall any, but he'd ask the dwarves.

Standing there staring at the book, he made his decision. "It's not like I'd be limited to one trade. If we manage to upload, I'll potentially have decades to learn as many crafts as I want. It's good to be the king!"

Smiling, he opened the book. His eyes unfocused as the words on the pages seemed to swirl together and stream directly into his mind. He felt momentarily dizzy, reaching out to steady himself with one hand on the bookshelf as knowledge of soils, hardening elements, and pigments flooded through him. He knew how to construct a kiln, how hot to make it when firing different mixtures, and what minerals made good glazes. He understood how to work simple pottery and the proper way to use wire and carving tools to cut and shape his work.

When it was over, he blinked a few times, feeling steady on his feet again. "That was *awesome!*" He wanted to get started on testing and leveling this new skill right away.

"Hobbes, do you have a blueprint for a ceramics workshop?"

"I do not, Majesty. I do have a potter's shop, which may suit your purposes."

"Close enough. Can you construct a potter's shop inside the wall?" He considered for a moment. "Maybe attach it to my residence? Do we have the stone resources?"

"Of course, Majesty. I can construct it wherever you like. And you currently have more than enough stone resources. If you like, you can always add more stone units by removing stone from the mountain itself. My current limit is two hundred units per day."

Mace thought about the size and location of the residence that had been set aside for Shari and himself. Adding a shop of any significant size might interfere with Shari's planning for the city. Block a road or an alley or something. And if they were going to make this into a true capital city, they were going to need to have a palace worthy of receiving visiting dignitaries and hosting large gatherings.

"Hobbes... can you create rooms within the stone? And would that speed up your resource gathering rate?"

It took a moment for the AI to answer. *"I can indeed do so, Majesty. Though I was not aware of that ability until you asked."* Mace suspected Elysia had just made an adjustment on the fly to allow it. She was, after all, connected to his brain. She probably saw what he had in mind and made it possible.

"It seems that construction within the stone of the mountain is not only possible, but it allows me to deposit the stone removed to make voids without a daily limit. In addition, the process is faster than construction of the type I have been completing outside. Did you have a blueprint in mind?"

"What do you have for palace blueprints?"

"I have three complete palace blueprints available. Here is the first." Mace's attention was drawn to the pedestal, above which a three-dimensional hologram of a palace had appeared. It was a fancy thing with tall, slender towers topped by elaborate spires. Narrow stairs climbed up to walkways that curved in graceful arches between the towers. Fancy windows and ornate stonework abounded.

"Shari would probably love this, but it's not what I'm looking for. What else have you got?"

The hologram blinked out for a moment and was replaced by a more militant looking fortress. It was all sharp edges with thick walls that came together at severe angles. The towers were simple, rounded things at each corner with arrow slots every few yards. Mace tried to ignore the exterior appearance, focusing on what the interior spaces would look like. His plan was to build it *inside* the mountain, after all.

"Show me the last one please, Hobbes."

The hologram blinked again, and this time the palace reminded him of something he might see in one of the old movies about King Arthur and Camelot. Massive walls that curved around a graceful structure that spoke of strength and power while somehow retaining its beauty. Mace was instantly drawn to it. The towers were wide and rounded, with arched windows beginning on the third floor and balconies starting on the fifth.

The lower levels were made for defense, with narrow windows that let in light and air without being large enough for attacking soldiers to gain access.

"Can you show me the interior, Hobbes?"

The hologram expanded toward him, and it seemed as if he were flying over the walls and into the massive double front entry doors. He found himself in a grand hallway that extended to the left and right, while ahead of him was a sort of receiving area. Beyond that was another set of doors, slightly smaller, that led to a massive main hall/throne room that could easily host a gathering of two hundred people or more.

Mace let Hobbes guide him through the structure room by room. The main building was four stories tall, with the ground floor being mostly public and administrative space. Besides the main hall, there was a large kitchen and a second smaller kitchen next to a more private dining room, a meeting room, a library, several offices, an armory, a barracks, and an entire wing of servants' quarters. The second floor was a combination of more offices, these being larger than those on the ground floor, and more spacious living quarters. Some were a combination of both. These were meant for higher level administrators who would both live and work in the palace. The suites featured a sitting room, a formal office, and a large bedroom with its own private bath.

The simple living quarters would serve nicely for visiting ambassadors, merchants, or other non-royal guests.

The third floor was made up exclusively of a dozen luxury suites. Each featured a formal sitting area, three small servants' quarters, a private dining room, a study, and a large bedroom with en suite bathrooms that featured large soaking tubs as well as showers.

Back down on the ground floor, the right-hand hallway led to one of the towers meant to house the king and queen and their personal staff. The first level of the tower featured a formal sitting area and dining room with a butler's pantry. In the back was a small armory and sleeping rooms for guards and servants. The second level featured a large 'war room' with an inlaid floor featuring a map of the kingdom (such as it was) and several tables with chairs. Next to it was a library with a seating area and long reading table. On the next two levels, Mace found retainers' quarters and more servants' quarters. The retainers' quarters were simple but comfortable, with a sitting area, bedroom, and a bathroom in each. These were meant for the queen's ladies mostly, so that they might be close by if needed. There was another butler's pantry here, as well as a small kitchen that might be used to warm food or make hot drinks.

The fifth level was the monarch's residence. The entire floor was taken up by a formal sitting room, an informal sitting room, three small bedrooms and a huge master, each with their own bathroom, fireplace, and balcony, a study, a meeting room, a game room, and at least a dozen closets. There was also a guardroom near the top of the stairs.

Mace had seen enough. "Hobbes, I'd like you to build this inside the mountain. Please show me the map of the area inside the wall?"

The hologram switched to an overhead view of the city, including the existing buildings—and a dotted outline for the buildings Shari had planned but hadn't constructed yet. The main gate in the wall faced directly toward the mine entrance, so Mace needed to offset the palace a bit. To the east along the wall was where the farmers had put their temporary fields, and where there would eventually be orchards. He didn't want to interfere with that. So, to the west it was. He picked a spot about five hundred feet west of the mine entrance. That would put his palace over the top of the dwarves' caverns, the library he was standing in, and the dungeon. This worked out well, as it would allow him to create a direct passage down from the monarch's tower to the dungeon and the portals.

He pointed to the spot he had chosen. There was no direct route from the main gate to this location, but a road could be created from the main road to the palace gate without interfering with any of the buildings Shari had planned.

"Hobbes, please place the palace doors here. Follow the blueprint, with a few changes. Obviously, the guest quarters on the north side won't have balconies, as they'll face directly into the center of the mountain. So

I'd like you to shift some of the guest suites into a secondary tower." He went through a short list of other changes he wanted to see, including a few secret passages that he wouldn't be telling anyone but Shari about. As he spoke and pointed, Hobbes made the hologram reflect the changes. The main and secondary towers would stand out slightly from the stone, as would the front face of the palace and the balconies. When he was done, he asked, "About how long will all of this take for you to cut out of the mountain and construct?"

"In all, it will take approximately one week. May I make a recommendation or two, Majesty?"

"Of course, Hobbes. I'm always interested in your input."

"Thank you, Majesty. I suggest starting with the main entry, corridors, and great hall. I can transfer the stone units I remove from those large spaces and immediately begin construction of your residence tower. Those can be completed by this evening. Also, I would remind you that you began this exercise because you wished to construct a potter's shop. As that is a facility that requires good ventilation, I could construct it either just outside your tower, attached via a short, covered walkway, or in the tower itself. Possibly on the level above your quarters?"

"Excellent advice, Hobbes! Thank you. Let's do as you suggest. And I think on the ground next to the tower is fine for the shop. That will give me room to expand it, should I take on apprentices or choose to add other professions."

"You are most welcome, Majesty. It shall be done as you command. I might add that I could assist the dwarven mining crew by removing stone for the ramp down to the dungeon."

Mace chuckled. "No, thank you, Hobbes. I think they're having too much fun down there. We might just make them angry. We have time before we need to be moving goods down to the portals. That does bring up a question, though. Can you alter the structures within the dungeon? Is that possible?"

"I can, Majesty, to a very limited extent. Right now, the dungeon retains its original core, to which I do not have access. In fact, my initial attempts to communicate with the core after you claimed the dungeon along with the territory around it were met with some hostility. I can force some minor cosmetic changes at the command of the king, because technically the core is now one of your subjects. For example, I can smooth out the path from the dungeon entrance down to the portal room. Remove any debris, traps, and the like."

Hobbes paused, and a map of the dungeon appeared as a hologram. A bright red dot appeared in what Mace thought he recalled as the treasure room off the portal cavern.

"If you were to remove the current dungeon core and replace it with one containing my essence, you would have complete control of every aspect of the dungeon through me."

Mace's pulse quickened slightly. Being able to control a dungeon? He could add levels, set up each level with more difficult monsters and better loot than the last. It could become a perfect training ground for his people. Low-level citizens could start at level one and fight angry frogs and fluffy bunnies, while he and Shari and the others could bypass straight to level 5 where the mobs were higher level than him.

But he was also curious about the dungeon core. "Hobbes, you said the existing dungeon core was hostile toward you. Does that mean it's sentient?"

"Yes, Majesty. Every dungeon has a sentient core. They are what protects and grows the dungeon from its inception. Some are more… evolved than others. The one in question is quite old, and it was inhabited by nothing but underground wildlife and undead. It is… antisocial?"

And if I remove the core, will it be… killed?"

"That is up to you, Majesty. Dungeon cores are generally a stone or a gem, and they are well protected. They can certainly be destroyed, but removing it from its dungeon should not do so. Should you remove it, you have several options. You could place it somewhere and allow it to

grow a new dungeon. You could place it here, for example, to replace me as the city's AI. You could allow me to drain its energy, adding it to the city and greatly increasing my power—it would provide enough points to make this a Level 2 City and get us close to Level 3—or you could destroy it outright. Though that would be a tremendous waste of valuable resources."

Mace sat on one of the stools near the bookshelf. "While I love the idea of you being able to control the dungeon, I want to speak with this core before I make any decisions. If it is sentient, I don't want to rip it from its home and potentially destroy it without at least trying to communicate with it.

"Very commendable, Majesty. I shall provide you with a replacement gem, in case you choose that option when you reach the core. One moment."

There was a glow in the pedestal, and a moment later, an opaque crystal about the size of Mace's fist rose up from the surface.

"Simply place this crystal in the core's bed if you choose to replace it."

"Awesome! Hobbes, you are the *man!*" Mace took the slightly warm crystal and put it into his inventory ring. "I'll try and have a little chat with the core. If it wants to cooperate, great. If not, I can always plant it somewhere else. If it turns out to be hostile, we'll just level you up a bit!"

"Good luck, Majesty. I have commenced construction on the palace. Your tower will be ready in approximately seven hours."

Mace flashed a thumbs-up at the pedestal, not knowing whether Hobbes could see it or would understand it.

Taking the books he'd selected with him, he made his way back to the surface with a spring in his step. Visions of modifying the dungeon, and potentially growing a second one somewhere in his kingdom, danced through his mind. And he thought having a new palace to decorate and organize might please Shari. Get her mind off the morning's trauma.

He found her still playing with the children. Two very small dwarves were riding Snuffles around as he mock-charged invisible enemies. Several more were conquering Ursus, who was on his back with his eyes closed and tongue out, playing dead as the victors romped around on his belly. Mion was swooping about, casting heals on the tiny warriors as they accumulated bumps and scratches.

Shari sat cross-legged in the grass, a tired infant orcling asleep in her lap. Mace was glad to see her smiling as she 'commanded' the troops. He quietly took a seat next to her and leaned in to kiss her cheek.

"Quite the victory, General HotShari." He winked at her.

"I have an enthusiastic and seemingly tireless army." She smiled at him, then looked down in her lap. "Except for this one, who has missed half the battle."

The two of them sat there for a few minutes, just watching and relaxing. Mace hated to admit it, but the morning hadn't been easy for him either. It was just in his nature to bury his feelings and move on. So, the simple joy and innocence of the children's play helped to untie the knot in his gut a bit, as well.

Eventually, he took Shari's hand in his. "So, you know those folks who used to be household staff? The ones you're loaning out to the various supervisors?"

"Sure. You need a few them for a project?" She turned to him, curious.

"Maybe all of them. As we speak, Hobbes is building us a proper palace. I think you're going to need them starting in the morning. And I would guess you'll have plenty of work for the crafters, too. Going to need furniture, artwork, carpets, table settings…" He stopped when she leaned over and kissed him.

"That's wonderful! Thank you, my love." Her eyes gleamed, and there was a hint of tears forming. "It'll take me weeks to get it all straightened out and running properly." He could see her mind already spinning into action.

"That's not all. It seems when we claimed this place, we also claimed the dungeon, which we sort of already knew. But, apparently, the dungeon has a sentient core, and it's a little grumpy..." He went on to share with her what he'd learned from Hobbes. Her eyes got wider and wider as he spoke. She immediately grasped the potential advantages of having their very own tame dungeon within the city.

And when he spoke to her about taking up *Ceramics* as a trade, she got excited for him. As the children began to tire, she called for them to nap, and she and Mace brainstormed about potential uses for the material.

"You've had quite the busy day," she eventually said.

"As have you. You've exhausted your army, defeated the monstrous beast." He paused when Ursus snorted at him, opening one eye and letting his tongue loll out. "And become the mistress of your very own castle."

She smiled sweetly at him, pulling him in for a very careful hug, so as not to disturb the sleeping infant. "You should go pass out those books. When these little ones are awake, I'll return them to their families with a small victory bonus for each. Then I'll begin rounding up the staff we'll need and get them ready to start work in the morning."

Mace nodded and left her to the snoring horde.

He sought out the farmers first, as they were easily found out in the small plots of land they'd been given to work. He spoke with them for some time, asking after which of them was most experienced. It turned out that one of the dwarves had over a hundred years of farming under his belt. When Mace offered him the manual, he refused.

"Thank ye, Majesty. Er, Mace. Ye do me a great honor with the offer o' this gift. But I'll be refusing. Give it ta one o' the young ones. It might teach me a thing or two, but no more. If'n they learn somethin' from the book that I ain't knowin', they can share it with me. Better to have two with the knowledge than one."

Mace nodded his head and handed the book to the dwarf anyway. "You are a much better judge than I am when it comes to this. Give it to the one you think has the most potential." After a quick goodbye, he left the farmers in deep discussion

He suspected Griff and Lisa were down in the mine with the dwarves, so he went in search of Tommaso. After asking around here and there, he found the man at the smithy, placing minor enchantments on some of the mid-grade weapons the smiths had produced.

When Mace produced the book and showed it to Tommaso, the man cried out, "You found one! I am deeply honored that you would entrust me with this." He nearly wept as he took possession of the book, kneeling as the entire smithy went quiet and all eyes focused on him. "I swear by the goddess Elysia that I will serve you as we agreed in return for this wonderful gift."

Golden light swirled around him as Elysia bound them both with the agreement, then again after he opened the book and absorbed the knowledge. There was applause in the smithy, and several of those present clapped him on the back in congratulations. It took about thirty seconds for Brahm to ask, "So, what new enchantments can you place on my weapons?" Much to the amusement of Mace and the others.

Tommaso just grinned and sat down at the bench where he'd been working. "Bring me a weapon, and let us see!"

Mace left them to it, walking into the mine, through the former slave pens cavern, and down the partially completed ramp to find Lisa. When he caught up to the miners, he was impressed with their progress. Not only had they mined a significant amount of iron ore as they worked, but based on the distance he'd traveled down from the top, Mace estimated they were more than halfway to the dungeon portal.

"Mace!" Lisa stopped swinging her pick when she caught sight of him. Walking over, she beamed up at him from chest height. "My mining skill is up to Journeyman level 2 already!"

He returned her smile, resisting the urge to muss her hair like he would a kid. "That's what happens when you spend days in a dark hole swinging that thing! Keep up this pace and you'll be ahead of Griff soon."

"Already am! He keeps taking breaks to 'listen to the stone' for long periods of time. I think he's trying for some special skill or something. But he's only a Journeyman level 1 right now, so I win!"

"And don't you ever let him forget it!" Mace gave her a thumbs-up, then mentally reached into his inventory and pulled out the leatherworking book. "Are you still planning on leveling up your leather crafting?"

When she nodded, staring at the book, he grinned. She never saw it, her focus lasered in on the title. When he pushed it into her hands, she caressed the cover reverently. "Thank you, Mace. This will save me a *ton* of hours sewing basic leather vests and small leather bags to raise my skill."

Just as with the others, as she opened the book to read it, the knowledge was imparted directly into her head while a golden glow surrounded her.   The light caught the attention of the others in the tunnel, including Griff.   He walked over, calling out as he moved, "Did ya just trick me girl into promising something, ya rascal?"

Mace grinned at him. "Mmmmaybe! But you're too late. You saw the light. Elysia has bound her to her oath, and now she is committed to marrying Stonehand."

Griff stopped dead in his tracks, a stricken look on his face. "Wha… what're ye sayin'?" His face fell as he turned his focus on Lisa, who was smiling like a giddy schoolgirl over all the new knowledge. Griff took it to mean she was happy about the match, and a dark cloud began to darken his visage and his fists clenched.

Realizing things had quickly gone too far, Mace held up both hands. "No! No, I was joking, man. She just read a leatherworking trainer book."

He watched as Griff took a couple deep breaths, calming down. When a sheepish grin appeared on his face, Mace couldn't resist. "And what's all this about *your girl*? When did that happen? You should have made some kind of formal announcement or something!" He waggled a finger at the dwarf as if he were a scolding mother. "So, you two… hooked up?"

Griff adopted a mock-offended look. "Whether or not we be playin' hide the gherkin be none o' yer business!" He winked as he spoke.

Lisa must have come back to her senses at a point in that conversation that allowed her to hear that statement. "Griff!" She blushed cutely. "We just sort of…happened," she said to Mace. "Griff has taken such good care of me. He's real gentlemen, he is."

Now it was Griff's turn to look shy. Mace was enjoying this immensely, the grin on his face widening so much it began to ache.

"Besides," Lisa continued, a wicked smile on her face as she cast a sideways look at her boyfriend. "It ain't like I've a lot of choices just layin' around. His might be the last live gherkin left on the island!"

Mace snort-laughed, as did many of the dwarves in the mining crew. Griff was a good sport and just thumped his chest, sticking his tongue out at Lisa.

They chatted for a bit, then Mace decided to let them resume their mining and stone-whispering or whatever Griff was doing. As he was getting ready to leave them, he said, "Let's be ready to go to Svartholm and locate the duergar first thing in the morning."

Both nodded to him after sharing a brief look. Griff unconsciously checked his wrist, where in the real world his watch would be.

"You guys still getting used to being on the US east coast server time?"

"Aye. It ain't so hard, really. We're underground, so we don't see the sun anyway. We've had Peabody reset all the clocks in the facility to match your time, except the one by the elevator. Just a make sure we don't walk outside in the dark by accident," Griff answered.

"Speaking of going outside…" Mace filled them in on his and Shari's morning food run. Lisa had tears in her eyes when he was through, and she immediately started running up the ramp to find Shari.

She called out over her shoulder as she ran, "Why didn't ye tell me this earlier?"

Looking to Griff, Mace spoke quietly. "I know you guys had a bad time on your last food run, but it might be a good idea for you to do what we did. Get a truck and load up as much as you can. Then just stay inside until we're ready to upload."

Griff nodded slightly, stroking his beard in thought. "Aye, it's been a few days. Mebbe them big beasties has been consumed by little ones by now? The question becomes whether any o' *them* is still there."

"Might be worthwhile finding another grocery store or warehouse or something. Lisa lived there before everything ended. Surely she knows another one?"

"Aye, I'll ask her tonight. Tomorrow we'll do that damned escort quest…" Mace chuckled as Griff gave him a dirty look. "Then the next day we'll make a food run."

"Take whatever weapons you can. If you have to make some noise to survive, do it. Get the supplies, then retreat to safety once and for all. If something follows you, even breaks into the building, you can just have Peabody lock down the elevators and seal the levels above you. You should be fine."

Mace left Griff to his mining and returned to the surface. He found Shari and Lisa sitting and talking quietly, so he left them to it. Looking around, he saw everyone busy with one job or another. His people seemed happy enough.

Having no pressing duties in the city, Mace waved at Shari and logged out. He wanted to spend some hours working the pod software, and he already knew tomorrow was going to be a long day in the game.

Chapter 17

The next morning, Mace and Shari woke to find a message from Tex. Mace had worked for several hours the evening before, then transmitted what he'd done to Tex. Apparently, something in there had triggered an inspiration in Tex. His excited message said he was going to be working on the code all day, maybe for several days, and not to disturb him.

Mace grinned at that last part. He knew the feeling of getting into a zone and working for a full day or two straight through without realizing.

After a healthy breakfast of granola bars, powdered eggs mixed with hot sauce and dried minced onion, and pickles—because for some reason Shari wanted them—they cleaned up and crawled into their pods.

It was just after sunrise in their city, and the residents were already starting their daily routine. The smell of breakfast was in the air, and already the faint ring of hammering at the smithy echoed down the street.

Both were excited to see the status of their new palace. The royal residence tower would have been completed during the night, as well as the great hall. Turning toward the mountain face to the north, Mace wasn't disappointed. On the contrary, he was impressed by the height and girth of the tower!

As Shari took his hand and practically dragged him toward it, he noted that the base was easily a hundred feet in diameter, and it looked solid enough to support the mountain itself. Only half of the tower existed outside the mountain, looking as if it had grown organically from the stone.

The huge main doors were in place as well, and Shari found her staff waiting for her just outside. She greeted everyone with a hug, then led the whole group inside. Mace stood back and watched as they gasped in wonder at the wide, high-ceiling hallways extending off to either side. Walking forward through the waiting area and the double doors to the great hall, Mace had to admit he was impressed. The hall echoed with the sound of footsteps as they entered. Well, not his. He never made a sound when he walked. The ceiling when they first walked in was only about fifteen feet high. But ten or so paces into the room it soared up to the three stories in height. Holes in the ceilings somehow allowed sunlight to filter in through shafts that led outside. Mace made a mental note to ask Hobbes how he accomplished that. He suspected mirrors.

The floor of the hall was polished marble, with matching columns that ran down either side and supported a second-floor gallery that formed a horseshoe around the back of the room. There was a raised dais at the other end with two ornately carved stone thrones. Mace and Shari crossed the room hand in hand, and he helped her up the three steps and into her seat before taking his own. Immediately the staff who had followed them in bowed low and held themselves in that position.

"None of that!" Shari gently scolded them. "There will be no bowing and curtsying in this hall unless we're entertaining official visitors." The staff all straightened up and bobbed their heads in acknowledgment. Shari frowned. She was going to have a hard time curing them of lifetimes of slave mentality.

Mace thrust his nose up in the air, looking sideways at Shari next to him. "Well, look at us! Aren't we just all snooty and royal!" He pretended to roll down a window between his throne and hers. "Pardon me, m'lady… but would you happen to have any delicious stone-ground spicy mustard?"

It took her a moment to get the joke as the staff just looked at each other, confused. "Dork!" she whispered at him. "Go away. You have a fancy escort quest to start. I've got plenty to do here!"

Mace held both hands to his heart, leaning back in his chair and looking wounded. He cried out, "Not even five minutes in our new home, and I'm exiled!" He stuck out his bottom lip and tried to look hurt. The staff looked alarmed as well as confused now.

"Hush. You'll scare the children," she whispered at him, smacking his arm playfully. When he didn't move, she got up from her seat and leaned over him, planting a long soft kiss on his lips. There were sighs of relief and a few quiet claps from behind her.

Mace grinned, reaching up as if to pull her into his lap and continue the show, but she slapped his hands away and pointed toward the doors. "Go!"

Grinning, he leaped up from the chair and scooped her into his arms, tilting her back into a long, deep kiss. When he brought her back upright, she gasped slightly, blushing. He let her go and leapt from the dais, causing the staff to scatter. "Until I return, my love!" he called out, waving goodbye as he backed through the doors and closed them.

Outside he found the dwarves and Layne gathered by the mine entrance. "Good morning, my fellow adventurers!" he called out cheerfully. Most of them instantly got suspicious looks on their faces. Lisa was the first to ask, "What's got into ya this morning?" She looked behind him at the new palace tower. "Or should I be askin' what ye got into?" The wicked grin on her face got the others laughing.

Mace didn't answer except to give her an exaggerated wink as he passed by. They followed him into the mine and down through the dungeon to the portal room. As they walked, he explained their path.

"One of the portals leads to a tunnel that's a few hours' walk from Svartholm. We can get there by noon, find the duergar, and hopefully get them ready to move first thing in the morning." He paused, looking at his companions.

"Keep in mind this is a duergar city, in the underground. Most of the citizens there will slit your throat for a single gold piece or just for being a surface dweller. Nobody goes anywhere alone, and it would be better if you all stay near me until I get you someplace safe. There's a very nice inn that I stayed at last time I was there. Ideally, you'll all remain there for the duration of our visit. The alternative is to have you wait outside the city. But there you might be attacked by duergar patrols or creatures of the underground."

"It'd be good ta stay in a proper inn," Griff suggested, and the others nodded their agreement.

"So be it." Mace led the way through the portal, stepping to one side and scanning the area with his natural drow dark vision to make sure it was clear. To assist the others, he cast a light globe and set it to float near the ceiling. It would have the added advantage of annoying any rock spiders that might be waiting in ambush. Most creatures of the dark didn't react well to light.

When the others were all through the portal, he had them pause to mark the location on their maps, and to make sure they knew exactly where it was located on the wall. They might be in a hurry when they returned and not have time to search for it.

The trip through the underground was mostly uneventful. They ran into a goblin scouting party, but the little monsters were partially blinded by the light and didn't offer much resistance. Griff slammed his shield into the front few mobs as they approached, then hurled insults at them to make sure he had aggro. Jo burned them with fire, then Lisa and Meg mowed them down with blades. Mace just stood and watched, letting them gain some experience working together. The goblins were all level twenty to twenty-five, so the dwarves got a good bit of xp from the fight.

Twice they were ambushed from above by rock spiders. Jo took a nasty bite when one of them landed on her, and she suffered a *poisoned* debuff. Leroy was quick with a cure poison potion and healing spells. Mace harvested the rock spider meat, as it would have some value as a trade good. It couldn't hurt to try and make allies with the duergar of Svartholm while he was here. And it would be better than having a potential enemy at your back, so to speak.

When they finally reached the massive cavern that surrounded Svarthold, the dwarves muttered and whistled at the construction. The massive center column was impressive, even to Mace who had seen it before. Layne asked for a short pause so she could sketch the city from a distance, and Mace obliged. It only took a few minutes, and he was surprised at how accurate the sketch was when she showed it him.

"I shall fill in the colors later, or perhaps create a whole new image based on this. The sketch is just to provide reminders if my memory fades," Layne explained as she put the sketch pad back into her inventory.

Mace led the procession, reminding them to be cautious as they neared the gate. "Keep your heads down as much as possible, and try not to make eye contact. Put all your jewelry and such in your inventory. If you're attacked, call out immediately. If any fighting needs to be done, leave it to me. Few will be willing to take on a Darkblade, but surface dwarves and a light elf? Races that are normally only seen as slaves down here. You'd start a riot if you draw weapons."

When he was sure they understood the situation, they walked the short distance remaining to the gate. The duergar guards looked him up and down, then inspected his companions. "These be yer slaves, drow?"

Mace leaned in close to the guard and growled, "These are no slaves. I am King Mace of Styrke, and these are my free subjects. You will show them, and me, proper respect."

The guard growled back, drawing a wicked looking one-handed axe from his belt. Mace instantly had blades in both of his hands, and he was ready to exterminate the guard, when another stepped between them, his back to Mace.

"Hold! I hear'd o' this one. Word came with the last caravan from the drow city. He be a Darkblade. Stole hisself a kingdom from them Black Flame slavers. Killed every one o' them while he were at it." He paused to look over his shoulder at Mace and his weapons. "They say he be favored o' the drow queen."

The first guard's face went blank, and his mouth moved a few times without making any sound. He took a step back, putting away his weapon. The second guard turned to face Mace and gave a slight bow. "Apologies, yer lordship. Had we know'd ye were visitin', we'd have made arrangements."

Mace relaxed a bit, sheathing his weapons. "No apology necessary. Though I would appreciate it if you would spread the word about me and my companions to the rest of the guards. I do not wish to have to kill any of your people, but I will if pressed."

The guard nodded his head. "I'll be passin' word along, do no' fear. Can I help ye find an inn or a particular shop?"

"I stayed at a very nice inn up in the central column last time I visited with Master Krieger…" He didn't think it would hurt to drop a name or two. "So I'm all set there, thank you. But I wonder if you can help me with something else? I'm looking for the duergar refugees from Steinhalle. Might you know any of them? Or where they might be within the city?"

The guard turned to his chastened companion and they exchanged a questioning look. Turning back to Mace, he said, "I hear'd that some o' me cousins had been run out by rock trolls. But I dinna meet any o' them that I know of." The other guard shook his head, implying he hadn't either. "I'll send word around that yer lookin' for 'em, and we'll have them find ye at yer inn. That'd be the Pissed Ogre on level seventeen, yes?"

Mace grinned, remembering the sign with ogre making a rude gesture. "That's the one, yes. Thank you." He produced ten gold and handed it to the guard. "For all your assistance."

The guard's eyes widened slightly before the gold disappeared. Mace noted that he didn't share it with his companion and winked. The guard coughed once, then waved them through the gate. "Enjoy yer visit, King Mace!" he called out loudly enough for all those nearby to hear.

Immediately, a buzz arose ahead of Mace, and the crowd parted as he pressed up the street. Layne caught up to him, whispering, "That guard wasn't kidding about spreading the word."

Mace snorted. "Not exactly tactful, but effective enough." He did his best to look kingly as they walked, adopting a sort of stately stride while keeping an angry look on his face. The whispered comments that drifted over to him included 'Darkblade' and 'Assassin King'. He thought that one had a nice ring to it.

The others gawked at the city as they passed up the main road toward the central spire. Mace constantly checked to make sure they were all still behind him. When they reached the chaos of the market where he'd first met Minx, he paused to group them up a bit tighter. "Layne, Jo, Leroy, right behind me. Meg, Lisa, you next, and Griff take up the rear. Stay close. And don't touch anything."

The crowds continued to part ahead of him, the chatter getting louder and louder as more people were informed of his presence. The gossip spread like wildfire pushed by a strong breeze ahead of him. So every eye was on him and his party as they made their way across the market.

A dagger flew out of the crowd to his right, speeding toward Layne's head. Mace spun and reached out with his left hand, catching the hilt of the weapon less than a foot from her face. As the crowd gasped, amazed by the speed of his reaction more than the attack itself, Mace finished his spin and hurled the dagger back in the direction it had come. He'd seen a drow arm finishing the throwing motion a millisecond after noticing the airborne weapon.

The would-be assassin was caught by surprise and didn't dodge quickly enough. The dagger caught him in the shoulder, the force of the throw knocking him off balance. Mace didn't give him the chance to recover. He leapt through the widening crowd and landed a kick to the drow's face. When his target fell dazed to the ground, Mace placed a foot on his throat and paused to look around.

Seeing no additional foes, he called out. "This is what happens to those who attack me or mine!" Lifting his boot, he stomped the drow's throat. There was an audible snap as the drow's spine broke. Now paralyzed, his victim barely twitched as Mace held up his soul dagger. "This is going to hurt. In fact, it will be excruciating. Your soul is now mine!" He slammed the dagger into the drow's gut, watching him try to scream as he was drained.

The assassin died with a whimper, paralyzed and unable to draw enough air into his lungs for anything else. Mace looted his body without even looking at what he received and rejoined his people.

They continued through the market without incident after that. Mace ushered them into an elevator and pushed the button that read '17'. As soon as they got off on the correct floor, he led them to the inn.

The innkeeper appeared to remember him, and he nodded his head. Mace approached the bar. "I need rooms for myself and all my companions. And a couple of sturdy guards to make sure we're not disturbed."

The duergar nodded, counting the bodies behind Mace. "That'll be ten gold per night. How long will ya be stayin'?"

"Hopefully just tonight." He slid a small bag with twenty gold across the bar. "Make sure my people are well fed. And that the guards don't sleep on the job."

"Of course, sir."

"That's 'Your Majesty' to you." Layne did her best to sound gruff and aloof.

"What'd ye say to me, ye uppity pointy-eared…" the innkeeper growled at the elf, reaching under the bar for a weapon.

"I said you have the honor of speaking to King Mace of Styrke, and you will address him as 'Your Majesty' or 'King Mace' or I will serve your tongue to the next kobolds that cross your doorstep." Layne glared at the duergar.

Several of the patrons in the tavern stood and placed hands on their weapons upon hearing a slave speak to the innkeeper in such a manner. Most were duergar, with a few kobolds and gnomes mixed in, and a small party of drow at one table. At the same time, the innkeeper himself raised an empty hand from under the bar and held it up, reaching instead for the coin. He nodded his head slightly. "King Mace."

Seeing this, Mace turned his back to the duergar behind the bar and drew both daggers. "Who wishes to test their skills against a Darkblade today?"

All but a few of the duergar and the drow party took their seats. The duergar that remained standing looked unsure of themselves while the drow just observed with stony faces. One of the duergar, a large specimen with a mining pick in his hand, shouted. "Drow don't have no kings!" To which several others called out their agreement. From somewhere in the back a shrill voice shouted, "Gnomes rule!", making Mace grin.

"I am the first in a very long time. Maybe the first ever." Mace smiled at him, giving him a mock bow. "At your service."

The one who had spoken turned to the drow. "This be true?" As one, the drow nodded their heads, not speaking. The duergar put his pick away, mumbling, "If ye be a king, ye should know ta keep yer slaves on a tighter leash!"

Happy with the de-escalation and finding himself with an audience, Mace opted not to push the issue. Instead, he asked, "I seek the duergar of Steinhalle. We have urgent business to discuss. Do any of you know where I might find them?"

The innkeeper coughed once, and Mace turned in time to catch him shaking his head while looking at his patrons. Not one of them spoke. Leaning partway over the bar, he whispered to the innkeeper. "I mean them no harm. Just the opposite. My people and I have eliminated the rock trolls at Steinhalle, and we wish to help its original inhabitants reclaim their homes."

The duergar innkeeper stared at him for a long moment. "Yer a drow. I'd not believe ye if ye told me ye had ta piss."

"I am also an outworlder, and not your normal drow. If I were, I'd have cut your throat by now."

The innkeeper chuckled. "Aye, ye got me there." Raising his gaze to a young duergar sitting down the bar, he jerked his head toward the door. The youngling leapt from his stool and raced out the door. "I've just sent word ta their chieftain, who be an acquaintance o' mine." He looked around the room, then at Mace's companions. Handing Mace several keys, he added, "Might be best if yer friends waited in their rooms. I'll have food and drink sent up at supper time."

Mace passed out the keys, and Griff led the procession up the stairs. At another nod from the innkeeper, two beefy duergar in plate armor took up station at the top of the stairs behind them.

Mace took a seat at the end of the bar where he could lean his back against the wall and keep the entire room in sight. Just for show, he twirled both daggers before making them disappear into their sheaths. "Bring me some c'irliq," he commanded.

The innkeeper looked surprised at the request, then did as he was told. A bottle of the clear liquid and a clean glass were placed in front of Mace. He decided to try again with the innkeeper. After taking a drink to make sure it was the good stuff, he held up a finger to hold the innkeeper's attention.

"I'd like to purchase several barrels of this to take home with me. Can you supply them, or should I inquire with a distributor somewhere?"

"I sell it in bottles or kegs. There be no barrels." The innkeepers attitude was still gruff.

"Fine. Then I will need… a hundred kegs. I have a thirsty city full of hard-working dwarves and orcs and minotaurs. Not to mention the centaurs, who can drink a keg each with ease."

The innkeeper coughed in surprise, his eyes wide. Mace was sure he'd never sold that much in a single transaction. The duergar recovered quickly and blurted out, "Ten gold each keg. One thousand gold total," eyeing Mace as he said it.

Mace snorted. "You believe because I was generous with my gold earlier, I'm some kind of fool? I was inclined to be friendly, but that was before you insulted me. And now you insult me again with that price. I'll take my business elsewhere." He emptied his glass and slid a single silver coin across the bar to make his point.

The innkeeper took the coin and the remainder of the bottle and walked away. Mace waited patiently, the booze creating a pleasantly warm tingle in his gut. He was just starting to regret letting the rest of the bottle get away when a larger than normal duergar burst through the door with the youngling trotting behind. After a quick look around, he made straight for Mace, stomping his way across the floor.

"What be this I hear about me village? Who're ye ta demand ta see me?"

"I am Mace, King of Styrke, the kingdom that now includes your former village. Who might you be?"

"I be Balen Boulderhugger, Chieftain o' the Steinhalle Duergar! And ye ain't my king!"

"I wasn't when you got run out by the rock trolls. In fact, I only claimed my kingdom just a few days ago. I will return your village to you, but only if you accept that you will become citizens of Styrke and swear an oath of loyalty. You and each of your people."

Mace pulled the letter that he'd found with the sword and handed it to Balen. The chieftain took one look and his face went pale. "This were written by me da! He died, defendin' our backs as we fled. Where'd ye get it!?"

Mace took a moment to tell the story about the rock troll attack, their journey underground to finish the quest, and his discovery of the hidden alcove. He also produced the troll champion's head, creating a stir as everyone in the bar crowded closer to look and listen.

Balen looked at him, fury on his face. "So what yer sayin' is ye stole a relic weapon belongin' ta me and mine, then ye stole our damned home, and now yer here to demand we serve ye!"

Mace tried to be patient and resist the urge to just kill the chieftain and deal with his replacement.

"No, I did not steal anything. I found the sword with this note, and I fulfilled your father's wish by killing all the rock trolls that stole your home. I *liberated* your village, which lies within the boundaries of *my kingdom.* And I do not demand you serve me unless you choose to return to *my kingdom* and live there." The grey dwarf was turning redder the longer Mace spoke.

He felt Minx's tail tighten around his neck, and her voice came to him.

"Heart. Give him the heart. For quest."

Initially, Mace's mind was blank. It took him several seconds of listening to Balen rant about taking his village back before he remembered looting a duergar's heart from the black flame fighters, and the quest it gave him.   Reaching into his bag, he pulled out the heart and held it out in front of him.

Balen instantly went silent. As did every other duergar in the room. Mace just stared at him, giving what he hoped was a threatening look. "This heart belonged to the last duergar who thought he could attack me. He had fifty Black Flame fighters with him. They died in less than two minutes."

Mace slammed the heart on the bar.   Being preserved inside his inventory, it still had fresh blood in it, and that blood now leaked in a widening pool on the bar top.

"Black Flame, ye say?" Balen reached out to touch the heart even as the other duergar in the room drew weapons. He lifted the heart in his hand and closed his eyes. A moment later, he opened his eyes and spat on the heart. The others all gasped and began to protest.

"SILENCE!" he roared. He held the heart up in the air, and the crowd quieted. "This be the heart o' me second cousin, whose name I will not speak. He were stricken from the clan roles. He be the reason Steinhalle fell ta them filthy trolls!"

Turning, he flung the heart into a nearby fireplace. Several duergar shouted and scrambled toward the flame to save it, but Balen roared, *"THE FIRST ONE O' YA TOUCHES THAT HEART DIES BY ME OWN BLADE!"*

The others stopped, but they didn't look happy about it, and there was much grumbling. Mace asked, "What's going on here?"

Balen looked angry, but he answered the question. "Since ye bring'd me that heart, I'll tell ye. Me second cousin were a complete ass. Not satisfied with hard work like the rest o' us. He left the village ta seek out fame and fortune. No one in the village, not even his own family, liked him, and none wept at his leavin'. But they wept sure enough when he returned. Six months after his leavin', he brought back a band o' slavers called Black Flame. He'd told 'em our village were easy pickin's. Sold us out fer a share o' the loot and profits."

There was some louder angry grumbling from the duergar present. The drow simply sat at their table and listened.

"We fought 'em off, killed a good number o' them bastards. But it cost us dear. We wasn't a large settlement, barely a hundred strong. We lost a dozen good fighters that day, includin' his own brother. So, when them filthy troll beasties came a week later, we were no' strong enough ta withstand the attack."

A notification flashed across Mace's UI, but he mentally waved it aside. It was likely the completion of the Duergar's Heart quest.

"But what about throwing the heart in the fire? And why were the others so upset about it?

Balen spat on the floor and took his time answering. "We be duergar. If, when we're killed, one o' the brothers can recover our heart, it can be buried in the stone. Eventually, years later, we will be reborn, our bodies good as new. But the arse whose heart ye give'd me has earned eternal death!" There were several shouts of agreement around the room. Others just remained quiet. Clearly, eternal death was a frightening concept to these grey dwarves.

"Then I'm glad you've had your revenge. Now, if you're finished yelling and stomping around, I am here to offer to escort you and your people safely back to Steinhalle. All you have to do is swear the oath, and be loyal, productive citizens of Styrke. You would be welcome in our city as fellow citizens or traders. We will help your people recover from your losses, and even to thrive."

Balen was silent for a long while. His gaze went to the burning heart withering in the coals, then back to Mace. Finally, he said, "I'll swear yer damned oath, if me people agrees. I'll need ta gather 'em and talk it over."

Mace relaxed slightly. "You have until morning. If you're going home, I'll be at the gate right after breakfast, let's say the eighth bell. Have your people there, and we'll escort you to your village. If you're not there by the ninth bell, then Steinhalle will remain mine, and I shall find others to settle there. Maybe the gnomes we met in the tunnel nearby."

Ignoring Balen, who turned and left without a word, Mace looked to the innkeeper. "I'll give you one more chance as well. One hundred kegs for three hundred gold. Take it or leave it."

Mace wasn't sure if it was the price, or the fact that he'd made the offer in front of so many witnesses, but the innkeeper accepted. "Lemme see yer gold. I'll have the lads line up the kegs for ye by mornin'."

Mace stacked three rectangular plates of gold, each worth one hundred gold coins, onto the bar. There were several comments from the peanut gallery and a few whistles. Few citizens of Elysia had held that much gold at once. Most of them were either successful merchants or bankers.

Remaining at the bar, he took a moment to look over his notification from earlier. The rewards for completing the *Duergar's Heart* quest were okay – fifty thousand xp and a reputation gain with Steinhalle, raising him up to neutral. The escort quest had updated after he located Balen, but the current stage wouldn't be complete until he returned them to their home.

The clock on his UI told him he had some time before supper would be served, so he exited the inn and returned to the elevator. He had been dissuaded from his plan to speak to the smith who'd created his soul blade by Krieger and Jervis. Instead, he headed down to the market. The last time he'd been there he'd found Minx, so he considered the place to be good luck. Reaching up, he gently scratched Minx's belly as she purred on his shoulder.

The market was filled with items of every conceivable type. Useful to ridiculous, colorful to bland, and delicious smelling to outright rank and offensive. There were a few specific things he wanted to find as he browsed the stalls. Any crafting books would be priority items. Also blueprints and schematics for anything from weapons to entire buildings that he could take back to his people. He hadn't thought to get extra gold from Shari, so he was down to the 600 or so gold in his own inventory. But he carried bags of jewels from the alcove and other items of value that he could barter with.

He also kept a lookout for Felina the catwoman that had sold him Minx. If he saw her, he wanted to thank her for introducing them. As if reading his mind, Minx's voice came to him.

"Felina not here. Sad."

"I'm sorry, little one. I hoped to see her too. Maybe next time. Or, once we establish trade in our city, maybe she'll visit there. I'll be sure to tell the guards she should be welcomed as an honored guest and brought to the palace to see you." He smiled as Minx tightened her tail a bit and resumed purring. A passing gnome gave Mace an odd look, as it seemed he was speaking to no one as he walked. He just ignored the gnome and continued on.

Toward the far side of the market square, there was a row of permanent shops that included a bookstore. Mace hurried over and stepped inside. The first thing he noticed was the dust and dusky smell of old paper. Minx sneezed on his shoulder, becoming visible briefly as she rubbed her nose with one tiny paw and gave him a disgruntled look.

A female duergar emerged from behind a bookcase. She carried a book in one hand and a feather duster in the other. "Pardon the dust, master drow. My late husband never felt the need to clean this place. How can I help you?"

Mace rubbed his own nose. The dust cloud was really quite annoying. "Perhaps I can help you first. Is there a back door or window to this place?"

She looked at him with suspicion, then nodded. "Please go and open it, and I'll clear the dust for you."

She did as he requested, opening an office door that led to the back, then an outer door to the alley behind the building. Mace stood near the front and mumbled *Ventus!* while moving his hands to control the summoned wind. He directed the flow of air down one aisle after another, casting the spell repeatedly as he pushed the dust back through the shop and out the door. In less than a minute, the cloud of dust was gone, and both he and Minx were breathing easier.

"I thank ye fer that," the shopkeeper said. "Would have taken me all day."

"You can thank me by telling me if you have any training manuals for crafting. Or spellbooks? Or schematics?"

She looked at him like he was stupid. "This be a book shop. What else would I be havin' here?"

Mace shot back at her. "Let me guess. Your late husband dealt with the clients?"

"Ha! Ye got me there. Ain't never been one to mollycoddle nobody." She grinned at him. "Bad fer business, likely. No matter, I be plannin' ta sell the shop anyway and move on. This were never my choice. I be a tailor by trade." She shook her head, looking around. "What craftin' trade be ye lookin' for?"

He shrugged. "Any of them? All of them. I have a city to build and citizens to train in nearly every craft."

Light dawned in her eyes. "Ah, ye be *that* drow. I hear'd about ye in the market square. The new king." She waved an arm at a whole wall of books on shelves behind the sales counter. "These be the most valuable books. Spell books, class trainers, craft trainers, recipes fer alchemy, and such."

Mace stepped to the counter and leaned over, inspecting the titles. She was right, they were everything she said and more. He picked a book at random, a spell book for fire mages, which were popular in the underground. "How much for the fire mage book?"

Her eyes unfocused for a moment as she checked some kind of inventory or price list. "That one be one hundred fifty gold."

He had suspected as much. Training books were worth their weight in gold in Elysia. That was the reason Brahm and Captain Charles had been so thankful for the books they received. Even with the gems in his inventory, he didn't have enough wealth to buy all the books he wanted. But he had an idea.

"I take it business has been slow? Since your husband passed, I mean."

"Aye, and before that. This were more like a hobby fer him. Made enough ta feed us, but me tailorin' pays the mortgage. That book be priced at one hundred fifty gold, but it cost him one hundred twenty ta buy it. And we might sell a book a week."

"I have a proposal for you. I'm sorry, I didn't catch yer name?"

"I didn't throw it!" She grinned at him. "I be Ella." She held out a hand, which he shook. "Should I be callin' ye king? Or majesty?"

"Maybe later." He grinned at her. "I'm not used to the formality yet. You mentioned that you want to sell the shop. How would you like to open up a shop in my new city? You can do both books and tailoring. I'll give you a building large enough for both, plus room for your living space. No charge, no mortgage. It's a city full of people who'll break their backs trying to earn the gold to buy your books." He paused to take a calming breath. She wasn't shaking her head no, and he was getting excited.

"You can sell this shop, the building, I mean. Would it bring enough to pay off your mortgage?"

"Aye, that it would…" She wasn't convinced yet, but she was playing along.

"I'm escorting the Steinhalle duergar back to their village in the morning. We could locate a wagon or two, load up all your inventory, and bring you along. I would require two things from you in return."

Her face instantly turned suspicious again. "And what'd those be?"

"First, you swear an oath of loyalty, same as all my other citizens. And second, you keep the prices on the books reasonable. No big markups. My people are trying to grow a city, and it would benefit you to help them do so. You could grow right along with us. We will become a major trade hub in the coming years."

She shook her head, and his heart sank a little. He'd thought he had her.

"It be a good offer, King. But there be no way I could pack up all this by mornin'."

"How about if I bring help? I have a party of hardworking dwarves with me. We could have this place loaded up in a matter of hours." He checked his inventory. He still had two of the storage rings that held one hundred items each sitting empty in there. And some room in the ring he was wearing. "I don't suppose you have a couple storage bags or rings that would help?"

She nodded her head. "Aye, me late husband had a couple, fer when he went to buy books. 'Twas easier than drivin' a cart everywhere he went."

Mace felt his plan coming together. His people would be earning much more gold than normal during dungeon runs and for completing quests. They would be able to purchase books relatively quickly. He looked at Ella. "Would you excuse me for one second?"

Stepping outside, he sent a message to Shari. *"Hey, hun, could you do me a favor? Ask Hobbes if he has a blueprint for a bookshop? Or any shop with a lot of shelves."*

He waited a minute or so before she answered. *"Yep. He has a bookshop. What's up?"*

He quickly explained to her what he planned, and about Ella's needs for a twin shop with living area.

"Hahaha! You just work the angles wherever you go, don't you, my love? That's brilliant! One minute, let me talk to Hobbes." Mace paced back and forth in front of the shop, making a few passersby more than a little curious. A couple minutes later, Shari's voice sounded in his ear again. *"So, we cobbled together a building with a large shop and workshop for the tailoring, as well as living quarters. Only two bedrooms, but I assume that's okay for a widow?"*

"One sec, I didn't ask if she has any kids." Mace dashed back inside the shop, startling Ella who was pulling a book down from the 'expensive' shelf.

"Ella, is it just you? Do you have any kids? Would two bedrooms in the living space be enough?"

"It be just me. Our daughter be grown and gone, with kids o' her own now." Ella smiled gently, thinking of her grandkids. "I could use tha' extra bedroom fer me tailoring…"

Mace shook his head. "Nope. My queen has designed a dual shop for you, with room to display the books *and* your tailored goods. With a workshop in the back for you and living quarters upstairs."

Ella got a strange look on her face. "Yer… queen? Ye bothered yer queen fer a grumpy ol' seamstress?"

Mace chuckled. "Oh, trust me, it was no bother. She simply *loves* this town building stuff. And she's looking forward to meeting you, if you'll join us?"

Ella turned her back and seemed to be wiping a tear from her eye. When she turned back to face him, she nodded once. "Aye. Go get yer packing crew. I'll need to close up for an hour or so. There be an alchemist, been tryin' ta buy me shop fer months. I'll go make that deal and pay off me debt. Meet ya back here. Ye'll have ta make arrangements fer a wagon and lizards. Need a big wagon fer all these shelves and books..."

"No need to bring the shelves. Your new shop will have sturdy stone shelves. You can sell these to your alchemist for a few extra gold. You can use one of your rings to store all your bedroom furniture and crafting stuff. Then we'll use both your rings and mine to store as many books as we can. The rest will go into the wagon."

He held out a hand for her to shake, but she gathered him up in a bear hug that made a few of his vertebrae pop. "Thank ye, Yer Kingness." She sniffled slightly, not looking up at him.

"Thank *you,* Ella. I think you'll make a wonderful addition to our community. As soon as you get settled in your new home, I'm sure Shari will want to have you over for dinner. She's a *Scribe* and a *Cartographer* and will be probably try to buy a few of your best books before the others get to them." He smiled. Reaching into his inventory, he pulled out three of the diamonds from the alcove. "Which reminds me. Take these. In case you don't get as much from the alchemist as you need. Use them to cover your mortgage if you need to. If you don't need them, return them to me."

She looked up at him, her eyes wide and puffy. "Ye'd... ye'd trust me with these? Must be worth... two hundred gold each."

"Would you start your relationship with your new king, who is also a Darkblade by the way, by stealing from him?"

"Nay, I wouldn't." She shook her head emphatically. "Ye've been right kind and honest with me. I'll not repay ye with deceit."

"Good!" Mace patted her shoulder. "I'll go gather my crew, feed them, and meet you back here in... two hours? And since we'll be packing up your bed and things, I'll reserve you a room at our inn."

"Bah! No need. I'll pack the bed last. One last night in me home, to say g'bye." She shooed him toward the door. "Off with ye!"

Mace returned quickly to the inn and told the innkeeper to have everyone's meals sent to his room. The innkeeper shook his head. "The table in there be not big enough. Ye can use me private dining room. No charge." Mace accepted, and he went upstairs to round up his party.

Back in the dining room, with their two guards standing outside the door, he explained to them about Ella. The others were all excited about potentially having access to more knowledge, and they were happy to help her pack up. With eight bodies working, it would be done quickly.

The food was served, along with a complimentary bottle of c'irliq and a couple of pitchers of ale. It was roasted petramander in a mushroom sauce that gave a buff of +4 to stamina for four hours. They made plans for the escort quest as they ate, betting amongst themselves whether the Steinhalle dwarves would even show up.

Mace stuck his head out the door to speak with the guards, asking about where he might get a wagon and petramander or two to pull it. One of the guards knew a merchant whose business was on a downturn that might sell a wagon. Mace gave him a hundred gold and instructed him to get a large wagon with a healthy team and to meet them at the bookshop.

Their meal finished and stomachs full, the party set off for Ella's shop. When they hit the market, everyone slowed to take in the sights again. Mace didn't blame them. Before today, none of the dwarves had been to any sort of big city. He and their second guard kept watch as they did a little shopping.

They still reached the shop a few minutes before Ella. She came bustling up, out of breath from rushing back. "It be all settled!" She grinned at him, passing the three diamonds back to him discreetly. "Thank ye, fer the trust."

She let them in, and they got to work. She took one of her storage rings upstairs, left the other with Layne. Mace pulled out his two empty rings and handed them to Griff and Lisa. "Big stuff first. I don't know how big the wagon is going to be. Don't take the shelves, just the inventory," he said.

As they got to work, he got another idea. Stepping back out to the market, he moved toward a leatherworker's stall. "Do you have any bags of holding? Or other items for storage?"

The gnome running the stall nodded her head. "I have these bags here." She held up one of three bags sitting on her table. "Each holds fifty items. I don't have anything larger. Fifty gold each."

"I'll give you forty each. And a bonus if you can refer me to someone who has more or better."

"Deal!" She handed over the three bags, and he held up one of the diamonds, one eyebrow raised. "Go see Bonnie. She's a gnome like me, around the corner and five or six stalls down. She has storage rings. Big ones. But they'll be expensive. Tell her Eden sent you." Mace handed her the diamond and hurried to follow her directions.

He found the jewelry stall with no problem. It was indeed run by a gnome, and it was guarded by two hobgoblins in full armor. He approached, asking, "Are you Bonnie? Eden said I might find you here."

"I am." The gnome smiled up at him. She must have been standing on a crate or something to see over her countertop. "What can I do for you?"

"I need storage rings, or whatever other storage devices you have. The bigger the better."

She pointed to a ring mounted in a small black velvet box. "That one holds five hundred items. I have two of them." Next, she pointed to a thick metal bracelet engraved in a leaf pattern. "This one's elvish. Loot from one of the wars long ago. It holds one thousand items."

"How much for all three?" Mace asked. As far as he was concerned, you could never have too much inventory space.

She looked thoughtful. "Since Eden sent you, I'll make you a deal. Two hundred each for the rings, three hundred for the bracelet."

Mace looked them over. He was going to buy them, he just wanted to see if he could level his *Trade* skill. "How about… five hundred for all three, and an open invitation to trade in my city, tax-free. I'll provide you with a stall in the market, or an empty storefront if you prefer, for one month for free. After that, you pay rent and taxes like everyone else. Or I'll offer you a deep discount if you'd like to purchase a permanent shop."

"So, you'd be the new drow king everyone's whispering about?" she asked.

He nodded his head. "King Mace of Styrke, at your service."

"And how many jewelry shops do you have in your city?"

"Darkstone had zero jewelry shops when I left yesterday. We're a growing city. Many of my residents are former slaves, just starting a new life." To add a little encouragement, he pulled the bag of diamonds from his inventory and poured several out onto his palm, making sure to jiggle the bag a good bit so Bonnie could judge its weight. Selecting two diamonds, he poured the others back in the bag and put it away. He then removed one of the hundred-gold plates and set it on her counter, placing the diamonds neatly on top.

"What do you say? Do we have a deal?"

"I've never been to a surface city. Might be interesting. Can I bring Eden with me?"

Mace grinned, briefly. "Sure. And two or three others. But that's it. We're still a small city, I can't have an army of merchants invading. I'll be limiting the number of visiting traders to six at a time, for now."

They both knew he meant visiting traders from the underground, where they were just as likely to be thieves and murderers as honest merchants. She gave him a wink and took the payment, making it disappear up a sleeve. "I'll see you in Darkstone, then." After a pause, she said, "Where IS this city?"

He had her open up her map, and he shared the location with her, along with the route he took up to the surface with the kobolds. From there, he told her just to follow the mountain range and it would lead her right to the city walls. "I'm afraid there are no roads, yet. I'm working on building one soon."

He took the storage devices and nodded his head before walking away. Just a few steps toward the book shop, he paused. Turning back, he said, "Or, if you like, we're escorting a bunch of duergar back to Steinhalle in the morning. It's within the boundaries of my kingdom, and a few hours' walk from the city, if you're not carrying a heavy load. You're welcome to join us. Then you can map a surface route back at your leisure.

She shook her head. "This is a busy time for me here. But thank you."

"We'll be at the gate at eight bells, leaving by nine bells if you change your mind.

Back at the bookstore, he put the bracelet on his wrist and handed storage rings to Jo, and Meg, who both gaped at the rings when they saw the capacity. Mace handed Leroy the three bags with fifty slots each.

Now everyone in their packing crew had storage devices to work with, except Layne. She took a seat on a stool in a corner and began to play a tune that increased stamina regeneration and generally put them all in a good mood. Books disappeared off the shelves at a rapid pace. They made every effort to keep them organized in the same way that they'd been on the shelves. Mace focused on the most expensive books, the ones behind the counter. He started by jumping atop the counter and reaching up to the upper left shelf, then working his way across.

Reading the titles as he went, he practically drooled over the accumulated knowledge on those shelves. He'd need to figure out some kind of bulk discount with Ella and use city funds to buy as many of them as he could.

When Lisa was finished filling her ring, she went to assist Ella, taking one of the unused bags from Leroy. The druid was spending more time watching Meg reach and bend than he was filling his bags. Mace didn't scold him, as they were clearly going to be finished quickly enough. Eight people boxing and moving things could empty a space pretty quickly. Take away the need to move anything by simply sucking it into a ring or a bag, and the process sped up considerably.

The guard arrived with the wagon and a team of young petramanders. The wagon was huge! Nearly long enough for two drow to lay end to end in the bed. Or one rock troll. Mace stepped outside to speak with him for a moment.

"Yer lordship." The guard bowed his head. "I grabbed ye the largest he had. And these lizards be a breeding pair, in case ye wanted ta start a herd o' yer own." He lifted a sack of gold coins. "There be nearly fifty left over fer ye. The merchant was desperate fer gold." He grinned. Mace suspected there had been some intimidation involved as well.

He held up a hand. "Split what is left between the two of you," he said as he nodded toward the other guard. "I'm sure the innkeeper doesn't pay you what you're worth. And I may need your assistance loading some large items shortly."

The two guards exchanged looks, and the one who had remained with Mace cleared his throat. "Yer pardon, lordship. But would ye be needin' guards fer yer journey to Steinhalle?"

Mace looked both of them in the eye. He detected no deceit from either of them, but they were grey dwarves. Though not as purely evil as drow, the average grey dwarf would still murder without hesitation given a chance to get away with it.

"I'm afraid not." He shook his head, and both guards looked disappointed as they nodded their acceptance. "But I could always use more guards in my city. It won't pay as well as this job, and you'll have to swear an oath of loyalty, which Elysia herself will bind you to. Breaking the oath would mean your death."

The first guard asked, "What I hear'd ya say to Ella, that bit about crafting. I could learn a craft? Other than smashin' heads?"

Mace nodded. "Of course. You'd have to earn some gold, either working as a guard, running dungeons, or ideally both. And you could either apprentice under one of the masters in your free time or purchase one of Ella's books and learn that way. All citizens that join us in these early days receive a free place to live, and you could use that as your crafting shop at first. Or build yourself a real one. There will be many opportunities for growth."

The other guard, the one who'd brought the wagon, asked, "And we'd not owe ye a debt?"

"Only your oath of loyalty. And your willingness to work hard to improve the community."

Mace left them to think, saying, "I'll shout if we need a hand inside. In the meantime, please make sure nobody bothers us, and that the wagon and team are safe." The two guards bowed their heads, and Mace stepped back inside.

He found the place basically empty. There was some items underneath the counter that still needed to be stored. And Leroy had moved back to the back room to help Griff and Jo round up crafting tools and materials.

Ella came downstairs with Lisa behind her. "Everything be packed up." She smiled as she took in the empty shelves. "You lot've been busy down here."

Mace said, "Take a look around, make sure we've got everything. The wagon's outside, but I don't think we'll need it."

Ella poked around, examining all the shelves. Mace noticed her eyes darting toward his people and then down toward the floor. She looked nervous about something. He thought he knew what it was about.

"Thanks, guys, everybody hop in the wagon. We'll ride back in luxury. I'll be right out."

When the others had left, he hopped up on the counter and sat with his heels thumping the wooden front. "Nobody took anything they shouldn't; my people are honest. And no secret compartments have been opened. I'll leave that to you, if you like. Do you have space enough in your ring?"

Ella looked embarrassed. "That's just it. I dunno. Me late husband said he had a secret place where he stashed some gold and our most precious items. But I do no' know where it is. I've looked for it often since he died, but I've had no luck."

Mace nodded. "I can probably find it for you, if you like." He thumbed his chest. "Darkblade. Trained for that kind of thing, ya know." His smile seemed to relax her some. When she nodded, he activated his *Mage Sight* and began searching the room. Finding nothing in the front room, he worked his way to the back. There was a faint blue glow underneath the floorboards in one corner. Using a disposable throwing dagger, he pried the board up. Underneath he found a leather satchel that glowed a bright blue.

He stepped back after checking to make sure there were no traps. Ella bent down and lifted the pack and carried it to the other room to set it on the counter. Searching inside, she frowned, then looked confused. "I do no' think this be me husband's."

She pulled a bag from the pack and dumped its contents on the floor. Large gems of several different types rattled across the boards, each engraved with symbols of some kind. Next, she opened a box filled with what looked like crafting ingredients. There was also a wrapped leather sheath filled with fine tools, and lastly, a small book with a worn cover. Opening the book, she read for a few moments. "Ah, I see. Ye found old Harmon's treasure. He were an enchanter, lived here two hunnert years at least. Died suddenly when he attempted some kind o' ritual." She lowered her voice to a whisper and winked at him as she added, "Some say he were tryin' ta summon himself a succubus ta play with. Burned up half this place in the process." She gathered the items and put them back into the pack. "That be why me late husband purchased this shop. He did no' mind a little work, and he got it cheap because o' the damage."

Mace nodded. "So then you're husband's stash is still here someplace. I'll continue the search. In the meantime, would you consider selling Harmon's treasure to me? I know an enchanter who'd make good use of it."

She handed him the pack. "My gift to ya. Fer all yer doin' to help me."

Mace bowed slightly in thanks as he accept the gift. "Thank you, Ella." He moved on to the stairs and continued to search with his *Mage Sight.* In the upstairs bathroom, he spotted a glow behind a mural on the wall above the toilet. It was an odd mural, featuring a duergar riding a large bull. The bull's eyes were wide, and it was snorting in fear or anger. The glow of whatever was behind the wall made the bull's eyes glow to Mace's enhanced eyes.

"I think your husband had a sense of humor." He pointed to the mural, but Ella just looked confused. Smacking his forehead, he cast *Mage Sight* on her as well. Her mouth dropped open, and she looked around in wonder. "The glow that you see is something magic behind the wall. But he placed it so that the bull's eyes glow. Funny." Mace grinned as she caught on.

"Ha! He thought he was funny, but no one ever laughed at his jokes." She sniffed a little. "This be exactly the kind o' thing he'd do." She stepped forward and touched the mural gently, tracing the bull's face and horns with light fingers. "Be a shame to destroy this."

Mace examined it more closely, finding what he was looking for after just a few moments. "No need to destroy it." He pressed a cracked tile and the mural popped open, the door's edges matching the outline of the bull's body exactly.

Ella snorted, laughing at the ridiculous thing. "Ah, I do miss him some days." She sighed when she caught her breath. Reaching into the open space, she found a matched pair of thick leather-bound books, a wooden box with a silver clasp, and two bags filled with coins. She looked surprised at the weight of the bags and promptly put the coins in her inventory. If they were gold, Mace thought Ella's husband had done better than she'd figured.

Setting the books down carefully, she opened the clasp on the wooden box and lifted the lid. Inside were a few hand-written notes, a men's handkerchief, a pair of engraved cufflinks, and a few other items Mace couldn't make out. Ella touched each one of them briefly. Sniffling again as she closed the box and hugged it to her chest, her voice wavered slightly. "Sentimental old fool. Them's all gifts I give'd him when we were younglings. And notes. Me da didn't approve of him, and we had ta meet in secret. I left him notes under a stone ta tell him where ta find me."

Mace stayed silent, not wanting to intrude on her memories. After a while, she set the box down and retrieved one of the books. "These be his journals. He was always writin' a lil somethin' before he came to bed." She opened the large book, and Mace could see tightly packed written words filling the pages front and back. "Seventy years o' his scribblin's…"

Mace coughed. "I think maybe you've got some reading to do. You have enough room in your ring for your bed and these other items?" When she nodded absently, he said, "Then I wish you a pleasant evening, Ella. We'll stop here and pick you up on our way to the gate. Eight bells?"

She nodded again, and Mace left her to her reminiscing. He joined the others outside, and they rode the wagon up to the main column. The guard who'd secured the wagon led the team away to a nearby stable while the rest rode the elevator up to the inn and retired for the evening.

Chapter 18

Morning found Mace, Griff, Lisa and the others up early and having a full breakfast in the private dining room. The same waitress he'd failed to earn a smile from during his first visit served them bacon, eggs, freshly baked bread lightly toasted and buttered, some kind of citrus fruit that had a sweet and tangy taste, and a light ale.

They ate quickly, the guards joining them for the meal this time. Both had informed Mace that they wished to take the oath and join him. One of them left ahead of the group to fetch the wagon and lizard team, the other escorted Mace as he took a detour to the back alley where his hundred kegs were stacked in several rows. He took them all into his bracelet and returned to the others without any hassles. On the way out, the innkeeper actually smiled at Mace, saying, "Hope to you see you again, Majesty." The smile made Mace want to test the contents of the kegs.

Piling into the wagon, they worked their way down through the market to Ella's shop. She was there, just handing over a set of keys to another duergar that Mace assumed was the alchemist. Griff hopped off the wagon and helped Ella up, and they were off again in less than a minute.

Upon reaching the gates, they found a small crowd of people milling around just inside and to the left of the exit. There were half a dozen wagons, a few smaller carts all piled high with items, and maybe sixty duergar men, women, and children.

Balen Boulderhugger stepped forward to meet them as they approached. His face still looked angry, but he stuck out a hand, which Mace shook. "We be waitin' on a few stragglers, if ye don't mind."

Mace looked around. All eyes seemed to be on him, some with hope in them, others with fear. He tried to look at their mission as more than just another escort quest. These were actual families, even if they were only NPCs. After all, if he had his way, he'd become an NPC too.

"Of course, Chieftain Boulderhugger. I said we'd wait as late as nine bells. It's only just past eight, so you have some time yet." Looking again at the overloaded carts, he added, "We've got an empty wagon here. All but Ella can walk, and she can ride up front with the driver. Would your people like to transfer some of their loads?"

Balen shook his head. "We be fine. My people ain't trustin' no drow with their goods," he grumped at Mace.

"Bah! Hush, ye backwater dillweed!" Ella scolded him. "King Mace be an honorable outworlder and me new friend! He be more trustworthy than you 'n' yer lot!"

Balen's gaze dropped to his feet. He took a few deep breaths, then spoke. "Our wagons be fine ta carry our goods. But we've a few elders and wee ones that could do with a ride."

Mace tried to be as gracious as possible. "That would be fine. Send them over, maybe with a few packs or blankets to use as cushions? We've got plenty of room."

Balen nodded as all but Ella hopped out of the wagon. He walked back to his people, and a few minutes later, a trickle of Steinhalle duergar began to flow toward the wagon. A few ancient-looking elders that Ella whispered to Mace were nearing three hundred years of age were the first to approach. They were gently helped into the back of the wagon, where boxes were placed and padded with a folded blanket for them to sit on. A few additional less venerable elders followed, and they were quickly outpaced by a pack of ten children who raced toward the wagon and vaulted up into the back. Ella and the others quickly settled them, making room for the remaining elders to ride comfortably.

By the time all were loaded, the stragglers had arrived. Balen shouted that all who'd be making the trip were present. Mace nodded once, and the caravan set off. They exited the gate without ceremony, other than a polite wave from the guards, and were on their way.

Mace let Balen lead the way with a small company of his own fighters. He walked along about midway back along the line with Layne next to him strumming a refreshing tune that gave everyone including the lizards pulling the wagons a stamina buff. Griff, Lisa and the others were grouped at the back of the caravan, right behind the wagonload of children. As always, in the underground, an attack is most likely to come from above or behind.

With Layne's buff, they kept a good pace. Mace expected the trip to take a full day based on a quick estimate of the distance on his map. And with a time allowance to deal with ambushes or roving goblin patrols. His map was mostly blank, though, so he didn't know if there was a direct route to Steinhalle, or whether they'd have to meander around a while.

The first bit of excitement came when a rock spider dropped onto Mace's wagon, opting for the juicy young duergar as targets. Jo instantly hit it with a fireball, causing it to scream as its fur caught fire. Meg shoved it off the side of the wagon with her halberd, jamming the blade deep into its side toward Mace, who plunged his soul dagger into its head and drained it.

The dagger gave a slight feeling of contentment, but it wasn't much appeased by the low-level soul. The duergar, however, were much impressed with the speed and efficiency of the party's response. The elders clapped their hands, and the children cheered. Mace looted the meat and other bits, and they moved on without ever having stopped the wagons.

After three hours of travel, two more rock spiders, a pack of feral petramanders, and a squod attack, they stopped in a small cavern filled with giant mushrooms and a burbling stream for a lunch break. The duergar broke out some travel rations and ale, and everyone simply sat on the ground to eat. Mace remained on his feet, patrolling the area with his *Mage Sight* activated. He cast it on Griff and Lisa as well, so they could help keep watch. He'd offered the same to Balen, but the gruff duergar had refused.

When the meal was through, the duergar rose without a word and resumed their trek. Mace moved to the front of the line and walked to the stream. He called out, "*Frigus!*" and moved his hands, directing a cold blast that created a short ice bridge, enabling the wagons and carts to cross.

They moved along for three hours encountering only minor skirmishes with the denizens of the underground, and Balen called for another break. This time in a larger cavern that was bare of anything except a thick carpet of moss on the floor and some scattered boulders. When Mace caught up to him, he asked, "Why are we stopping here?"

Balen grimaced. "We be close to our home. This cavern be the edge of our hunting grounds. Used ta be giant moles and feral petramanders here. Along with a crop o' mushrooms." He waved his arm in a sweeping motion that took in the entire cavern. "In the weeks before we were driven out, three o' me hunters came here and dinno' return. Me guess be there's a new predator here."

Mace swept the cavern, finding no signs of life. He activated his *Mage Vision* and checked again, still finding nothing. Which in itself was worrying. Caverns in the underground were nearly always occupied. Often crowded. Each was a microcosm of the larger world, with insects feeding on plant life, snakes and small creatures feeding on the insects, larger creatures, eating them, and so forth.

He turned to Balen. "I don't detect anything. We'll move forward, but carefully. Get all your people off the wagons and walking alongside with weapons ready. Tell them to be ready to hide underneath if we're attacked. We'll move slow and quiet, so the elders can keep pace."

Balen simply nodded and turned away, motioning silently to his fighters who dispersed down the line. Mace was impressed with how quickly and quietly the duergar prepared themselves. Even the frail elders seemed eager for a little adventure, using one hand on the wagon to steady themselves as they walked.

The caravan seemed to inch forward as they crept across the open space. They moved silently, Layne forgoing her usual traveling tune for the moment. Balen stayed in the lead, though his fighters were now more spread out along the line. Mace moved his group to mix in with them, and he took up the rear. The whole caravan was stretched just a couple hundred feet from front to rear, so he could see what was happening up ahead.

Three-quarters of the way across the cavern every head snapped upward as a keening, chittering sound echoed through the space. Mace instantly cast a light globe up toward the ceiling, causing the keening to rise in pitch and volume. It revealed a giant centipede dangling from a hole in the ceiling.

> *Megapede Elite*
> *Level 60*
> *Health: 40,000/40,000*

Its head hung down maybe five feet below the ceiling, the rest of its body disappearing in the hole above. It had two wicked pincer mandibles that clicked together in agitation, each one as long as Mace's leg. Jo sent a fireball upward to smash into its face, but the attack did little damage. Most of the flames rolled right off the chitin exoskeleton.

"Go! This is our fight!" Mace shouted at the duergar. Balen and his fighters each grabbed a lizard's harness and began to pull them forward. Griff and Lisa physically lifted the elders and tossed them unceremoniously into the wagon bed. The children raced alongside their parents, fear making them silent and a bit faster than normal.

Mace held up his hands, shouting, "*Ventus!*" and making a slashing motion at the same time. A blade of air sliced into the megapede, and there was an audible crunch as the chitin cracked on the rear of its head segment.

The megapede began to run across the ceiling, more and more of its body emerging from the hole. By the time its tail emerged with its smaller but no less deadly pincers, Mace could see that the creature was about twenty feet long. The body was segmented and had fifty legs on each side. The middle forty legs on each side ended in thick insectoid feet that gripped the stone effortlessly as it moved along the ceiling. The remaining legs, five on each side in the front and back, ended in wickedly barbed spear points made of the same chitin as its exoskeleton. The clicking sounds of its many feet striking the stone as it moved sounded like war drums in the otherwise silent underground cavern.

Jo continued to send fireballs after it, though many of them missed as it moved with great dexterity down the curve of the ceiling to the nearest wall. Those that hit shaved off a few points of health, but the creature didn't seem to notice.

Lisa took aim with her crossbow and fired a bolt that actually penetrated the chitin covering one of its many abdominal sections. Likewise, Layne's arrows managed to do some damage, mainly because with her superior skill and experience she was able to target the joints between segments.

Mace aimed another lash of his wind blade at the same spot, cracking the chitin further and exposing the bleeding flesh beneath. He took a moment to check on the duergar, who were nearly to the cavern's exit despite their limited pace.

"Retreat! Slowly, but steadily. Let's try not to get too far from our duergar. Something else might attack them while we're dealing with this bug." Mace began to walk backward even as he called out, *"Frigus!"* and pushed both hands toward the descending mob. A trail of ice formed on the floor of the cavern between himself and the wall, then began to climb up toward the megapede. When the two met approximately twenty feet up the wall, the monster lost its grip and fell. Landing on its back with a crunch, it quickly contorted its body and righted itself. Still on the ice sheet, its movement was slowed as the propulsion feet slid on the slippery surface.

"We need to lure it into the tunnel. Take it away its ability to use that tail pincer." Mace and his group continued to back away from the thing, remaining between it and the fleeing duergar. Lisa fired again, this time directly into the monster's face as it approached. She scored a critical hit, the bolt slamming into one of its dozen compound eyes and doing significant damage.

Megapede Elite
Level 60

Health: 31,800/40,000

Jo fired a massive fireball directly into its face, still not doing much damage, but causing it to pause and shake away the flames. The damaged eye boiled and exploded from the heat.

The combination of the ice, the damage, and the delay from the fire attacks allowed the duergar to escape into the tunnel. Mace and his people turned and raced after them, stopping just inside the tunnel entrance to make a stand. With his people safe, Balen left his fighters to guard the front of the caravan and joined Mace and the others at the rear to fight the elite mob.

Griff waited until the megapede was almost to the tunnel before activating his *Shield Rush* ability. He shot forward, shield slamming into the monstrous head that was larger than Griff himself. Metal struck chitin with a resounding clang, but the dwarf's size and momentum were not enough to have much of an effect on the megapede. Griff staggered back from the impact, shaking his head and groaning. Leroy sent him a heal, and he seemed to recover his wits. Planting his shield in the stone, he started yelling, "C'mon, ye big prickly puss bucket! Yer father was an inchworm, and yer mother was a porcupine!"

The rest of the group paused to look at the angry tank, and Lisa snorted. "Lame!" She winked at him when he turned to look at her. "We need to practice your taunts!"

Rolling his eyes, he returned his attention to the elite monster just as it latched onto his shield with its mandibles. The chitin screeched across the metal as it lifted the front segments of its body up toward the ceiling, taking Griff and his shield with it. The dwarf, now hanging by his shield arm with most of his body exposed, was quickly impaled by two of the sharp forelegs. He screamed in pain, letting go of his shield and dangling a foot above the floor with the two legs protruding through his shoulder and gut.

Leroy began frantically healing their tank as Meg charged forward with her halberd blade. Using her momentum and every ounce of strength she could muster, she drove the pointed end spike into the creature's face.

It found the soft spot around its mouth, driving inward a full ten inches. She quickly began twisting and pushing at the same time, doing as much damage as she could. Lisa and Balen were right behind her, hacking and slashing at the beast with swords and axe as they dodged thrusts of the pointed forelegs and the snapping mandibles.

Mace ran forward and grabbed Griff, yanking him back off the spiked feet. The barbs in the spikes snagged on the tank's armor and ripped large chunks of his flesh away as he fell.

The megapede began to lower its front segments, trying to crush the melee fighters under its body, but Meg had the presence of mind to plant the butt end of her halberd's shaft against the stone floor. The harder the monster pushed, the deeper the weapon penetrated, its own weight working against it. Leaving the weapon jammed in place, she drew her throwing spear from her inventory and began to jab at the monster's face.

After dragging Griff back to a safe distance, Mace left him for Leroy to take care of. Using his natural drow agility, he charged at the monster. Shifting to one side, he ran partway up the wall and pushed himself off, the boost allowing him to land atop the writhing megapede. Laying flat on his belly, he slammed his left-hand dagger into the weakened spot on the back of its head segment and used it as an anchor to keep himself atop the beast as it thrashed.

Below him, he heard Meg scream as one of the sharp forelegs penetrated her side. It lifted her off the ground, her feet dangling and unable to find purchase. Grunting in pain and effort, she continued to jab at it with her spear even as crimson jets of blood watered the floor under her.

"Noooo!" Leroy abandoned Griff, who was back up to sixty percent health, and began to cast heals on his beloved. Her health bar hovered around thirty percent as she continued to bleed and take damage from the barbs on the leg as it thrashed her around while Leroy cast heal after heal. He practically screamed at her, "Stop jabbin' and drink a potion, dammit! I can't keep ye alive on me own!"

She did as she was told, pulling a potion from her bag and gulping it down. The thrashing of the leg caused some of it to spill, but her health bar rose above fifty percent.

Mace slammed his soul dagger into the weakened chitin near his first dagger. "Die, you creepy bastard!" Immediately the surge of energy roared up his arm and into his body. The dagger cried out in joy as it drained the elite monster.

"Yessss!"

The megapede began to thrash furiously, the high-pitched keening deafening everyone nearby as it slammed its body left and right. Without warning, it charged forward, its center legs propelling it even with its upper legs in the air. Lisa and Balen were bowled over and trampled even as Leroy, Jo and Layne dove to either side of the tunnel to avoid the same fate. Meg was thrown free of the leg that impaled her in a spray of blood before slamming into a wall and dropping to the ground.

Frantic to kill the beast before it wiped his whole party, Mace let go of the dagger in his left hand and withdrew the legendary blade Duskshadow from his inventory. Using the soul dagger as his anchor now, he slammed Duskshadow through the cracked chitin and activated its enchantment. The eight-inch dagger blade instantly became a thirty-inch shadow blade that ripped through the megapede's brain.

Using the strength that his soul dagger was stealing from the beast and pouring into him, Mace withdrew the long blade and slammed it back in, again and again. In the throes of agony, the monster slammed its head upward, crushing Mace against the tunnel ceiling and stunning him. He felt a few of his ribs break against a protruding rock, and he lost his grip on the shadow sword. The beast's head fell back down, and Meg's halberd, which was still deeply embedded in the underside of its head segment, was thrust upward as the butt end struck the stone floor. The spike erupted through the top of the megapede's head and into Mace's gut.

Mace tried to scream in pain, but couldn't get the air in his lungs. His chest had been compressed by the impact with the ceiling, and he was still stunned. All that came out was a weak groan accompanied by a trickle of blood.

The damage to its head and brain finished the creature, its health bar dropping to zero. Mace's stun wore off, and he pulled both the soul dagger and Duskshadow from its head. The pain of those movements nearly blinded him. He tried to roll off, but the spike from Meg's halberd held him in place. Gritting his teeth, he put away his weapons and used his arms to push himself up off the creature's head, feeling the spike pull out of his gut and hearing the splash of blood as he did. The energy from the soul dagger had kept his health above fifty percent, but his UI showed a stacked *bleeding* debuff.

He couldn't see Leroy anywhere from where he was, which meant the healer couldn't see him either. Laying on his side, Mace pulled a health potion from his inventory and drank it. The sounds of Leroy frantically calling Meg's name, and many others calling out for Lisa and Balen, prompted him to check the party display on his UI.

Lisa was greyed out. He thought the megapede must have crushed her. Meg's health bar was back to full, so she must have leveled up. Balen was barely holding on, his health bar just a sliver. Jo and Leroy had been slightly injured, as was Layne. Griff was recovered from his wounds, but he was moving slowly. The dwarves' health bars had all refilled when they leveled. His own health bar was above half and holding, the bleeding having been stopped by the potion.

Rolling off the monster's back, he landed on unsteady feet and took in the scene. A dozen or more duergar were gathered along one side of the monster, each of them having taken hold of one leg, and were trying to lift the beast. Mace could make out Balen's bloodied head and one arm underneath. One of them was pouring a health potion down his throat, but Mace couldn't tell if he was swallowing it.

He quickly cast *Levitate* on the corpse. The spell didn't raise the elite mob off the floor on its own, but it did provide enough of an assist that the duergar were able to lift it and pull Balen free. A few excited shouts got Leroy's attention long enough for him to use the last of his mana on a heal for Balen.   The dwarf druid immediately gulped a mana potion and went back to healing.

With all the living healed enough to be out of danger, Mace took a moment to loot the corpse. He was awarded with eighty-five gold, a hundred sixty pieces of megapede meat, seventy pieces of megapede chitin, all twenty of its spiked feet, both mandibles, and a set of chitin pincers. He shook his head. If he'd killed this same beast a month earlier, he might have gotten a tenth of these items. A little meat, a couple pieces of chitin for armor, and a spike or two.

It turned out that nearly all the dwarves and duergar had leveled up when the megapede died. The exception being Balen, who was apparently a much higher level than the others. Layne and Mace hadn't earned new levels either.

Each of them was able to loot the mob's corpse, except of course for Lisa, who was in limbo waiting to respawn. Mace hoped she had the sense to wait and respawn at her body, instead of choosing to immediately respawn back at the inn in Svartholm where she'd spent the previous night. He didn't have a way to communicate with her in limbo – a game mechanic that prevented players who were, for example, killed during successful sneak attacks on a fortress or guild house, from alerting their comrades before they respawned.

While the requisite ten minutes passed for Lisa, Mace had the dwarves and duergar physically harvest all they could from the megapede. Chitin armor was cracked up and peeled away in large chunks to be used in crafting armor. Thick chitin feet from the eighty unsharpened legs were harvested as well. These could be shaped into spikes or other useful items. One of the duergar females asked if she could take one for carving a figurine. Mace gave her two.

Finally, Lisa respawned. The golden glow of a level increase immediately engulfed her.

"Damn, that hurt," was the first thing she said. "I could no' get out o' the way fast enough. Got meself squished. Damned heavy thing, stepped right on me face." She grinned sheepishly at Griff. The tank hung his head.

"That's my fault. I failed to hold aggro," he mumbled.

"Bah!" Balen walked up and slapped the dwarf on the shoulder. Now fully healed, the duergar chieftain was all smiles. "I see'd ya take on the big beastie! It skewered ye like a hunk o' petramander kabob. I'd not have gotten back up after that if it were me. Yer tougher than ye look, dwarf!"

Griff bowed his head briefly. Grinning at the duergar, he replied, "How'd it smell under there? From the look on yer face, I'm guessin' not good."

Balen rolled his gaze up the ceiling and placed both hands dramatically over his heart. "It weren't the weight o' the beastie that nearly did me in, it were the stench!"

Both of them chuckled, the others around them joining in. Lisa looted the corpse, and they prepared to get on their way. As they were moving back toward the caravan, Balen caught up with Mace.

In a voice so quiet only Mace could possibly have heard it, he said, "I seen what ye did with Duskshadow. I were wrong before. Ye be a true champion, and worthy o' wielding that weapon.

"Thank you, Balen. That means a lot to me." Mace looked at the weapons slot on his character sheet. The weapon showed as equipped for his left hand, and it was now soulbound. He'd been holding off equipping the weapon since finding it, and he had contemplated giving it to Lila. In the heat of battle, the decision had been made for him.

The duergar's spirits were high as they resumed the trip. They were close to home, which they'd be able to reclaim, and the unknown creature that had been killing off their food supply, and their hunters, had been destroyed.

Nothing else attacked them on the final leg of their journey. When Balen led them through the broken gates of Steinhalle, all of Mace's party got quest completion notifications. This time all of them leveled up, including Mace and Layne.

> **Quest Complete: Steinhalle Dungeon Part II**
> *You have safely returned sixty of the Steinhalle duergar to their rightful homes. You lost zero Steinhalle duergar during the journey from Svartholm. Bonus experience awarded!*
> **Reward**: *Quest completion xp; 100,000, Bonus xp; 1,000 per citizen x 60 = 60,000xp; Reputation gain with Steinhalle +100. You are now Friendly with the duergar in the village.*

The duergar spread out through the village, inspecting the damage. Some of them shouted with joy, others wept over their losses. Balen, his face set in an unreadable mask, waited in the center square for Mace and the others as they entered at the rear of the column.

"Thank ye, all of ye, fer returning our home ta us." He shook hands with each of them.

> **Your reputation with the Steinhalle duergar has increased by +100! You are now Respected.**

Mace was last to shake his hand. "Now that you're here and safe, we'll leave you to rebuild. We just have one little formality to deal with…"

Balen nodded his head. "Aye, an agreement is an agreement."

He raised his hands and shouted, "All of ye! Come here, right now!"

His people didn't waste any time returning to the center of the village. When all of them were present, he took a knee. Each of them followed suit, and they repeated his words as he took the oath.

"I, Balen Boulderhugger of the Steinhalle duergar, do be pledgin' me loyalty to King Mace and the Kingdom o' Styrke. I'll take no action against king or kingdom, on pain o' death."

The swirling magic that bound them to the oath appeared around each of them, and it was done.

"Welcome to Styrke!" Mace shouted, raising a fist in the air. "As my first task as your king, I will help to make sure your home remains safe." He pulled up his city UI and, sure enough, there was a tab for Steinhalle. After a few mental clicks, the sound of grinding stone and bending metal could be heard as the bent and broken gates began to repair themselves.

The duergar all got to their feet and clapped or gave muted cheers. Mace waved at them in what he thought was a kingly manner, though both Griff and Lisa snorted with amusement. Lisa turned on Griff, punching him in the shoulder. "Ya shouldn't be laughin' at nobody, mister 'yer mother was a porcupine'!"

This time everyone laughed. Griff shrugged. "I was improvising."

Mace turned his attention back to the duergar. "Balen Boulderhugger, I invite you and your people to join us to live in Darkstone, our city on the surface. You certainly are welcome to remain here if you choose, but I want you to know you have options."

Balen shook his head. "Fer now, we'll be stayin' here. This be my home, the home o' me father and grandfather. It weren't easy to give it up, and now that it be ours again, we'll be stayin'."

Mace looked at the wagon with the petramander team. There was no way to get them back to the surface on the route they'd be taking. And walking them all the way back to the portal would take hours.

"Would you be so kind as to take care of our wagon and team? I'm told the lizards are a breeding pair. Maybe you have someone here that can breed them?"

"Aye, we can handle that. Give us a month, and we'll be havin' a herd o' pregnant females." The chieftain thumped his chest. "There be other caverns here that'll have feral lizards."

"If you run into problems with food sources, or more enemies, send a runner up to the surface." He shared the route on his map with Balen, being careful not to show the portal room or the dungeon at all. "We will send what help we can."

They said goodbye to the duergar and set off on the journey home. After Mace had levitated everyone up through the first of the chutes to the next level corridor, the familiar clank of many feet on stone rang out. Mace cast another light globe and waited.

A moment later, the same party of gnomes jogged into the light, weapons bared. When the lead gnome saw Mace and halted abruptly, the others crashed into him and each other, causing a pile-up in the tunnel.

"Gnomes…" Mace greeted them.

"King Drow!" the same lead gnome from before called out. He instantly raised both his empty hands in the air as if surrendering. His companions quickly followed suit. "We been sent to find you."

"Suicide mission!" the enthusiastic young gnome in the back shouted. Several of the others smacked him on and about the head. Mace tried not to grin.

"Were you sent to try and collect that toll after all?" he growled, causing every gnome to take a step back.

"No!" the lead gnome squeaked. Grimacing, he cleared his throat and tried again. "No. Sent with an invitation. Our big boss, the Head Gadgeteer, wishes to honor you. Thank you for killing the rock trolls. Invites you to visit our city, Tinkeropolis!"

Mace couldn't resist the grin this time. "Are you not worried I'll steal the treasure under your fountain?"

"Dammit, Pidge! You and your big mouth!" One of the gnomes in the back kicked the one who had mentioned the fountain during their last encounter. Pidge kicked back, and a free-for-all melee erupted. Cursing, punching, kicking, and biting spread as all but the leader jumped into the fray.

The lead gnome rolled his eyes. "We forgot to tell the boss that you know about the treasure. That might change things. We'll have to go ask him." He turned and started shouting at his troops, throwing more than a few kicks himself. When the last of them calmed down and all were back on their feet, Mace held up a hand.

"Oh, valiant gnome warriors. Please tell your Head Gadgeteer that I have no desire to steal your treasure. I would be honored to visit your city. If I am still welcome after you've spoken to him again, come find me at Darkstone City on the surface."

The leader nodded once, thumping his fist to his chest in salute, then he turned and ran back the way they came. The others followed, quickly disappearing into the darkness as one of them shouted: "Munchkins Rule!"

Shaking his head, Mace led the others back to their home without further incident.

*****

The next morning, Griff and Lisa woke before sunrise in their underground home. Today was the day they planned to make a food run.

Both of them were quiet as Griff heated some water and poured packs of maple and brown sugar instant oatmeal into bowls. Their thoughts couldn't help but turn to the last time they'd been outside, and the nearly deadly encounter with the monstrous zombie creatures.

Finally, Lisa spoke. "D'ya think it'll be safe ta go back to the same Tesco? Or do we find a new one?"

Griff paused, about to pour steaming water into one of the bowls. "I've been thinkin' about it. I think we go back. We know our way around that one. If the double doors are still sealed, we should be fine. I don't like the idea of drivin' halfway across town to a store we've not seen before."

Lisa looked doubtful, but she nodded her head once. "But we'll check it out first, right? Like, drive around? Look inside, mebbe make a bit o' noise to see what happens?"

"O' course. If something comes chargin' out, we can escape in the truck. Which reminds me, we should try and find a larger truck, like Mace and Shari suggested. One more big load o' food, so we never again have to stick our pretty heads out there for them beasties to bite off."

The two of them returned to their rooms and donned their outside gear. Five minutes later, they were climbing into the Jeep and heading outside, one last time.

*****

Mace and Shari logged in about the same time Griff and Lisa were climbing into the Jeep. Shari wanted to show off the progress on the new palace, and Mace patiently followed her around, nodding and complimenting her choices. He didn't really care about the decorations much, but it made him happy that she was happy. And she really was doing an excellent job.

When the tour was over, he hugged her tight. Kissing her forehead, he said, "I'll leave you to it, my queen. I think I'm going to head down to the portal room and explore one of the ones we haven't checked yet."

She looked concerned. "By yourself? Which one are you going to pick?"

"I'm thinking the one up on the cliff that looks down over a town. See if maybe we can find another ally or even annex a whole town."

"Just be careful. And good luck!" She patted his behind like he was a baseball player going up to bat, then turned and began issuing orders to the new household staff.

Mace checked his gear as he made the journey down through the mine, into the dungeon, and through to the portal room. The circle of portals remained just as it was when he'd first activated them. He stood in the center near the pedestal and slowly turned in a circle. The one he'd chosen sat between the waterfall portal that Griff had brought the dwarves and orcs through, and the sea cave portal.

Moving to stand in front of it, he gazed through at the scene beyond. From a high vantage point atop a hill or cliff, it looked down into a luscious green valley filled with a town of red-roofed buildings. On either side, were steep mountains rising higher than the portal's location.

Taking a deep breath, Mace stepped through the portal. The disorientation lasted less time with each trip through the portals, and this time he barely faltered when he stepped onto the grass on the other side. He felt Minx's tail tighten briefly as she too compensated for the imbalance. Reaching up to stroke her fur without even thinking, he felt her relax and begin to purr.

He immediately turned around to face the portal. It wasn't what he'd expected. Rather than a cliff face or wall, the portal seemed to have been set into the trunk of a massive old ironwood tree. The elder giant stood at least a hundred fifty feet tall, and its branches extended out nearly as far. The trunk was easily wide enough to drive a wagon through if one were to hollow it out. If the tree were to fall, one could carve a small ship from its trunk in one single piece.

Not needing to worry about being able to find the giant landmark again, Mace took a throwing dagger from his inventory and embedded it in the earth with a flick of his wrist to mark the exact location on the trunk. Something about the aura of the elder tree made him not want to carve a sign in its trunk.

Turning back to the town below, he began to descend the slope. It was a gradual, grass-covered slope with boulders and rocky outcroppings scattered here and there. With nearly a mile to walk, Mace took a moment to open the map on his UI as he walked. He hoped to find that the portal had led him to a town in reasonable proximity to his kingdom.

His hopes were dashed as the map filled in around his location, but everything out of range of his sight was a ghostly grey. He tried zooming out, and still there was nothing but grey. Finally, he zoomed out far enough that most of the continent was visible. Far to the west, he saw the parts of the map he had filled in. The entrance to the underground where he'd first emerged, the kobold village, the centaur village, Lakeside, Darkstone, as well as the lake, river, and the cities of Port Bjurstrom and Graf.

The town he was approaching had not been labeled as yet. He supposed he would need to ask someone where he was. It was so far east of his kingdom that it was near the eastern coast. As he got closer, he saw that the buildings were constructed of both wood and stone, and a few tendrils of smoke wound upward from fireplaces.

Mace was scanning the shoreline on his map, wondering if the sea cave was somewhere nearby, when an impact to his chest knocked him off balance. As he stumbled, Minx screamed and became visible as she was impaled by an arrow that flung her off his shoulder. Her tail briefly tightened on his neck, but the force of the impact pulled her free. Her icon on his UI, constantly there below his own avatar's face, went grey as she hit the ground, already dead.

Another impact struck Mace's leg, then another in his gut. Looking up, he saw arrows speeding toward him from behind the rocks in every direction. A second later, one pierced his eye, and his health bar plummeted. As he fell dying upon the grass, he heard, "We got him! We killed the filthy drow!"

As he appeared in limbo, the first words out of his mouth were, "Well, shit."

End Book Three

Acknowledgements

As always, I want to thank my alpha readers, my family, who spend endless hours reading and re-reading my nonsense, seeking out plot holes and typos. And who occasionally provide original monsters to play with. Some of them are characters in this very book! And a big thank you to my beta readers, who mostly just screw around and suggest wild plot twists and insult each other, but also help me find the outstanding mistakes and fix them.

My thanks to Paul at Dominion for editing this mess of words and random commas. A big thanks to Richard Sashigane for the portalicious cover. And to Bonnie Price for her awesome typography.

For semi-regular updates on books, art, and just stuff going on, check out my Greystone Guild FB https://www.facebook.com/greystone.guild.7 or my website www.davewillmarth.com where you can subscribe for an eventual newsletter.

And don't forget to follow my author page on Amazon! That way you'll get a nice friendly email when new books are released. You can also find links to my Greystone Chronicles and new Shadow Sun books there! https://www.amazon.com/Dave-Willmarth/e/B076G12KCL

PLEASE TAKE A MOMENT TO LEAVE A REVIEW!

Reviews on Amazon and Goodreads are vitally important to indie authors like me. Amazon won't help market the books until they reach a certain level of reviews. So please, take a few seconds, click on that (fifth!) star and type a few words about how much you liked the book! I would appreciate it very much. I do read the reviews, and a few of my favorites have led to friendships and even character cameos!

You can find information on lots of LitRPG/Gamelit books on Ramon Mejia's LitRPG Podcast here https://www.facebook.com/litrpgpodcast/. Also thank you to Ramon for early feedback on this book when I was thinking about discarding it, and some good advice. You can find his books here. https://www.amazon.com/R.A.-Mejia/e/B01MRTVW3O

There are a few more places where you can find me, and several other genre authors, hanging out. Here are my favorite LitRPG/GameLit community facebook groups. (If you have cookies, keep them away from Daniel Schinhofen).

https://www.facebook.com/groups/LitRPGsociety/

https://www.facebook.com/groups/LitRPG.books/

https://www.facebook.com/groups/GameLitSociety/

https://www.facebook.com/groups/litrpgforum/

https://www.facebook.com/groups/541733016223492/

There are a couple new young authors that you should check out. We met at an IHOP not so long ago for brunch and hung out a bit. Both are good guys, with bright futures ahead of them. When they're famous and signing movie deals, I'm totally taking credit.

The first is Richard Hummel, my almost-neighbor and brand new daddy who despite getting no sleep, still found time to write the second book in this series... https://www.amazon.com/Radioactive-Evolution-Dystopian-Post-Apocalyptic-Adventure-ebook/dp/B07KLMTZBW/

And check out this one by Frank Albelo, who swears he's not mob'd up, but I'm not sure I believe him. https://www.amazon.com/Hall-Book-Muraglen-Saga-ebook/dp/B07HL8Y9K6/

www.ingramcontent.com/pod-product-compliance
Lightning Source LLC
Chambersburg PA
CBHW080723020726
47503CB00010B/2767